TO THE HILT

TO THE HILT

DICK FRANCIS

MICHAEL JOSEPH
LONDON

MICHAEL JOSEPH LTD
Published by the Penguin Group
27 Wrights Lane, London w8 5tz
Viking Penguin Inc., 375 Hudson Street, New York, New York 10014, USA
Penguin Books Australia Ltd, Ringwood, Victoria, Australia
Penguin Books Canada Ltd, 10 Alcorn Avenue, Toronto, Ontario, Canada m4v 3b2
Penguin Books (NZ) Ltd, 182-190 Wairau Road, Auckland 10, New Zealand

Penguin Books Ltd, Registered Offices: Harmondsworth, Middlesex, England

First published in Great Britain 1996
Second impression before publication

'Disobedience' from WHEN WE WERE VERY YOUNG
by A A Milne, first published by Methuen
Children's Books (1924), by permission of
Reed Consumer Books

Set in 12/14pt Monotype Sabon by
Rowland Phototypesetting Ltd, Bury St Edmunds, Suffolk
Printed in England by Clays Ltd, St Ives plc

A CIP catalogue record for this book is available from the British Library

ISBN 0 7181 3754 X

BEDE'S DEATH SONG

Fore thaem neidfaerae   naenig uuirthit
thoncsnotturra,   than him tharf sie
to ymbhycggannae aer   his hiniongae
hwaet his gastae   godaes aeththae yflaes
aefter deothdaege   doemid uueorthae.

Before that sudden journey no one is wiser in
thought than he needs to be, in considering,
before his departure, what will be adjudged to
his soul, of good or evil, after his death-day.

From *The Earliest English Poems*,
translated by Michael Alexander
(Penguin Books, Third Edition 1991)

Chapter 1

I don't think my stepfather much minded dying. That he almost took me with him wasn't really his fault.

My mother sent me a postcard – 'Perhaps I'd better tell you your stepfather has had a heart attack' – which I read in disbelief outside the remote Scottish post office where I went every two weeks to collect my letters. The postcard had lain there unread for approximately ten days.

Somewhat distractedly, though my stepfather and I were hardly intimate, I went back into the cluttered little shop and begged use of the telephone.

'You'll be reimbursing us as usual, Mr Kinloch?'

'Of course.'

Dour old Donald Cameron, nodding, lifted a flap of counter and allowed me through to his own jealously protected and wall-mounted instrument. As the official public telephone, thoughtfully provided outside for the few surrounding inhabitants, survived vandalism for roughly thirty minutes each time it was mended, old Donald was accustomed to extending to customers the courtesy of his own phone. Since he charged an extra fee for its use, I privately reckoned it was Donald himself who regularly disabled the less profitable technology on his doorstep.

'Mother?' I said, eventually connected to her in London. 'This is Al.'

'Alexander,' she corrected automatically, not liking my abbreviation, 'are you in Scotland?'

'I am, yes. What about the old man?'

'Your stepfather,' she said reprovingly, 'is resting.'

'Er . . . *where* is he resting?' In hospital? In *peace*?

'In bed,' she said.

'So he is alive?'

'Of course he's alive.'

'But your postcard . . .'

'There's nothing to panic about,' she said calmly. 'He had some chest pains and spent a week in the Clinic for stabilisation and tests, and now he is home with me, resting.'

'Do you want me to come?' I asked blankly. 'Do you need any help?'

'He has a nurse,' she said.

My mother's unvarying composure, I sometimes thought, stemmed from a genuine deficiency of emotion. I had never seen her cry, had never heard tears in her voice, not even after her first husband, my father, had been killed in a shooting accident out on the moors. To me, at seventeen, his sudden loss had been devastating. My mother, dry-eyed, had told me to pull myself together.

A year later, still cool at the ceremony, she had married Ivan George Westering, baronet, brewer, pillar of the British Jockey Club, my stepfather. He was not domineering; had been generous, even; but he disapproved of the way I lived. We were polite to each other.

'How ill is he?' I asked.

'You can come if you like,' my mother said. 'It's entirely up to you.'

Despite the casual voice, the carefully maintained distance, it sounded closer to a plea than I was used to.

'I'll arrive tomorrow,' I said, making up my mind.

'If you're sure?' She betrayed no relief, however; no welcome.

'I'm sure.'

'Very well.'

I paid the phone call's ransom into Donald's stringy outstretched palm and returned to my laden, ancient and battered four-wheel drive outside. It had good gears, good brakes, good tyres and little remaining colour on its thin metal flanks. It contained, at that moment, food for two weeks, a big cylinder of butane gas, supplies of batteries, bottled water and insect killer and three brown cardboard boxes, parcel delivery, replenishing the tools of my trade.

I painted pictures. I lived in a broken down long-deserted shepherd's hut, known as a bothy, out on a windy Scottish mountainside, without electricity. My hair grew to my shoulders. I played the bagpipes. My many and fairly noble relations thought me weird.

Some are born weird, some achieve it, others have weirdness thrust upon them. I preferred solitude and paint to out-thinking salmon and shooting for food; I had only half inherited the country skills and courtesies of my ancestors. I was the twenty-nine-year-old son of the (dead) fourth son of an earl and I had no unearned wealth. I had three uncles, four aunts and twenty-one cousins. Someone in such a large (and conventional) family had to be weird, and it seemed I'd been elected.

I didn't mind. Mad Alexander. Messes about with paints. And not even *oils*, my dear, but those frightfully common *acrylics*.

If Michelangelo could have laid his hands on acrylics, I said, he would have joyfully used them. Acrylics were endlessly versatile and never faded. They out-virtued oils by furlongs.

Don't be *ridiculous*, Alexander.

I paid my uncle (the present earl, known as 'Himself') a painting a year as rent for the ruin I inhabited on his estate. The painting was done to his choice. He mostly asked for portraits of his horses and dogs. I quite liked to please him.

Outside the post office, on that dry cloudy cold morning in September, I sat in my old jeep-type jalopy and did my paperwork, opening my letters, answering them and sending off the replies. There were two cheques that day for work delivered, which I despatched to the bank, and an order from America for six more paintings to be done at once – like yesterday.

Ridiculous, mad Alexander, in his weird way, actually, quietly prospered; and I kept that fact to myself.

The paperwork done, I drove my wheels northwards, at first along a recognisable road, then a roughly gravelled stretch, then up a long, rutted and indistinct track which led nowhere but to my unnamed home in the Monadhliath Mountains. 'Between Loch Ness and Aviemore,' I usually explained, and no, I hadn't seen the monster.

Whoever in the mists of time had first built my bothy had chosen its position well: it backed straight into an elbowed granite outcrop that sheltered it from the north and east, so that winter blizzards mostly leap-frogged over the top. In front lay a sort of small stony plateau that on the far side dropped away steeply, giving me long views of valleys and rocky hills and of a main road far below.

The only problem with the road, that served to remind me that an outside world existed, was that my dwelling was visible *from* it, so that far too often I found strangers on my doorstep, hikers equipped with shorts, maps, half-ton walking boots and endless energy. There was nowhere left in the world unpenetrated by inquisitive legs.

On the day of my mother's postcard I returned to find four of the nosy species poking around without inhibitions. Male. Blue, scarlet, orange backpacks. Glasses. English regional voices.

The days when I'd offered tea, comforts and conversation were long gone. Irritated by the invasion I drove onto the plateau, stopped the engine, removed my keys from the ignition and walked towards my front (and only) door.

The four men stopped peering into things and ranged themselves into a ragged line ahead of me, across my path.

'There's no one in,' one of them called. 'It's all locked up.'

I replied without heat, 'What do you want?'

'Him as lives here,' one said loudly.

'Maybe that's you,' said another.

I felt the first tremble of something wrong. Their manner subtly wasn't the awkwardness of trespassers caught in the act.

There was no shuffling from foot to foot. They met my eyes not with placating apology, but with fierce concentration.

I stopped walking and said again, 'What do you want?'

The first speaker said, 'Where is it?'

I felt a strong primitive impulse to turn tail and run, and wished afterwards that I'd listened to the wisdom of pre-history, but somehow one doesn't easily equate knobbly-kneed hikers with positive danger.

I said, 'I don't know what you mean,' and I made the mistake of turning my back on them and retracing my steps towards the jeep.

I heard their heavy feet scrunching on the stony ground behind me but still didn't truly believe in disaster until they clutched and spun me round and purposefully and knowledgeably punched. I had a sort of splintered composite view of intent malevolent faces, of grey daylight reflecting on their incongruous glasses, of their hard bombarding fists and of a wildly slanting horizon of unhelpful mountains as I doubled forward over a debilitating pain in the abdomen. Neck chop. Jabs to the ribs. Classic pattern. Over and over. Thud, merciless thud.

I was wearing jeans, shirt and sweater: they might as well have been gossamer for all the protection they offered. As for meaningful retaliation, read non-existent. I couldn't find breath. I swung at them in anger but fought an octopus. Bad news.

One of the men kept saying insistently, 'Where is it? Where is it?' but his colleagues made it impossible for me to answer.

I wondered vaguely if by 'it' they meant money, of which I carried little. They were welcome to it, I thought groggily, if they would stop their attentions. I unintentionally dropped my small bunch of keys and lost it to a hand that grabbed it up with triumph.

Somehow or other I ended with my back against the jeep: no further retreat. One of them snatched handfuls of my hair and banged my head against metal. I clawed blood down his

5

cheek and got a head-butt in return that went straight from my skull to my knees, buckling them like butter.

Events became unclear. I slid to the ground, face down. I had a close view of grey granite stones and short dry struggling blades of grass, more brown than green.

'Where is it?'

I didn't answer. Didn't move. Shut my eyes. Drifted.

'He's out,' a voice said. 'Fat lot of help you are.'

I felt hands roughly searching my pockets. Resistance, as an option, promised only more bruises. I lay still, not wholly conscious, inertia pervading, angry but helplessly passive, nothing coordinating, no strength, no will.

After a time of floating I felt their hands on me again.

'Is he alive?'

'No thanks to you, but yes, he is. He's breathing.'

'Just leave him.'

'Chuck him over there.'

'Over there' turned out to be the edge of the plateau, but I didn't realise it until I'd been dragged across the stones and lifted and flung over. I went rolling fast and inexorably down the steep mountain slope, almost bouncing from rock to rock, still incapable of helping myself, unable to stop, dimly aware of flooding with whirling comprehensive pain.

I slammed down onto a larger rock and did stop there, half on my side, half on my stomach. I felt no gratitude. I felt pulverised. Winded. Dazed. Thought vanished.

Some sort of consciousness soon came crazily back, but orderly memory took much longer.

Those bastard hikers, I thought eventually. I remembered their faces. I could draw them. They were demons in a dream.

The accurate knowledge of who I was and where I was arrived quietly.

I tried to move. A mistake.

Time would take care of it, perhaps. Give it time.

Those bastards had been *real*, I realised, demons or not. Their fists had been real. 'Where is it?' had been real. In spite of everything, I ruefully smiled. I thought it possible that they hadn't known what they were actually looking for. 'It' could have been whatever their victim valued most. There was no guarantee in any case that delivering up 'it' would save one from being thrown down a mountain.

It occurred to me to wonder what time it was. I looked at my left wrist, but my watch had gone.

It had been about eleven o'clock when I'd got back from the post office . . .

Hell's teeth, I thought abruptly. *Mother. Ivan. Heart attack.* I was supposed to be going to London. Or the moon.

The worst thing I might feel, I considered, was nothing.

Not the case.

With fierce concentration, I could move all my fingers and all my toes. Anything more hurt too much for enthusiasm. Outraged muscles went into breath-stopping spasms to protect themselves.

Wait. Lie still. I felt cold.

Bloody stupid, being mugged on one's own doorstep. Embarrassing. A helpless little old lady I was not, but a pushover — literally — just the same.

I found the casual callousness of the walkers extraordinary. They had appeared not to care whether I lived or died, and had in fact left it to chance. I supposed they could truthfully say, 'He was alive when we saw him last.' They could dodge the word murder.

The ebb tide in my body finally turned. Movement could at last be achieved without spasm. All I had to do from then on was scrape myself off the mountain and go and catch a train. Even the thought was exhausting.

I was sure, after a while, that by immense good fortune I had broken no bones in my helter-skeltering fall. I'd been a rag doll. Babies got lucky through not trying to help themselves. Same principle, I supposed.

With an unstoical groan, I raised from prone to kneeling on my rock and took a look up at where I'd come down. The edge of the plateau was hidden behind outcrops but was alarmingly far above. Looking down was almost worse, though from five or more years of living there, I understood at once where I was in relation to the bothy above. If I could traverse to the right without losing my footing and plunging down another slope, I would come eventually to the uneven but definable path that meandered from the road below up to my home: the challenging half-hidden ascent that brought walkers to my door.

The four hiker-demons had probably come up that way. I certainly didn't want to meet them if they were on their way down. Hours had probably passed, though. I knew I had lain helpless for a long time. They must surely by then have left.

Realistically, I was going nowhere except uncontrollably downwards again unless I could reach that path. Hikers or not, it was the only possible route. Trying to go in the opposite direction, to reach the track up from the post office, was pointless, as it involved an overhang and a perpendicular rock climb, neither of which could be managed without gear.

I was well used to moving alone in the mountains, and I was always careful. I would never normally have attempted what now confronted me without an axe and crampons, let alone with every move a wince, but fear of a less lucky fall, of a broken leg or worse, kept me stuck like glue, with finger-nails and tiny cautious shifts of weight, to every protruding scrap of solid rock. Loose stones rattled and bounced away. Scrubby earth gave too little purchase. Rock was all.

I made the journey sitting down, looking out over the perilous drops to the valley, digging in with my heels; careful, careful . . . *careful*.

The path, when at last I reached it, was by comparison a broad highway. I sat on one of its rocky steps and felt as weak as thankful: sat with my forearms on my knees, head hanging, trying to be cool about a degree of strain and discomfort far beyond the easily bearable.

Those *bastards*, I thought. The helpless rage of all victims shook in my gut. My physical state was shaming and infuriating. Somehow or other I should surely have put up a better fight.

From where I sat I could see most of the long path down to the road. No scarlet, orange or blue backpacks moved on it anywhere. Curse them, I thought; and damn them; and *shit*.

There was silence behind and above me and I had no sense of anyone being there. The inescapability of having to go up for a look was only a shade worse than actually making the effort; but I couldn't stay where I was for ever.

With reluctant muscles and a fearful mind I got laboriously to my feet and began the climb.

No evil faces grinned over the plateau above. My instinct that I was alone proved a true one, and I crawled the last bit on hands and knees and raised my head for a cautious look without anyone pouncing on me with a yell and kicking me back into space.

The reason for the silence and the absence of attackers was immediately obvious: my jeep had gone.

I stood erect on the plateau, figuratively groaning. Not only had I lost my transport, but the door of my home stood wide open with heaps of my belongings spilling out of it – a chair, clothes, books, bedclothes. I walked wearily across the plateau and looked in at a sickening mess.

Like all who live purposefully alone without provision for guests, my actual household goods were few. I tended to eat straight out of the frying pan, and to drink all liquids from a mug. Living without electricity, I owned none of the routinely stolen things like television, stereo or computer, nor did I have a mobile phone because of not being able to recharge the batteries. I did own a portable radio cassette for checking that interstellar war hadn't broken out, and for playing taped music if I felt like it, but it was no grand affair with resale value. I had no antique silver. No Chippendale chairs.

What I did have was paint.

When I'd moved into the tumbledown building five and a half years earlier I'd made only the centre and largest of its three divisions habitable. About fifteen feet by nine, my room had been given a businesslike new roof, a large double-glazed window, and a host of anti-damp preservation measures in its rebuilt walls and flooring. Light, heat and cooking were achieved with gas. Running water came from a small clear burn trickling through nearby rocks, and for a bathroom I had a weathered privy a short walk away. I'd meant at first to stay on the mountain only during the long northern summer days, but in the end had left my departure later and later that first year until suddenly the everlasting December nights were shortening again, and I'd stayed snug through a freezing January and February and had never since considered leaving.

Apart from a bed, a small table, a chest of drawers and one comfortable chair, the whole room was taken up by three easels, stacked canvases, a work stool, a wall of shelves and the equivalent of a kitchen table covered with pots and tubes of paints, and other essentials of my work like jugs of brushes and painting knives and jamjars full of clear or dirty water.

Lack of space and my own instincts dictated order and overall tidiness, but chiefly the disciplined organisation was the result of the very nature of the acrylics themselves: they dried so fast when exposed to air that lids *had* to be replaced, tubes had to be capped, only small quantities could be squeezed onto a palette at a time, brushes had to be constantly rinsed clean, knives wiped, hands washed. I kept large amounts of clean and dirty water in separate buckets under the table and used tissues by the jeep-load for keeping mess at bay.

Despite all care, I had few clothes free of paint stains and had to sand down the woodblock floor now and then to get rid of multicoloured sludge.

The mess the four demons had made of all this was spectacularly awful.

I had left work in progress on all three easels as I often painted three pictures simultaneously. All three were now face down on the floor, thoroughly saturated by the kicked-over buckets. My work table lay on its side, pots, brushes and paints spilling wide. Burst paint tubes had been squashed underfoot. My bed had been tipped over, chest of drawers ransacked, box files pulled down from the shelves, ditto books, every container emptied, sugar and coffee granules scattered in a filthy jumbled chaos.

Bastards.

I stood without energy in the doorway looking at the depressing damage and working out what to do. The clothes I was wearing were torn and dirty and I'd been bleeding from many small scrapes and scratches. The bothy had been robbed, as far as I could see, of everything I could have raised money on. Also my wallet had gone and my watch had gone. My cheque-book had been in the jeep.

I had said I would go to London.

Well . . . so I bloody well *would*.

Mad Alexander. Might as well live up to the name.

Apart from moving back into the room the chair and other things that were half out of the doorway, I left the scene mostly as it was. I sorted out only the cleanest jeans, jersey and shirt from the things emptied out of the chest of drawers, and I changed into them out by the burn, rinsing off the dried trickles of blood in the cold clean water.

I ached deeply all over.

Bloody bastards.

I walked along to the privy, but there had been nothing to steal there, and they had left it alone. Of the two original but ruined flanks to my habitable room, one was now a carport with a grey camouflage-painted roof of corrugated iron, the other, still open to the skies, was where I kept the gas cylinders (in a sort of bunker) and also rubbish bins, now empty, as I had taken the filled black bags down to the post office for disposal that morning. Let into one tumbledown wall there were the remains of what might have been a fireplace with a small oven above. Perhaps the place had once been a kitchen or bakehouse, but I'd been happier with gas.

Nothing in these two side sections had been vandalised. Lucky, I suppose.

From the jumble on the main bothy floor I harvested a broken stick of charcoal and slid pieces of it into my shirt pocket, and I found a sketch-pad with some clean pages; and armed with such few essentials I left home and set off down the wandering path to the road.

The Monadhliath Mountains, rising sharply to between 2500 and 3000 feet, were rounded rather than acutely jagged, but were bare of trees and starkly, unforgivingly grey. The steep path led down to heather-clad valley slopes and finally to a few pine trees and patches of grass. The transition from my home to the road was always more than a matter of height above sea level: up in the wild taxing granite wilderness, life – to me at any rate – felt simple, complete and austere. I could work there with concentration. The clutching 'normal' life of the valley diminished my awareness of something elemental that I took from the paleolithic silence and converted into paint: yet the canvases I sold for my bread and butter were usually full of colour and lightheartedness and were, in fact, mostly pictures of golf.

By the time I reached the road there was a hint in the quality of light of dusk hovering in the wings getting ready to draw together the skirts of evening. It was the time of day when I stopped painting. As it was then September, watch or no watch, I could pretty accurately guess at six thirty.

Even though it had been by-passed by the busy A9 artery from Inverness to Perth, there was enough traffic on the road for me to hitch a ride without much difficulty, but it was a shade disconcerting to find that the driver who stopped to pick up a long-haired jeans-clad young male stranger was an expectant-eyed fortyish woman who put her hand caressingly on my knee half a mile into the ride.

Lamely I said, 'I only want to go to Dalwhinnie railway station.'

'Boring, aren't you, dear.'

'Ungrateful,' I agreed. And bruised, tired and laughing inside.

She took the hand away with a shrug. 'Where do you want to go?' she asked. 'I could take you to Perth.'

'Just Dalwhinnie.'

'Are you gay, dear?'

'Er,' I said. 'No.'

She gave me a sideways glance. 'Have you banged your face?'

'Mm,' I said.

She gave me up as a prospect and dumped me half a mile from the trains. I walked, ruefully thinking of the offer I'd declined. I'd been celibate too long. It had become a habit. Bloody feeble, all the same, to pass up a free lunch. My ribs hurt.

Lights were going on everywhere when I reached the station and I was glad of the minimum shelter of its bare ticket office, as the air temperature was dropping alarmingly towards night. Shivering and blowing on my fingers I made a telephone call, endlessly grateful that this instrument at least was in fine working order and not suffering from a clone of Donald Cameron.

A reverse charge call via the operator.

A familiar Scots voice spluttered at the far end, talking first to the operator, then to me. 'Yes, of course I'll pay for the call ... Is that really you, Al? What the heck are you doing at Dalwhinnie?'

'Catching the night train to London. The Royal Highlander.'

'It doesn't go for hours.'

'No ... What are you doing at this moment?'

'Getting ready to leave the office and drive home to Flora and a good dinner.'

'Jed ...'

He heard more in my voice than just his name. He said sharply, 'Al? What's the matter?'

'I ... um ... I've been burgled,' I said. 'I'd ... um ... I'd be very glad of your help.'

After a short silence he said briefly, 'I'm on my way,' and the line went quiet.

Jed Parlane was my uncle's factor, the man who managed the Kinloch Scottish estates. Though he'd been in the job less than four years we had become the sort of friends that took goodwill from each other for granted. He would come. He was the only one I would have asked.

He was forty-six, a short stocky Lowland Scot from Jedburgh (hence his name), whose plain common sense had appealed to my uncle after the turmoil stirred up by an arrogant predecessor. Jed had calmed the resentful tenants and spent maintenance money oiling many metaphorical gates, so that the huge enterprise now ran at a peaceful profit. Jed, the wily Lowlander, understood and used the Highlander's stubborn pride; and I'd learned more from him about getting my own way than perhaps he realised.

He came striding into Dalwhinnie station after his twelve or more mile drive to reach me, and stood four-square in front of where I sat on a brown-painted bench against a margarine wall.

'You've hurt your face,' he announced. 'And you're cold.'

I stood up stiffly, the overall pain no doubt showing. I said, 'Does the heater work in your car?'

He nodded without speaking and I followed him outside to where he'd parked. I sat in his front passenger seat while he re-started the engine and twiddled knobs to bring out hot air, and I found myself unexpectedly shuddering from the physical relief.

'OK,' he said, switching on the car's internal light, 'so what's happened to your face? You're going to have a hell of a black eye. That left-hand side of your forehead and temple is all swollen...' He stopped, sounding uncertain. I was not, I guessed, my usual picture of glowing good health.

'I got head-butted,' I said. 'I got jumped on and bashed about and robbed, and don't laugh.'

'I'm not laughing.'

I told him about the four pseudo hill-walkers and the devastation in the bothy.

'The door isn't locked,' I said. 'They took my keys. So tomorrow maybe you'll take your own key along there – though there's nothing left worth stealing...'

'I'll take the police,' he said firmly, aghast.

I nodded vaguely.

Jed pulled a notebook and pen from inside his jacket and asked for a list of things missing.

'My jeep,' I said gloomily, and told him its number.

'Everything in it . . . food and stores, and so on. From the bothy they took my binoculars and camera and all my winter padded clothes and four finished paintings and climbing gear and some Glenlivet . . . and my golf clubs.'

'*Al!*'

'Well, look on the bright side. My bagpipes are in Inverness having new bits fitted, and I've sent my passport away for renewal.' I paused. 'They took all my cash and my credit card . . . I don't know its number, though it's somewhere on file in your office – will you alert them? – and they took my father's old gold watch. Anyway,' I finished, 'if you have a credit card with you, will you lend me a ticket to London?'

'I'll take you to a hospital.'

'No.'

'Then come home to Flora and me. We'll give you a bed.'

'No . . . but thanks.'

'Why *London?*'

'Ivan Westering had a heart attack.' I paused briefly, watching him assimilate the consequences. 'You know my mother . . . though I suppose you don't actually know her all that well . . . she would never ask me to help her but she didn't say *not* come, which was as good as an SOS . . . so I'm going.'

'The police will want you to give a statement.'

'The bothy is a statement.'

'Al, don't go.'

'Will you lend me the fare?'

He said, 'Yes, but –'

'Thanks, Jed.' I fished a piece of charcoal stick out of my shirt pocket and opened the sketch-pad I still carried. 'I'll draw them. It'll be better than just describing them.'

He watched me start and with a touch of awkwardness said, 'Were they looking for anything special?'

I glanced across at him with half a smile. 'One of them kept saying "Where is it?"'

Anxiously he said, 'Did you tell them?'

'Of course not.'

'If you'd told them, they might have stopped hitting you.'

'And they might have made sure I was dead, before they left.'

I drew the four men in a row, face on: knees, boots, glasses, air of threat.

'Anyway,' I said, 'they didn't *say* what they were looking for. They just said "Where is *it*?" so *it* might have been *anything*. They might have been fishing for anything I valued. For what I valued most, if you see what I mean?'

He nodded.

I went on, 'They didn't call me by name. They'll know it now, because it was all over things in the jeep.' I finished the composite sketch and turned to a clean page. 'Do you remember those hikers who preyed on holidaymakers last year in the Lake District? They robbed trailers, mobile homes.'

'The police caught them,' Jed agreed, nodding. 'But those hikers didn't *beat* people and throw them down mountains.'

'Might be the same sort of thing, though. I mean, just opportunist theft.'

I drew the head of the 'Where is it?' man, as I remembered him the most clearly. I drew him without glasses.

'This is their leader,' I explained, shading planes into the bony face. 'I'm not good at voices and accents, but I'd say his was sloppy south-east England. Same with them all.'

'Hard men?'

'They'd all done time in a boxing gym, I'd say. Short-arm jabs, like at a punch-bag.' I swallowed. 'Out of my league.'

'Al . . .'

'I felt an utter fool.'

'That's illogical. No one could fight four at once.'

'Fight? I couldn't even *connect*.' I broke off, remembering. 'I scratched one of their faces . . . He was the one who crashed his head against mine.' I turned to a fresh page in the sketch-pad and drew again, and his face came out with a clawed cheek, eyes glaring through round glasses and a viciousness that leaped off the paper.

'You'd know him again,' Jed said with awe.

'I'd know them all.'

I gave him the sketch-pad. He looked from drawing to drawing, troubled and kind.

'Come home with Flora and me,' he repeated. 'You look bad.'

I shook my head. 'I'll be all right by tomorrow.'

'The next day is always the worst.'

'You're a laugh a minute.'

After a while he sighed heavily, went into the station and returned with tickets.

'I got you a sleeper for tonight, and an open return for whenever you come back. Ten oh one from here, arrives at Euston at seven forty-three in the morning.'

'Thanks, Jed.'

He gave me cash from his pockets. 'Phone me tomorrow evening.'

I nodded.

He said, 'They've put the heater on in the waiting-room here.'

I shook his hand gratefully and waved him away home to his comfortable Flora.

CHAPTER 2

Best to forget that night.

The face that looked back from an oblong of mirror as the train clattered over the points on the approach to Euston was, I realised, going to appeal to my mother's fastidious standards even less than usual. The black eye was developing inexorably, my chin bristled, and even I could see that a comb would be a good idea.

I righted what I could with the help of Jed's cash and a chemist's shop in the station but my Mama predictably eyed me up and down with a pursed mouth before dispensing a minimum hug on her doorstep.

'Really, Alexander,' she said. 'Haven't you *any* clothes free of paint?'

'Few.'

'You look thin. You look ... well, you'd better come in.'

I followed her into the prim polished hallway of the architectural gem she and Ivan inhabited in the semi-circle of Park Crescent, by Regent's Park.

As usual, she herself looked neat, pretty, feminine and disciplined, with short shining dark hair, and a hand-span waist, and as usual I wanted to tell her how much I loved her, but didn't, because she found such emotion excessive.

I'd grown tall, like my father, and had been taught by him

from birth to look after the delicately boned sweet-natured centre of his devotion, to care for her and serve her and to consider it not a duty but a delight. I remembered a childhood of gusty laughter from him and small pleased smiles from her, and he'd lived long enough for me to sense their joint bewilderment that the boy they'd carefully furnished with a good education and Highland skills like shooting, fishing and stalking was showing alarming signs of non-conformity.

At sixteen, I'd said one day, 'Dad . . . I don't want to go to university.' (*Heresy*.) 'I want to paint.'

'A good hobby, Al,' he'd said, frowning. He'd praised for years the ease with which I could draw, but never taken it seriously. He never did, to the day he died.

'I'm just telling you, Dad.'

'Yes, Al.'

He hadn't minded my liking for being alone. In Britain the word 'loner' flew none of the danger signals it did over in the United States, where the desirability of being 'one of a team' was indoctrinated from pre-school. 'Loners' there, I'd discovered, were people who went off their heads. So maybe I was off mine, but anything else felt wrong.

'How's Ivan?' I asked my mother.

'Would you like coffee?' she said.

'Coffee, eggs, toast . . . anything.'

I followed her down to the basement-kitchen where I cooked and ate a breakfast that worked a change for the better.

'Ivan?' I said.

She looked away as if refusing to hear the question and asked instead, 'What's the matter with your eye?'

'I walked into . . . well, it doesn't matter. Tell me about Ivan.'

'I er . . .' She looked uncharacteristically uncertain. 'His doctors say he should slowly be resuming his normal activities . . .'

'But?' I said, as she stopped.

'But he won't.'

After a pause I said, 'Well, tell me.'

There was then this subtle thing between us: that shadowy

moment when the generations shift and the child becomes the parent. And perhaps it was happening to us at an earlier age than in most families because of my long training in care of her, a training that had been in abeyance since she'd married Ivan, but which now resurfaced naturally and with redoubled force across her kitchen table.

I said, 'James James Morrison Morrison Weatherby George Dupree . . .'

She laughed, and went on, 'Took great care of his Mother, though he was only three.'

I nodded. 'James James said to his Mother, "Mother," he said, said he, "You must never go down to the end of the town if you don't go down with me."'

'Oh, *Alexander*.' A whole lifetime of restraint quivered in her voice, but the dammed up feelings didn't break.

'Just tell me,' I said.

A pause. Then she said, 'He's so *depressed*.'

'Er . . . *clinically* depressed?'

'I don't know what that means. But I don't know how to deal with it. He lies in bed most of the time. He won't get dressed. He hardly eats. I want him to go back into the Clinic but he won't do that either, he says he doesn't like it there, and Dr Robbiston doesn't seem to be able to prescribe anything that will pull him out of it.'

'Well . . . has he a good reason for being depressed? Is his heart in a bad state?'

'They said there wasn't any need for by-passes or a pace-maker. They used one of those balloon things on one of his arteries, that's all. And he has to take pills, of course.'

'Is he afraid he's going to die?'

My mother wrinkled her smooth forehead. 'He just tells me not to worry.'

'Shall I . . . um . . . go up and say hello?'

She glanced at the big kitchen clock, high on the wall above an enormous cooker. Five to nine.

'His nurse is with him now,' she said. 'A male nurse. He doesn't really *need* a nurse, but he won't let him go. Wilfred,

20

the nurse – and I don't like him, he's too obsequious – he sleeps on our top floor here in those old attics, and Ivan has had an intercom installed so that he can call him if he has chest pains in the night.'

'And does he have chest pains in the night?'

My mother said with perplexity, 'I don't know. I don't think so. But he did, of course, when he had the attack. He woke up with it at four in the morning, but at the time he thought it was only bad indigestion.'

'Did he wake you?'

She shook her head. She and Ivan had always slept in adjoining but separate bedrooms. Not from absence of love; they simply preferred it.

She said, 'I went in to say good morning to him and give him the papers, as I always do, and he was sweating and pressing his chest with his fist.'

'You should have got a message to me at once,' I said. 'Jed would have driven over with it. You shouldn't have had to deal with all this by yourself.'

'Patsy came . . .'

Patsy was Ivan's daughter. Sly eyes. Her chief and obsessive concern was to prevent Ivan leaving his fortune and his brewery to my mother and not to herself. Ivan's assurances got nowhere: and Patsy's feelings for me, as my mother's potential heir, would have curdled sulphuric acid. I always smiled at her sweetly.

'What did Patsy do?' I asked.

'Ivan was in the Clinic when she came here. She used the telephone.' My mother stopped for effect.

'Who did she want?' I prompted helpfully.

Amusement glimmered in my mother's dark eyes. 'She telephoned Oliver Grantchester.'

Oliver Grantchester was Ivan's lawyer.

'How blatant was she?' I asked.

'Oh, straight to the jugular, darling.' Patsy called everyone darling. She would murder, I surmised, with a 'Sorry, darling' while she slid the stiletto into the heart. 'She told Oliver,' smiled my mother, 'that if Ivan tried to change his Will, she would contest it.'

'And she meant you to hear.'

'If she hadn't wanted me to, she could have called him from anywhere else. And naturally she was sugar-candy all over the Clinic. The loving daughter. She's good at it.'

'And she said there was no need for you to bring me all the way from Scotland while she was there to look after things.'

'Oh dear, you know how *positive* she is . . .'

'A tidal wave.'

Civility was a curse, I often thought. Patsy needed someone to be brusquely rude about the way she bullied everyone with saccharine; but if ever openly crossed she could produce so intense an expression of 'poor little me-dom' that potential critics found themselves comforting her instead. Patsy at thirty-four had a husband, three children, two dogs and a nanny all anxiously twitching to please her.

'And,' my mother said, 'there's some sort of serious trouble at the brewery, and also I think he's worried about the Cup.'

'What cup?'

'The King Alfred Cup, what else?'

I frowned. 'Do you mean the race?' The King Alfred Gold Cup, sponsored by Ivan's brewery as a great advertisement for King Alfred Gold beer, was a splendid two-mile steeplechase run every October, a regular part now of the racing year.

'The race, or the Cup itself,' my mother said. 'I'm not sure.'

At that inconclusive point the kitchen was abruptly invaded by two large middle-aged ladies who heavily plodded down the outside iron steps from road level to basement and let themselves in with familiarity.

'Morning, Lady Westering,' they said. A double act. Sisters, perhaps. They looked from my mother to me expectantly, awaiting an explanation, I thought, as much as an introduction. My gentle mother could be far too easily intimidated.

I stood and said mildly, 'I am Lady Westering's son. And you are?'

My mother told me, 'Edna and Lois. Edna cooks for us. Lois cleans.'

Edna and Lois gave me stares in which disapproval sheltered sketchily behind a need to keep their jobs. Disapproval? I wondered if Patsy had been at work.

Edna looked with a critical eye at the evidence of my cooking, an infringement of her domain. Too bad. She would have to get used to it. My father and I had historically always done the family meals because we'd liked it that way. It had started with my mother breaking a wrist: by the time it was mended, feeding the three of us had forever changed hands; and as I'd understood very early the chemistry of cooking, good food had always seemed easy.

My mother and Ivan had from the beginning employed a cook, though Edna – and also Lois – was new since my last visit.

I said to my mother, 'Wilfred notwithstanding, I'll go up now and see Ivan. I expect I'll find you upstairs in your sitting-room.'

Edna and Lois hovered visibly between allegiances. I gave them my most cheerful non-combative smile, and found my mother following me gratefully up the stairs to the main floor, quiet now but grandly formal with dining-room and drawing-room for entertaining.

'Don't tell me,' I teased her, once we were out of the kitchen's earshot, 'Patsy employed them.'

She didn't deny it. 'They're very efficient.'

'How long have they worked here?'

'A week.'

She came with me up to the next floor, where she and Ivan each had a bedroom, bathroom and personal day-room, in his case a study-cum-office, in hers the refuge they used most, a comfortable pink and green matter of fat armchairs and television.

'Lois cleans very well,' my mother sighed as we went in there, 'but she will *move* things. It's almost as if she moves them deliberately, just to prove to me that she's dusted.'

She shifted two vases back to their old familiar position of one at each end of the mantelshelf. Silver candlesticks were returned to flank the clock.

'Just tell her not to,' I said, but I knew she wouldn't. She didn't like to upset people: the opposite of Patsy.

I went along to see Ivan, who was sitting palely in his study while noises from his bedroom next door suggested bed-making and the tidying of bottles.

He wore a crimson woollen dressing-gown and brown leather slippers and showed no surprise at my presence.

'Vivienne said you were coming,' he said neutrally. Vivienne was Mother.

'How are you feeling?' I asked, sitting in a chair opposite him and realising with misgiving that he looked older, greyer and a good deal thinner than he had been on my last visit in the spring. Then, I'd been on my way to America with my mind full of the commercial part of my life. He had made, I now remembered, an unexpected invitation for my advice, and I had been too preoccupied, too impatient and too full of doubt of his sincerity to listen properly to what he'd wanted. It had been something to do with his horses, his steeplechasers in training at Lambourn, and I'd had other reasons than press of business to avoid going there.

I repeated my question, 'How are you feeling?'

He asked merely, 'Why don't you cut your hair?'

'I don't know.'

'Curls are girlish.'

He himself had the short-cut shape that went with the businessman personality: with the baronetcy and membership of the Jockey Club. I knew him to be fair-minded and well respected, a middling man who had inherited a modest title from a cousin and a large brewery from his father and had done his best by both.

It was a sadness with him that he had neither son nor any male relative: he was resigned to the baronetcy dying with him.

I'd often flippantly asked him, 'How's the beer, then?', but on that morning it seemed inappropriate. I said instead, 'Is there anything I can do for you?' and regretted it before the last words were out of my mouth. Not Lambourn, I thought. Anything else.

But 'Look after your mother,' was what he said first.

'Yes, of course.'

'I mean ... after I've gone.' His voice was quiet and accepting.

'You're going to live.'

He surveyed me with the usual lack of enthusiasm and said dryly, 'You've had a word with God, have you?'

'Not yet.'

'You wouldn't be so bad, Alexander, if you would come down off your mountain and rejoin the human race.'

He had offered, when he'd married my mother, to take me into the brewery and teach me the business, and at eighteen, with chaotic visions of riotous colours intoxicating my inner eye, I'd learned the first great lesson of harmonious stepson-ship, how to say no without giving offence.

I wasn't ungrateful and I didn't dislike him: we were just entirely different. As far as one could see, he and my mother were quietly happy together and there was nothing wrong with his care of her.

He said, 'Have you seen your uncle Robert during the last few days?'

'No.'

My uncle Robert was the earl – 'Himself'. He came to Scot-land every year in late August and stayed north for the shooting and fishing and the Highland Games. He sent for me every year to visit him, but although I knew from Jed that he was now in residence, I hadn't so far been summoned.

Ivan pursed his lips. 'I thought he might have wanted to see you.'

'Any time soon, I expect.'

'I've asked him –' He broke off, then continued, 'he'll tell you himself.'

I felt no curiosity. Himself and Ivan had known each other for upwards of twenty years, drawn together by a fondness for owning racehorses. They still had their steeplechasers trained in the same yard in Lambourn.

Himself had approved of the match between Ivan and the widow of his much-loved youngest brother. He'd stood beside me at the wedding ceremony and told me to go to him if I ever needed help; and considering that he had five children of his own and half a clan of other nephews and nieces, I'd felt comforted in the loss of my father and in a deep way secure.

I had managed on my own, but I'd known that he was *there*.

I said to Ivan, 'Mother thinks you may be worried about the Cup.'

He hesitated over an answer, then asked, 'What about it?'

'She doesn't know if it's troubling you and making you feel worse.'

'Your dear mother!' he deeply sighed.

I said, 'Is there something wrong with this year's race? Not enough entries, or something?'

'Look after her.'

She'd been right, I thought, about his depression. A malaise of the soul, outwardly discernible in weak movements of his hands and the lack of vigour in his voice. I didn't think there was much I could do to improve things, if his own doctor couldn't.

As if on cue a fifty-to-sixty, thin, moustached, busy-busy person hurried into the room in a dark flapping suit announcing that as he was passing on his way to the Clinic he had called in for five minutes to check on his patient. 'Morning, Ivan. How's things?'

'Good of you to come, Keith.'

Ivan drifting a limp hand in my direction, I stood up with parent-inculcated politeness and was identified as 'My stepson'.

Dr Keith Robbiston rose in my regard by giving me a sharp glance and a sharper question, 'What analgesic have you been taking for that eye?'

'Aspirin.' Euston station aspirin, actually.

'Huh.' Scorn. 'Are you allergic to any drugs?'

'I don't think so.'

'Are you taking any other drugs?'

'No.'

'Then try these.' He produced a small packet from an inner suit pocket and held it out to me. I accepted it with gratitude.

Ivan, mystified, asked what was going on.

His doctor briskly answered while at the same time producing from other pockets a stethoscope and blood-pressure monitor. 'Your stepson . . . name?'

'Alexander Kinloch,' I said.

'. . . Alexander, your stepson, can't move without pain.'

'What?'

'You haven't noticed? No, I suppose not.' To me he said, 'The reduction and management of pain is my speciality. It can't be disguised. How did you get like this? It can't be organic if you're not taking medicine. Car crash?'

I said with a flicker of amusement, 'Four thugs.'

'Really?' He had bright eyes, very alert. 'Bad luck.'

'What are you talking about?' Ivan said.

I shook my head at Dr Robbiston and he checked around his heart-threatened patient with effective economy of movement but no comment on my own state.

'Well done, Ivan,' he said cheerfully, whisking his aids out of sight. 'The ticker's banging away like a baby's. Don't strain yourself, though. But walk around the house a bit. Use this strong stepson as a crutch. How's your dear wife?'

'In her sitting-room,' I said.

'Great.' He departed as abruptly as he'd arrived. 'Hang in there, Ivan.'

He gave me a brief smile on his quick way out. I sat down again opposite Ivan and swallowed one of the tablets the doctor had given me. His assessment had been piercingly on target. Punch-bags led a rotten life.

'He's a good doctor, really,' Ivan told me defensively.

'The best,' I agreed. 'Why do you doubt him?'

'He's always in a hurry. Patsy wants me to change . . .' He tapered off indecisively; only a shadow seemed left of his former chief-executive decisiveness.

27

'Why change?' I asked. 'He wants you to be well, and he makes house calls, a miracle these days.'

Ivan frowned. 'Patsy says he's hasty.'

I said mildly, 'Not everyone thinks or moves at the same speed.'

Ivan took a tissue out of a flat box on the table beside him and blew his nose, then dropped the used tissue carefully into a handy waste-paper basket. Always neat, always precise.

He said, 'Where would you hide something?'

I blinked.

'Well?' Ivan prompted.

'Er . . . it would depend what it was.'

'Something of value.'

'How big?'

He didn't directly answer, but I found what he said next more unusual than anything he'd said to me since I'd known him.

'You have a quirky mind, Alexander. Tell me a safe hiding place.'

Safe.

'Um,' I said, 'who would be looking?'

'Everyone. After my death.'

'You're not dying.'

'Everyone dies.'

'It's essential to tell *someone* where you've hidden something, otherwise it may be lost for ever.'

Ivan smiled.

I said, 'Are we talking about your Will?'

'I'm not telling you what we are talking about. Not yet. Your uncle Robert says you know how to hide things.'

That put me into a state of breathlessness. How *could* they? Those two well-intentioned men must have said something to someone somewhere that had got me beaten to buggery and thrown over the next best thing to a cliff. Nephew of one, stepson of the other . . . I shifted in undeniable pain in that civilised room and acknowledged that for all their worldliness they had no true conception of the real voracious jungle of greed and cruelty roughly known as mankind.

'Ivan,' I said, 'put whatever it is in a bank vault and send a letter of instruction to your lawyers.'

He shook his head.

Don't give anything to me to hide, I thought. Please don't. Let me off. I'm not hiding anything else. Every battered muscle protested.

'Suppose it's a horse,' he said.

I stared.

He said, 'You can't put a horse in a bank vault.'

'What horse?'

He didn't say. He asked, 'How would you hide a horse?'

'A racehorse?' I asked.

'Certainly.'

'Then . . .' I paused a moment, 'in a racing stable.'

'Not in an obscure barn miles away from anywhere?'

'Definitely not. Horses have to be fed. Regular visits to an obscure barn would be as good as a sign saying "treasure here".'

'Do you believe in hiding things where everyone can see them but they don't realise what they're looking at?'

I said, 'The snag with that is that in the end someone *does* understand what they're looking at. *Someone* spots the rare stamp on the envelope. Someone spots the real pearls when the mistletoe berries wither.'

'But you would still put a racehorse among others?'

'And move it often,' I said.

'And the snag to that?'

'The snag,' I said obligingly, 'is that the horse can't be raced without disclosing its whereabouts. Unless, of course, you're a crook with a ringer, which would be unlike you, Ivan.'

'Thank you for that, Alexander.' His voice was dryly amused.

'And if you didn't race the horse,' I went on, 'you would waste its life and its value, until in the end it wouldn't be worth hiding.'

Ivan sighed. 'Any more snags?'

'Horses are as recognisable as people. They have faces.'

'And legs . . .'

After a pause I said, 'Do you want me to hide a horse?' and I thought, What the *hell* am I saying?

'Would you?'

'If you had a good reason.'

'For money?'

'Expenses.'

'Why?'

'Do you mean, why would I do it?' I asked.

He nodded.

I said feebly, 'For the interest,' but in fact it would be because it might lighten his depression to have something other than his illness to think about. I would do it because of my mother's anxiety.

He said, 'What if I asked you to *find* a horse?'

He was playing games, I thought.

'I suppose I would look for it,' I said.

The telephone on the table by his elbow rang but he merely stared at it apathetically and made no attempt to pick up the receiver. He simply waited until it stopped ringing and then showed exasperated fatigue when my mother appeared in the doorway to tell him that someone to do with the brewery wanted him.

'I'm ill. I've told them not to bother me.'

'It's Tobias Tollright, dear. He says it's essential he talks to you.'

'No, no.'

'Please, Ivan. He sounds so worried.'

'I don't want to talk to him,' Ivan said tiredly. 'Let Alexander talk to him.'

Both my mother and I thought the suggestion pointless, but once he got the idea in his head Ivan wouldn't be budged. In the end I walked over and picked up the phone and explained who I was.

'But I *must* speak to Sir Ivan himself,' said an agitated voice. 'You simply don't understand.'

'No,' I agreed, 'but if you'll tell me what's the matter, I'll relay it to him for an answer.'

'It's ridiculous.'

'Yes, but um . . . fire away.'

'Do you know who I am?' the voice demanded.

'No, I'm afraid not.'

'I am Tobias Tollright, a partner in a firm of chartered accountants. We audit the King Alfred Brewery accounts.'

'Right,' I said.

'There are discrepancies . . . Really, Sir Ivan is Chairman and managing director and majority shareholder . . . it is *unethical* for me to speak to you instead of him.'

'Mm,' I said, 'I do see that. Perhaps you'd better write to him.'

'The matter is too urgent. Remind him it is illegal for a limited company to go on trading when it is insolvent, and I fear . . . I really fear that measures must be taken at once, and only he can authorise them.'

'Well, Mr Tollright, er . . . hold on, while I explain.'

'What is it?' my mother asked anxiously. Ivan didn't ask but looked deeply exhausted.

He knew.

I said to him, 'There are things that only you can sign.'

Ivan shook his head.

I went back to Tollright, 'Can any of your urgent measures save the day?'

'I have to discuss it with Sir Ivan. But perhaps, yes.'

'What if he gives me power of attorney to act for him in this matter? Would that do the trick?'

He hesitated. It might be a legal move, but he didn't like it.

I said, 'Sir Ivan is still at an early stage of convalescence.'

I couldn't say in front of Ivan that too much worry might kill him, but it seemed as if Tobias's mental cogs abruptly engaged in a higher gear. How soon, he wanted to know without any more protest, could he expect to see me.

'Tomorrow?' I suggested.

'This afternoon,' he contradicted positively. 'Come to our

31

main offices in Reading.' He told me the address. 'This matter is very urgent.'

'Ultra?'

He cleared his throat and repeated the word as if he'd never used it before. 'Well . . . yes . . . ultra.'

'Just hold on, would you?' I lowered the receiver and spoke to my unwilling stepfather. 'I can sign things if you give me the authority. Is that what you really want? I mean, you'll have to trust me a lot.'

He said wearily, 'I do trust you.'

'But this is . . . well, *extreme* trust.'

He simply flapped his hand.

I said into the phone, 'Mr Tollright, I'll see you as soon as I can.'

'Good.'

I put down the receiver and told Ivan that such trust was unwise.

He smiled faintly. 'Your uncle Robert said I could trust you with my life.'

'You just more or less did.' I did a double-take. '*When* did he say that?'

'A few days ago. He'll tell you about it.'

And *who else* had they told? Alexander can hide things . . . *Shit*.

'Ivan,' I said, 'It's more solid if a power of attorney is signed and witnessed in front of a lawyer.'

'Phone Oliver Grantchester. I'll talk to him.'

He was vague, however, with his lawyer, telling him only that he wanted to draw up a power of attorney, but not saying what for. Extremely urgent, though, he emphasised; and, as he still felt wretchedly ill, would Oliver please come to his house so that everything could be completed at once.

Oliver Grantchester, it seemed, easily agreed to instant action, but Ivan's gloom nevertheless intensified. How on earth, I wondered, but didn't ask, had a brewery as well known as King Alfred's tied itself in financial knots?

Standing close outside Wantage, the ancient town of the

great king's birth, King Alfred's Brewery supplied most of southern England and half of the Midlands with King Alfred's Gold (a fine light brew) and King Alfred's Bronze (a brew more bitter) which flowed by the frothy lakeful down grateful throats.

Ivan had shown me round his brewery. I'd seen the Kingdom and the Crown that I'd declined. He had offered them again and yet again, and he couldn't understand why I went back to the mountains every time.

The phone call done, Ivan seemed grateful when a thin man in a short white cotton jacket came in from the next-door bedroom and told him respectfully that everything was clean and tidy for the day. The obsequious Wilfred, I presumed.

Out in the hallway a vacuum cleaner began whining. At the noise Ivan's fragile tolerance looked on the absolute brink of disintegration. Wilfred went out into the hallway. The vacuuming stopped but an aggrieved female voice could be heard saying, 'It's all very well, but I've got my job to do, you know.'

'Oh dear,' my mother said, and went to pour oil.

'I can't stand it all,' Ivan said.

He stood up, swaying unsteadily and knocking the box of tissues from the table to the floor. I picked up the box, noticing it had numbers written on its underside, one a series that I recognised as Himself's phone number in Scotland.

Seeing me looking at it, Ivan said, 'There's a pencil by the phone but that new cleaner keeps moving my notepad over onto the desk. It drives me mad. So I use the tissue-box instead.'

'Why don't you tell her?'

'Yes, I suppose I should.'

I offered him my arm for balance, which he accepted.

'Think I'll just rest until Oliver comes,' he said, and I went with him through to his wide bed, where he lay down on the covers in his dressing-gown and slippers and closed his eyes.

I went back into his study and eased down into the chair I'd occupied before. Dr Robbiston's tablet had at least diminished the persistently acute stabs of muscular pain to an overall

33

ache. I could no longer feel anything but a general soreness round my left eye. Think of something else, I told myself. Think of how to hide a bankruptcy . . .

I was a *painter*, dammit. Not a fixer. Not a universal rock. I should cultivate an ability to say no.

My mother came back. The vacuum remained silent. She perched in Ivan's chair and said, 'You see? You see?'

I nodded. 'I see a man who loves you.'

'That's not . . .'

'That's what's the matter. He knows his brewery is in trouble, is maybe on the edge. The brewery is the base of his life. It may be that the brewery's troubles brought on his heart attack in the first place. He may feel a loss of prestige. He may think he's failed you. He can't bear that.' I paused. 'He told me to look after you.'

She stared at me. 'But,' she said, 'I would live with him in poverty, and comfort him.'

'I think you need to tell him.'

'But –'

'I know you find it hard to put feelings into words, but I think you should do it now.'

'Perhaps . . .'

'No,' I said, 'I mean *now*. This minute. He talks about dying as if it would be a haven. He's told me twice to look after you. I will, but if that's not what you want, go and put your arms round him. I think he's ashamed because of the brewery. He's a good man – he needs saving.'

'I don't . . .'

'Go and love him,' I said.

She gave me a wild look and walked into Ivan's bedroom as if not sure of her footing.

I sat in a sort of hiatus, waiting for the next buffet of fate and wishing that all I had to decide that day was whether to pick Hooker's green or emerald for the colour of the grass of the eighteenth hole at Pebble Beach. Golf was peaceful and well mannered and tested one's honesty to disintegration. I painted the passions of golf as much as its physical scenery, and I'd learned it was the raw emotion, the conflict within the self, that sold the pictures. If I painted pretty scenery without feeling moral tension in my own mind, it quite likely wouldn't sell. It was golfers who bought my work, and they bought it for its core of struggle.

The four completed paintings stolen from the bothy had all been views of play on the great courses at Pebble Beach, California, and represented not only time spent and future income, but also an ingredient of anguish that I couldn't quantify or explain. Along with the canvas and the paint, the demon hikers had taken psychic energy, and although I could produce other and similar work again and again, never exactly *those* brushstrokes, *those* slanting shadows, *those* understandings of the flow of determination in the seconds before the striking of the ball.

The comparative peace of half an hour came to an end with the arrival of Oliver Grantchester who brought with him a frail-looking young woman hung around with computer, printer and bag of office necessities.

Oliver Grantchester and I had met about twice over the years, neither of us showing regret that it hadn't been oftener. My presence in Ivan's study was stiffeningly unwelcome to him, raising not a smile but a scowl.

He said not 'Good morning' but, 'I thought you were in Scotland.'

Ivan and my mother, hearing his voice, came through from the bedroom and gave him the friendly welcome he hadn't got from me.

'Oliver!' my mother exclaimed, offering her cheek for a routine kiss. 'So good of you to come.'

'Yes, good of you,' Ivan echoed pianissimo, taking his customary chair.

'Any time, Ivan,' Oliver Grantchester said heavily. 'You know that.'

The lawyer's large grey-suited body and authoritative voice somehow took up a lot of room and made the study seem smaller. Perhaps fifty, he had a bald crown surrounded by greying dark hair and a large fleshy mouth with chins to match. I wouldn't have been able to make him look out of a portrait as a friendly, warm-eyed philanthropist, but that could have been because I, Alexander, prompted no smile in *him*.

He introduced his assistant dismissively as 'Miranda', and it was my mother who settled her helpfully at Ivan's desk against one wall, and made space for her to set out her portable machines.

Grantchester said to Ivan, 'You want to draw up a power of attorney? Very wise of you, if I may say so, in view of your health. I brought with me a basic document. You have that ready, Miranda?' Miranda meekly nodded. Grantchester went on, 'It's a pity more people aren't as thoughtful as you, my old friend. Life must go on. A temporary power of attorney will smooth things over nicely until you're back to your old self again.'

Ivan meekly agreed.

'So who is to act for you?' Grantchester asked. 'You know I would be honoured to help you in any way I can. However, you might prefer to have Patsy. Yes, your daughter will be eminently suitable. I expect you've already discussed it with her.' He looked round the room as if expecting her to materialise. 'Patsy it is, then.' To Miranda he said in explanation, 'Draw up the document, naming Mrs Patsy Benchmark, Sir Ivan's daughter.'

Ivan cleared his throat and said to her, 'No. Not Mrs Benchmark. I'm giving the power of attorney to my stepson, here. Write Alexander Kinloch.'

Oliver Grantchester's mouth opened wide, but no sound came out. He looked utterly astounded and also angry.

'Alexander Robert Kinloch,' Ivan repeated to Miranda, and spelled out my last name letter by letter so that there should be no mistake.

The lawyer, finally finding his voice, said, 'You *can't*.'

'Why not?' Ivan asked.

'But he's . . . he's . . . *look* at him.'

'He has long hair,' Ivan agreed. 'I wish he would cut it. All the same –'

36

'But your *daughter*,' Grantchester protested, 'what will she say?'

What Patsy would say raised anxious lines on Ivan's forehead. He gave me a long look of doubt, and I looked back with calm, allowing the decision to be his alone. If Patsy got her busy fingers on his affairs, I thought, he would never get them back.

Ivan looked at my mother. 'Vivienne, what do you think?'

She clearly felt, as I did, that he would have to make up his own mind. She said, 'The choice is yours, my dear. Your judgment is best.'

Ivan said to me, 'Alexander?'

'Whatever you want.'

'I advise Mrs Benchmark,' Oliver Grantchester said firmly. 'She's the natural person. She's your heir.'

Ivan dithered. The post-heart-attack Ivan dithered where once he would have dominated. The brewery's predicament had knocked his certainties to pulp.

'Alexander,' he said finally, 'I want *you*.'

I nodded, giving him a tacit promise.

'Alexander,' he said to Grantchester. 'I'll give the power of attorney to *him*.'

'You could have both of them,' his lawyer said, desperately. 'You could have both of them, acting jointly.'

Even he could see, though, that such a path would lead to chaos.

'Only Alexander,' Ivan said.

His lawyer wouldn't accept it without a struggle. I listened to him trying to persuade Ivan with heavy legal arguments to change his decision, and I thought frivolously that, never mind my stepfather, it was Oliver himself who didn't want to have to deal with Patsy raging.

Ivan, true at least to part of his nature, wouldn't be budged. Miranda typed my name on the document and Grantchester told me crossly to sign it, which I did. Ivan, of course, signed it also.

'Make certified copies,' Ivan said. 'Make ten.'

With irritation, the lawyer waved at Miranda who made ten copies on a portable fax machine. Grantchester himself signed them all, thereby, I gathered, certifying that the power of attorney had been properly drawn.

'Also,' Ivan said tiredly, 'I will write a letter to the brewery's Company Secretary making Alexander my Alternate Director, which will give him authority to act on my behalf in all business decisions at the brewery, not just my personal affairs, that are covered by the power of attorney.'

'You can't!' Grantchester said explosively. 'He knows nothing at all about business.'

Ivan looked at me calmly. 'I think he does,' he said.

'But he's . . . he's an *artist*.' Grantchester filled the word with an opinion near contempt.

Ivan said obstinately, 'Alexander will be my Alternate Director. I'll write the letter at once.'

The lawyer scowled. 'No good will come of it,' he said.

CHAPTER 3

My mother gave me her National Westminster Bank card for getting cash from machines and told me her secret number: a very extreme manifestation of trust.

I used the card and then bought a train ticket to Reading although I didn't, as she'd begged, acquire some 'decent' clothes before arriving at the offices of Pierce, Tollright and Simmonds.

I took with me from Ivan's study a folder containing the power of attorney, the certified copies, and a copy of Ivan's handwritten letter appointing me his Alternate Director.

Tobias Tollright looked me up and down, inspected the power of attorney and Ivan's letter and telephoned my mother.

'This person who says he's your son,' he asked her, 'would you please describe him.'

He had his office phone switched to conference, so I could hear her resigned reply.

'He's about six feet tall. Thin. He has chestnut hair, wavy, curling onto his shoulders. And, oh yes, he has a black eye.'

Tobias thanked her and disconnected, his enthusiasm for my appearance still bumping along at zero in a way that I was used to from men in suits.

'What is wrong', I asked, plunging in, 'at the brewery?'

Once he'd come to terms with the way I looked, he proved both astute and helpful. In my turn I ignored his fussy little mannerism of digging round his teeth with a succession of wooden picks and making sucking noises, and concentrated on understanding the mumbled nasal voice that by-passed the cleaning. He was barely ten years older than myself, I reckoned. Not enough age gap, anyway for him to pull much advantage of seniority. After the first ten minutes we got on fine.

His office was a boring functional box with a view of railway lines from a stark window, and strip lighting overhead that developed bags under the youngest eyes. Interesting to paint (a thin glaze of ultramarine perhaps, over yellow ochre) but terrible to live with.

'Basically,' he said, 'the man in charge of the brewery's finances has milked the cow and done a bunk to Brazil or some such haven with no extradition treaties. The brewery cannot in consequence meet its obligations. The creditors are restive, to put it mildly, and as auditor I cannot at the moment give King Alfred an OK to continue trading.'

More than enough, I thought, to give Ivan a heart attack.

I asked, 'How much is missing?'

He smiled. 'How big is a fog?'

'You mean, you don't know?'

'Our embezzler was the *Finance Director*. He worked the three-card trick. Find the queen ... but she's gone to a nice anonymous bank account for ever and all you have left is debts.'

I frowned. 'You're not being awfully precise.'

'I warned Sir Ivan last year that I thought he had an open drain somewhere, but he didn't want to believe it. Now he's so ill, he still won't face it. I'm sorry to say it, but there it is. And he would rather cover up the theft, if he can, than admit to the world that he – and his whole board of directors – has been careless and even stupid.'

'And he's not the first down that road.'

'Far, far from it.'

'So, what are your life-belt measures?'

He hesitated, picking away at the teeth. 'I can *advise* you,' he said, 'but I cannot act for you. As an auditor I must keep a certain distance from my clients' affairs. In effect, I can only point out a course of action you might wish to take.'

'Then please point.'

He fiddled some more with his mouth and I felt sore and in need of sleep and not scintillatingly bright.

'I would suggest,' he said carefully, 'that you might call in an insolvency practitioner.'

'A who?'

'Insolvency practitioner. Someone to negotiate for you.'

'I didn't know such people existed.'

'Lucky you.'

'Where do I find one?' I asked blankly.

'I'll give you a name. I can do that at least.'

'And,' I asked gratefully, 'what will he do?'

'She.'

'Oh, well, what will she do?'

'If she thinks the brewery can be saved – and to do that she will have to make her own independent assessment of the position – if she thinks there's still life in the corpse she'll set up a CVA.'

He looked at my face. 'A CVA,' he explained patiently, 'is a creditors' voluntary arrangement. In other words, she will try to call together a meeting of creditors. She'll explain to them the scope of the losses, and if she can persuade them that the brewery can go back to trading at a profit, they will together work out a rate at which the debts can be paid off bit by bit. Creditors will always do that if possible, because if they force a firm into total liquidation, they don't get paid much at all.'

'That,' I said, 'I understand.'

'Then,' Tobias went on, 'if the committee, acting with the brewery, can produce to me a budget and a forecast that will satisfy me as auditor that the brewery has a viable future, then I can sign the audited accounts, and it can continue to trade.'

'Well . . .' I thought for a bit, then said, 'What are the chances?'

'Fairly reasonable.'

41

'No higher?'

'It depends on the creditors.'

'And ... er ... who are they?'

'The usual. The bank. The Inland Revenue. The pension fund. The suppliers.'

'The bank?'

'The Finance Director organised a line of credit for expansion. The money's gone. There's no expansion and nothing in the bank to service the loan. To pay the interest, that is to say. The bank has given notice that they will not honour any more cheques.'

'And the tax people?'

'The brewery hasn't paid its employees' national insurance contributions for six months. The money's vanished. As for the pension fund, it's evaporated. The suppliers, in comparison, are small beer – if you'll excuse the dreadful pun – but the can suppliers are berserk.'

'What a mess,' I said. 'Aren't there any ... er ... *assets*?'

'Sure. The brewery itself. But there's an outstanding loan on that too, and nothing left to service it with. The bank would foreclose at a loss.'

'What about the pubs the brewery owns?' I asked.

'The tied houses? The Finance Director mortgaged the lot. To put it briefly, that money's gone too.'

'It sounds *hopeless*.'

'I've known worse.'

'And what about the King Alfred Cup?'

'Ah.' He concentrated on his teeth. 'You might ask Sir Ivan where it is.'

'At Cheltenham,' I said, puzzled. 'They run it at Cheltenham a month on Saturday.'

'Ah,' he said again, 'you're talking about the *race*.'

'Yes. What else?'

'The Cup itself,' he said earnestly. 'The King Alfred Gold Cup. The chalice. Medieval, I believe.'

I rubbed a hand over my face. Bruises were catching up.

'It's extremely valuable,' Tobias said. 'Sir Ivan should really consider selling it to offset some of the debt. But there is some doubt as to whether it belongs to the brewery or to Sir Ivan personally and . . . I say,' he broke off, 'are you feeling all right?'

'Yes.'

'You don't look it. Would you like some coffee?'

'Very much.'

He bustled about, organising what turned out to be tea.

I took another of Keith Robbiston's pills and slowly stopped sweating. The tea was fine. I smiled feebly to allay Tobias's kind concern and explained I'd travelled all night on the train, which seemed to him reason enough for faintness in the afternoon, even without the rainbowed eye.

'Actually,' I said, getting a better grip on things, 'I was wondering about the race itself, not the trophy. The race is part of the brewery's prestige. A sign of its success. Would . . . er . . . would the creditors agree to go ahead on the basis of keeping up public confidence in the brewery, even though the prize money will have to be found, and also the money for an entertaining tent and lunch and drinks for maybe a hundred guests? It's the brewery's best advertisement, that race. Cancelling it now, at this late stage, when the entries are already in, would send a massive message to all and sundry that the company's in a shaky state . . . and there's nothing like an ill wind for blowing a dicky house to rubble.'

He gazed at me. 'You'll need to say all that to the committee.'

'She . . . your insolvency angel, couldn't she say it?'

His gaze wandered over my hair and down to my paint-marked jeans, and I could see him thinking that the race had a better chance of survival with a more conventional advocate.

'You'll need to convince her.' He smiled briefly. 'You've convinced *me*.' He paused. 'Incidentally, among the brewery's possible assets there is a *racehorse*. That's to say, it's unclear again whether it belongs to the brewery or to Sir Ivan himself. I'd be glad if you could clarify it.'

'I?'

'You are in total charge. Your comprehensive powers of attorney make that unquestionably clear.'

'Oh.'

'Sir Ivan must have absolute faith in you.'

'In spite of how I look?'

'Well . . .' He gave me suddenly a broad grin. 'Since you mention it, yes.'

'I'm a painter,' I explained, 'and I look like one. You don't find droves of painters in pinstripes.'

'I suppose not.'

I drank a second cup of tea and asked idly, 'What is the name of the horse?'

'How do you hide a horse, Alexander . . . ?'

Hide a horse. Ye gods.

'It's called Golden Malt,' Tobias said.

Yesterday morning, I thought morosely, I was leading the peaceful if eccentric life of a chronicler of the equally eccentric compulsion to hit a small white ball a furlong or two and tap it over lovingly landscaped grass until it dropped into a small round hole. Yesterday morning's sensible madness now lay the other side of a violent robbery, an aching body, an edge-of-the-grave stepfather, his ordeal by domesticity and his shift onto my shoulders of ever-expanding troubles.

Ivan, I saw, wanted me to keep his horse hidden away from the clutches of bankruptcy. Ivan had given me the legal right to commit an illegal act.

'What are you thinking?' Tobias asked.

'Um . . . um . . . How is the brewery going to pay its workers this week?'

He sighed. 'You do have a way of cutting down to the essentials.'

'Will the bank cough up?'

'They say not. Not a penny more.'

'Do I have to go to them on my knees?'

He said with compassion, 'Yes.'

It was by then Wednesday afternoon. Payroll day at the brewery, as in most business enterprises, was Friday. On the

Tollright telephone I engaged the professional services of the lady negotiator and also made an appointment with the bank for the following morning.

I asked Tobias how much was needed to keep the ship afloat until the creditors could set up the rescue operation – if they would – and he obligingly referred to King Alfred's ledgers and told me a sum that made Ivan's heart attack seem a reasonable response to the information.

'You can only do your best,' Tobias observed, busy with a toothpick. 'None of this is your fault. It appears you've just been dumped into it up to the hilt.'

I didn't know whether to wince or smile at the familiar phrase. Up to the hilt – in one particular way I'd been in jeopardy up to the hilt for the last five years. It had taken five years for the demons to arrive at my door.

I said, 'About that horse – Golden Malt, did you say? – why is there a doubt about who owns it?'

Tobias frowned. 'You'll have to ask Sir Ivan. The horse isn't listed as an actual asset of the brewery. There's been no annual claim for depreciation, as if it were office equipment, but the brewery has paid the training fees and claimed them against tax as an advertising expense. As I said, you'll need to sort it out.'

For the next hour he tracked with me through the past year's accounts, item by item. I could see, as he demonstrated, that but for the perfidy of the man in charge of the cash flow, the beer business would have fermented its yeast to its usual profitable heights.

'The head brewer's the best asset,' Tobias said. 'Don't lose him.'

I said helplessly, 'I know nothing about brewing beer.'

'You don't have to. You are the overall strategist. I'm simply advising you as an outsider, and I can tell you the brewery's share of the market has risen perceptibly since they appointed this particular brewmaster.'

'Thank you.'

'You do look exhausted,' he said.

'I was never that good at maths.'

'You're doing all right.'

He produced papers for me to sign. I read them and did my best to understand, but trusted a lot to his good faith. As Ivan had trusted his Finance Director, no doubt.

'Good luck with the bank tomorrow,' Tobias said, shuffling the papers together and sucking his toothpick. 'Don't let them mug you.'

They wouldn't be the first, I thought. 'Will you come with me?'

He shook his head. 'It's your job, not mine. I wish you good luck.'

I said, 'There's one other thing . . .'

'Yes?'

'How do I get from here to Lambourn nowadays, without a car?'

'Taxi.'

'And without much money.'

'Ah,' he said. 'Same as ever. Bus to Newbury. Bus from there to Lambourn.' He summoned a timetable from reception. 'Bus from Newbury to Lambourn leaves at five forty-five.'

'Thanks.'

'What you need,' he said, 'is the out-patients department of the Royal Berkshire Hospital.'

I caught the bus instead. I even had time at Newbury to spend some of my mother's cash on a new pair of jeans and to discard the old paint-stained denims in the bus station's gents. In fractionally more respectable mode, therefore, I arrived on a Lambourn doorstep that I would have been happier to avoid.

My stepfather's horses – and that included Golden Malt – and also my uncle Robert 'Himself's' horses, were trained at the racing town of Lambourn by a young woman, Emily Jane Cox.

She said at the sight of me, 'What the hell are you doing here?'

'Slumming.'

'I hate you, Alexander.'

The problem was that she didn't, any more than what I felt for her could at worst be described as lust, and at best as unrealistic Round Table chivalry. Worse than hate or love, we had come near to apathy.

I had walked, feet metaphorically dragging, from the bus stop to the stable on Upper Lambourn Road. I had arrived as she was completing her evening rounds of the stable, checking on the welfare of each of the fifty or so horses entrusted to her care.

It was true, as jealous detractors pointed out, that she had inherited the yard as a going concern from a famous father, but it was her own skill that continued to turn out winners trained by Cox.

She loved the life. She loved the horses. She was respected and successful. She might once also have loved Alexander Kinloch, but she was not going to dump a busy and fulfilled career for solitude on a bare cold mountain.

'If you love me,' she'd said, 'live in Lambourn.'

I'd lived with her in Lambourn for nearly six months, once, and I'd painted nothing worth looking at.

'It doesn't matter,' she'd consoled me early on. 'Marry me and be content.'

I had married her and after a while left her. She'd never used my name, but had become simply Mrs Cox.

'What are you doing here?' she repeated.

'Er . . . Ivan has had a heart attack.'

She frowned. 'Yes, I read about it in the papers. But he's all right, isn't he? I telephoned. Your mother said not to worry.'

'He's not well. He asked me to look after his horses.'

'You? Look after them? You don't know all that much about horses.'

'He just said . . .'

She shrugged. 'Oh, all right then. You may as well set his mind at rest.'

47

She turned away from me and walked back across her stable yard to an open door where a lad was positioning a bucket of water.

She had dark hair cut like a cap and the sort of figure that looked good in trousers. We were the same age almost to the day, and at twenty-three had married without doubts.

She'd always had a brisk authoritative way of talking that now had intensified with the years of responsibility and success. I had admired – loved – her positive energy, but it had drained my own. Even if I'd still loved her physically, I couldn't have forever bowed to her natural habit of command. We would have quarrelled if I'd stayed. We would have fought if I'd ever tried to return. We existed in a perpetual uncontested truce. We had met four times since I'd left, but never alone and never in Lambourn.

Ivan had three horses in training in Emily's yard. She showed me two unremarkable bays and one bright chestnut, Golden Malt. Somewhat to my dismay he had noticeably good looks, two white socks and a bright white blaze down his nose: great presence as an advertisement for a brewery, not such a good idea for disappearing without trace.

'He's entered for the King Alfred Gold Cup,' Emily said with pride, patting the horse's glossy neck. 'Ivan wants to win his own race.'

'And will he?'

'Win?' She pursed her lips. 'Let's say Golden Malt's running for the news value. He won't disgrace himself, can't put it higher than that.'

I said absently, 'I'm sure he'll do fine.'

'What's the matter with your eye?'

'I got mugged.'

She nearly laughed, but not quite. 'Do you want a drink?'

'Good idea.'

I followed her into her house, where she led the way through the much lived-in kitchen, past her efficient office and into the larger sitting-room where she entertained visiting owners and, it seemed, revenant husbands.

48

'Still Campari?' she enquired, hands hovering over a tray of bottles and glasses.

'Anything.'

'I'll get some ice.'

'Don't bother,' I said, but she went all the same to the kitchen.

I walked across the unchanged room with its checked wool sofas and dark oak side tables and stood before a painting she'd hung on the wall. It showed a view of windswept links with a silver slit of sea in the background; with grey scudding clouds and two golfers doggedly leaning face-against the gale, trudging and pulling their golf clubs behind them on trollies. In the foreground, where long dry grass bent away from the wind, there lay a small white ball, invisible still to the players.

I'd sent the painting as a sort of peace offering: it was one of the first I'd painted in the bothy after I'd left, and seeing it again brought sharply back not just the feel of the paint going onto the canvas but also all the guilt and joyous sense of freedom of that time.

Emily said behind me, 'One of my owners brought a friend with him a few weeks ago who spotted that painting from across the room and said, "I say, is that an Alexander?"'

I turned. She was carrying two tumblers with ice in and looking at the picture. 'You'd signed it just Alexander,' she said.

I nodded. 'I always do, as you know.'

'Nothing else?'

'Alexander's long enough.'

'Anyway, he recognised it. I was very surprised, but he turned out to be some sort of art critic. He'd seen quite a lot of your work.'

'What was his name?'

She shrugged. 'Can't remember. I said you always painted golf, and he said no you didn't, you painted the perseverance of the human spirit.'

God, I thought, and I asked again, 'What was his name?'

'I told you, I can't remember. I didn't know I was going to

see you so soon, did I?' She walked over to the bottles and poured Campari and soda onto ice. 'He also said you might be going to be a great painter one day. He said you had both the technique and the courage. The courage, I ask you! I said what courage did it take to paint golf and he said it took courage to succeed at *anything*. Like training horses, he said.'

'I wish you could remember his name.'

'Well, I can't. He was a round little man. I told him I knew you and he went on a bit about how you'd got those tiny red flecks into the stems of the dry grass in the foreground.'

'Did he tell you how?'

'No.' She wrinkled her forehead. 'I think the owner asked me about his horse.'

She poured gin and tonic for herself, sat down and waved me to a sofa. It felt extraordinarily odd to be a guest where once I'd been host. The house had always been hers, as it had been her father's, but it had felt like my home when I'd lived there.

'That art man,' Emily said after a large swallow of gin, 'also said that your paintings were too attractive at present to be taken seriously.'

I smiled.

'Don't you mind?' she asked.

'No. Ugly is *in*. Ugly is considered *real*.'

'But I don't want ugly paintings on my walls.'

'Well . . . in the art world I'm sneered at because my paintings sell. I can do portraits, I accept commissions, I can draw – all unforgivable.'

'You don't seem bothered.'

'I paint what I like. I earn my bread. I'll never be Rembrandt. I settle for what I can do, and if that is to give pleasure, well, it's better than nothing.'

'You never said anything like that when you were here.'

'Too much emotion got in the way.'

'Actually,' she rose to her feet and crossed back to the picture, 'since that Sunday morning I've been looking at the grass.

So how did you get those tiny red flecks on the stalks? And the brown flecks and the yellow flecks, come to that.'

'You'd be bored.'

'No, actually, I wouldn't.'

Campari tasted sweet and bitter, a lot like life. I said, 'Well, first I painted the whole canvas bright red.'

'Don't be silly.'

'I did,' I assured her. 'Bright solid cadmium red, all over.' I rose and walked over to join her. 'You can still see horizontal faint streaks of red in the silver of the sea. There's even some red in the grey of the clouds. Red in those two figures. All the rest is overpainted with the colours you can see now. That's the chief beauty of acrylic paint. It dries so fast you can paint layer on layer without having to wait days, like with oils. If you try to overpaint oils too soon the layers can mix and go muddy. Anyway, that grass . . . I overpainted that once with raw umber, which is a dark yellowish brown, and on top of that I put mixtures of yellow ochre, and then I scratched through all the layers with a piece of metal comb.'

'With *what?*'

'A comb. I scratched the metal teeth through the layers right down to the red. The scratches lean as if with the wind . . . they are the stalks. The scratches show red flecks and brown flecks from the layers. And then I laid a very thin transparent glaze of purple over parts of the yellow, which is what gives it all that ripple effect that you get in long grass in a strong wind.'

She stared silently at the canvas that had hung on her wall for more than five years, and she said eventually, 'I didn't know.'

'What didn't you know?'

'Why you left. Why you couldn't paint here.'

'Em . . .' The old fond abbreviation arose naturally.

'You did try to tell me. I was too hurt to understand. And too young.' She sighed. 'And nothing's changed, has it?'

'Not really.'

She smiled vividly, without pain. 'For a marriage that lasted barely four months, ours wasn't so bad.'

I felt a great and undeserved sense of release. I hadn't wanted to come to Lambourn again: I'd avoided it from guilt and unwillingness to risk stirring Emily to an ill will she had in fact never shown. I had shied away habitually from the memory of her baffled eyes.

Her actual words to me had been tough. 'All right then, if you want to live on a mountain, bugger off.' It had been her eyes that had begged me to stay.

She'd said, 'If you care more for bloody paint than you do for me, bugger off.'

Now, more than five tranquillising years later, she said, 'I wouldn't have given up training racehorses, not for anything.'

'I know.'

'And you couldn't give up painting.'

'No.'

'So there we are. It's OK now between us, isn't it?'

'You're generous, Em.'

She grinned. 'I quite enjoy saintly forbearance. Do you want something to eat?'

It was she who made mushroom omelettes in the kitchen, though when I'd lived there I'd done most of the cooking. We ate at the kitchen table. She still had a passion for ice cream: strawberry, that evening.

She said, 'Do you want a divorce? Is that why you came here?'

Startled, I said, 'No. Hadn't thought of it! Do you?'

'You can have one any time.'

'Do you want one?'

'Actually,' she said calmly, 'I find it quite useful sometimes to be able to mention a husband, even if he's never around.' She sucked her ice-cream spoon. 'I'm used to being in charge. I no longer want a live-in husband, to be frank.'

She stacked our plates in the dishwasher, and said, 'If you don't want a divorce, why did you come?'

'Ivan's horses.'

'That's crap. You could have asked on the phone.'

The Emily I'd known had been forthrightly honest. She had

rid herself of some of the owners she'd inherited from her father because they'd sometimes wanted her to instruct her jockeys not to win. There was a world of difference, she'd said, between giving a young horse an easy race to get him to like the game, and trying to cheat the racing public by stopping a horse from winning in order to come home next time out at better odds. 'My horses run to win,' she said robustly, and the racing world, with clear-eyed judgment, gave her its trust.

It was tentatively, therefore, that I said, 'Ivan wants me to make Golden Malt disappear.'

'What on earth are you talking about? Do you want some coffee?'

She made the coffee in a drip-feed pot, a new one since my days.

I explained about the brewery's financial predicament.

'The brewery,' Emily said tartly, 'owes me four months training fees for Golden Malt. I wrote to Ivan personally about it not long before his heart attack. I don't like to bitch, but I want my money.'

'You'll get it,' I promised. 'But he wants me to take the horse away from here, so that it doesn't get sucked in and sold prematurely.'

She frowned, 'I can't let you take it.'

'Well . . . yes you can.'

I stretched down the table to reach the folder I'd brought with me and handed her one of the certified copies of the power of attorney, explaining that it gave me authority to do as I thought best regarding Ivan's property, which one way or another definitely included Golden Malt.

She read the whole thing solemnly and at the end said merely, 'All right. What do you want to do?'

'To ride the horse away from here tomorrow morning, when the town and the Downs are alive with horses going in all directions.'

She stared. 'Firstly,' she said, 'he's not an easy ride.'

'And I'd fall off?'

'You might. And secondly, where would you go?'

'If I tell you where, you'll be involved more than maybe you'd want to be.'

She thought it over. She said, 'I don't see how you can do it without my help. At the very least you need me to tell the lads not to worry when one of the horses goes missing.'

'Much easier with your help,' I agreed.

We drank the coffee, not talking.

'I like Ivan,' she said finally. 'Technically he's still my step-father-in-law, same as Vivienne is still my mother-in-law. I see them at the races. We're on good terms, though she's never effusive. We send each other Christmas cards.'

I nodded. I knew.

'If Ivan wants the horse hidden,' Emily said, 'I'll help you. So where do you plan to go?'

'I bought a copy of *Horse and Hound* in Newbury,' I said, taking the magazine out of the folder and opening at the pages of classified advertisements. 'There's a man here, over the Downs from here, saying he looks after hunters at livery and prepares horses for hunter 'chases and point-to-points. I thought about phoning him and asking him to take my hack for a few weeks. For four weeks, in fact, until a day or two before the King Alfred Gold Cup. The horse would have to come back here, wouldn't he, so he could run with you as trainer?'

She nodded absently, looking where my finger pointed.

'I'm not sending Golden Malt to *him*,' she announced. 'That man's a bully, horses go sour on him, and he thinks he's God's gift to women.'

'Oh.'

She thought briefly. 'I have a friend, a woman, who offers the same service and is a damn sight better.'

'Is she within riding distance?'

'About eight miles across the Downs. You'd get lost on the Downs, though.'

'Er . . . you used to have a map of the tracks and gallops.'

'Yes, the Ordnance Survey map. But my map must be seven years old. There are a lot of new roads.'

'Roads may change, but the tracks are seven *thousand* years old. They'll still be there.'

She laughed and fetched the map from the office, spreading it out on the kitchen table. 'Her yard is west of here,' Emily said, pointing. 'She's quite a good way away from Mandown, where most people exercise the Lambourn strings. She's *there*, see, outside the village of Foxhill.'

'I could find that,' I said.

Emily looked doubtful, but phoned her friend.

'My yard's so full,' she said, 'could you take an overflow for me for a week or two? Keep him fit. He'll be racing later on . . . You can? Good . . . I'll send one of my lads over with him in the morning. The horse's name? Oh, just call him Bobby. Send me the bills. How are your kids?'

After the chit-chat she put down the receiver.

'There you are,' she said. 'One conjuring trick done to order.'

'You're brilliant.'

'Absolutely right. Where are you sleeping?'

'I'll find a room in Lambourn.'

'Not unless you want to advertise your presence. Don't forget you lived here for six months. People know you. We got married in Lambourn church. I don't want tongues wagging that you've come back to me. You can sleep here, on a sofa, out of sight.'

'How about,' I said impulsively, 'in your bed?'

'No.'

I didn't try to persuade her. Instead, I borrowed her telephone for two calls, one to my mother to tell her I would be away for the night but hoped to have good news for Ivan the next day, and one to Jed Parlane in Scotland.

'How are you?' he said anxiously.

'Living at a flat-out gallop.'

'I meant . . . anyway, I took the police to the bothy. What a *mess*.'

'Mm.'

'I gave them your drawings. The police haven't had any other complaints about hikers robbing people around here.'

'Not surprising.'

'Himself wants to see you as soon as you return. He says I'm to meet you off the train and take you straight to the castle. When are you coming back?'

'With luck, on tomorrow night's Highlander. I'll let you know.'

'How is Sir Ivan?'

'Not good.'

'Take care, then,' he said. 'So long.'

Emily, deep in thought, said, as I put down the receiver, 'I'll send my head lad out with the first lot, as usual, but I'll tell him not to take Golden Malt. I'll tell him that the horse is going away for a bit of remedial treatment to his legs. There's nothing wrong with his legs, actually, but my lads know better than to argue.'

They always had, I reflected. Also, they faithfully stayed. She trained winners; the lads prospered, and did as she said.

She wrote, as she always did, a list of which lad would ride which horse when the first lot of about twenty horses pulled out for exercise at seven o'clock the next morning, and which lad would ride which horse in the second lot, after breakfast, and which lad would go out again later in the morning with every horse not yet exercised. She employed about twenty lads – men and women – for the horses, besides two secretaries, a house-keeper and a yard man. Jockeys came for breakfast and to school the horses over jumps. Vets called. People delivered hay and feed and removed manure. Owners visited. I'd learned to ride, but not well. The telephone trilled incessantly. Messages whizzed in and out by computer. No one ever for long sat still.

I had been absorbed into the busy scenery as general cook/dogsbody, and runner of errands, and although I'd fitted in as best I could, and for a while happily, my own internal life had shrivelled to zero. There had been weeks of self-doubt, of wondering if my compulsion to paint were mere selfishness, if the belief in talent was a delusion, if I should deny the promptings of my nature and be forever the lieutenant that Emily wanted.

Now, more than five years later, she put her newly written list for the head lad in the message box outside the back door. She let out her two labradors for a last run and walked round the stable yard to make sure that all was well. Then she came in, whistled for the dogs to return to their baskets in the kitchen, and locked her doors against the night.

All so familiar. All so long ago.

She gave me two travelling rugs to keep warm on the sofa and said calmly, 'Goodnight.'

I put my arms round her tentatively. 'Em?'

'No,' she said.

I kissed her forehead, holding her close. 'Em?'

'Oh,' she said in exasperation. 'All *right*.'

CHAPTER 4

She no longer slept in the big bedroom we'd shared, but in the old guest room, in a new queen-sized romping ground suitable for passing fancies.

She had slotted a new luxurious bathroom into what had once been her father's dressing-room. Downstairs the house might be as I remembered it, but upstairs it was not.

'This is not a precedent,' Emily said, taking off layers down to a white lace bra. 'And I don't think it's wise.'

'Bugger wise.'

'You obviously haven't been getting enough.'

'No, I haven't.' I switched off the lights and drew back the curtains, as I'd always done. 'How about you?'

'I'm known as a dragon. There aren't many with the guts of St George.'

'Do you regret it?'

She rustled out of the rest of her clothes and slid naked between the sheets, her curved shape momentarily silhouetted against a window oblong of stars. I took off my clothes and felt ageless.

'Rumours run round Lambourn like the pox,' she said. 'I'm bloody careful who I let into this room.'

We stopped talking. We had never, I supposed, been inventive or innovative lovers. There had been no need. Front to front with hands and lips and tongues we had shivered with sensual intense arousal, and that at least hadn't changed. Her body to my touch was long known and long forgotten, like going back to an abandoned building: a newly explored breast, familiar concave abdomen, hard mound of pelvis, soft dark warm mystery below and beyond, known secretly but never explored by spotlight since, in spite of her forthright public face, she was privately shy.

I did what I knew she liked, and as ever my own intensest pleasure came in pleasing her. Entry was easy, her readiness receptive. Movement strong and rhythmic, an instinct shared. When I felt her deep pulse beating, then too I took my own long moment; sometimes in the past it had been as good as that, but not always. It seemed that in that way also we had grown up.

'I've missed you,' she said.

'I, too.'

We slept peacefully side by side, and it was in the morning in the shower that she looked at my collection of bruises with disbelief.

'I told you,' I said mildly. 'I got mugged.'

'Trampled by a stampede of cows, more like.'

'Bulls.'

'OK, then. Bulls. Don't come downstairs until the first lot has gone out.'

I'd almost forgotten I was there to steal a horse. I waited until the scrunching hooves outside had diminuendoed into the distance and went down for coffee and toast.

Emily came in from the yard, saying, 'I've saddled and bridled Golden Malt. He's all ready for you, but he's pretty fresh. For God's sake, don't let him whip round and buck you off. The last thing I want is to have him loose on the Downs.'

'I've been thinking about anonymity,' I said, spreading honey on toast. 'Have you still got any of those nightcaps you put over their heads in very cold weather? A nightcap would hide that very white blaze down his nose. And perhaps boots for his white socks . . .'

She nodded, amused. 'And you'd better borrow a helmet from the cloakroom, and anything else you need.'

I thanked her and went into the large downstairs cloakroom where there was always a haphazard collection of jackets, boots, gloves and helmets for kitting out visitors. I found some jodhpur boots to fit me (better than trainers for the job) and tied my hair up on the top of my head with a shoelace before hiding the lot under a shiny blue helmet. I slung round my neck a pair of jockeys' goggles, the big mica jobs they used against rain and mud . . . fine disguise for a black eye.

Emily, still amused, said no one would recognise the result. 'And do borrow one of those padded jackets. It's cold on the Downs these mornings.'

I fetched a dark-coloured jacket and said, 'If anyone comes looking for the horse, say I had authority to take him, and I took him, and you don't know where he is.'

'Do you think anyone will come?' She was curious more than worried, it seemed.

'Hope not.'

Golden Malt eyed me with disillusion from inside his night-cap. Emily gave me a leg-up onto his back and at this point looked filled with misgiving.

'When the hell did you last sit on a horse?' she asked, frowning.

'Er . . . some time ago.' But I got my feet into the stirrups and collected the reins into a reasonable bunch.

'How often have you actually ridden since you left here?' Emily demanded.

'It's all in the mind,' I said. Golden Malt skittered around unhelpfully. It looked a long way down to the ground.

'You're a bloody fool,' she said.

'I'll phone you if anything goes wrong . . . and thanks, Em.'

'Yes. Go on, then. Bugger off.' She was smiling. 'I'll kill you if you let him get loose.'

I'd reckoned that the first three hundred yards might be the most difficult from the point of view of my deficient riding ability as I had to go that distance along a public road to reach the track that led up to the Downs; but I was lucky, there were few cars on the road and those that were had drivers who slowed down for racehorses. I touched my helmet repeatedly in thanks and managed to steer a not-too-disgraceful course.

No one wound down a window and called to me by name or linked the camouflaged horse to Emily. I was just on one of hundreds of Lambourn equine residents, large as life but also invisible.

Golden Malt thought he knew where he was going, which helped at first but not later. He tossed his head with pleasure and trotted jauntily up the rutted access to the downlands which spread for fifty miles east to west across central southern England – from the Chilterns to Salisbury Plain. I felt more at home on the Downs than in Lambourn itself, but even there solitude was rare: strings of horses cluttered every skyline and trainers' Land Rovers bumped busily in their wake. Lambourn's industry lay out there on the sweeping green uplands in the wind and the prehistoric mornings. I had thought that they would be world enough: that I could live and work there . . . and I'd been wrong.

Golden Malt began to fight when I turned him to the west at the top of the hill, instead of continuing to the east. He ran backwards, he turned in small circles, he obstinately refused to go where I tried to point his head. I didn't know whether expert horsemen with legs of iron would have forced him to obey in a long battle of wills: I only knew that I was losing.

I remembered suddenly that one day I'd stood beside Emily on the trainers' stand at a race meeting watching one of her horses refuse to go down to the start. The horse had run backwards, cantered crabwise, turned in circles, ignored every instruction and used his vast muscle power to make a fool of the slight man on his back. And that man had been a tough experienced jockey.

Across the years I heard Emily's furious comment, 'Why doesn't the bloody fool get off and *lead* him?'

Oh *Em*, I thought. My dear wife. Thank you.

I slid off the stubborn brute's back and pulled the reins over his head, and *walked* towards the west, and as if his entire nature had done an abracadabra, Golden Malt ambled along peacefully beside me so that all I had to worry about was not letting him step on my heels.

Emily's anxiety that I would get lost on the bare rolling grassland didn't take into consideration the boyhood training I'd had in following deer across unmapped Scottish moorlands. The first great rule was to determine the direction of the wind, and to steer by its angle on one's face. Stalking a deer was only possible if one were down wind of him, so that he couldn't smell one's presence.

The wind on that particular September day was blowing steadily from the north. I headed at first straight into it and then, when Golden Malt was used to its feel, veered slightly to the left, plodding purposefully across the green featureless sea as if I knew my bearings exactly.

I could see glimpses of villages in the lower distances, but no horses. When I'd walked about a mile I tried riding again, scrambling clumsily back into the saddle and gathering the reins; and this time, as if unsure in his isolation from sight and sound of his own kind, Golden Malt walked docilely where I asked.

I risked another trot.

No problem.

I crossed a footpath or two and skirted a few farms, setting dogs barking. There was no great need for pin-point accuracy at that stage of the journey because somewhere ahead lay the oldest path in Britain, the Ridgeway, that still ran east–west between the Thames at Goring Gap to West Kennet, a village south-west of Swindon. Although from there on it had disappeared, it was likely the Druids had walked it to reach Stonehenge. True to its name, it ran along the highest ground of the hills because once, long before the Romans came with Julius Caesar, the valleys had been wooded and prowled by bears.

In the age of cars, the Ridgeway path beckoned walkers, and to lone horse-thieves it was a broad highway.

When I reached it I almost missed it: trotted straight across and only belatedly realised that I'd been expecting more of a production than a simple rutted track. Indeed, I retraced my steps and stopped Golden Malt for a rest while I looked around for helpful signposts, and found none. I was on high ground. The track ran from east to west, according to the wind. It was definitely a *path*. It had to be the right one.

Shrugging, I committed the enterprise and turned left, to the west, and trotted hopefully on. All paths, after all, led *somewhere*, even if not to Stonehenge.

I had chosen a longer route than essential in order to avoid roads, and it was true that the Ridgeway didn't represent the straightest line from A to B, but as I didn't want to get lost and have to ask the way and draw attention to myself, I considered the extra time and miles well spent.

The path turned south-west at roughly where I expected and led across a minor road or two and, to my relief, proving to be the real thing, delivered me to Foxhill.

Emily's friend took my quiet arrival for granted.

'Mrs Cox,' I said, 'says she will call by in a day or two to pick up the saddle and bridle.'

'Fine.'

'I'll be off, then.'

'Right. Thanks. We'll look after the old boy.' She patted the chestnut neck with maternal and expert fondness, and nodded to me cheerfully as I left, not querying my assertion of thumbing a lift back to Lambourn.

I thumbed a lift to Swindon instead, however, and caught a train to Reading, and called on a powerful area bank manager who wasn't expecting a padded jacket, jodhpur boots and a shiny blue riding helmet with jockeys' goggles.

'Er . . .' he said.

'Yes. Well, I'm sorry about the presentation but I'm acting for my stepfather, Sir Ivan Westering, and this is not my normal world.'

'I know Sir Ivan well,' he said. 'I'm sorry he's ill.'

I handed him a certified copy of the power of attorney and Ivan's Alternate Director letter which, although much creased by now through having been folded into my shirt pocket for the cross-country expedition, worked its customary suspension of prompt ejection, and, smooth man that he was, he listened courteously to my plea for the workers at the brewery to receive their wages as usual for this present week, and for the pensioners to be paid also, while the insolvency practitioner, Mrs Morden, tried to put together a committee of creditors for a voluntary arrangement.

He nodded. 'I've already been approached by Mrs Morden.' He paused thoughtfully, then said, 'I've also talked to Tobias Tollright. He told me you would come here on your knees.'

'I'll kneel if you like.'

The faintest of smiles twitched in his eye muscles, and vanished. He said, 'What do you get out of this personally?'

Surprised, I didn't know what to say, so I didn't say anything, a feeble absence of answer that seemed not to bother him.

'Hmph.' He sniffed. He looked at his fingers. He said, 'All right. The wages cheques will be honoured for this week. We'll allow the pensioners seventy-five per cent. Then we'll see.' He stood up, holding out a smooth white hand. 'A revelation doing business with you, Mr Kinloch.'

I shook his hand and breathed deeply with relief on the way out.

With an hour and a half to spare before the intimidating prospect of my appointment with Mrs Margaret Morden, fairy godmother to near-bankrupt Cinderellas, I bought more throwaway razors, a small tube of shaving cream and another comb – the Euston collection being still in London – and in a pub tried to put a tidier face on things. Nothing but time, though, would unblack the eye. I drank half a pint of King Alfred Gold to get reacquainted with what I was trying to save and turned up promptly on the lady's threshold.

A word or two had gone ahead of me, I gathered, as she knew at once who I was and welcomed me without blinking. The power of attorney was yet again carefully inspected, a certified copy accepted and ready to be filed away, and a copy of Ivan's letter taken, as had been done also at Tollright's

64

firm, and the bank. Mrs Morden gave me back Ivan's open-sesames and requested me, in my turn, to sign an authorisation for her to act for the brewery. This was not handshake-gentleman's-agreement-land, this was paper-trail responsibility.

Mrs Margaret Morden looked somewhere in the ageless forties, and was not the severe businesswoman I'd expected. True, her manner was based on self-confidence, and formidable intelligence shone in steady grey eyes, but she was dressed not in a suit but in a soft calf-length dress of pink and violet printed silk, with a ruffle round the neck.

Involuntarily I smiled, and from her satisfied change of expression realised that that was exactly the aim of her clothes; to encourage, to soften prejudice, to mediate, to persuade.

Her office was spacious, a cross between functional grey and leather-bound law books, with a desk-like shelf the whole length of one wall, bearing six or seven computer monitors, all showing different information. A chair on castors stood ready before them, waiting, it seemed, to roll her from screen to screen.

She sat down in a large black chair behind a separate executive-sized desk and waved me to the clients' (slightly smaller) chair facing. There were brewery papers already spread out on the desk: she and Tobias between them had obviously wasted no time.

She said, 'We have here a serious situation . . .'

The serious situation was abruptly made worse by the door crashing open to admit a purposeful missile of a man, with a flustered secretary behind him bleating (as in a thousand film scripts), 'I'm very sorry, Mrs Morden, I couldn't stop him.'

The intruder, striding into centre-stage, pointed a sharp finger at my face and said, 'You've no right to be here. *Out.*' He jerked the finger towards the door. 'Any negotiations needed by the King Alfred Brewery will be performed by *me.*'

He was quivering with rage, a thin fiftyish man going extensively bald and staring fiercely through large glasses with silvery metal rims. He had a scrawny neck, a sharp adam's apple and megawatt mental energy. He told me again to leave.

Mrs Morden asked calmly, 'And you are . . . ?'

'Madam,' he said furiously, 'in the absence of Sir Ivan Westering I am in charge of the brewery. I am the acting managing director. This wretched young man hasn't the slightest authority to go round interviewing our auditor and our bank manager, as I hear he's been doing. You will disregard him and get rid of him, and *I* will decide whether or not we need your services at all, which I doubt.'

Mrs Morden asked non-commitally, 'Your name?'

He gasped as if amazed that she shouldn't know it. 'Finch,' he said sharply, 'Desmond Finch.'

'Ah, yes.' Mrs Morden looked down at the papers. 'It mentions you here. But I'm sorry, Mr Finch, Mr Kinloch has an undoubted right to act in Sir Ivan's stead.'

She waved a hand towards the certified copy of the power of attorney, which lay on her desk. Finch snatched it up, glanced at it, and tore the page across. 'Sir Ivan's too ill to know what he's doing,' he pronounced. 'This farce has got to stop. *I* am in charge of the brewery's affairs and I alone.'

Mrs Morden put her head on one side and invited my comment. 'Mr Kinloch?'

Ivan, I reflected, had deliberately by-passed Desmond Finch in giving me his trust, and I wondered why. It would have been normal for him to have passed his power to his second-in-command. If he hadn't done so – if he had very pointedly not done so – then my obligation to my stepfather was absolute.

'Please continue with your work, Mrs Morden,' I said without heat. 'I will check again with Sir Ivan, and if he wants me to withdraw from his affairs, then of course I will.'

She smiled gently at Finch.

'It's not good enough,' he said furiously. 'I want this . . . this usurper out *now*. This minute. At *once*. Mrs Benchmark is adamant.'

Mrs Morden lifted her eyebrows in my direction, no doubt seeing the arrival of total comprehension in my face.

'Mrs Benchmark,' I explained, 'is Patsy Benchmark, Sir Ivan's daughter. She would prefer me out of her father's life. She would prefer me . . . er . . . to evaporate.'

'Let me get this right,' Margaret Morden said patiently, 'Sir Ivan is Mrs Benchmark's actual father, and you are his stepson?'

I nodded. 'Sir Ivan had a daughter, Patsy, with his first wife, who died. He then married my widowed mother when I was eighteen, so I am his stepson.'

Finch, loudly and waspishly, added, 'And he is trying to worm his way into Sir Ivan's fortune and cut out Mrs Benchmark.'

'No,' I said.

I couldn't blame Margaret Morden for looking doubtful. Patsy's fear was obsessive but real.

'Please try to save the brewery,' I said to Mrs Morden. 'Sir Ivan's health may depend on it. Also, the brewery will be Patsy's one day. Save it for her, not for me. And she won't thank *you*, Mr Finch, if it goes down the tubes.'

It silenced them both.

Finch gaped and made for the door, and then stopped dead and came back to accuse with venom: 'Mrs Benchmark says you have stolen the King Alfred Gold Cup. You've stolen the golden chalice and you're hiding it, and if necessary she will take it back by force.'

Hell's teeth. '*Where is it?*'

My ribs ached.

The King Alfred Gold Cup. *It*. The *it* that the demons had been looking for. The *it* that I didn't have, not the *it* that I did have.

'You look tired, Mr Kinloch,' Mrs Morden said.

'*Tired!*' Finch was deeply sarcastic. 'If he's tired he can go back to Scotland and sleep for a week. Better, a month.'

Good suggestion, I thought. I said, 'Was the Cup kept at the brewery?'

Desmond Finch opened and closed his mouth without answering.

'Don't you know?' I asked with interest. 'Has there been a rumpus, with policemen flourishing handcuffs? Or did Patsy just *tell* you I'd taken it? She does have a galvanic way of neutralising people's common sense.'

The second-in-command of the brewery made an exit as unheralded as his entry. When the air had settled after his departure, Mrs Morden asked if by any chance I had a replacement certified copy of the power of attorney which, owing to Ivan's foresight in giving me ten, I had. I gave her one: five left.

'I need further instructions,' she said.

'Such as, carry on?'

'I am willing to, if you will give me a handwritten assurance releasing me from any proceedings arising from work done on your say-so. This is by no means a normal request, but little about this particular insolvency now seems normal.'

I wrote the release to her dictation, and signed it, and she had it witnessed by her secretary as being supplemental to the authorities to act that I'd already given her.

'I hope to bring together the brewery's main creditors on Monday,' she said. 'Telephone me tomorrow for a progress report.'

'Thank you, Mrs Morden.'

'Margaret,' she said. 'Now, these depressing numbers . . .'

I walked back to Pierce, Tollright and Simmonds, where the auditor and I became Tobe and Al and went out for an early beer.

I told Tobias of Desmond Finch's visit to Margaret Morden, a tale that resulted in much vicious chewing of an innocent toothpick but an otherwise diplomatic silence.

'Have you met him?' I asked, prompting.

'Oh yes. Quite often.'

'What do you think of him?'

'Off the record?'

'This whole pub,' I said, 'is off the record.'

Even so, his caution took its time. Then he said, 'Desmond Finch gets things done. He's a very effective lieutenant. Give him a programme he understands, and he will unswervingly carry it out. His energy pumps the blood round the brewery, and it is his persistence that makes sure that everything that ought to be done, is done.'

'You approve of him, then?'

He grinned. 'I applaud his work. I can't stand the man.'

I laughed. 'Thank God for that.'

We drank in harmony. I said, 'What was Norman Quorn like?' Norman Quorn was the Finance Director that had vanished with the cash. 'You must have known him well.'

'I thought I did. I'd worked with him for years.' Tobias took out a toothpick and swallowed beer. 'The last person, I would have thought, to do what he did. But then, that's what they always say.'

'Why was he the last person?'

'Oh. He was coming up to retirement. Sixty-five. A grey, meticulous accountant. No fun in him. Dry. We went through the firm's books together every year. Never a decimal out of place. It's my job of course to pull out invoices at random and make sure that the transactions referred to did in fact take place, and in Quorn's work there was never the slightest discrepancy. I'd have bet my reputation on his honesty.'

'He was saving everything up for the big one.'

Tobias sighed. Another toothpick took a mauling. 'He was clever, I'll give him that.'

'How did he actually steal so much? I've been reeling at the figures with Margaret Morden.'

'He didn't go round to the bank with a sack, if that's what you mean. He didn't shovel the readies into a suitcase and disappear through the Channel Tunnel. He did it the new-fashioned way, by wire.' He sucked noisily. 'He did it by electronic transfer, by routing money all over the place via ABA numbers – those are international bank identification numbers – and by backing up the transactions with faxed authorisations, all bearing the right identifying codes. He was too damned clever. I may have believed I could follow any tracks, but I've lost him somewhere in Panama. It's a job for the serious fraud people, though Sir Ivan wants to hush up the whole thing and won't call them in, and of course it wouldn't save the brewery if he did. Margaret Morden is the best hope for that. The only hope, I'd say.'

We refilled the half-pints in suitable gloom.

I said tentatively, 'Do you think Quorn could have stolen the King Alfred Cup? The actual gold chalice?'

'*What?*' He was astonished. 'No. Not his style.'

'But electronic transfers *were* his style?'

'I see what you mean.' He sighed deeply. 'All the same . . .'

'Desmond Finch says that Patsy Benchmark – have you met Ivan's daughter? – is accusing *me* of having stolen the Cup. She's persuasive. I may yet find myself in Reading Gaol.'

'Writing ballads à la Oscar Wilde?'

'You may jest.'

'I've met her,' Tobias said. He thought through another toothpick. 'The fact that no one seems to know where this priceless gold medieval goblet actually *is*, does not mean that it's been stolen.'

'I drink to clarity of mind.'

He laughed. 'You'd make a good auditor.'

'A better slosher-on of paint.'

I considered his friendly harmless-looking face and imagined the analytical wheels whirring round as fast in him as they were in me. Benevolent versions of Uncle Joe Stalin's vulpine smirk hid unsmiling intents from presidents to peasants and all points in between. Yet trust had to begin somewhere, or at least a belief in it.

I asked, 'What happened first? The disappearance of Norman Quorn, or your realisation that the books were cooked, or my stepfather's heart attack? And when was the Cup first said to be missing?'

He frowned, trying to remember. 'They were all more or less at the same time.'

'They can't have been simultaneous.'

70

'Well, no.' He paused. 'No one seems to have seen the Cup for ages. Of the other three . . . I told Sir Ivan one morning about two weeks ago . . . he was in his London house . . . that the brewery was insolvent, and why. He told me to cover it up and keep quiet. Quorn had already gone away for a few days' leave, or so the brewery secretaries said. Sir Ivan collapsed in the afternoon. I could get no instructions after that from anyone until you came along. The whole financial mess simply got worse while Sir Ivan was in hospital because no one except him could make decisions and he wouldn't talk to me. But the bank wouldn't wait any longer.'

'What about Desmond Finch?'

'What about him?' Tobias asked. 'Like I told you, he's a great lieutenant but he needs a general to tell him what to do. He may say now he's in charge, but without Mrs Benchmark prodding him from behind he'd be doing the same as he's been doing for the past two weeks, which is telling me he can't act without Sir Ivan's orders.'

It all, in a way, made sense.

I said, 'Margaret Morden says I don't have to go to the creditors' meeting on Monday.'

'No, better not. She'll persuade them if anyone can.'

'I asked her to root for the race.'

'Race? Oh yes. King Alfred Gold Cup. But no trophy.'

'The winner only ever gets a gold-plated replica. Never the real thing.'

'Life,' he said, 'is full of disillusion.'

When I reached the house in Park Crescent, Dr Keith Robbiston was just leaving, and we spoke on the steps outside with my mother holding the door open, smiling while she waited for me to go in.

'Hello,' Robbiston greeted me fast and cheerfully. 'How's things?'

'I finished the pills you gave me.'

'Did you? Do you want some more?'

'Yes, please.'

He instantly produced another small packet: it seemed he carried an endless supply. 'When was it,' he asked, 'that you fell among thieves?'

'The day before yesterday.' It felt more like a decade. 'How is Ivan?'

The doctor glanced at my mother and, clearly because she could hear, said briefly, 'He needs rest.' His gaze switched intensely back to me. 'Perhaps you, you strong young man, can see he gets it. I have given him a powerful sedative. He needs to sleep. Good day to you now.' He flapped a hand in farewell and hurried off in a life taken always at a run.

'What did he mean about rest?' I asked my mother, giving her a token hug and following her indoors.

She sighed. 'Patsy is here. So is Surtees.'

Surtees was not the great nineteenth-century story-teller of that name, but Patsy's husband, whose parents had been book-worms. Surtees Benchmark, tall, lean and of the silly-ass school of mannerism, could waffle apologetically while he did you a bad turn, rather like his wife. He saw me through her eyes. His own never twinkled when he smiled.

My mother and I went upstairs. I could hear Patsy's voice from the floor above.

'I *insist*, Father. He's got to go.'

An indistinct rumble in return.

As her voice was coming from Ivan's study I went up and along there with my neat mother following.

Patsy saw my arrival with predictable rage. She too was tall and lean, and stunningly beautiful when she wanted to charm. The recipients of her 'Darling!' greetings opened to her like sunflowers: only those who knew her well looked wary, with Surtees no exception.

'I have been telling Father,' she said forcefully, 'that he must revoke that stupid power of attorney he made out in your name and give it to *me*.'

I put up no opposition but said mildly, 'He can of course do what he likes.'

Ivan looked alarmingly pale and weak, sitting as ever in his dark red dressing-gown in his imposing chair. The heavy sedative drooped already in his eyelids, and I went across to him, offering my arm and suggesting he should lie down on his bed.

'Leave him alone,' Patsy said sharply. 'He has a nurse for that.'

Ivan however put both hands on my offered forearm and pulled himself to his feet. His frailty had worsened, I thought, since the day before.

'Lie down,' he said vaguely. 'Good idea.'

He let me help him towards his bedroom and, short of physically attacking me, Patsy and Surtees couldn't stop me. Four practised thugs had been beyond my fighting capabilities, but Patsy and her husband weren't, and they had sense enough to know it.

As I went past him, Surtees said spitefully, 'Next time you'll *scream.*'

My mother's eyes widened in surprise. Patsy's head snapped round towards her husband and with scorn she shrivelled him verbally, 'Will you keep your silly mouth *shut.*'

I went on walking with Ivan into his bedroom, where my mother and I helped him out of his dressing-gown and into the wide bed where he relaxed gratefully, closing his eyes and murmuring, 'Vivienne . . . Vivienne.'

'I'm here.' She stroked his hand. 'Go to sleep, my dear.'

He couldn't with so powerful a drug have stayed awake. When he was breathing evenly my mother and I went out into the study and found that Patsy and Surtees had gone.

'What did he mean?' she asked perplexed. 'Why did Surtees say, "Next time you'll scream"?'

'I dread to think.'

'It didn't sound like a joke.' She looked doubtful and worried. 'There's something about Surtees that isn't . . . oh dear . . . that isn't *normal.*'

'Dearest Ma,' I said, teasing her, 'almost no one is normal. Look at your son, for a start.'

Her worry dissolved into a laugh and from there to visible

happiness when from the study phone I told Jed Parlane that I would be staying down south for another twenty-four hours.

'I'll catch tomorrow night's train,' I said. 'I'm afraid it gets to Dalwhinnie at a quarter past seven in the morning. Saturday morning.'

Jed faintly protested. 'Himself wants you back here as soon as possible.'

'Tell him my mother needs me.'

'So do the police.'

'Too bad. See you, Jed.'

My mother and I ate the good meal Edna had cooked and left ready, and spent a peaceful, rare and therapeutic evening alone together in her sitting-room, not talking much, but companionable.

'I saw Emily,' I said casually, at one point.

'Did you?' She was unexcited. 'How is she?'

'Well. Busy. She asked after Ivan.'

'Yes, she telephoned. Nice of her.'

I smiled. My mother's reaction to my leaving my wife had been as always calm, unjudgmental and accepting. It was our own business, she had implied. She had also, I thought, understood. Her sole comment to me had been, 'Solitary people are never alone,' an unexpected insight that she wouldn't enlarge or explain, but she had long been accustomed to the solitary nature of her son's instincts, that I had tried – and failed – to stifle.

In the morning, when everyone had slept well, I talked for much longer than previously with Ivan.

He looked better. He still wore pyjamas, dressing-gown and slippers, but there was muscle tone and colour in his face, and clarity in his mind.

I told him in detail what I'd learned and done over the two days I'd spent in Reading. He faced unwillingly the whole frightening extent of the plundering of the brewery and

74

approved of the appointment of Margaret Morden as captain of the lifeboat to save the wreck.

'It's my own fault things got so bad,' Ivan sighed. 'But, you know, I couldn't believe that Norman Quorn would rob the firm. I've known him for years, moved him up from the accounts department, made him Finance Director, gave him a seat on the Board ... I *trusted* him. I wouldn't listen to or believe Tobias Tollright. I'll never be able to trust my own judgment again.'

I said, intending to console, 'The same thing happens to firms every year.'

He nodded heavily. 'They say the greater the trust the safer the opportunity. But *Norman* ... how *could* he ... ?'

His pain was more personal than financial, the treachery and rejection harder to bear than the actual loss, and it was the heartlessness of that personal treachery that he couldn't endure.

'I wish,' he said with feeling, 'that you would take over and run the brewery. I've always known you could do it. I hoped when you married that efficient and attractive young woman that you would change your mind and come in with me. So *suitable*. You could live in Lambourn in her training stables and manage the brewery in Wantage, only seven miles away. *Perfect*. A life most young men would jump at. But no, you have to be different. You have to go off and live on your own, and *paint*.' His voice wasn't exactly contemptuous, but he found my compulsion wholly incomprehensible. 'Your dear mother seems to understand you. She says you can't keep mountain mist in a cage.'

'I'm sorry,' I said inadequately. I could see the sense of the life path he'd offered. I didn't know why I couldn't take it. I did know it would result in meltdown.

I changed the subject and said I'd asked Margaret Morden to get the creditors if possible to keep the Cheltenham race alive; to get them to realise that the seventeenth running of the King Alfred Gold Cup would underpin public faith in the brewery and boost the sales that would generate the income that alone would save the day.

Ivan smiled. 'The Devil would like you on his side.'

'But it's true.'

'Truth can subvert,' he said. 'I wish you were my son.'

That silenced me completely. He looked as though he were surprised he had said it, but he let it stand. A silence grew.

In the end I said tentatively, 'Golden Malt . . . ?'

'My horse.' His gaze sharpened on my face. 'Did you hide it?'

'Did you mean me to?'

'Of course I did. I hoped you would, but . . .'

'But,' I finished when he stopped, '*you* are a member of the Jockey Club and can't afford to be in the wrong, and the creditors may want to count Golden Malt an asset and sell him. And yes, I did steal him out of Emily's yard but any sleuth worth his salt could find him, and if he has to vanish for more than a week I'll have to move him.'

'Where is he?'

'If you don't know, you can't tell.'

'Who does know, besides you?'

'At present, Emily. If I move him, it will be to shield her.' I paused. 'Do you have any proof that you personally own him? Bill of sale?'

'No. I bought him as a foal for cash to help out a needy friend. He paid no tax on the gain.'

'Tut.'

'You can't see that six years down the road your good turn will bite you.'

The telephone buzzed at his elbow, and he made a gesture asking me to answer it for him. I said 'Hello?' and found Tobias Tollright at the other end.

'Is that you, Al?' he asked. 'This is Tobe.' Fluster and insecurity in his voice.

'Hi, Tobe. What's up?'

'I've had this man on the phone who says Sir Ivan has revoked your powers of attorney.'

'What man?'

'Someone called Oliver Grantchester. A solicitor. He says he's in charge of Sir Ivan's affairs.'

'He certified all the copies of the power of attorney,' I said. 'What's wrong with them?'

'He says they were a mistake. Apparently Patsy Benchmark got Sir Ivan to say so.'

'Hold on,' I said, 'while I talk to my stepfather.'

I rested the receiver on the table and explained the situation to Ivan. He picked up the receiver and said, 'Mr Tollright, what is your opinion of my stepson's business sense?'

He smiled through the reply, then said, 'I stand by every word I signed.' He listened, then went on, 'My daughter misinformed Mr Grantchester. Alexander acts for me in everything, and I give my trust to no one else. Clear?' He gave me back the telephone and I said to Tobias, 'OK?'

'My God. That woman. She's dangerous, Al.'

'Mm ... Tobe, do you know any good, honest, discreet private investigators?'

He chuckled. 'Good, honest and discreet. Hang on ...' There was a rustle of pages. 'Got a pencil?'

There was a pencil on the table but no notepad. I turned over the box of tissues, in Ivan's fashion, and wrote on the bottom of it the name and phone number of a firm in Reading. 'Thanks, Tobe.'

'Any time, Al.'

I disconnected and said to Ivan, 'Patsy is also going around telling people I've stolen the chalice, the King Alfred Cup.'

'But,' he said, undisturbed, 'you do have it, don't you?'

CHAPTER 5

After a moment of internal chill I said carefully, 'Why do you think I have the Cup?'

He looked astonished but not yet alarmed. 'Because I sent it to you, of course. You are good at hiding things, Robert said. I sent it to you, to keep it safe.'

Hell's teeth, I thought. Oh God. Oh *no*.

I said 'How? How did you send it to me?'

For the first time he seemed to realise that however good his plans had been, somewhere along the line the points had got switched. He frowned, but still not with anxiety.

'I gave it to Robert to give to you. That's to say, I told him where to find it. Are you listening? Stop looking so blank. I asked your uncle Robert to take the damned Cup to Scotland for you to take care of. So don't tell me you don't have it.'

'Er . . .' I said, clearing my throat, 'when did you send it to Scotland?'

'I don't know.' He waved a hand as if the detail were unimportant. 'Ask Robert. If you haven't got the Cup, then he has.'

I breathed slowly and deeply, and said, 'Who else knew you were sending the Cup to me?'

'Who? No one else. What does it matter? Robert will pass the Cup to you when you go back to Scotland, and you can keep it safe for me until the brewery's affairs are settled because, like the horse, the Cup belongs to *me*, and I don't want to see it counted as a brewery asset and sold for a drop in the ocean.'

'Bill of sale?' I suggested hopelessly.

'Don't be ridiculous.'

'No.'

I asked with artificial absence of urgency, 'When did all this happen? When did you ask Himself to take the Cup to Scotland?'

'When? Oh, sometime last week.'

'Last week . . . while you were still in the Clinic?'

'Of course while I was in the Clinic. You're being very dense, Alexander. I was feeling very ill and I'd had so many drugs and injections, I was *thinking* double, let alone seeing, and Robert came to visit me while I was worried sick by Tobias Tollright, and he, Robert, of course, not Tollright, said he was leaving the next day for Scotland for his annual shooting and fishing, and for the Games, and it made sense to ask him to look after the Cup, and he said he would, but better still he would entrust it to *you*. I asked if he trusted you enough . . . and he said he would trust you with his life.'

Hell, I thought, and asked, 'Which day was that?'

'I can't possibly remember. Why do you think it matters?'

His own illness had been painful and traumatic but he hadn't, I thought, had a lot of fists thudding like ramrods into his ribs and abdomen until he could hardly breathe, he hadn't been head-butted and bounced half unconscious down a mountain and he hadn't spent three days bruised, aching and sorry for himself, swallowing Keith Robbiston's pills to make life tolerable.

By that Friday morning, as it happened, the waves of overall malaise had receded; only individual spots were at that point sore to the touch. I felt more or less normal.

Next time you'll scream.

I relaxed into my chair and asked conversationally, 'Did you tell Patsy that I was looking after the Cup?'

Ivan said, 'I do wish you and Patsy could like each other. Your dear mother and I are so fond of each other, but with our children we are not a successful family. You and Patsy

79

both have such strong characters, it's such a shame you can't be friends.'

'Yes, I'm sorry,' I said, and it was true that I was. I would actually have liked to have a sister. I went on, 'She did, though, tell Desmond Finch that I'd stolen the Cup, and he believes it and is spreading it about, which is unfortunate.'

'Oh, Desmond,' Ivan said indulgently. 'Such a good man in so many ways. I rely on him, you know, to get things done. He's thorough, which so many people are not these days. At least through all this troubling time I can be sure that the brewing and sales are running as they should.'

'Yes,' I said.

The spurt of returning health that had carried Ivan through the morning began to fade, and we sat quietly together, taking life at his pace, which was slow to negligible. I asked him if I could bring him anything, like coffee, but he said not.

After a while, in which he briefly dozed, he said with weakness, 'Patsy couldn't have been sweeter when I was in the Clinic. She came every day, you know. She looked after my flowers . . . I had so many plants, people were so kind. Everyone in the Clinic said how lucky I was to have such a loving, thoughtful and beautiful daughter . . . and perhaps she was in and out when Robert came, but I can't think how she thought you had *stolen* the Cup. You must be mistaken about that, you know.'

'Don't worry about it,' I said.

Armed with generous cash from my mother I trekked back by rail to Reading and went to see the firm of Young and Uttley, the investigators recommended by Tobias. An unprepossessing male voice on the telephone having given me a time and a place, I found a soulless box of an office – outer room, inner room, desks, filing cabinets, computers and coat stand – with an inhabitant, a man of about my own age dressed in jeans, black hard boots, a grubby singlet with cut-out armholes and a heavy black hip-slung belt shining with aggressive studs. He

80

had an unshaven chin, close-cropped dark hair, one earring dangling – right ear – and the word HATE in black letters across the backs of the fingers of both hands.

'Yeah?' he said, when I went in. 'Want something?'

'I'm looking for Young and Uttley. I telephoned—'

'Yeah,' said the voice I'd heard on the phone. 'See. Young and Uttley are *partners*. That's their pictures on the wall, there. Which one do you want?'

He pointed to two glossy eight-by-ten-inch black and white photographs drawing-pinned to a framed cork board hanging on a dingy wall. Alongside hung a framed certificate giving Young and Uttley licence to operate as private investigators, though to my understanding no such licence was necessary in Britain, nor existed. A ploy to impress ignorant clients, I supposed.

Mr Young and Mr Uttley were, first, a sober dark-suited man with a heavy moustache, a striped tie and a hat, and secondly, a wholesome fellow in a pale blue jogging suit, carrying a football and a whistle and looking like a dedicated schoolteacher going out to coach children.

I turned away, smiling, and said to the skin-head watching me, 'I'll take you as you are.'

'What do you mean?'

'Those pictures are both you.'

'Quick, aren't you?' he said tartly. 'And Tobe warned me, and all.'

'I asked him for someone good, honest and discreet.'

'You got him. What do you want done?'

I said, 'Where did you learn your trade?'

'Reform school. Various nicks. Do you want me or not?'

'I want the discreet bit most of all.'

'Priority.'

'Then I want you to follow someone and find out if he meets, or knows where to find, four other people.'

'Done,' he said easily. 'Who are they?'

I drew them for him in a mixture of pencil and ball-point, having somewhere lost my charcoal. He looked at the drawings, one of Surtees Benchmark, and one of each of my four attackers.

I told him Surtees's name and address. I said I knew nothing about the others except their ability to punch.

'Are those four how you got that eye?'

'Yes. They robbed my house in Scotland, but they have south-east England voices.'

He nodded. 'When did they hit you?'

'Tuesday morning.'

He mentioned his fee and I paid him a retainer for a week. I gave him Jed's phone number and asked him to report.

'What do I call you?' I asked.

'Young or Uttley, take your pick.'

'Young and Utterly Outrageous, more like.'

'You're so sharp, you'll cut yourself.'

I went grinning to the train.

I spent the later part of the afternoon shopping, accompanied by my long-suffering mother, who paid for everything with her credit cards.

'I suppose,' she said at one point, 'you weren't *insured* against the loss of your winter clothes and your climbing gear and your paints?'

I looked at her sideways, amused.

She sighed.

'I did insure the jeep,' I said.

'That's something, at least.'

Back at Park Crescent I changed into some of the new things and left the jodhpur boots, padded jacket, crash helmet and goggles for return to Emily sometime, and I told Ivan (having checked with Margaret Morden) that so far the brewery's creditors were earning haloes and had agreed to meet on Monday.

'Why don't you stay here?' he said, a shade petulantly. 'Your mother would like it.'

I hadn't told him about the attack on the bothy so as not to trouble him and he hadn't persisted in asking how I'd hurt my eye. I explained my departure in the one way that would satisfy him.

'Himself wants me up there . . . and I'd better do something about the Cup.'

Relaxing, he nodded. 'Keep it safe.'

The three of us tranquilly ate an Edna-cooked dinner, then I shook Ivan's hand, hugged my mother warmly, humped my bags and boxes along to Euston, boarded the Royal Highlander and slept my way to Scotland.

Even the air at Dalwhinnie smelled different. Smelled like home. Cold. Fresh. A promise of mountains.

Jed Parlane was striding up and down to keep warm and blowing on his fingers. He helped carry my clutter out to his car and said he was relieved to see me and how was I feeling.

'Good as new.'

'That's more than can be said for the bothy.'

'Did you lock it?' I asked, trying not to sound anxious.

'Relax. Yes, I did. In fact I got a new lock for it. Whatever was there when you left is still there. Himself asks me to drive over and check every day. No one is sniffing around, that I can see. The police want to interview you, of course.'

'Sometime.'

Jed drove me not to the bothy but, as arranged, straight to Kinloch Castle to talk to Himself.

The castle was no fairy-tale confection of Disney spires and white-sugar icing, but like all ancient Scottish castles had been heavily constructed to keep out both enemies and weather. It was of thick and plain perpendicular grey stone with a minimum of narrow windows that had once been arrow slots for archers. Built on a rise to command views of the valley at its foot, it looked dour and inhospitable and threatening even on sunny days, and could chill the soul under nimbostratus.

My father had grown up there, and as a grandson of the old earl I'd played there as a child until it held no terrors: but times had changed and the castle itself no longer belonged to

83

the Kinloch family but was the property of Scotland, administered and run as a tourist attraction by one of the conservation organisations. Himself, who had effected the transfer, had pronounced the roof upkeep and the heating bills too much for even the Kinloch coffers, and had negotiated a retreat to a smaller snugger home in what had once been the kitchen wing with living quarters for a retinue of dozens.

Himself would on occasion dress in historic Highland finery and act as host to visiting monarchs in the castle's vast main dining-hall, and it had been after one such grand evening, about six years earlier, that an enterprising band of burglars in the livery of footmen had lifted and borne away an irreplaceable gold-leafed eighteenth-century dinner service for fifty. Not a side plate, not a charger, had surfaced since.

It had been less than a year later, when a second theft had deprived the castle of several tapestry wall-hangings, that Himself had thought of a way of keeping safe the best known and most priceless of the many Kinloch treasures, the jewel-encrusted solid gold hilt of the ceremonial sword of Prince Charles Edward Stuart, Bonnie Prince Charlie.

It had, of course, meant taking the hilt out of its supposedly thief-proof display case and replacing the real thing with a replica. Ever since he had whisked the genuine article to safety, Himself had politely refused to tell the castle's administrators where to find it. It belonged to *him*, he maintained, as it had been given personally by Prince Charles Edward to his ancestor, the earl of Kinloch at the time, and had been handed down to him, the present earl, in the direct male line.

So had the castle, the administrators said. The hilt belonged to the nation.

Not so, Himself argued. The castle transfer documents had not included personal property and had in fact specifically excluded the hilt.

There had been hot debates in newspapers and on television as to when, if ever, a gift to one man became the property of all.

Moreover, as Himself pointed out, the hilt had been given

84

as thanks and appreciation for hospitality, horses and provisions. The facts were well attested. Prince Charles Edward, on his long retreat northwards (after his nearly successful campaign to win the English crown) had stayed for two nights at Kinloch Castle, had been comforted and revictualled, his retinue rested and re-horsed, for which services he had passed on to the then earl the hilt of his ceremonial sword, the blade having been earlier snapped off short in an accident.

The sword had never been used in nor intended for battle: it was too heavy and too ornate, a symbol of power and pomp only. The Prince, his dreams shattered like the blade, had left it behind and ridden on towards Inverness, to what proved to be his army's last decisive defeat at Culloden.

The Prince, tougher in flight, had famously escaped across Scotland to the Western Isles, making it safely back to France. The Earl of Kinloch, not so lucky, had been beheaded by the English for his allegiance (like poor fat old Lord Lovat) but had by then passed the splendid hilt to his son, who passed it to *his* son, and so on down the generations. It had become known as the 'Honour of the Kinlochs', and Himself, the present earl, though he had had to cede his castle, had finally won a declaration in the courts (still disputed) that the hilt, for his lifetime at least, belonged to *him*.

Since he had 'disappeared' the hilt, the castle had been further robbed of a display of Highland artifacts: shields, claymores and brooches. Himself, in residence in London at the time of that break-in, had made sarcastic remarks about bureaucrats being hopeless custodians of treasures. Ill-feeling flew like barbs in the air. The castle's bruised administrators were now hell-bent on finding the hilt, to prove that Himself was no better at guarding things than they were.

Under guise of rewiring and refurbishing the castle, including Himself's wing, they were inching with probes everywhere, determined on uncovering the cache. All they had wrung out of Himself was a promise that the Honour of the Kinlochs had not left his property. The ill-feeling and the search went on.

Jed having decanted me at the private wing's seldom-locked door I went inside and found my uncle in his dining-room, dressed in tweeds despite the early hour and pouring coffee from a pot on the sideboard.

He gave me, as always when we met after an interval, the salutation of my whole name, to which I replied with old and easy formality.

'Alexander.'

'My lord.'

He nodded, smiled faintly, and gestured to the coffee.

'Breakfast?'

'Thank you.'

He took his cup over to the table and began eating toast. Two places had been laid at the table, and he waved me to the free one.

'That's laid for you,' he said. 'Your aunt stayed in London.'

I sat and ate toast and he asked me if I'd had a good journey.

'I slept all the way.'

'Good.'

He was a tall man, topping me by at least four inches, and broad and large without looking fat. At sixty-five he had grey hair showing a white future, a strong nose, heavy chin and guarded eyes. His physical movements tended to be unco-ordinated and clumsy; his mind was as tough and solid as an oak. If it were true that he'd told Ivan he would trust me with his life, then the reverse in general was also true, but like many good men he tended to trust too many people, and I wouldn't have staked my life on his absolute silence, even though any indiscretion would have been unintentional.

He said, spreading marmalade, 'Jed told me what happened at the bothy.'

'Boring.'

He wanted me to tell him in detail what had happened, so I did, though with distaste. I told him also about Ivan giving me the power of attorney, and my experiences in Reading.

He drank three cups of coffee, stretching as if absently for slice after slice of toast.

Eventually I asked him calmly, 'So do you have the King Alfred Gold Cup? Is it here?'

He answered broodingly, 'I did tell Ivan you were good at hiding things.'

'Mm.' I paused. 'Probably someone heard you.'

'God, Al.'

I said, 'I think it was the chalice, not the hilt, that those men were trying to find at the bothy. I also think they hadn't been told precisely what they were looking for. They kept saying "Where is it?" but they didn't say what they meant by *it*. I thought at the time they meant the hilt, because I didn't know Ivan had given you the Cup, but also it seemed possible they were simply fishing for anything I valued.' I sighed. 'Anyway, I'd say now the *it* was definitely the Cup.'

He said heavily, 'Jed said they'd hurt you badly.'

'That was Tuesday. Today's Saturday, and I'm fine. Don't worry about it.'

'Was it my fault?'

'It was the Finance Director's fault for running off with the brewery's cash.'

'But mine for suggesting you to Ivan.'

'It's history.'

He hesitated. 'I still have to decide what to do with that damned lump of gold.'

I did not make instant glad-eyed offers to keep it safe.

He listened to my silence and gave me a rueful shake of the head.

'I can't ask it of you, I suppose,' he said.

Next time you'll scream . . . There would be no next time.

I said, 'Patsy has told a few people that I already have the Cup. She's saying I stole it from the brewery.'

'But that's nonsense!'

'People believe her.'

'But you've never been to the brewery. Not for years, anyway.'

I agreed. 'Not for years.'

'Anyway,' said my uncle, 'it was Ivan himself who took the

Cup out of the brewery, on the day before his heart attack. He told me he was feeling deeply upset and depressed. His firm of auditors – what's that chap's name . . . Tollright? – were warning him he was on the point of losing everything. And you know Ivan . . . he was worried both about his workpeople losing their jobs and about himself losing face and credibility. He takes his baronetcy and his membership of the Jockey Club very seriously . . . he could not bear having his whole life collapse in failure.'

'But it wasn't his fault.'

'He appointed Norman Quorn to be Finance Director. He says he no longer trusts his own judgment. He's taking too much guilt onto his own shoulders.'

'Yes.'

'So when he could see bankruptcy and disgrace ahead, he simply walked out with the Cup. Sick at heart was the phrase he used. Sick at heart.'

Poor Ivan. Poor sick heart.

I asked, 'Did he take the Cup to Park Crescent? Is that where you collected it from?'

My uncle half laughed. 'Ivan said he was afraid it would be as accessible in Park Crescent as in the brewery. He wanted to keep it out of any asset-pool and he didn't want to leave a paper-trail, like renting a bank vault, so he left it . . . you'll laugh . . . he left the treasure in a cardboard box in the cloakroom of his club. Left it in the care of the door-keeper.'

'Hell's teeth.'

'I fetched it from his club. Gave the doorman a thank you. Brought the Cup up here, in my car. James and I drove up here together as usual, you see. The family flew up, of course.'

James was his eldest son, his heir.

'I didn't tell James what I'd got,' Himself observed thoughtfully. 'James doesn't understand the word secret.'

James, a friendly fellow, liked to talk. Life, to my cousin James, was mostly a lark. He had a pretty wife and three wild children, 'all away sailing this week,' explained Himself, 'when they should be back at school.'

My uncle and I left the dining-room and walked outside round the whole ancient complex, as he liked to do, our feet quiet on the sheep-cropped grass.

'I asked Ivan how much the King Alfred Cup was actually worth,' he said. 'Everyone tends to refer to it as priceless, but it isn't, of course. Not like the hilt.'

'How much did Ivan say?'

'He said it was a symbol. He says you can't put a price on a symbol.'

'I suppose he's right.'

We walked a way in silence, then he said, 'I told Ivan I wanted to get the Cup valued. If he wanted me to get you to look after it, I had to know its worth.'

'What did he say?'

'He got very agitated. He said if I took it to a reputable valuer he would end up losing it. He said it was too well known. He began panting with distress. I had to assure him I wouldn't take it to anyone that would recognise it.'

'But,' I said, 'no one else could give you a reliable estimate.'

He smiled. We rounded the southernmost corner and turned our faces into the endless wind.

'This afternoon,' he said, raising his voice, 'we'll find out.'

The valuer summoned to the castle was neither an auctioneer nor a jeweller, but a thin eighty-year-old woman, a retired lecturer in English from St Andrew's University, Dr Zoë Lang, with a comet tail of distinguished qualifications after her name.

My uncle explained he had met her 'at some function or other', and when she arrived, gushing but overwhelmingly intellectual, he waved a vague hand in my direction and introduced me as 'Al, one of my many nephews'.

'How do you do?' Dr Lang asked politely, giving me a strong bony handshake with her gaze elsewhere. 'Cold day, isn't it?'

Himself made practised small-talk and led the way into the dining-room, where with gentle ceremony he sat his guest at the table.

'Al,' he said to me, 'there's a box in the sideboard, right-hand cupboard. Put it on the table, would you?'

I found and carried across a large brown cardboard box stuck all over with sticky tape and conspicuously marked in big black handwritten capitals, 'Books. Property of Sir I. Westering'.

'Open it, Al,' Himself instructed without excitement. 'Let's see what we've got.'

Dr Lang looked politely interested, but no more.

'I have to warn you again, Lord Kinloch,' she said in her pure Scots voice, 'that almost no significant works of goldsmiths' art survive from the ninth century in England. I have done as you asked and kept your request private, which has been no hardship as the last thing you want, I'm sure, is ridicule.'

'The last,' Himself agreed gravely.

Dr Zoë Lang had straight grey hair looped back into a loose bun on her neck. She wore glasses and lipstick, and clothes too large for her thin frame. There was a small gold brooch but no rings. Something about her, all the same, warned one not to think in terms of dry old virginal spinster.

I ripped off the sticky tape and opened the box, and found inside, as promised, books: old editions of Dickens, to be precise.

'Keep going, Al,' my uncle said.

I lifted out the books and underneath came to a grey duster-cloth draw-string bag enclosing another box. I lifted that out also.

The inner box, in size a twelve-inch cube, was of black leather with gold clasps. Between the clasps, stamped in small gold letters, were the words MAXIM, London. I freed the box from its protecting bag and pushed it across the table to Himself.

'Dr Lang,' he said courteously, pushing the box on further into her reach, 'do us the honour.'

Without flourish she undid the clasps and opened the box, and then sat as still as marble while I felt her surprise in mental gusts across the table.

'Well,' she said finally, and again, '*Well . . .*'

Inside the box, supported by white satin-covered cushioning, the King Alfred Gold Cup lay on its side. I had never actually seen it before and nor, from his expression, had my uncle Robert.

No wonder, I thought, that Ivan had wanted to keep that Cup for his own. No wonder he wanted it hidden and kept safe. That Cup must have come to mean as much to him as Prince Charles Edward's sword hilt had come to mean to the earls of Kinloch, the affirmation that the personal stewardship of symbolic treasures should not be whisked away by ephemeral grey-faces, who wouldn't, down the decades, care a jot.

King Alfred's Cup, bigger than I'd imagined, was in shape a wide round bowl on a sturdy neck with a spreading foot. The rim of the bowl was crenellated like many castles (Windsor, but not the Kinlochs'): its sides glittered with red, blue and green inlaid stones and overall it shone with the warm unmistakable golden glow of twenty-two carats at least.

With almost reverence Dr Lang lifted out the astonishing object and stood it on the polished wood of the table, where it gleamed as if with inner light.

Dr Lang cleared her throat and said as if pulling herself down to earth, 'King Alfred never saw this, of course. It's shaped like a chalice, but if King Alfred ever used anything like this to take communion, it would have been much smaller and, of course, very much lighter. This cup must weigh five or more pounds. No . . . sad as I am to say it, this cup is modern.'

'*Modern?*' Himself echoed, surprised.

'Certainly not medieval,' regretted the expert. 'Almost certainly Victorian. Eighteen-sixty, or thereabouts. Very handsome. Beautiful, even. But not old.'

The cup had what looked like a pattern engraved right round the top below the crenellations and again round the lower third of the bowl. Dr Lang looked attentively at the patterns and smiled with obvious enjoyment.

'The cup is engraved with a poem in Anglo-Saxon,' she said. 'No trouble spared. But it's still Victorian. And I doubt if those coloured stones are rubies and emeralds, though you'd need to get an informed opinion for that.'

'Can you read the poem?' I asked.

She glanced at me briefly. 'Of course. I taught Anglo-Saxon for years. Wonderful vigorous poetry, what little's left of it. No printing presses or copying machines then, of course.' She fingered the bands of engraving. 'This is Bede's Death Song. Very famous. Bede died in 735, long before Alfred was born.' She turned the cup round, searching with her fingers for the beginning of the verse. 'In literal translation it says, "Before that sudden journey no one is wiser in thought than he needs to be, in considering, before his departure, what will be adjudged to his soul, of good or evil, after his death-day."'

Her old voice held the echo of years of lecturing to students; the authority of confident scholarship. At seventeen I had run away from that sort of slightly didactic tone and deprived myself of much enlightenment in consequence, and all these years later I found I still irrationally resented her perfectly justifiable consciousness of the high ground of superior knowledge.

Be ashamed of yourself, Al, I thought. Be humble. Bede's Death Song's message was of taking stock of the good and evil one did on earth because hell after death was a certainty. Unimaginable centuries later I believed that the only real hell was on earth and usually undeserved: and I was not going to discuss it with Zoë Lang.

I took it for a certainty that Ivan knew what teaching was engraved on his Cup. He had judged and found himself culpable and was harder on himself precisely because his standard for his own probity had been set so high. I wondered if he valued the Cup more for what was inscribed on it than for its intrinsic worth.

'So how much,' Himself was asking his expert, 'should one insure this Cup for?'

'Insure?' She pursed her lips. 'You could weigh it and multiply by the current price of gold, or you could maintain it is a valuable and interesting example of Victorian romanticism, or you could say it's worth dying for.'

'Not that.'

'People die in defence of their property all the time. It's a powerful instinct.' She nodded as if to emphasise the point. 'I don't think you could insure this Cup for any more than its worth in gold.'

Its weight in gold wouldn't save the brewery or go anywhere near subtracting even a significant nought.

My uncle thoughtfully restored the Cup to its box and closed the lid. The whole room looked a little darker at its eclipse.

'The accounts of King Alfred burning the cakes and suffering from haemorrhoids were all tosh,' Dr Lang said in her lecturing voice. 'King Alfred suffered from spin-doctors. But the fact remains, he is the only king in Britain ever to be called great. Alfred the Great. Born in Wantage, Berkshire. He was the fifth son, you know. Primogeniture wasn't supreme. They chose the fittest. Alfred was a scholar. He could read and write, both in Latin and his native tongue, Anglo-Saxon. He freed southern England – Wessex – from the rule of the invading Danes, first by appeasement and sly negotiation, then by battle. He was *clever*.' Her old face shone. 'People now try to make him a twentieth-century thinking social worker who founded schools and wrote new good laws, and the probabilities are that he did both, but only in the context of his own times. He died in 899, and no other well-authenticated king of that whole first millennium is so revered or honoured, or even remembered. It's a great pity this remarkable gold chalice here isn't a genuine ninth-century treasure, but of course it would have been either stolen or lost when Henry VIII devastated the churches. So many old treasures were buried in the fifteen-thirties to keep them safe, and the buriers died or were killed without telling where the treasures were hidden, and all over England farmers still to this day find gold deep in their fields, but not this Cup. Alas, it wasn't around in the days of Henry VIII. I think, actually, that the proper place for it now is in a museum. All such treasures should be cared for and displayed in museums.'

She stopped. Himself, who disagreed with her, thanked her warmly for her trouble and offered her wine or tea.

'What I would like,' she said, 'is to see the Kinloch hilt.'

Himself blinked. 'We have only the replica on show.'

'The real one,' she said. 'Show me the real one.'

After less than three seconds he said, smiling, 'We have to keep it safe from Henry VIII.'

'What do you mean?'

'I mean we have had to bury it to keep it.' He was making a joke of it and, unwillingly, she smiled tightly and settled for a sight of the copy.

We walked down the long passage where once relays of footmen had hurried with steaming dishes from kitchen to Great Hall, and Himself unlocked the weighty door that let us into the castle proper.

The Great Hall's walls, thanks to the theft of all the tapestries, were now for the most part grimly bare. The display cases, since the disappearance of the priceless dinner service, were unlit and empty. The long centre table, where once fifty guests had dined in splendour, bore a thin film of dust. Without comment my uncle walked down the long room under its high vaulted ceiling until he came to the imposing grilled glass display unit at the far end that had once held the true Honour of the Kinlochs.

Himself flicked a switch. Lights inside the glass case came to brilliant life and beamed onto the gold-looking object inside.

The replica hilt lay on black velvet and, even though one knew it was not the real thing, it looked impressive.

'It is gold plated,' its owner said. 'The red stones are spinel, not ruby. The blue stones are lapis lazuli, the green ones are peridots. I commissioned it and paid for it, and no one disputes that this is mine.'

Dr Zoë Lang studied it carefully and in silence.

The hilt itself, though larger than a large man's fist, looked remarkably like the King Alfred Gold Cup, except that there were no crenellations and no engraving. There was instead the pommel, the grip that fitted into the palm of the hand: and instead of the circular foot, only the neck into which the snapped-off blade had been fastened.

The ceremonial sword that Prince Charles Edward had hoped to use at his coronation as rightful King of England and Scotland had been made for him in France (and, amazingly, paid for by him personally) in 1740. It had been his own to give, and on impulse, in gratitude and despair, he had given it.

Dr Lang, with fervour and unexpected fanaticism, said intensely, 'This imitation may be your own, but I agree with the castle's custodians that the real Honour of the Kinlochs belongs to Scotland.'

'Do you think so?' Himself asked politely, good manners and jocularity in his voice. 'I would argue with you, of course, and I would defend my right of ownership . . .' He paused provocatively.

'Yes?' she prompted.

He smiled sweetly. 'To the hilt.'

CHAPTER 6

'Al,' Himself asked thoughtfully, as we walked back from seeing Zoë Lang out to her taxi, 'how far would you actually go
in defending the Honour of the Kinlochs?'

'Up to and including the hilt?'

'I'm not joking, Al.'

I glanced at his heavy troubled face.

'The answer,' I said, 'is that I don't know.'

After a pause he asked, 'Would you have given up the hilt
to the four men who attacked you if they'd told you what they
wanted and had used more than their fists?'

'I don't know.'

'But how much urge did you have anyway to tell them where
to look?'

'None,' I said. 'I didn't like them.'

'Al, be serious.'

'They made me angry. They made me feel futile. I would
have denied them anything I could.'

'I don't ask for you to suffer to keep that thing safe. If they
attack you again, don't let them hurt you. Tell them what they
want to know.'

I said with humour, 'You wouldn't have said that two
hundred years ago.'

'Times change.'

We went peacefully into his house and into his dining-room,

where the black cube containing the King Alfred Gold Cup still lay on the table. We checked briefly to make sure that the gold prize was still inside, and I ran a finger over the faint indentations of Bede's Death Song: consider the evil one does on earth, because a reckoning awaits.

Was it good or evil, in changing times, to pay for physical relief on earth with one's eternal honour?

Where did common sense begin?

At what point did one duck the scream?

I had no need to ask such questions aloud. Himself – my august uncle, my hereditary clan chief – was the product of the same ancient ethos and conditioning that I had received from his brother, and I had willy nilly inherited the mainstream Kinloch mind, stubbornness and all.

Himself and I re-enclosed the black cube in its draw-string bag and replaced it in the cardboard box with the copies of Dickens on top. I restuck it all as best I could with the wide brown fastening tape, though the result couldn't be called secure, and we put the box back in the sideboard for the want of anywhere better.

'We can't leave it there for ever,' my uncle said.

'No.'

'Do you trust Dr Lang?'

I was surprised by the question, but said, 'I would trust her to be true to her beliefs.'

'Think of somewhere better for the Cup, Al.'

'I'll try.'

At his own request I hadn't told him to the inch where to find the hilt, though he knew it was somewhere at the bothy. After much consideration we had, as a precaution against us both inconveniently dying with our secret untold, like Henry VIII's evaders, entrusted Jed with the basic information.

'If you have to,' Himself had said to him, 'dig around and pull the bothy apart stone by stone. Otherwise, forget what we've told you.'

Jed couldn't, of course, forget it although he had never alluded to it since except to say once that he felt overwhelmed by our faith in his loyalty. If Jed had been going to betray us to the castle's administrators he could have done it at any time in the past few years, but instead had taken the game of hide and seek into his own private world in enjoyment, and it was certainly the basis of the solid friendship between the two of us.

Jed came back to the castle late in the afternoon, still with my gear in the boot of his car, wanting to know if he could drive me home to the bothy.

'No,' Himself said decisively. 'Al will stay here tonight. Sit down, Jed. Get yourself a drink.'

We were by then in the room my uncle considered his own private domain, a severe predominantly brown room with walls bearing stuffed fish in glass cases and deers' antlers from long-past battles on the hills. There were also three of my paintings of his racehorses and one painting of his favourite gun-dog, much loved but now dead.

Jed fixed a glass of whisky and water and sat down on one of the elderly hard-stuffed chairs.

Himself as usual made the decisions. 'I see Al seldom enough. He will stay here tonight and tomorrow night to please me, and on Monday morning you can take him to the bothy and the police station, and anywhere else you care to. I'll be fishing the Spey next week. I have guests Monday, Tuesday and Wednesday. Thursday and Friday I'll be out on the moor with the guns . . .' He outlined his plans. 'James returns from sailing tomorrow. He'll be staying on here. His wife will take the children back to school. All clear, Jed?'

'Yes, sir.'

Jed and he discussed estate affairs for a while and I listened with half an ear and tried to imagine a good temporary home for Bede's Death Song engraved in gold.

I had asked Zoë Lang to read the poem aloud in Anglo-Saxon, and with enjoyment she had done so, her love of the old language giving the words shape and meaning and new life. I couldn't understand a syllable, but I could hear the throb and the pulse and the strong alliteration, and when I commented on it she'd told me a shade patronisingly that all Anglo-Saxon poetry had been written to be spoken, not read. The excitement, even the *intoxication*, she said, was engendered by the rhythmic beat as much as by the vivid imagery of the words. The poems describing battle could set sword-arms twitching. 'The Dream of the Rood' would make a Christian of an atheist.

Himself and I had listened respectfully, and I thought how much the outward appearance of age could colour one's expectation of a person's character. I wanted to paint her as young, vibrant, fanatical, with the ghost of the way she looked now superimposed in thin light grey lines, like age's cobwebs.

I strongly sensed a singular individual powerful entity that might have intensified with time, not faded. We were dealing with that inner woman, and should not forget it.

If I underpainted thickly in Payne's grey mixed with titanium white, I thought, and then brought the essential person to glowing life with strong bone structure in a faithful portrait, no colour tricks or linear gimmicks, and then scratched down into the grey for the unthinkable future . . . then with a steady hand and a strong vision I might produce a statement of terrible truth – or I might finish with a disaster fit only for the bin. To have the technique and the courage weren't always enough. Apart from vision as well, one needed luck.

Hide King Alfred's Gold Cup . . . my mind wandered back to the task in hand.

Hiding the Cup, for all its worth in gold, wasn't in the same sphere as hiding the hilt. Ivan might prize the Cup for reasons of his own, but as a symbol it wasn't entangled with history and an earl's beheading and generations of clan honour. The King Alfred Gold Cup had been fashioned a thousand years after the great king's days of glory: a tribute to him, undoubtedly, but never his own property.

The King Alfred Cup might be worth killing for . . . but not suffering for, or dying.

And yet . . . I asked myself again if I would have given the demon walkers that Cup if I'd known what they were looking for, if I'd had it to give, and I thought quite likely not. Anger . . . pride . . . *cussedness*.

Mad, weird, ridiculous Alexander.

The problem with hiding anything in the castle was that Himself was rarely in residence, while the administrators were not only in and out all the time but were also actively hunting treasure. In the family's private wing lived a full-time overall caretaker with his housekeeper wife, a conscientious worker who eviscerated private cupboards in the name of spring cleaning. The sideboard in the dining-room wouldn't shelter even a peanut for long. The discovery on the premises of a golden wonder, even if not the hilt, would have leaked into informed circles like burst pipes. If hiding the Cup involved hiding also any awareness of its existence, as I supposed it did, then the castle was out.

The castle grounds were out also, thanks to an efficient gardener.

So where?

Any thoughts anyone might have had about a peaceful evening were at that point blasted apart by the earthquake arrival of my friendly cousin James, who had listened to a gale-and-rain weather forecast and decided to run for port a day early, along with his boisterous family, who habitually lived fortissimo at Indy-car speed.

When the invasion stampeded upstairs to arrange bedrooms, I telephoned my mother and asked after Ivan. Things were no worse. There had been no further agitated crisis in the brewery's affairs: insolvency had gone into hiatus for the weekend.

'And Patsy?' I asked.

'Not a sound from her since yesterday morning.'

'My uncle Robert sends his regards.'

'And ours to him,' my mother said.

James, red haired and freckled, wandering by with gin and tonic in fist, asked amiably how the 'old boy' was doing.

'Depressed,' I said.

'Father says someone decamped with the brewery's nest egg.'

'Nest egg, chickens, battery hens, the lot.'

'What a lark, eh? How long are you staying?'

'Till Monday.'

'Great. Father's always saying we don't see enough of you. How are the daubs?'

'In abeyance,' I said, and gave him a lightweight account of the trouble at the bothy.

'Good Lord!' He stared. 'I didn't think you had much there worth stealing.'

'Jeep and golf clubs, and bits and pieces.'

'What rotten luck.'

His sympathy was genuine enough. James would always summon nurses to patch up one's wounds.

'Did they take your pipes?' he asked, concerned.

'Luckily they're in Inverness. The bag had sprung a leak.'

'Are you entering the contests this year?'

'I'm not good enough.'

'You don't practise enough, that's all.'

'The winners are nearly always army pipe majors. You know that. Why do I bother to say it?'

'I just like to encourage people,' he said, beaming; and I thought that that in truth was his great gift, to make people feel better about their lives.

The piping contests, held every autumn, took place from the far north all the way south to London. I had once or twice tried my hand in a piobaireachd competition, but it had been like a novice downhill skier taking on Klammer or Killy, an interesting experience memorable only for not having made an absolute fool of oneself.

Besides, I had political problems with some of the pibrochs, the ancient laments for the deaths and defeats of history. I couldn't – wouldn't – play 'My King has landed at Moidart', because the King that had landed was Prince Charles Edward, rightful King of England by descent, but disqualified (since Henry VIII's quarrel with the Pope) because of being Roman Catholic. Prince Charles Edward landed at Moidart in the Western Isles to begin his fateful march towards London, a thrust for the Crown, however understandable, that had led to the ruination of Scotland. In the wake of Prince Charles Edward's defeat at Culloden, the English, to remove the threat of a third upheaval (the 1715 and 1745 rebellions having been barely unsuccessful), had notoriously chased the Scots from their lands and had tried to wipe out nationhood by outlawing the speaking of Gaelic, the wearing of the tartan and the playing of the pipes. Scotland had never recovered. Sure, the tartan, the pipes and the slightly sentimental allegiances had crept back, but they were tourist attractions contrasting affectedly with the drab slab functional housing round the commercially regenerated modern city of Glasgow.

The direct descendant of Mary, Queen of Scots, had brought ruin, still unresolved, to most of Scotland – though even at Culloden, sixty per cent of those fighting *against* the Bonny Prince had been Scots themselves, not English – and although to please my uncle I guarded the lethal gift to my ancestor, I couldn't feel anything but fury for the inept, selfish, vain and ultimately faint-hearted Prince. I played laments for those he'd damaged. I played laments for the damage he'd done. I never felt love for the man.

Saturday evening passed in the chaos indigenous to James's family, and in the morning when I went downstairs in search of coffee I found Himself in the dining-room looking around him as if in bewilderment at an empty cardboard box, old faded leather-bound copies of Dickens, an empty black cube with white satin lining and a grey draw-string duster bag all lying about haphazardly on the floor.

The sideboard door stood open. The King Alfred Gold Cup had gone.

There were squeals from the kitchen next door. Children's voices. High.

Dazedly my uncle opened the connecting door and I followed him into the large unmodernised kitchen, an expanse of black and white tiling still called on old castle plans 'the cold preparation room'. Shades of old vegetables, I thought. Food nowadays mostly arrived at the castle in caterers' vans, wrapped in film and ready to heat and eat.

James was leaning against the sink, coffee mug in hand, indulgent smile in place.

His three unruly children – two boys and a girl – scrambled around on the floor, all of them wearing large saucepans on their heads with the handles pointing backwards. Spacewatch good guys, we were told.

The King Alfred Cup also stood on the floor, upside down. Himself bent from the waist and picked it up, finding it heavier than he expected.

'Hey,' objected his elder grandson, standing up to face him, 'that's the galactic core of M.100 with all its Cepheid variables in those red stones. We have to keep it safe from the black-hole suction mob.'

'I'm glad to hear it,' his grandfather said dryly.

The boy – Andrew – was eleven years old and already rebellious, hard-eyed and tough. If time took its normal course he would one day succeed James as earl. James might be open to soft persuasion but I wanted to know for sure about his son.

I said, 'Andrew, if you had a favourite toy, something you really valued, and someone tried very hard to take it away from you ... suppose he even threatened to hurt you if you didn't give it to him, what would you do?'

He said promptly, as if he thought the question feeble, 'Bash his face in.'

My uncle smiled. James said with mild protest, 'Andy, you would talk it over and make a deal.'

His son repeated stalwartly, 'I'd bash his face in. Can we have the Cepheid monitor back?'

'No,' his grandfather said. 'You shouldn't have taken it out of its box.'

'We were looking for something worth fighting for,' Andrew said.

James defended them. 'They haven't done it any harm. What is it, anyway? It can't be real gold.'

Himself thrust the Cup into my arms, where its weight again surprised. 'Put it away safely,' he said.

'OK.'

'It's a racing challenge trophy,' my uncle explained unexcitedly to his son. 'I can't keep it for more than a year and I need to give it back without dents in.'

The explanation satisfied James entirely and he told his children to look for a substitute galactic goody.

On an impulse I asked him if he would like to spend some of the day playing golf. We both belonged to the local club where, with varying success, I quite often walked after the elusive white ball, but there were seldom days when we could go out together.

He looked pleased, but said, 'I thought you said your clubs were stolen.'

'I might buy some new ones.'

'Great, then.'

He phoned the club, who found a slot for us in the afternoon, and we drove over in good time for the pro shop to kit me out with better clubs than the ones I'd lost: and, for good measure, I acquired snazzy black-and-white shoes with spikes on, and gloves and balls and umbrellas: also a lightweight blue waterproof bag to carry things in and a trolley like James's to pull everything along on wheels. Thus re-equipped I went out with my cousin into the wind and rain, which had arrived as forecast, and got happily soaked to the skin despite the umbrellas.

'Will you paint this?' James asked, squelching on wet grass.

'Yes, of course.'

'You're not really as weird as we all think, are you?'

I putted a ball to the rim of a hole, where it obstinately stopped.

'I paint frustration,' I said, and gave the ball a kick.

James laughed, and in good spirits we finished the eighteen holes and went back to the castle for the nineteenth.

My hands-on relationship with golf was essential to my work, I'd found. It wasn't that I had much skill, but in a way the failures were more revelatory than success: and I particularly liked to play with James who laughed and lost or won with equal lack of seriousness.

The only really warm room in the whole castle complex (apart from the caretaker's quarters) was the home of the vast hot water tank, where ranks of airers dried out the persistent Scottish rains. James and I accordingly showered, changed, and left all our wet things steaming, including my sopping new shoes and golf bag, and then ambled back to the dining-room for tinctures.

James's children were in there. The King Alfred Cup, though still in its white satin nest, lay in full glorious view on the polished table under a chandelier's light.

'You didn't say we couldn't *look* at it,' Andy objected to his father's mild rebuke. 'We couldn't find *anything else* worth fighting a space war for.'

I said to James, 'What about the hilt?'

'Oh yes.' He thought it over. 'But we'd only see the replica, and anyway, I can't let the children through into the castle proper. I promised Himself I wouldn't.'

'Let's ask him,' I said. So we found him in his own room and asked, with the result that all of us, Himself, James, James's wife and children and I, walked the length of the Great Hall and stood round the grilled glass cage, staring down at its floodlit treasure.

'*That,*' Andrew decided, 'would be worth fighting a galactic space war for. If it was real, of course.'

'And you, James,' Himself asked, 'would you too fight for it?'

James, no fool, answered soberly, making what must have been to him an unwelcome commitment, 'If I had to, I suppose so, yes.'

'Good. Let's hope it's never necessary.'

'Where is the real one?' Andrew asked.

His grandfather said, 'We have to keep it safe from the black-hole suction mob.'

Andy's face was an almost unpaintable mixture of glee and understanding. A boy worth fighting for, I thought.

Himself carefully didn't look at me once.

*

It was still raining on Monday morning. James took his family to set off south, Himself left to meet his guests and ghillies at Crathie to bother the silver swimmers in the Spey, and Jed arrived to pick me up and set my normal life back on course.

He brought with him a replacement credit card and cheque-book which he had had sent to his house for me, and he'd heard from Inverness that my bagpipes were ready for collection. He had freed one of the estate's Land Rovers for my temporary use, and he lent me a fully charged portable phone to put me in touch with events in London and Reading. Reception was poor in the mountains, but better than nothing, he said.

I said inadequately, 'Thanks, Jed,' and he shook his head and grinned, shrugging it off.

'There's a new lock on the bothy, like I told you, and here are two keys,' he said, handing them over. 'I have a third. There aren't any others.'

I nodded and went out of doors with him, and found the boxes from London that I'd left in his car on Saturday evening already piled into the Land Rover. I'd taken into Himself's house only clothes in a paper carrier and I left with them (dry) in an all-purpose heavy duty duffle bag from the gun-room. The bag smelled of cartridges, moors and old tweed: very Edwardian, very lost world.

Jed commented on my new clubs.

'Yes,' I said, 'but this time I'm storing my kit in the club house. Where do you propose I should keep my pipes?'

Jed said awkwardly, 'Are you afraid the robbers will come back?'

'Would you be?'

'You can always stay with Flora and me.'

'Have you noticed,' I asked, 'how people tend to rebuild their earthquaked houses in the same place on the San Andreas fault? Or in the path of hurricanes?'

'You don't have to.'

'Call it blind faith,' I said.

'Call it obstinacy.'

I grinned. 'Definitely. But don't worry. This time I'll install a few burglar alarms.'

'There isn't any electricity.'

'Tins on strings with stones in.'

Jed shook his head. 'You're mad.'

'So they say.'

He gave up. 'The police are expecting you. Ask for Detective Sergeant Berrick. He came out with me to the bothy. He knows what the vandalism looks like.'

'OK.'

'Take care, Al. I mean it. Take care.'

'I will,' I said.

We drove off together but parted at the estate gates, from where I headed towards the bothy, stopping only once, briefly, to pay with a replacement cheque for the new golf gear, and unload it into a locker, which I would have done better to have done oftener in the past.

The new keys to the bothy door opened my way into the same old devastation that I'd left there six days earlier.

Nothing looked better. The only overall improvement was that it no longer hurt to move, a plus, I had to concede, of significant worth. With a sigh I dug out of the mess an unused plastic rubbish bag and, instead of its normal light load of paint-cleaning tissues, filled it with the debris of ruined acrylics and everything small but broken.

It was still raining out of doors. Indoors my mattress and bedding were soaked and smelling from a bucketful of dirty paint water. I wasn't sure what they'd done to my armchair, but it, too, smelled revolting.

Bastards.

Out of rainy-day habit I'd run the Land Rover into the shelter of the carport when I'd arrived, but at that point I backed it out again, and bit by bit stacked my ruined possessions in the dry space, painstakingly looking for anything *not* mine that might have been left behind by my attackers. When I'd finished, all that was left in the room was the bare metal and coiled wire bedstead, the chest of drawers (empty), one shelf of salvaged books, a frying pan with cooking tools and one easel (two broken). I swept the floor and collected coffee, sugar and sundry debris into a dustpan and gloomily looked at the dozens of superimposed paint-laden footprints on my wood-blocks, all left by the types of trainers sold by the million throughout Britain and useless for identifying the wearers.

In spite of the thoroughness of my search, the only thing I found that I hadn't had before was not a helpful half-used matchbook printed with the address and phone number of a boxing gym, but a pair of plastic-framed glasses.

I put them on and everything close went blurry. For long distances, they were sharp.

The prescription was stamped into one of the earpieces: -2.

They were, I thought, the sort of aid one could buy off revolving-stand displays all over the world. They were the sort of glasses worn by my attackers. A disguise. A theatrical prop. I wrapped them in a piece of tinfoil from a roll I sometimes used for instant makeshift palettes: one didn't have to scrape off old dry paint but could simply scrunch the whole thing up and throw it away. Some poverty-afflicted painters used old phone books that way all the time.

I carted the bags and boxes of new gear into the bothy from the Land Rover and stacked everything unopened on the bare springs of the bed. Then I locked the door, sat for a while in the Land Rover, thinking, and finally drove off in search of Detective Sergeant Berrick.

Within five minutes of my arrival, the Detective Sergeant had told me he implacably disliked drug dealers, prostitutes, Englishmen, the Celtic football team, the Conservative party, anyone educated beyond sixteen, all superior officers, paperwork, rules forbidding him to beat up suspects, long-haired gits – and in particular long-haired gits who lived on mountains and got themselves duffed up while eating hand-outs from people with titles who ought to be abolished. Detective Sergeant Berrick, in fact, revealed himself as a typical good-hearted aggressive Scot with a strong sense of justice.

He was thin, somewhere in the tail-end thirties, and would probably soon be promoted to become one of the superiors he despised. His manner to me was artificially correct and a touch self-righteous, a long way from the paternal instincts of his friendly old neighbourhood predecessor who had turned bad boys into good citizens for years but was now flying a desk in far off Perth, made useless by age regulations and the reclassification of paternalism as a dirty word.

Sergeant Berrick told me not to expect to get my goods back.

I said, 'I was wondering if you might have some luck with the paintings.'

'What paintings?' He peered at a list. 'Oh yes, here we are. Four paintings of scenes of golf courses.' He looked up. 'There was paint all over your place.'

'Yes.'

'And you painted those pictures yourself?'

'Yes.'

'Is there any way we could recognise them?'

'They had stickers on the back, in the top left-hand corner,' I said. 'Copyright stickers giving my name, Alexander, and this year's date.'

'Stickers can be pulled off,' he said.

'These stickers can't. The glue bonds with the canvas.'

He gave me a don't-bother-me stare but punched up my file on a computer.

'Copyright stickers on backs,' he said aloud, typing in the words. He shrugged. 'You never know.'

'Thanks,' I said.

'You could put another sticker over the top,' he said.

'Yes, you could,' I agreed, 'but you might not know my name is printed in an ink that shows up in X-rays.'

He stared. 'Tricky, aren't you?'

'It's a wicked world,' I said, and got an unpremeditated smile in return.

'We'll see what we can do,' he promised. 'How's that?'

'I'll paint your portrait if you find my pictures.'

He spread out on his desk the drawings I'd done at Dal-whinnie station of my assailants, and changed his challenging attitude to one of convinced interest.

'Paint my wife,' he said.

'Done.'

A few doors along from the police station I visited a shop that was a campers' heaven aimed at tourists, and there acquired a sleeping bag and enough essentials to make living in the stripped bothy possible, and then drove a long detour to Donald Cameron's far-flung post office to see if any letters had arrived for me in the past week, and to stock up, as I usually did, with food and a full gas cylinder.

'Will you be wanting to use my telephone, Mr Kinloch?' old Donald asked hopefully. 'There's something amiss with the one outside.'

I bet there is, I thought; but to please the old beggar I made one call on his instrument, asking the bagpipe restorers if there was any chance of their delivering my pipes either to Jed Parlane's house or to Donald Cameron's shop.

Old Donald practically snatched the receiver out of my hand and told the pipe people he would be going to Inverness on Wednesday and would collect my pipes for me personally: and so it was arranged. Donald, restoring the phone to its cradle, beamed at me with expectation.

'How much?' I asked, resigned, and negotiated a minor king's ransom.

'Always at your service, Mr Kinloch.'

It rained all the way up the muddy track to the bothy. Once there I sat in the comparative comfort of the Land Rover outside my locked front door and made inroads into the battery power of Jed's portable phone. Poor reception, but possible.

It was still office hours in Reading. I tried Tobias Tollright first with trepidation, but he was reasonably reassuring.

'Mrs Morden wants to talk to you. She held the meeting of creditors. They did at least attend.'

'And that's good?'

'Encouraging.'

I said, 'Tobe . . .'

'What is it?'

'Young and Uttley.'

Tobias laughed. 'He's a genius. Wait and see. I wouldn't recommend him to everyone, or everyone to him, but you're two of a kind. You both think sideways. You'll get on well together. Give him a chance.'

'Did he tell you that I engaged him?'

'Er . . .' The guilt of his voice raised horrible doubts in my mind.

'He surely didn't tell you what I asked him to do?' I said.

'Er . . .'

'So much for discretion.'

Tobias said again, lightheartedly, 'Give him a chance, Al.'

It was too late by then, I thought ruefully, to do anything else.

I phoned Margaret Morden and listened to her crisp voice.

'I laid out all the figures. The creditors all needed smelling salts. Norman Quorn took off with every last available cent, a really remarkable job. But I've persuaded the bank and the Inland Revenue to try to come up with solutions, and we are meeting again on Wednesday, when they've had a chance to consult their head offices. The best that one can say is that the brewery is basically still trading at a profit, and while it still has the services of Desmond Finch and the present brewmaster, it should go on doing so.'

'Did you . . . did you ask the creditors about the race?'

'They see your point. They'll discuss it on Wednesday.'

'There's hope, then?'

'But they want Sir Ivan back in charge.'

I said fervently, 'So do I.'

'Meanwhile you may still sign for him. He is adamant it should be you and no one else.'

'Not his daughter?'

'I asked him myself. He agreed to speak to me. Alexander, he said. No one else.'

'Then I'll do anything you need, and . . . Margaret . . .'

'Yes?'

'What are you wearing today?'

She gasped, and then laughed. 'Coffee and cream.'

'Soft and pretty?'

'It gets subliminal results. Wednesday – a gentle practical dark blue, touches of white. Businesslike but not threatening.'

'Appearances help.'

'Indeed they do . . .' her voice tailed off hesitantly. 'There's something odd, though.'

'Odd about what?'

'About the appearance of the brewery's accounts.'

Alarmed, I said 'What exactly is odd?'

'I don't know. I can't identify it. You know when you can smell something but you don't know what it is? It's like that.'

'You worry me,' I said.

'It's probably nothing.'

'I trust your instincts.'

She sighed. 'Tobias Tollright drew up the audit. He's very reliable. If there were anything incongruous, he would have noticed.'

'Don't alarm the creditors,' I pleaded.

'They are interested only in the future. In getting their money. What I feel – a whisper of disquiet – is in the past. I'll sleep on it. Solutions often come in the night.'

I wished her useful dreams, and sat on my Scottish mountainside in the rain-spattered Land Rover realising how little I knew, and how much I relied on Tobe and Margaret and Young (or Uttley) for answers to questions I hadn't the knowledge to ask.

I wanted to paint.

I could feel the compulsion, the fusing of mental vision with the physical longing to feel the paint in my hands that came always before I did any picture worth looking at: the mysterious impetus that one had to call creation, whether the results were worth the process or not.

Inside the bothy there was an old familiar easel and the new painting supplies from London, and I had to instruct myself severely that two more phone calls had to be made before I could light a lamp (new from the camping shop) and prepare a canvas ready for morning.

Tack cotton duck onto a stretched frame. Prime three times with gesso to produce a good surface, let it dry. Lay on the Payne's grey mixed with titanium white. Make working drawings. Plan. Sleep. Dream.

I phoned my mother.

Ivan was no worse, no better. He had agreed to talk to some woman or other about saving the brewery, but he still wanted me to act for him, as he couldn't yet summon the strength.

'OK,' I said.

'The real trouble at present,' my mother said, 'is Surtees.'

'What about him?'

'He is *paranoid*. Patsy is furious with him. Patsy is furious about *everything*. I do wish you would come back, Alexander, you're the only person she can't bully.'

'Is she bullying Ivan?'

'She bullies him terribly, but he can't see it. He told Oliver Grantchester he wants to write a codicil to his Will, and it seems Oliver mentioned it to Patsy, and now Patsy is demanding to know what Ivan wants a codicil for, and for once Ivan won't tell me, and oh *dear*, it's so bad for Ivan. And she's practically *living* here, she's at his elbow every minute.'

'And Surtees? Why is he paranoid?'

'He says he's being followed everywhere by a skinhead.'

I said weakly, '*What?*'

'I know. It's stupid. No one else has seen this skinhead. Surtees says the skinhead disappears whenever he, Surtees, is with other people. Patsy's livid with him. I do wish they wouldn't crowd in here all the time. Ivan needs rest and quiet. Come back, Alexander . . . please.'

The overt uncharacteristic plea was almost too much. Too

many people wanted too much. I could see that they needed someone to decide things – Ivan, my mother, Tobias, Margaret, even my uncle Robert – but I didn't feel strong enough myself to give them all strength.

I wanted to *paint*.

To my mother I said, 'I'll come back soon.'

'When?'

Dear heaven, I thought, and said helplessly, 'Wednesday night.'

We said goodbye and, finally, I phoned Jed.

He said 'All hell has broken loose at the castle.'

'What sort of hell?'

'Andy – Himself's young grandson – has run off with the King Alfred Gold Cup.'

CHAPTER 7

I laughed.

'Well,' Jed said, 'I suppose it's quite funny.'

'What exactly happened?'

It seemed that soon after Himself and his guests returned to the castle for a good Scots afternoon tea of hot scones and fortified cups, Dr Zoë Lang had made an unheralded return visit, bringing with her an expert in precious and semi-precious stones. She couldn't rest, she said, while her evaluation of the King Alfred Cup had been incomplete.

Himself, Dr Lang, the jeweller and the fishing guests had all accordingly gone into the dining-room in the quest for truth.

The cardboard box had been retrieved from the sideboard and the copies of Dickens removed. The black leather cube had been lifted out and the gold clasp undone, and in the white satin nest . . . nothing.

My cousin James, who had returned from seeing his family onto the air shuttle from Glasgow to London, had instantly said he would tan the hide off his elder son, who had been fascinated by the Cup, but the Spacewatch good guy could not at that moment be reached for questioning, as he was by then somewhere on the road back to boarding school with his mother, who had no phone in her car.

Jed said, 'I called in to see Himself about estate business, and I found this old lady rather rudely telling him he shouldn't be trusted to keep the Kinloch hilt safe from robbers if he couldn't guard things from his own grandson, and Himself just stood there benevolently agreeing with her, which seemed to make her even crosser. Anyway, after she'd gone, he asked me to ask you if you thought he ought to worry about Andrew, so do you?'

'No.'

Jed's sigh was half a chuckle.

'I told Himself you had carried out of the castle one of those big old game-bags from the gunroom, and he beamed. But what's it all about? They were saying that that Cup is a racing challenge trophy, that's all. Is it really worth a lot?'

'It depends where you stand,' I said. 'It's gold. If you're rich, it's just an expensive bauble. If you're a thief, it's worth murder. In between – you balance the greed against the risks.'

'And to you? To Himself? To Sir Ivan?'

When I didn't reply at once, he said, 'Al, are you still there?'

'Yes . . . I don't know the answer, and I don't want to find out.'

On Tuesday morning a cold front swept the sky dramatically, clearing away the grey rain and leaving a high washed pale blue cosmos with a northern yellowish tint of sunlight. The bothy faced west, which often gave me long mornings of near-perfect painting light, followed by warm afternoon glows that I'd at first subconsciously translated into mellowing glazes and then, when I found out those pictures sold most quickly, into commercial technique. I did paint for a living: I also earned money so that I could paint to please only myself, when I wanted to.

On that Tuesday, on the grey-white underpainting, I lightly drew in pencil the head of a still-young woman, with a face already strongly defined by character, a face of good bone structure, of intelligence, of purpose. I drew her not looking straight ahead but as though she saw something to her right, and I drew her not smiling, not disapproving, not arrogant, not self-conscious, but simply *being*.

When the proportions and the expression were near to what I intended, I painted the whole head in light and dark intensities of ultramarine blue, mostly transparent, mixed with water. I painted dark blue shadows round the edges of the canvas, leaving light areas round the head itself, and worked dark shadows round the eyes and under the chin until I had a fairly complete monochrome portrait in blue on light grey.

She looked as I thought Dr Lang might have looked forty years earlier.

I had learned my trade from four different painters, one in Scotland, one in England, one in Rome and one in California, and had watched and assimilated and practised until I knew what paint would do, and what it wouldn't. Unable to afford art school, with a father dead and a mother newly married and rebuilding her own life, I had offered my services as cook, cleaner, gofer and dogsbody to the four accomplished painters in turn, asking only for payment in food, a patch of floor to sleep on, and scraps of paper and paint.

After three years of such profitable drudgery I'd received a surprise enquiry from my uncle: what, he wanted to know, would I like for a twenty-first coming-of-age birthday present? I'd asked for the use of a tumbledown shed on the mountainous part of his estate and a pass to give me an occasional game on the local golf course (which he owned).

He'd given me the use of the hut (once an overnight shelter for shepherds at lambing time), full membership of the golf club and some money for paints. Two years later he'd sent me to Lambourn to make portraits of the horses he had in training with Emily Jane Cox.

After I'd run from Lambourn he'd moved me from the hut to the sturdier but ruined bothy and had paid for it to be made habitable; and a year after that he'd asked me to take care of the Honour of the Kinlochs.

I couldn't have refused him, even if I'd wanted to, which I hadn't.

I had all my younger life been in awe of him. It was only during the last five years that I'd grown old enough for a more adult understanding. He had of course taken the place of the father I'd lost, but much more than that he had become friend, partner and ally: and never would I trade on that privilege, either with him or within the family.

Brooding over my blue woman, I ate a cheese and chutney sandwich and in the afternoon overpainted the background with browns and crimsons, glazing and rubbing together the colours in the method called scumbling until I had a deep rich background that wasn't identifiably blue or brown or red but which receded from the eye, leaving the face itself startlingly near and clear.

Tuesday night I slept again on the floor in the sleeping bag and dreamed of colours, and early on Wednesday, as soon as it was light, began overpainting flesh onto the blue bones, working from light areas to dark, giving her strength and brain but not a peach-skin luminous beauty. By afternoon she was a woman who would both excel in an academic world and comfort a strong man in bed . . . or so, in my mind, I saw her.

At about the time when every day Jed could be found in the estate office writing notes on current affairs, I phoned him.

'Are you OK?' he asked.

'Any news of Andrew and the Cup?'

'The poor little bugger swore he didn't take it. Himself says he believes him. Anyway, the damned thing seems to have vanished.'

'Are you alone in the office?' I asked.

'You guessed right. I'm not.'

'Well, listen. I'm going back to London tonight from Dalwhinnie. Can you meet me there, and if so, when? And could you bring with you an old bedsheet?'

'Er . . .'

'A bedsheet,' I repeated. 'People I see in London will know I am not in the bothy. While I'm in London, the bothy is as secure as one blow from a sledgehammer on that nice new lock.'

'*Al.*'

'I've been painting a picture that I really do *not* want stolen or ruined. Please could you bring a sheet to wrap it in? Please will you keep it safe for me?'

'Yes, of course,' he said hesitantly, 'but what about . . . anything else?'

'No one will find anything else. I just don't want to lose the picture.'

After barely a pause he said, 'How about nine thirty?'

'Perfect. Could you bring Flora, to drive your own car home? You can have the estate's Land Rover back.'

'How long will you be gone?'

'How long is a piece of string . . . ?'

Reliable as always, he brought Flora and a bedsheet to the station, and drove away in the Land Rover with the well-wrapped picture and all my new climbing gear and paints and winter clothes (in duffle bag) and also my bagpipes, newly ransomed from the old fleecer, Donald Cameron, on his return from Inverness.

Jed swore on his mother's grave to keep my belongings safe (she was still alive) and Flora laughed and kissed me, and with minimum luggage I yet again rocked down the rails and hugged my mother before breakfast.

The Park Crescent house felt as claustrophobic as it had the previous week. The cleaner, Lois, relentlessly vacuumed, her expression mulish. She and Ivan's male nurse, Wilfred, had reached head-tossing terms. Edna the cook tut-tutted over the evidence of my hot fried breakfast. My mother put up with it all instead of chucking the whole lot out.

Although it was by then more than three weeks since Ivan's heart attack, he had still not summoned will or strength enough to dress in day clothes. As if time had been suspended since I'd left, I found him, in gown and slippers, looking equally exhausted in his armchair. He greeted me with a weak smile and an instant and relieved transference to me of all decision-making.

'That woman wants you to phone her,' he said, pointing at

the tissue-box, so I turned it over and found Margaret Morden's number written beside the one-word message – NOW.

I phoned her 'now'.

'Sir Ivan said you'd be coming to London.'

'I'm here.'

'Oh, good.' She sounded relieved. 'Can you hop down to my office?'

'How did it go yesterday?'

'Quite well. I need Sir Ivan's agreement. If he can't come here, perhaps you could carry papers to London for his signature.'

'Great idea,' I said with enthusiasm, but Ivan flapped a no-no hand and said into the receiver when I held it out for him, 'Alexander will sign things. Advise him as you would advise me. He's fairly bright . . .' He waved the telephone away and Margaret Morden said in my ear, 'But your daughter . . .'

'You're talking to Al,' I said. 'What about Patsy?'

'She and that brewery manager, Desmond Finch, very nearly wrecked the negotiations yesterday by crashing the creditors' meeting. And she had her husband with her . . . he's a menace. I shouldn't say it, but if the brewery survives it will be in *spite* of Mrs Benchmark. I don't understand her. The brewery will be hers, you'd think she would be the first to want the rescue operation to succeed.'

'She wants me, personally, dead.'

'You don't mean that!' she protested.

'Well, she doesn't want me to be instrumental in saving the day.'

'I can agree with *that*. How soon can you get here?'

'An hour and a half.'

'Right,' she said. 'I'll clear the decks.'

I spent over half an hour with Ivan, during which he told me several times not to bother him with details (such as, would his brewery survive), but to stick to *essentials* (namely, the safe-keeping of his best horse and his Gold Cup).

'Bede's Death Song,' I said casually, and watched astounded as my stepfather's eyes filled with tears.

'Look after your mother,' he said.

'You are *not* going to die.'

'I think so.' He wiped the tears away with his finger. 'Probably.'

'No. She needs you.'

'I am adding a codicil to my Will,' he said. 'Don't let anyone stop me.'

'By "anyone", do you mean Patsy?'

'Patsy,' he nodded. 'And Surtees, and Oliver.'

'Oliver Grantchester?' I asked. 'Your lawyer?'

'Patsy gets him to tell her things.'

I said with dismay, 'Did you tell Oliver Grantchester you wanted to add a codicil, and *he* told Patsy?'

'Yes.' His voice held defeated acceptance. 'Oliver says she's family.'

'He should be struck off.'

'He won't be, though, will he? I asked him to come tomorrow morning, so please, Alexander . . .'

'I'll be here,' I promised, frowning, 'but –'

'She's so *strong*, you see,' he interrupted. 'So sweet and kind. But she gets her own way.'

'If I were you,' I said, 'I would take a piece of paper here and now and simply write down in your own handwriting what you want, and then get Wilfred and Lois in here to witness you signing – unless of course they are recipients –' He shook his head. '– and then the codicil would be done and legal and you wouldn't have to endure any arguments tomorrow.'

He wasn't a man to whom simple solutions came naturally. He relied on accountants and lawyers and formality. His first strong instinct was to disregard my suggestion as frivolous, and it was only after about five quiet minutes, during which I did nothing to persuade him, that he saw the attraction of the peaceful path.

'The only thing is,' I said, 'don't leave *me* anything. If you do the codicil will be declared void, as Patsy will say I influenced you.'

'But . . .'

'Don't,' I said.

He shook his head.

'I don't want you dead,' I said. 'Live and leave me nothing. Give me your word.'

He smiled weakly. 'You're as bossy as Patsy.'

I fetched paper and a pen from his desk and from across the room watched him write a scant half-page.

Then I sought out Wilfred and Lois, and Ivan himself lightly asked them to witness him signing and dating a simple legal document.

Ivan signed his paper and held his arm across the wording itself so that his witnesses couldn't read the details while they themselves signed: and, at his request, they added their home addresses.

Ivan thanked them courteously, giving their service little weight. With luck, I thought, Lois wouldn't report within five minutes to Patsy.

When Wilfred and Lois had gone (heads tossing at each other) I gave Ivan an envelope for his codicil; from cautious habit, when he'd stuck down its flap, he signed his name and the date twice across the join.

He held out the sealed envelope for me to take.

'Look after it,' he said.

'Ivan . . .'

'Who else?'

'If you promise I'm not in it.'

'You're not.'

'OK then.' I took the envelope. Horse, Cup, codicil, what else?

I was fifteen minutes later than I'd said for Margaret Morden but she made no comment. She wore a widely belted soft printed wool dress of dark reds and blues, accentuating the fairness of her fine and flyaway hair, and making sure one noticed the slenderness of her waist.

The creditors, she reported, had worked out a rate of

payment that they would accept. Their terms were stringent, which I should expect, but just about possible, if sales held up. The creditors conceded that good sales depended on the brewery's solid reputation, and they had included the King Alfred Gold Cup race's expenses in their calculations.

'*Great*,' I said. 'You're *brilliant*.'

'Yes, but they want a guarantee that if there is any shortfall in the expected receipts for the next six months, Sir Ivan will forfeit the Cup itself. The gold chalice is to be considered as an asset of the brewery, and may be sold.'

'Is that a fair arrangement?'

'I'd say so. I agreed subject to your approval. The same applies to the horse, Golden Malt.' She paused. 'Some of the creditors insisted the Cup and the horse be sold at once, but the certainty of negative publicity persuaded them to wait. Also no one at the brewery seems to know exactly where either the horse or Cup have got to.'

'Who's looking?'

'Desmond Finch. He is complaining bitterly about the creditors' terms. I told you he crashed the meeting. It is he who will have to implement the stringent measures. The creditors want the workforce reduced. Downsized – that's the fashionable term for sacked. Desmond Finch says he can't run the brewery with fewer people. He wants to sell the Cup.'

'Um.'

'You don't look convinced.'

'Well, when Ivan took the Cup out of the brewery he made it into the equivalent of a freely bouncing ball. I mean ... anyone who caught it might throw it on safely into trustworthy hands, who might bounce it some more ... but in its free state it could be caught by someone who would keep it for its value in gold. That Cup isn't worth enough to pay the brewery's debts but it is definitely worth stealing.'

Margaret listened without moving.

I went on, 'Ivan took his Cup and had a heart attack, so he gave his treasure into the keeping of his long-time friend, my uncle, Robert Kinloch. The two men decided to give the Cup to me to look after, but in their trusting way they spoke of that plan in front of listening ears, with the result that four robbers came to my door to find and steal the Cup.'

'So it's gone?'

'No. It wasn't there. It hadn't reached me. The four robbers . . . er . . . damaged me a bit.'

'That black eye last week? And all those winces?'

'Mm . . . Well, the Cup's still bouncing, so to speak, and I wouldn't stake my life on Desmond Finch returning it to the brewery if he got his hands on it.'

'That's probably slanderous – what would he do with it?'

'I'd say he would think it reasonable, if not proper, to give it to Patsy Benchmark.'

Margaret Morden's mouth opened.

I sighed. 'Patsy heard her father and my uncle plan to give the Cup to me.'

'My God. But . . . surely . . . she wouldn't send people to *harm* you.'

'She might. She might not. But how about Surtees, her husband?'

Margaret said, looking horrified, 'He was violent enough at that meeting yesterday for anything. But funnily enough, his violent way of speaking, and Mrs Benchmark's furious denunciation of you personally as a ruthless adventurer out for whatever you could get, well, they worked *against* them, and *for* you. When they'd gone the very senior bank manager put all his weight behind your trustworthiness, and it was he, too, who pushed for the race to be run. He said the bank would make the funds available.'

I could think of nothing to say.

'Fortunately the receivables are enough to more than cover the running costs this week. The pay cheques will be issued and honoured. You have to sign the agreements drawn up yesterday, but, if you do, Tobias Tollright will OK the audit, and King Alfred's Brewery will stay in business.'

I stood up blindly and walked to her window, and heard her voice behind me, 'Al?'

'Mm?'

'I thought you would be pleased.'

I didn't answer her, and she came questioningly to stand beside me. I put my arms round her silently and hugged her, and finally found voice enough to thank her in a more businesslike fashion.

She said, 'The bank manager said that nothing you have done is for your own benefit.'

'He's wrong. What benefits the brewery benefits Ivan, and what benefits Ivan benefits my mother, which benefits me.'

'Yes,' she said gravely, mocking me, 'I do see.'

She spread out the agreement papers on her desk and showed me where to put my name, bringing in her secretary to witness every signature. She then said she would have copies run off for all the creditors, which I would initial, and for Ivan and for Tobias, and for the brewery in the shape of Desmond Finch.

While all the copying was in hand she asked me why Ivan and my uncle had planned to send the King Alfred Gold Cup to *me*. Why to Alexander on his mountain?

I said I supposed it was because of Prince Charles Edward's sword hilt, and I told her of the ancient Honour of the Kinlochs, and about my uncle's ongoing disagreement with the castle's administrators.

'I'm afraid,' I said lightly, 'that now, owing to the incautious tongues of two men who would never knowingly harm me, any number of people may learn that whether or not I may know where to find the King Alfred chalice, I do have in my care the Kinloch golden hilt, which is infinitely more valuable, as apart from its historical uniqueness, it is oozing with emeralds and rubies.'

'Al!'

'So it looks as if it is time to bounce that on to someone else.'

'Immediately!'

Immediately. But to whom?

Not to James: and Andrew was too young.

Himself would have to decide.

Margaret's secretary returned with the copy agreements for copious initialling, and I asked if protocol would stretch to a pub lunch for three, Margaret, Tobias and me.

Margaret thought it might. Tobe, when telephoned, agreed. Accordingly we sat round a small table in a dark discreet corner and toasted the brewery's survival in a bottle of good Bordeaux.

I said to Margaret, 'You mentioned something to me about a twitch of unease. Is it for our auditor's ears?'

Margaret considered Tobias and slowly nodded. 'He might help.'

'What twitch of unease?' he asked, searching his pockets for toothpicks. 'To do with the brewery's prospects?'

'No, with its past.'

His search drew a blank. He walked over to the bar and returned with a whole small pot of picks. 'Go on, then,' he said. 'What twitch?'

'I think,' Margaret said tentatively, 'that Norman Quorn may have done a trial run.'

Tobias blinked. 'A what?'

'You remember I asked you for the accounts for the past five years?'

'Yes, you had them.'

Margaret nodded. 'Immaculate work. But I just got a teeniest whiff of what I call a "beach towel and hotel" job, only *that* one seems to have gone full circle, which of course doesn't usually happen, and didn't happen this time.'

'You've lost me,' I said. 'What's a "beach towel and hotel" job?'

I looked enquiringly at Tobias, but he shook his head. 'Never heard of it.'

Margaret, smiling, explained. 'I got the idea one day on holiday, while I was lying sunbathing on a beach chair round a hotel pool, watching people come and go. They would put a towel on a chair and go off and leave it, maybe for hours, and then come back and pick it up and wander off . . . and no one working for the hotel would think of asking who the towel belonged to. Do you see?'

'No,' I said, but Tobias thoughtfully nodded.

'Suppose,' Margaret said, 'that you were Norman Quorn, and you wanted to retire with a pension big enough to give you all the luxuries you'd never had – not just a bungalow on the south coast, counting the cost of things like postage stamps – but round-the-world cruises and a big new car and a bejewelled companion and caviare and playing the tables in a casino or whatever excites his dry conventional old bachelor mind. Suppose you got the sparkling explosive idea of taking enough for a glorious sunset, and you know how easy and fast it is now to send money whizzing round the world impersonally by wire . . . then you open small banking accounts here and there . . . you sort of book into hotels . . . and every so often you leave a beach towel on a sunbed for a while . . . and then move it onward to another hotel . . . and no one pays much notice, because the beach towel never goes missing, and comes safely home.'

'Only one day it doesn't,' Tobias said. 'I lost him in Panama.'

We drank the substantial red wine and ordered fried brie and cranberries with another half-bottle.

Margaret's job fascinated her. 'Almost everyone sees when their bankruptcy's looming,' she said, 'and nearly everyone makes the giveaway mistake of removing their most valuable possessions before torching the premises. Insurance fraud is the worst way out of bankruptcy. It never works. I won't take those cases. I tell them to go to jail and get it over with. Most insolvencies are caused by bad luck, bad management and changing times. Last year's rage is this year's ruin. And then sometimes you get a Norman Quorn. Ingenious, careful. A small trial run, to get the hotels used to the arrival of his beach towel . . . and they give the towel a sunbed to lie on for a day or so, and send it on unsuspectingly when the right instruction arrives – right codes, right signatures . . . lovely job.'

'And no one asks questions?' I said.

'Of course not. Millions of transactions take place round the world every day. Hotel guests arrive and leave by the hundred thousand.'

127

'And beach towels,' Tobias grinned, 'get sent to the laundry.'

I went to see Young and Uttley.

Neither Mr Young (moustache, suit and hat) nor Mr Uttley (football coach, ball and whistle) was in the office, and nor was the skinhead. Alone in occupation I found a secretary at work at a computer, a young woman with dark curly hair, black tights, short black skirt, loose bright blue sweater, scarlet lips and fingernails.

Giving me a flick of a glance, she said, 'Can I help you?' and went on working.

'Well . . .' I looked at her carefully, 'you can tell me why the hell you made sure Surtees Benchmark saw you following him?'

The busy fingers stilled. The bright eyes looked at my face. The familiar voice deepened and said in exasperation, 'How the shit do you *know*?'

'Eye sockets.'

'What?'

'I draw people. I look at their bones. Your eye sockets slant down in a particular way at the outer corners. Also your wrists are male. You should wear frilled cuffs.'

'Bugger you.'

I laughed. 'So why did you let Surtees see you?'

'Let him? I made sure he did, like you said, I got him real worried. See, if someone knows they're being followed, they're dead careful, but when they *don't* see their shadow they think they're safe, so they go at once and do what you could wait weeks for them to do otherwise, and you'd never know, either, what things he didn't care about anyone watching, and what he really wanted to keep hidden. See?'

'I guess I do.'

'So I got him busy looking out for a skinhead.'

'And,' I suggested, 'he then doesn't notice a secretary in a dark brown wig?'

'You got it.'

'What did the secretary see?'

'Ah.' Young, Uttley (and associates) enjoyed himself. 'Yon bonnie Surtees has a lady wife who keeps him on a throttling leash. Some men enjoy subjugation, I'm not saying they don't, but Wednesday afternoons it seems Mrs Surtees chairs some sort of local women's action committee and her Mister bolts into Guildford to consult his business colleague. Seems Surtees runs a stud farm that's half owned by his wife and half by someone else, the business colleague. Anyway, Wednesday afternoon – yesterday – Surtees drives round in a circle or two looking out for the skinhead, and when he thinks it's safe he steers not to any business office but to a terrace house on the outskirts of Guildford. That's to say, he parks in the next street and looks all around carefully – a dead giveaway, he's stupid – and then he walks to the little house and opens the front door with a key.'

I sighed.

'Don't you want to hear about it?'

'Yes, but I'd rather he'd visited four thugs in a gym.'

'Sorry about that. Anyway, yesterday Mr Young paid a visit to the house at Guildford, as soon as Surtees had left.'

'Mr Young in suit, hat, moustache?'

He nodded. 'The lot.'

'And?'

'And there's a poor little cow lives there that lets inadequates like Surtees pay to spank her before sex.'

'Damn.'

'Not what you hoped?'

'Too simple.'

'Do you want me to carry on?'

'Yes.' I brought a foil-wrapped packet out of a pocket and gave it to him. 'This is a pair of glasses left behind by one of the four robbers. They're the strength people take off when they want to read. I don't suppose they'll be much use, but it's all they left.'

He/she unwrapped the glasses without excitement.

'Also,' I said, 'see what you can find out about a goldsmith working in London in around 1850 or 60, called Maxim.'

After a short stare, he said 'Anything else?'

'How do you rate as a bodyguard?'

'That's extra.'

I paid him another week's retainer. Expenses and extras, he said, would fall due at the end.

Chapter 8

When Ivan spread out the creditors' agreements on his table and slowly took each of them onto his lap to read them carefully one by one, his overall reaction was one of relieved gloom.

When my mother came into his room, though, he lifted his head to her and smiled, and for the first time since his illness the worry dissolved from the lines on her forehead. She smiled back with the deep understanding friendship of a strong marriage, and I thought inconsequentially that if the area bank bighead had seen that exchange he would have counted it benefit enough for anything I had done.

'Our boy,' Ivan said (and I was usually '*your*' boy), 'has signed the brewery into chains and penury.'

'But . . .' my mother asked, 'why are you pleased?'

He picked up a thick batch of paper in a blue cover and waved it at her.

'This,' he said, 'is our annual audit. Tobias Tollright has signed it. It is our passport to continue trading. The creditors' terms for payment are tough, very tough, but they've been fair. We ought to be able to win our way back. And they've factored in the Cheltenham race! I was sure we'd have to cancel it. But the chalice and Golden Malt are still at risk . . . I'll not give them up. We *must* meet the payments. Increase sales . . . I'll call a board meeting.'

One could actually see his resolution trickling back.

'Well done, Alexander,' he said.

I shook my head. 'Thank Mrs Morden. It was all her work.'

We spent an easy, companionable evening, the three of us, but by morning Ivan's euphoria had mostly vanished and he was complaining that the brewery's shareholders would be receiving only tiny token dividends for the next three years. To do him justice he wasn't thinking of himself, although he was by far the major shareholder, but of various widows and relations left behind by time and mergers from the days before he'd inherited. Several widows relied on their dividends for existence, he said.

'If you'd have gone bankrupt,' I pointed out, 'they'd be lucky to get anything at all. A tiny lump sum and no dividends for ever.'

'But still . . .'

I'd hoped he would have had energy enough to dress, but he fretted instead about the widows. 'Perhaps I can afford . . . out of my own funds . . . heating bills this winter . . .'

My mother stroked his hand fondly.

I had expected, since he had written his codicil the day before, that he would have told his lawyer not to bother to come, but it seemed he had forgotten to cancel the meeting, and Oliver Grantchester, with his loud voice, bulky frame and room-filling presence arrived punctually at ten o'clock, the meek Miranda in tow.

Ivan began stuttering an embarrassed apology, to which Grantchester didn't listen.

The lawyer looked me up and down without favour and told Ivan that they didn't need my presence. He pointed to me and then to the door, giving me an unmistakable order. I might in fact have gone, but at that moment Patsy arrived like a ship in full sail, Surtees floundering foolishly in her wake.

Surtees the spanker: weak, pathetic and vicious.

'You are not making any codicil, Father, unless I'm sure Alexander' – Patsy spat the word – 'doesn't in any way benefit.'

'My dear,' Ivan told her pleasantly, 'I'm not writing any codicil this morning. None at all.'

'But you said . . . You arranged for Oliver to come . . .'

'Yes, I know, I'm sorry I forgot to tell him, but I wrote my codicil yesterday. It's all done. We can just have some coffee now.'

Ivan was naive if he thought coffee would quell a tempest. Patsy and Oliver both berated him. My mother stood like a shield beside him. Surtees glared at me as if his brains had seized up.

'It's perfectly simple,' Grantchester boomed. 'You can tear up yesterday's codicil and write another one.'

Ivan looked at me as if for help. 'But I don't need to write another one,' he said, 'do I?'

I shook my head.

The bombardment of voices went on. Ivan, upset, nevertheless held to his position: he had written his codicil, it expressed what he wanted, and there was no need to write it again.

'At least let me check it from the legal point of view,' Grantchester said.

Ivan with a touch of starch told him that he, Ivan, knew when a document had been correctly executed, and his codicil had.

'But perhaps I can see it . . . ?'

'No,' Ivan said, regretfully polite.

'I don't understand you.'

'I *do*,' Patsy said forcefully. 'It's quite clear that Alexander is manipulating you, Father, and you're so blind you can't see that everything he does is aimed at taking my place as your heir.'

Ivan looked at me with such troubled indecision that I quietly went out of his study and climbed the stairs to the room I'd slept in, to put together the few things I'd brought with me, ready for leaving. I'd done my best for the brewery – for Ivan, for my mother – but the biggest difference between my stepfather and me was the ease and extent of his mood swings and changes of opinions, and, good and honourable man though he might be, I never quite knew what he believed of me from one hour to the next.

133

It had seemed, since his illness, that he had relied on and believed in and made use of my good faith, but it had been a frail belief after all.

I could hear shouting going on downstairs, though I'd thought my departure would at least have stopped Patsy haranguing her father.

I stood at the window looking out towards Regent's Park and didn't hear my mother come upstairs until she spoke behind me.

'Alexander, Ivan needs you.'

I turned. 'I can't. I'm not fighting Patsy.'

'It's not just Patsy. That man who runs the brewery is here now too. Desmond Finch. Ivan thinks the world of him but he's a terrific fusspot, and he trots to Patsy with every complaint. They're all telling Ivan ... yelling at him ... that the terms you signed with the creditors are disgraceful and they could all have done better, and they want him to cancel your power of attorney retrospectively so that your signature on everything is void.'

I asked, 'Did Ivan send you to fetch me?'

'Well, no. But last night he was so *pleased* ...'

I sighed and put my arm round her slender waist. 'And,' I said, 'he can't legally make my signature void.'

We went down. Ivan looked hunted, harried by the pack. They all resented my reappearance, and I looked at them one by one, trying to put reasons to their antagonism.

Patsy, tall, good-looking, fierce and obsessed, had been an unappeasable foe since the day her father had fallen in love with my mother. Young women who felt possessive of their widowed fathers usually hated the usurper who displaced them, but Patsy's rage had skipped over her sweet-natured unthreatening stepmother and fastened inexorably on me. If she had ever stopped to make a sensible reckoning she would know that she had never lost anything at all because of me, let alone her father's love, but emotion ruled her entirely, and, after twelve years of her steadfast detestation, I didn't expect her to change.

She'd married Surtees two years after her father had married

134

my mother, and in the weak, good-looking Hooray-Henry had chosen a mate she could indoctrinate.

I looked at Surtees as he stood behind Ivan's chair; he was a person, I thought, who would always seek such a shield, who would never have the steel to stand out in the open and say 'Here I am. Judge me as I am.' Patsy had married a man she could bully and it had been very bad for both of them.

I found it less easy to understand Desmond Finch. He stood there glaring at me, thin, aggressive, flashing his large silver-rimmed glasses in sharp little head movements, his adam's apple actively jumping in his neck. I had no reason to doubt the general assessment I'd been given that he was efficient and energetic in his job, but I believed also in the evaluation that he would act only if given directions. It seemed plain that he danced to Patsy's instructions: plain also that he'd made no objective overview on the brewery's troubles, in spite of his own whole career being bound up in its financial health.

A limited man, I thought. Short-sighted mentally as well as optically. A voice baying in the pack. Not one to sink the teeth in first.

And Oliver Grantchester? He'd never liked me; I'd never liked him.

There he balefully stood, bulky, going bald, Ivan's legal adviser from way-back, consulted, wise – and enchanted by Patsy to the extent that his manner to me was always of suspicion, distrust and obstruction.

Ivan said weakly, 'Couldn't you have got a better deal for the brewery, Alexander?'

I smiled grimly. 'I'm sick of the brewery,' I said. 'Ivan, let Patsy loose on the creditors. I don't give a damn about the fact that she'll ruin her inheritance. Why should I care? The brewery is yours. It's rescued; it has problems that are basically solved, but which you can muck up in a moment. I'm a painter and I'm going back to my own work, and goodbye . . . a heartfelt goodbye to you all.'

Ivan said miserably, 'Alexander . . .'

'For you,' I said to him plainly, 'I've taken risks that I'll take

135

again, and I've begged and persuaded and bargained to save your good name. Because you sent me the chalice' – and I glanced at Patsy and Surtees, who stared as if transfixed – 'I got beaten beyond a joke. And I've had enough. I'll do anything on earth for my mother, but that's where it now ends. Do what you like, Ivan. Just count me out.'

My mother said, barely audibly, 'Oh no ... *please*, Alexander,' and Ivan looked exhaustedly strained.

Grantchester said heavily, 'Ivan tells us he gave you his codicil for safe-keeping. He now sees that this was a mistake. So hand it over.'

Into the silence that followed I said, 'Ivan?'

His eyes looked deep in their sockets. I understood the impossibility he faced. His faith in me was a disloyalty to his daughter; a disloyalty I had no right to coerce, even if I could.

'I'll get it,' I said, letting him off. 'It's upstairs.'

I went up and fetched the sealed envelope, and returning, put it into his hands.

'I'll take it,' Grantchester said authoritatively, but Ivan put the envelope on his knees and folded his hands on it, and shook his head.

'I'll keep it here, Oliver,' he said.

'But –'

'Then I can tear it up if I change my mind.'

I smiled into Ivan's troubled eyes and without weight said I would be upstairs for an hour or two more if he wanted me.

'He doesn't want you,' Surtees said spitefully. 'None of us do.'

I shrugged and left them and, shaking my head to my mother's pleading eyes, went back upstairs, looking out of the window and waiting.

They went on shouting, downstairs, but finally the angry voices came out of Ivan's study and descended to street level and left by the front door. When all was quiet I went out of my room and onto the stairs, and found Ivan on the landing below me, looking up. He made a gesture towards his study, a flip of the hand that was unmistakably an invitation, so I went down and followed him into his room, and sat opposite him in my usual chair.

My mother, looking as frail as her husband, stood beside Ivan, touching him as if to give him strength.

He said to me, 'Did you mean it, that you've had enough?'

For answer I asked, 'Did you cancel the power of attorney?'

'I . . . I don't know what to do.'

'No, he didn't,' my mother said. 'Ivan, tell Alexander . . . *Beg* Alexander to go on acting for you.' To me she said, 'Don't leave us.'

I had so recently vowed I would do anything on earth for my mother. So small a thing, to stay and field a few insults. I wilted inside from disinclination.

'What did you mean about being beaten?' Ivan said.

'That black eye I had last week . . .'

He frowned. 'Keith Robbiston said you were hurt.'

I told them about the robbers. 'I didn't want to worry you when you were so ill . . . so I didn't tell you.'

'Oh my God,' he said, 'I've done so much harm.'

'Nothing that isn't being put right.'

I poured brandy into two glasses standing ready on a nearby silver tray and handed one to Ivan, one to my mother. They both drank without protest, as if I'd given them medicine.

I said to Ivan, 'If you just leave things as they are, the brewery should be out of debt in three years. I know some of the terms are hard. They have to be. The debts are truly enormous. Mrs Morden has done a marvellous job, but she says the future depends greatly on keeping the services of your present brewmaster and on the managing energies of Desmond Finch. Desmond Finch wouldn't take a diamond-studded suggestion from me, but he's used to following your instructions, so that's what you have to do, Ivan. Go back to the brewery and instruct him.'

My stepfather nodded with resolution. And how long, I morosely considered, would that resolution last.

The telephone rang. Ivan's hand asked me to answer it, so I did.

A confident voice said, 'This is Detective Constable Thompson of the Leicestershire police. I want to speak to Sir Ivan Westering.'

Ivan, of course, wanted me to deal with whatever it was. I explained that Sir Ivan was recovering from a heart attack, and offered my services.

'And you are, sir?'

'His son.' Well, near enough.

After a pause a different voice, just as confident, identified himself as Detective Chief Inspector Reynolds.

'What is this about?' I asked.

The voice enquired whether Sir Ivan knew anyone named Norman Quorn.

'Yes, he does.'

The voice impersonally explained. I listened blankly. The Leicestershire police had for two weeks been trying to identify a body that they now had reason to believe was that of a Mr Norman Quorn. The Chief Inspector wanted Sir Ivan Westering, as Mr Quorn's long-term employer, to assist in making a positive identification, yes or no.

With shortened breath, I said, 'Doesn't he have any relations?'

'Only his sister, sir, and she is . . . *distressed*. The body is partly decomposed. The sister gave us Sir Ivan's name. So we would be grateful, sir . . .'

'He isn't well,' I said.

'Perhaps *you*, then?'

'I didn't know him.' I thought briefly. 'I'll tell my father. Give me a number to phone you back.' He told me a number, which I wrote out of habit on the bottom of the box of tissues. 'Right,' I said, 'five minutes.'

As emotionlessly as possible I gave Ivan the news.

'Norman!' he said disbelievingly. '*Dead?*'

'They want to know for sure. They ask you to go.'

'I'll go with you,' my mother said.

I phoned the Chief Inspector, told him I would be driving, and wrote his directions on the bottom of the tissue box.

138

In the end four of us went to Leicestershire in Ivan's Rover (retrieved from an underground garage), Ivan and my mother in the back with Wilfred sitting in the front beside me, a box of heart attack remedies on his lap. Wilfred read out the directions on the tissue-box so that fairly early in the afternoon we arrived at a featureless building in Leicester that housed a mortuary and investigating laboratories.

The detective chief inspector met us, shook hands with Ivan and my mother and me and was impressed into solicitude by Wilfred's presence and medical precautions. Ivan, though in suit and tie, looked almost greyer than in his dressing-gown.

Inside the building, in a small reception area that doubled as waiting-room, a large weeping woman was being comforted in the arms of an equally large uniformed policewoman. The chief inspector indicated that we should wait there while he took Ivan to see the body, but Ivan clutched my arm and wouldn't go without me, so, shrugging, the senior policeman settled for taking me too.

We were all then issued with disposable gowns, with gloves, overshoes and masks for our noses and mouths. Dead bodies, it seemed, could infect the living.

I hadn't been in such a place before, but it was curiously familiar from pictures. We went down a passage into a white painted room that was clean, brightly lit, not very large and smelled not unpleasantly of disinfectant. On a high centre table, under a white cover, lay a long quiet shape.

Ivan's hand shook on my arm but civic duty won the day. He looked steadily at the white face revealed when a gowned and masked mortuary attendant pulled back one end of the covering sheet, and he said without wavering, 'Yes, that's Norman.'

'Norman Quorn?'

'Yes, Chief Inspector. Norman Quorn.'

'Thank you, sir.'

I said, 'What did he die of?'

There was a pause. The policeman and the mortuary attendant exchanged eyebrow signals that I hadn't the code to read, and the policeman also looked assessingly at Ivan's physical state, and at mine, and came to a decision.

'I'll take you back to your wife, sir,' he said to Ivan, and offered his arm instead of mine, neatly leaving me behind alone to hear the answer to my question.

The mortuary attendant first of all identified himself as the pathologist who had carried out the original post mortem.

'Sorry,' I said.

'Don't be.' He casually pulled down his mask, revealing a young face, competent.

'So . . . what did he die of?' I asked.

'We're not sure.' He shrugged. 'There are no obvious causes of death. No gunshots, no stab wounds, no fractures of the skull, no signs of strangulation, no household poisons. No evidence of murder. He had been dead about two weeks when he was discovered. He didn't die where he was found, which was in a rubbish dump. I saw him *in situ*. He had been placed there after death.'

'Well . . .' I frowned, 'was he simply ill? Heart attack? Stroke? Pneumonia?'

'More likely one of the first two, though we can't know for sure. But there is an abnormality . . .' He hesitated. 'We showed it to his sister, and she fainted.'

'I'm not his sister.'

'No.'

He stripped back the sheet as far as the body's waist, showing the dark discolorations of decomposition and the efforts made to tidy up the radical post mortem incisions. I thought it no wonder the sister had fainted and hoped I wouldn't copy her.

'Look at his back,' the pathologist instructed, and with his gloved hands gripped the shoulders and half rolled the body towards him.

There were about a dozen or more rows of darker marks in the darkened flesh, and flecks of white.

The pathologist eased the body flat again.

'Those white bits – did you see them? – are his ribs.'

I felt nauseous, and swallowed.

The pathologist said, 'Those darker marks are burns.'

'*Burns?*'

'Yes. The skin and flesh have been burned away in a few places down to the ribs. He must have fallen into something very hot when he died. Something like a grating. People fall on electric fires in that way. Terrible burns, sometimes. This is like that. Any thoughts?'

My chief thought was how soon I could leave the mortuary.

'He was wearing a nylon shirt,' the pathologist said chattily, 'and there were man-made fibres in the lining and cloth of his suit jacket. They melted to some extent into his skin.'

In another minute, I thought, I would vomit.

I said, 'Could he have died from the burns?'

'I don't think so. As you saw, the burns extended only from below his shoulder blades to his waist. Several local burns, but not lethal, I don't think. It's mostly likely they occurred just after death, or anyway at about the same time. I would guess he had a stroke, fell unconscious on the fire, and died.'

'Oh'.

'Anyway,' the pathologist said with satisfaction, 'now that we have a positive identification we can have an inquest. The coroner's verdict will be "cause of death unknown" and the poor man can have a decent burial. I'll be glad to get him out of here, to be honest.'

I left him with relief and, stripping off the protective clothing, rejoined the group in the entrance area.

'Please tell us,' I said to the chief inspector, 'where exactly you found Mr Quorn.'

Instead of directly answering he explained that the still quietly weeping woman was Norman Quorn's sister. My mother had taken over from the policewoman the role of comforter although, true to form, she looked as if she would prefer saying 'Pull yourself together' to 'There, there.'

'Mr Quorn,' the chief inspector told us conversationally 'was found by council workers who went to clear away a decaying rubbish dump left behind on a farmer's land when a band of travellers moved on. We made lengthy enquiries among the travellers at their next place, but drew a total blank. We spent a great deal of time on it. The travellers pointed out that they were all much younger – we had told them the unknown body was elderly–'

'Sixty-five,' the sister sobbed.

'On the other hand, these travellers were accustomed to cook on home-made barbecues of brick supports with metal rods across, and there were signs that perhaps Mr Quorn had overbalanced backwards onto something like that. None of their current barbecues matched Mr Quorn's burns, but it was all inconclusive. There are absolutely no indications at all of foul play. So now we have your identifications, we can close the case. I'm sorry, but it isn't always possible to determine how things happened, and unless any other facts turn up . . .'

He left the sentence unfinished. Neither Ivan nor my mother told him that the brewery's funds had vanished with the Finance Director, and nor did I. Ivan would have to think it through, and decide.

Because of Wilfred's presence we were silent on the way back to London but spent the evening discussing nothing else.

Ivan was inclined to be glad that Norman Quorn hadn't after all run off with the money.

'We misjudged him,' he said sorrowfully. 'My dear old friend . . .'

'Your dear old friend,' I corrected regretfully, 'certainly did transfer the money out of the brewery. I've seen copies of about six huge withdrawals that he made just before he left. He did indeed, I'm afraid, send all the funds on their way to destinations still unknown.'

'But he didn't *go*!'

'No. He died. He didn't die on the rubbish tip. Someone put him there. Wherever he died, someone didn't report it to anyone, but just dumped him.'

Ivan's beliefs and intentions swung widely to and fro, but

his chief instinct, as before, was not to make public the brewery's loss. Norman Quorn dead, Norman Quorn living under palm trees . . . it made no difference. The theft existed and either way would be covered up.

I said, 'But don't you care who dumped him? Don't you want to know where he died?'

'What does it really matter? And as Norman was homosexual –' Ivan saw my surprise – 'didn't you know? No, I suppose you didn't, he was always discreet . . . but, you see, suppose he died where it was *awkward* for someone . . . do you see what I mean?'

I saw.

'And it wouldn't do Norman or the brewery any good to disclose his sexual preference or, oh dear, his theft.'

It was astounding, I thought, to find my starchy stepfather so tolerant of homosexuality, but my mother, who after all knew him better, took it for granted. 'Quite a lot of Ivan's friends,' she told me later, 'were "that way". Delightful friends,' she added. 'Good company always.'

Ivan asked me, 'If we tell the police that Norman stole the funds and was homosexual, would it affect the creditors' arrangements?'

'Well, I don't know. The creditors do know he stole the funds. They signed the agreements knowing that.'

'Well, then?'

'But they believe he skipped the country. They believe he's alive. They believe the money is with him . . . and it isn't.'

'So?'

'So where is it?'

A long silence.

By ten in the evening Ivan was saying we needed someone else's advice.

'OK,' I agreed, 'whose?'

'Perhaps . . . Oliver's?'

I said mildly, 'Oliver would ask you what I, Alexander, suggested, and then give you an opposite opinion.'

'But he knows the law!'

I had been careful always not to belittle Patsy to her father. Oliver was Patsy's man. So was Desmond Finch.

I asked, 'What did Patsy think of Norman Quorn?'

'She didn't like him. Always a sadness. Why do you want to know?'

'What would she expect you to do?'

Ivan dithered.

By midnight he had decided, in his law-abiding Jockey Club persona, that I should ask Margaret Morden whether Norman Quorn's death made any difference to the creditors, and that I, not Ivan, should tell Detective Chief Inspector Reynolds that the now-identified corpse had been probably an embezzler about to leave the country.

'Probably?' I echoed with scepticism.

'We don't know for sure.'

I thought he would have changed his mind again by morning, but it seemed my sensible mother had fortified his decision, as she agreed with it; so at nine o'clock Ivan, again in dressing-gown and slippers, instructed me to phone Leicestershire.

Slight snag. The policeman's phone number was written on the tissue box. The tissue box was still in the car. I trailed off to retrieve it and finally reached the necessary ear.

'Tell me on the phone,' he commanded when I suggested meeting.

'Better face to face.'

'I'm off duty at noon.'

'I'll get there. Where?'

'Do you remember the way to the mortuary? There then. It's on my way home.'

I refrained – just – from observing that the mortuary was on everyone's way home, and managed to trace Margaret Morden to hers.

'It's Saturday,' she said tartly.

'I do know.'

'Then it had better be important.'

'The King Alfred Brewery's Finance Director has turned up, still in England – but dead.'

'I agree,' she said slowly, 'that that is Saturday news. How did he die?'

'Stroke or heart attack, the pathologist thinks.'

'When?'

'About the time he disappeared.'

She thought briefly and said, 'Phone me in the office on Monday. And tell Tobias. But if what's bothering you most is the status of the creditors' agreements, my first impression is that they will stand.'

'You're a doll.'

'No, I'm definitely *not*.'

I put down the receiver with a smile and drove to Leicester.

The chief inspector's reaction was as expected. 'Why didn't you tell me this yesterday?'

'The brewery has hushed up the theft.'

'The body,' he said reflectively, 'was dressed in suit, shirt, tie, underpants, socks and shoes, all unremarkable. There was nothing in his pockets.'

'How did you identify him in the end?'

'One of our clever young constables took another look at the clothes. The shoes were new – on the sole of one was the name of a shop and the price. The shop was in Wantage, and they remembered the sale ... Mr Quorn was a regular customer. He was away from home, but a neighbour had the sister's address.'

'Neat.'

'But what he was doing in Leicestershire ... ?' He shrugged. 'It's possible he died out of doors, in a garden. There were a few blades of mown grass in his clothes. That would gel with him falling back onto a barbecue of some sort.'

'Hardly the right clothes for a barbecue.'

He looked me up and down in amusement. 'While you, sir, if I may say so, look more like a traveller.'

I acknowledged it in good humour.

'I'll complete my case notes with what you've told me,' the policeman said. 'It isn't by any means unknown for people to get rid of bodies when they've died inconveniently. I appreciate your help. Give my regards to Sir Ivan. He looks so ill himself.'

It was by then three and a half weeks since Ivan's heart attack (and four weeks and a day since Quorn had skipped with the cash) and what Ivan badly still needed and wasn't getting was complete untroubled rest. I drove back to London and for the remainder of that day and all of the next kept the house tranquil with the telephone switched into an answering machine and with simple meals, cooked by me, that needed no decisions. I gave Wilfred the rest of the weekend off and did his jobs: it was all peaceful and curative and its own reward.

On Monday I went by train again to Reading and did the rounds of the offices.

Life had moved on for Tobias and Margaret, who were already dealing with the next unfortunates down the line, but they each gave me half an hour and information.

'Old Quorn's dead!' Tobias exclaimed. 'Then where's the money?'

I said, 'I thought you might be able to work it out.'

He gave me his best blank outer stare concealing furious activity within.

'I followed him to Panama . . .' he said thoughtfully.

'How many stops to Panama?' I asked.

'Wait.' He turned to one of his three computer monitors, sorted out a disc from an indexed box, and fed it into a slot, pressing keys. 'Here we are. Wire transfer from the brewery to a bank in Guernsey . . . six transfers in one day, each from a different brewery account – it was as if he'd collected every-thing available into those six accounts, then he sent all six separately into the same account in Guernsey, and the bank there already had instructions to transfer the whole amount – multiple millions – to a bank in New York, which already held instructions to wire the money onward to a bank in Panama, and that bank cannot say where the money went from there.'

'Can't or won't?' I asked.

'Quite likely both. All these banks have unbreakable privacy laws. We only know the path to Panama because Norman Quorn had scribbled the ABA numbers on some rough paper and neglected to shred it.'

'Remind me about ABA numbers.'

Tobias chewed a toothpick. 'They identify all banks in the United States and roundabout areas like the Caribbean. They're part of the Fedwire system.'

'Tobe – what's Fedwire?'

'There are three huge worldwide organisations dealing with the international transfer of funds and information,' he said. 'Fedwire – ABA included – is the Federal Reserve Banks institution. They have nine-digit routing numbers, so any transfer with a nine-digit code is likely to have been seen to by Fedwire.'

I sighed.

'Then,' Tobe said, 'There's SWIFT – the Society for Worldwide Interbank Financial Telecommunication. And third, there's CHIPS – Clearing House Interbank Payments System, which is operated also through New York and has special identifier codes unique to their customers, ultra secret.'

'God.'

'Take your pick,' Tobias said. 'All the systems have identifying codes. The codes will tell you the bank, but not the account number. We know the brewery money went to a branch of Global Credit in Panama, but not into which account there.'

'But they must know,' I said. 'I mean, they can't have millions sent to them every day from New York. The amount, the dispatcher, the date . . . they could surely work it out.'

'Perhaps, but it's against their law to pass the information on.'

'Not to the police? Or the tax people?'

'Especially not to the police or the tax people. A lot of banks would be out of business at once if they did that.' Tobe smiled. 'You're an infant, Al.'

I acknowledged it. 'But,' I said, 'what if the money just sits in Panama for ever, now Norman Quorn is dead?'

'It may do,' Tobias nodded. 'There are billions and trillions of loot in unclaimed accounts sitting in banks all over the world, and you can bet your soul the banks profit from them and are in no hurry to look for heirs.'

'Henry VIII syndrome,' I said.

'What?'

I explained about gold church treasures hidden in fields.

'Just like that,' he said.

I left him pulverising a toothpick over someone else's problems and presented myself on Margaret Morden's doorstep.

I told her what few details I knew of Norman Quorn's exit.

'Poor man,' she said.

'So you don't think,' I asked, 'that the wages of sin is death?'

'*Are* death, surely? And where have you been for the last fifty years? The wages of sin nowadays are a few years of full board and lodging at the country's expense with a chance to study for a degree, followed by tender loving care from ex-prisoners' aid societies.'

'Cynical.'

'Realistic.'

'What about the victims?'

'The wages of a victim is to be blamed if at all possible for a crime committed against her – I regret it's often a her – and seldom to be offered compensation, let alone free board and lodging and a university education. The wages of a victim are poverty, oblivion and a lonely grave. It's the sinners the tabloids pursue with their cheque-books.'

'Margaret!'

'So now you know me better,' she said. 'Norman Quorn robbed little old widows of their pathetic dividends and I don't give a shit if he died of a guilty conscience.'

'Little old widows are a bit mawkish . . .'

'Not if you happen to be one.'

'Well . . . if the little old widows' dividends are languishing in a foreign bank somewhere, how do we find them?'

She said, 'What's in it for you?'

I looked at my hands. What could I say? She would consider it mawkish in the extreme whatever I said.

'I don't mean that, Al. I'm in a bad mood today. I'm dealing with yet another deliberate bankruptcy whose sole aim is to dodge paying small-scale creditors, who may themselves go out of business through the loss. The people I'm dealing with will dump the suppliers in the shit, declare the business bankrupt and closed, and go off and start all over again under another name.'

'But,' I said, 'is that legal?'

'Legal, yes. Moral, you must be kidding. I'm not used to people like you. Go away and leave me to my disillusions.'

'I wanted to ask you,' I said, 'about that possible trial run. Do you remember any of the trial's destinations?'

She frowned, then, as Tobias had done, consulted one of her row of computer faces and tapped instructions into the keys.

'It's possible,' she said finally, but with doubts, 'that Quorn sent a fairly small sum to a bank on an island in the Bahamas, who forwarded it to a bank in Bermuda, who sent it back to Wantage. The transactions weren't backed up by signed documentation, and half the information – like the actual account numbers – is missing. If the brewery's money is in either of those banks, which is doubtful, you're not going to find it.'

'Thanks a bunch.'

'Cheer up. First thing this morning I consulted your committee of creditors. The agreements they signed with you will remain unaltered by Norman Quorn's death.'

CHAPTER 9

I walked to the office of Young and Uttley, half expecting to find it locked, but when I knocked and turned the handle, the door opened.

I walked in. The occupant that day wasn't a skinhead or a secretary or Mr Young with moustache or even the football coach Uttley, but a straightforward-looking man of about my own age dressed much as I was myself in jeans, shirt and sweater: no tie, unaggressive trainers and clean hands. The chief difference between us was that he had very short light brown hair, while mine still curled on my shoulders.

I smiled at him slowly, and I said, 'Hello.'

'Hello.'

'What's your name?' I asked.

'Chris.'

'Chris Young?'

He nodded. 'I've done a bit of let-your-fingers-do-the-walking for you,' he said.

His accent was unchanged. The skinhead, the secretary and Chris Young all spoke with the same voice.

'And?' I asked.

'There was a goldsmith name of Maxim working in London in the eighteen hundreds. Like Garrard's or Asprey's today. Good name. Ritzy. Made fancy things like peacocks for table ornaments, gold filigree feathers with real jewels in.'

'Tobe promised me you were good,' I said.

'Just good?'

'Brilliant. A genius, actually.'

He grinned immodestly. 'Tobe told me you were a walking brain and not to be put off by your good manners.'

'I'll kill him.'

'Tobe told me you were raised in a castle.'

'It was cold.'

'Yeah. I drew an orphanage. Warm.'

We got on fine. I made a drawing of King Alfred's golden chalice, and he phoned back to his goldsmith informant with a detailed description. 'And it has engraved lines round it that look just like random patterns but are some sort of verse in Anglo-Saxon. Yeah, yeah, that's what I said, Anglo-bloody-Saxon. See what you can do.'

He put down the receiver. 'Those specs you gave me,' he said, 'you can buy them anywhere.'

I nodded.

'I'd use them myself for disguises, if I could see through them.'

'I reckon that's why the robber took them off.'

'That's another thing,' Chris Young said. 'Boxing gyms. Your spanking pal Surtees never goes near a gym. He's as unfit as a leaking balloon. I've tailed him until I've had it up to here with him, and besides, none of the gyms in his area have ever heard of him.'

'Fingers doing the walking?'

'Sure.'

'Suppose he uses a different name?'

Chris Young sighed. 'He's not the gym type, I'm telling you. Which leaves me – and don't point it out – with no option but to flash your drawings of your robbers all over the place hoping for a fist in the guts.'

I stared.

'An adverse reaction,' he said carefully, in his incongruous voice, 'is a positive indication of a nerve touched.'

'You've been reading books!'

151

'I've been bashed a few times. It always tells me something. Like being bashed told you quite a lot, didn't it?'

'I suppose it did.'

'See? If anyone bashes you again, learn from it.'

'I don't intend to be bashed again.'

'No? That's why you asked about bodyguards?'

'Exactly why.'

He grinned. 'I've a friend who's a jockey over the jumps. He's broken his bones about twenty times. It'll never happen again, he says. He says it every time.'

'Mad,' I agreed.

'Have you ever met a jump jockey?'

'I was married once to a trainer in Lambourn.'

'Emily Cox,' he said.

I was still.

'I like to know who I'm working for,' he said.

'And to check up on whether I would lie to you?'

'Most of my clients do.'

I would, I acknowledged to myself, have lied to him if I'd wanted to.

His telephone rang and he answered it formally, 'Young and Uttley, can I help you?'

He listened and said, 'Thank you' half a dozen times, and wrote a few words onto a notepad, and disconnected.

'Your chalice,' he said, 'was inscribed with something called Bede's Death Song. It sounds a right laugh. It was made in 1867 to the order of a Mr Hanworth Hill of Wantage, Berkshire, probably to impress the neighbours. It cost an arm and a leg because it was solid gold inlaid with emeralds, sapphires and rubies.'

'Real ones?' I exclaimed, surprised.

Chris consulted his notes. 'Cabochon gems, imperfect.' He looked up. 'What does cabochon mean?'

'It means polished but uncut. No facets. Rounded, like pebbles. Not made to sparkle.' I paused. 'They don't look real. They're big.'

'You mean, you've actually seen this thing?'

'I think it's what I got bashed for.'

'So where is it now?'

'You,' I said smiling, 'are – I hope – going to prevent anyone else from trying to bash that information out of me.'

'Oh.' He blinked. 'How difficult would it be to make you tell?'

'Fairly easy.' But, I thought, it might depend on who was asking.

'You'd fold? You surprise me.'

'The chalice isn't mine.'

'Reasonable. OK. I'll start on the gyms.'

'Be careful,' I said.

'Sure.' He sounded lighthearted. 'Black eyes will cost you extra.'

He wanted to know if I were serious about a bodyguard, and we agreed that identifying my robbers took priority.

Ah well.

Returning by train, tube and legs to Park Crescent I was met by my mother in a state of agitation: that is to say, she was looking out for me and told me calmly but at once that I should telephone Emily immediately.

'What about?'

'Golden Malt got loose.'

Damnation, I thought; *fuck it*.

'How's Ivan?' I asked.

'Not bad. Phone Emily, won't you?'

I phoned her.

'Golden Malt got loose on the Downs at Foxhill,' she said. 'He's not an easy ride, as you know. He bucked off the exercise lad and got loose and they couldn't catch him.'

'But racehorses often go home by themselves, don't they? Surely he'll turn up –'

'He *has* turned up,' she interrupted. 'He's found his way back *here*. Don't ask me how. He's been in this yard for five years, ever since Ivan bought him as a foal, and, first chance he got, he came home.'

'Bugger.'

'The thing is, what do you want me to do?'

'Keep him. I'll think.'

'I've had a phone call from Surtees. He says he's coming to collect him.'

'He said *what?*'

'He says the horse is Patsy's.'

I took a steadying breath. 'The horse is Ivan's.'

'Surtees says Patsy's going to sell the horse to prevent you getting your hands on it. He says you've stolen the King Alfred Cup and you'll steal Golden Malt and rob Patsy and the brewery. I said you wouldn't do that, but he's bringing a trailer to collect Golden Malt and take him to his stud farm for safe keeping.'

I tried to organise scattered thoughts.

'When do you expect him?' I asked.

'He'll be on his way already.'

I groaned. I'd just come from Reading, about thirty miles from Lambourn, and now, in London, it was nearer eighty.

'How did Surtees know you have the horse back?' I asked.

'I don't know. But he also knows he was in Foxhill. All my lads know, too. I can't send the horse back there.'

'Well, I'll come as soon as I can. Don't let Surtees take Golden Malt.'

She said despairingly, 'But how do I stop him?'

'Let down the tyres of the trailer. Build a Great Wall. Anything.'

I explained the problem briefly to my mother, who said at once that I could borrow Ivan's car.

Two hours at least by car. Roadworks and hold-ups in tortoise-slow traffic. Also, remembering the gauge from Saturday, I would have to stop for petrol.

I chose a train. I wasn't bad at trains. I ran and was lucky, catching an underground without waiting and a non-stop express from Paddington to Didcot junction and a taxi driver who hurried his wheels to Lambourn for a bonus. I took with me my mother's cash card and her phone card and all her available money, and my own new credit card and cheques, and also a zipped bag containing the things I'd borrowed ten days earlier from Emily – helmet, padded jacket, jodhpur boots – that my mother hadn't yet returned to her.

Helter-skelter though I went, Surtees had arrived first. He had brought with him not only a trailer for the horse but an assistant horse-handler in the shape of his nine-year-old daughter, Xenia.

Surtees, Emily, Xenia and Golden Malt were all out in the stable yard, Emily holding the horse by his bridle and arguing angrily with the others.

Emily's Land Rover stood in the driveway behind Surtees's trailer, effectively blocking his way out. The exit on the far side of the yard, the wide earth track used by the horses on their way out to exercise, was at present impassable as it seemed a lorry delivering hay had carelessly shed its load of bales there.

I paid the taxi driver his bonus and with reluctance walked into the angry scene. Emily looked relieved to see me, Surtees furious. Xenia gave me a head-to-toe sneer and in a voice just like her mother's said, 'What *do* you think you look like?'

'Good afternoon, Surtees,' I said. 'Having trouble?'

Surtees said with unthrottled rage, 'Tell your wife to get out of my way. That horse is Patsy's, and I'm taking it.'

I said, 'It's Ivan's, and I'm looking after Ivan's things, as you know.'

'Get out of my way!'

'The horse is officially in training here with Emily. It can't race from your stud farm. You surely know the rules.'

'Bugger the rules!'

Xenia, giving me the insolent stare she'd learned from her parents, said, 'You're a thief. Mummy says so.'

She was dressed in riding breeches, navy hacking jacket, polished boots and black velvet helmet, as if for a showground. Not a bad kid. Fair haired, blue eyed, hopelessly spoiled.

'Why aren't you in school?' I asked.

'I have riding lessons on Monday afternoons,' she answered

155

automatically, and then added, 'and it's none of your business.'

Surtees, presumably deciding that argument would get him nowhere, made a sudden rugger charge at me while my head and attention were turned towards Xenia, and with his shoulder cannon-balling into my stomach, knocked me over.

He fell on top of me, seeking to damage. Neither rugger nor any form of contact sport had ever been my choice or capability. I rolled over and over in the gravelly dirt with Surtees, scrambling for a weight advantage, trying to disconnect myself and stand up.

I could sense Xenia jumping up and down and screaming, 'Kill him, Daddy. Kill him.'

The whole situation was idiotic. Farcical. Killing me was definitely outside Surtees's imagination, but the prospect of offering Golden Malt to Patsy as a symbol of his virility and superiority over the hated step brother lent him a strength and viciousness hard to deal with.

Neither of us landed a decisive punch. Surtees, as Chris Young had sworn, wasn't the boxing-gym type.

Add in Xenia who, as befitted her clothes, carried a riding crop, and we arrived at a childish form of warfare in which a bodyguard would have lightened the load.

Surtees clutched my hair and tried to bang my head on the ground, which gave me the idea of doing it to him, with equal lack of effectiveness, while Xenia danced around us lashing out with the riding crop which usually landed on me though occasionally on her father, to his bellowing disgust.

I scrambled finally to my feet, but dragged Surtees up with me as he wouldn't leave go. Xenia hit my legs. Surtees tried a sweeping too-slow wide-armed clout to my head that gave me a chance to both duck the blow and get hold of his clothes and fling him with all my strength away from me so that he overbalanced and staggered backwards and, falling, cracked his head against a brick stable wall.

It stunned him. He slid to his knees. Xenia screamed, 'You've killed my Daddy,' though I clearly hadn't, and I wrapped my arms round her writing little body, lifting her off her feet, and yelled to Emily, 'Are any of these boxes empty?'

'The end two,' she shouted, and struggled to hold Golden Malt in control, the horse stamping around, upset by the noise.

The top half door of the end box stood open, the bottom half closed and bolted. I carried the frantically struggling child over there and dropped her over the lower half of the door, closing the top half and sliding home a bolt before she could climb out.

I unbolted and opened both halves of the vacant box next door and, grabbing the groggy Surtees by the back of his collar and by his belt, half ran him, half flung him into the space, closing both halves of the door and slapping home the bolts.

Xenia screeched and kicked her door. Surtees had yet to find his voice. Out of breath, I went over to Emily, whose expression was a mixture of outrage and laugh.

'Now what?' she said.

'Now I bolt you into Golden Malt's box so that none of this is your fault, and decamp with the horse.'

She stared. 'Are you serious?'

'None of this is serious, but it's not very funny, either.'

We could both hear Xenia's muffled shrieks.

'She'll upset all the horses,' Emily said, calming Golden Malt with small pats. 'I did think you might ride this fellow away again,' she said. 'I was just saddling him when Surtees came. The saddle is over there, in his box.'

I walked across the yard and found the saddle, which I carried back and fixed in place. There was a full net of hay in the box also, and a head collar for tying up a horse more comfortably than with a bridle. I carried them out and threaded them together with the zipped bag I'd brought, taking out the helmet but slinging the rest over the withers of the horse, in front of the saddle; like saddle bags of yore.

Then I took the reins from Emily and walked with her to the empty box. She went inside and I bolted the bottom half of the door.

'You'd better hurry,' she said calmly. 'The lads will arrive in less than half an hour for evening stables, and Surtees will have the police looking for you five minutes after that.'

I kissed her over the stable door.

'It will be dark in the next hour,' she said. 'Where will you go?'

'God knows.'

I kissed her again and bolted her into her temporary prison, and hauled myself into Golden Malt's saddle and, buckling on the helmet, set off again onto the Downs.

I needed the helmet for anonymity more than safety. So universal was the wearing of helmets that a head without one would have been remembered, even in a part of the country where horses were commoner than cows.

Golden Malt, to my relief, showed no reluctance to go along the stretch of road leading to the familiar track up to the training grounds, and seemed, if I understood him at all, to be reassured by being ridden and directed, not running loose and having to find his own way home.

Even at four in the afternoon there were other horses around in the distance. Golden Malt whinnied loudly and received an echoing response from afar, which caused him to nod his head as if in satisfaction: he went along sweetly, not trying to buck me off.

The problem was that I didn't know where to go. Surtees might indeed send the police after me, and although they wouldn't try to catch me on horseback like a Wild West posse, at some point or other I would very likely find myself vulnerably back on a road. Out of sight – that was the thing.

I tried to remember the map Emily and I had spread out in the kitchen, but I'd been concentrating on the way to Foxhill then, and I certainly couldn't go back there. Emily had a Patsy-informant in her yard – one of her lads making a little extra money from Surtees – and so, now, maybe, had her Foxhill friend. No good risking it.

The rolling sea of grass on Lambourn Downs was to my eyes featureless. I'd been up there fairly often with Emily in her Land Rover, but it had been five or six years ago. I looked back and could no longer distinguish the track home.

Think.

Monday, late afternoon. Time for all horses to go to their stables for food, for night.

I decided to be ordinary; to conform. It would be the abnormal, like an unhelmeted head, that would draw comment and attention and questions.

I thought again of the Ridgeway. I wouldn't get lost on it.

I might get *found* on it.

Golden Malt trotted happily the length of Mandown, his regular exercise ground. It was when I stopped at the far end and didn't turn his head back towards home that he grew restive.

I patted his neck and talked to him, as Emily would have done.

'Never mind, old fellow, we're safe out here,' I murmured over and over, and it was the lack of panic in the voice of confidence, that I think calmed him. I was afraid he would by-pass the false front and go instinctively for the underlying doubt, but he slowly relaxed and waited patiently, twitching his ears forward and back as untroubled horses do, leaving his future in my hands.

Unwelcome though the thought had been, I'd accepted that we might have to stay out on the Downs all night. I could otherwise amble into someone's stable yard or farm and ask for stabling until morning, but this wasn't normal any longer in the age of cars. There were motels but no horsetels; not anyway for unannounced strangers on thoroughbreds.

Shelter.

The weather was fine, though chilly. It wasn't too cold for Golden Malt's survival, but he was used to a snug box with food and drink provided, and perhaps a rug. An animal of racehorse calibre wouldn't stand quiet for even an hour if one simply tied his reins to a railing. He would break free and kick up his heels in a V sign as he galloped to the horizon. While red carpets might be out, four walls and water were essential.

There were two hours left until darkness. It took me nearly all of that time to find a place that Golden Malt would enter.

There were various huts on the Downs where the groundsmen kept equipment, but none of those would be big enough or empty enough, or would have running water. What I needed was the sort of shelter farmers built at a distance from their home yards, providing walls and roofs against hail and gales, and troughs for their stock to drink from.

The first two such shelters I came to were both filthy inside, thick with droppings. More importantly, Golden Malt wouldn't drink the water. He whiffled his nose and lips over the surface and turned his fastidious head away: and it was no good getting angry, I had to trust to his equine sense.

The third shelter I came to looked just as unappetising, but Golden Malt walked into it amiably and then came out and drank from the trough even before I'd removed bits and pieces from the water's surface.

Much relieved, I waited until he'd drunk his fill and then walked back in with him, and found a comfort in the shape of an iron ring let into the wall. Exchanging the head collar for the bridle I fastened the horse into his new quarters and positioned the hay net where he could eat when he wanted. I unsaddled him and took the saddle outside where he couldn't step on it, and finally – and resignedly – took stock of my own situation.

Like almost all such shelters, its windowless walls faced chiefly north and west and south against the prevailing winds. The east wall was pierced by the entry, which of course had no door. By good luck, although the air was always on the move on the uplands, there was no strong wind that evening, and although the temperature dropped with darkness, I felt more at home in the open than inside with the horse.

I unzipped the holdall and thankfully put on the padded jacket, which alone made the night enterprise feasible. Then I folded the holdall thickly to make a cushion and propped the saddle against the wall for a chair back, and reckoned I'd spent far worse hours on Scottish mountains.

After dark, the clear sky blazed with depths of stars, and in the folds of the Downs below me, little clumps of distant lights assured me that this solitude was relative: and solitude, to me, anyway, was natural.

Inside the shelter, Golden Malt steadily chomped on his hay and made me feel hungry. I'd eaten breakfast in London and a chocolate bar on the train to Didcot, but I hadn't had the foresight to fill the holdall with enough for dinner.

It couldn't be helped. I scooped a handful of water out of the trough and smelled it, and although it wasn't the cleanest ever, judged that if the horse had passed it, it wouldn't kill me. Cold water was never bad at anaesthetising hunger: and hunger was an odd sort of thing, not so much a grind in the stomach as an overall feeling of lassitude, and a headache.

I put my hands into the jacket pockets for warmth and slept sitting up, and soon after two o'clock (according to the luminous hands on the cheap watch I'd bought to replace my father's stolen gold one) awoke from cold. Everything was so quiet inside the shelter that I went in in some alarm, but Golden Malt was still there, safely tied up, asleep, resting a hock in mental twilight, his eyes open but no thoughts showing.

I walked around quietly outside to unstiffen and warm myself and after a while drank more water and sat down again to wait for dawn.

None of my thoughts was hilariously funny.

Surtees's second-hand dislike and spite towards me would now certainly have intensified into personal hatred, because he would think I had made a fool of him in front of his daughter. No matter that he had belligerently chosen to come to remove Ivan's horse, no matter that it was he who had rushed me first to knock me down, he would care only that Xenia had seen him fail on both fronts: the obnoxious Alexander had made off with the goods and left her father imprisoned in a box for horses, looking stupid.

Xenia, with whom I had no quarrel, could now be counted a foe for life. Her mother's consequently increased antagonism might really give a bodyguard work. *Someone* had sent the robbers to my bothy.

Next time you'll scream . . .

Bugger it, I thought. Even if I should dump Ivan and all his concerns (and with him, my mother) I wouldn't necessarily free myself from Patsy's obsession or revenge.

Surtees was Ivan's son-in-law. I was Ivan's stepson. Which of us, I wondered vaguely, took legal priority? Did priority exist?

I itched to paint, I longed to go back to my easel, to my silent room. Zoë Lang filled crevices in my mind to such an extent that in the middle of wondering if water were drinkable I would see the hollow under her cheekbone and think 'purple glaze on turquoise thinned with medium'. The face of the inner woman had to be built of glazes, of colour not as opaque as outer living skin might be, but still to be unmistakably the person who lived in that flesh, who thought and believed and confronted doubt.

I had set myself an unattainable ideal. Such human skill as I could summon wasn't enough for the job. I felt the suicidal despair of all who longed to do what they couldn't, what only a few in each century could – whether blessed or cursed in spirit. No achievement was ever finite. There was no absolute summit. No peak of Everest to plant a flag on. Success was someone else's opinion.

I drifted and dozed and woke again shivering in the first grey promise of light. Golden Malt was pawing the ground, his hooves thudding heavily on dirt, giving me the prosaic news that he had finished his hay. I undid his head collar and took him outside for a drink, and felt, if not exactly a communion with him, at least an awareness of being a fellow creature on a lonely planet.

Deciding that grass would do for breakfast he walked around a bit, head down, munching, while I held his rope and thought of coffee and toast. Then, as daylight more positively arrived, I saddled and bridled him in the shelter, and changed my trainers for jodhpur boots, to look and ride better, and finally, when the morning's first exercise strings would be peopling the landscape, heaved myself and gear onto his back and set about completing the disappearing trick.

I rode to the east, towards the strengthening light. I knew that the Ridgeway path lay to the north of me, also running west to east. Not far ahead I would come to the road from Wantage going south to Hungerford, and I wanted to cross that to reach the next wide expanse of open downland on the far side, where many trainers had their yards but wouldn't know by sight a conspicuous horse from Lambourn. Neither Emily nor I, in my rush to be gone before the lads arrived for evening stables, had given a thought this time to a hood and boots for hiding Golden Malt's white features.

I came to the main road and dismounted to walk the horse across, needing to open and shut gates on either side but, that done, I was free on the wide lands south of Wantage, with five or six miles available in most directions to find a suitable string of horses to attach myself to and follow.

I was looking for a small string of no more than four or five, as I reckoned I would get a more hospitable reception from a small-scale trainer: and so it proved. Just when I thought I'd drawn a blank and was in trouble I came across four horses plodding homeward, one of them being led by a lad on foot.

I followed at a distance and tried not to feel disconcerted when my leaders headed towards the heart of a village from where I could see ahead the huge swathe of the main north–south arterial road, the A34: impassable, if not impossible, for horses to walk across.

The road into the village led downhill. The string of four marched on, undaunted, and I found we were crossing the road *beneath* it, to a second half of the village on the far side. On through the village, the horses turned in between the peeling gates of a small stable yard.

A motor horsebox stood in the yard with a trainer's name and phone number painted on it. I retraced Golden Malt's steps to a phone box we had passed in the village and, juggling reins and coins, took the trainer away from his breakfast.

163

I was, I explained, an owner who was also an amateur jockey. I had just had a blazing row on the Downs with my trainer and had ridden off in a fury, and I was looking for somewhere to park my horse while I sorted things out. Could he help?

'Glad to,' he said heartily, and showed no less enthusiasm when I shortly arrived on a good-looking thoroughbred, offering generous cash for its board and lodging.

When I asked the trainer ('Call me Phil') the quickest way to London he said, 'By taxi to Didcot,' and I thought it ironic that I'd travelled three parts of an oval on Golden Malt and ended in the underpass village of East Ilsley which was actually nearer to Surtees's stud farm than to Emily's yard.

I would come to fetch my horse later that day, I told Phil, and he said not to hurry. He phoned for a taxi for me. We shook hands, in tune.

Back in London I met Ivan's and my mother's anxiety with perhaps more reassurance than I truly felt. Golden Malt, I assured them, was secure and well looked after, but it might be better to move him right away from the Berkshire Downs area where, to horse-educated eyes, he was as recognisable as a film star.

I asked Ivan to lend me his copy of *Horses in Training*, which gave the location amongst other details of every licensed trainer and permit holder in Britain, and I asked my mother to phone Emily and get her to go out shopping in Swindon or Newbury, as she often did, and to phone back to Park Crescent from a public phone there.

'But why?' my mother asked, puzzled.

'Emily's walls have ears, and Surtees is listening.' My mother looked disbelieving. 'And,' I added, 'please don't tell Emily I'm here.'

My obliging parent talked to Emily, who cheerfully said she would be going shopping soon, and forty-five minutes later she was telling my mother the number she was calling from in

Swindon. I took the number and my mother's phone card and jogged to the nearest outside line; and Emily wanted to know if all this cloak and dagger stuff were necessary.

'Probably not,' I said, 'but just in case.' I paused. 'What happened when I left?'

Emily almost laughed. 'The lads came for evening stables and let us all out. Xenia's tantrums turned to tears. Surtees was purple with fury and phoned the police, who arrived with a siren wailing that upset all the horses. Surtees told them that you'd stolen Golden Malt but fortunately the police had been to my yard before when we had a lot of saddles and bridles stolen, and they believed me when I said the horse was Ivan's and you had absolute authority to look after it in any way you thought best. I showed them the copy you gave me of the power of attorney and they told Surtees they wouldn't start a police hunt for you, which sent him practically berserk. He was yelling at the police, which did him no good at all with them, but I begged them to stay until he had gone because he was so violent I was afraid he would attack me or some of the horses. So they tried to quieten him and finally got him to drive his trailer away, but Xenia was crying out of control, and if Surtees reached home without causing an accident it will have been a miracle.'

'He's a fool.'

'He's a dangerous fool,' Emily said. 'All that silly-ass front of his has changed to pure poison. So take care, Al. I'm serious. You made him look stupid and he'll never forgive you.'

I said lightly, 'I'm engaging a bodyguard.'

'Al!' She sounded exasperated. 'Look out for Surtees. I mean it.'

'Yes,' I said. 'I want to talk to you, though, about Golden Malt.'

'Where is he?'

'Safe enough, but it will be better if I move him again, and I need your knowledge and advice. I've borrowed Ivan's copy of *Horses in Training* and sorted out four trainers who look possible, so if I tell you who they are, will you give me your opinion?'

'Fire away.'

I named the four trainers and again asked what she thought.

'Two of them would be OK,' she said slowly, 'but look up Jimmy Jennings.'

I looked him up and objected, 'He has too many horses.' I counted. 'Thirty-six.'

'Not any more. He's been ill. He's halved his yard . . . told some of the owners to take their horses away temporarily, but it looks as if it might be for ever. He and I are good friends. The real advantage of going to him is that he has two yards, and one of them is now standing empty. Tell me his phone number and I'll see what he says.'

I read out the phone number and asked, 'Would the horse be able to race from there in your own name as its trainer?'

'Well, Jimmy's a licensed trainer himself; no problem there. The horse could detour to my yard in Lambourn on the day of the race to pick up the colours and tack and his usual lad. I could inform the Jockey Club in advance, and as the owner, Ivan, is a member, I can't see there being any difficulty.' She thought briefly. 'From the secrecy point of view it's always the lads that are the leaky sieves. It's not deliberate disloyalty, they just talk in the pubs.'

'And one of your lads talks to Surtees.'

She sighed. 'If I knew which one, I would give him disinformation.'

'That's a thought.'

'Give me ten minutes and I'll phone you back.'

I waited quite a while by the phone, loitering and repelling a resentful woman who wanted to use the *end* instrument of the row, not one of the vacant others. She had fierce words to say. When Emily at last rang, the resentful woman still hovered, black beady eyes full of ill will.

'It's all fixed,' Emily said. 'Sorry I was so long. I told Jimmy the whole situation. He's a hundred per cent trustable if you trust him first. He says he'll put Golden Malt in his empty yard, and to avoid the chatty lad business, the horse will be cared for and exercised by Jimmy's sixteen-year-old daughter, who's already an amateur jockey and knows when to keep quiet. There's no need for his regular lads even to know Golden Malt is there. The yards are at opposite ends of the village. What's more, it's not a busy training area. Jimmy's gallops aren't the best, though it hasn't stopped him training a lot of winners in his time. I said you'd get there sometime this afternoon, and ... er ... I promised the training fee would be inflated. Jimmy didn't want to hear of it, but I insisted. He could do with a bit extra, though he's too proud to ask.'

'He'll get it,' I said.

'Yes. I knew you would agree.'

She gave me directions to the Hampshire village and said Jimmy had said I should look for a square white house with bronze flaming-torch gateposts, and I should ring the front door bell, not go round to the back.

'OK.'

'I'll phone Jimmy later for news. Don't worry, I won't do it from home. And I told him *not* to phone me.'

'Brilliant.'

'Do you *really* think my phone is bugged?'

'Don't take the risk.'

We said goodbye and the baleful old witch shouldered me out of the way to reach her preferred public phone. Everyone to their own obsession, I supposed. Impossible to dislodge fixed ideas. There were six unoccupied instruments she could have used.

I returned to Ivan's house, detouring to a newsagent for a copy of *Horse and Hound* and an up-to-date road map, and to my mother's and stepfather's bemusement I told them in detail about the shenanigans in Emily's yard and my travels with Golden Malt.

I said, 'Emily has arranged for a trainer friend of hers to look after your horse and keep him fit so he can run in the King Alfred Gold Cup. If you agree with what we've planned, I'll transfer Golden Malt to the trainer this afternoon. The horse will be in very good hands and it would be only by exceptionally bad luck that Surtees would discover where he is.'

Ivan said slowly, 'You've gone to a lot of trouble.'

'Well, the horse is yours. You asked me to look after your affairs, so . . . er . . . I try.'

'For your mother's sake.' A statement, not a question.

'Yes, but for yours, also. You don't approve of the way I live, but you have never been ungenerous to me, and you would have taken me into the brewery, and I don't forget that.'

He looked at his hands and I couldn't read his thoughts, but when I asked if I could borrow his car for the afternoon, he agreed without conditions.

Via the classified advertisements in *Horse and Hound* and the road map and the telephone, I arranged to meet a four-horse travelling horsebox (the smallest of a prestigious firm) in Phil's yard in East Ilsley, and there loaded Golden Malt for the last leg of his journey.

Phil and I shook hands again, mutually pleased and, asking the box driver of the top-class transport firm to follow Ivan's car as arranged, I led him southwards and eastwards along secondary roads until we arrived somewhere near Basingstoke in a village that looked as if it had never seen a racehorse. But there, in the village's main street, stood a square white house with bronze flaming torches on the gateposts.

I stopped the car, the horsebox braking to a halt behind me, and went to ring the front door bell, as instructed.

A thin, smiling middle-aged man opened the door in welcome. His skin had the grey tautness of terminal illness but his handshake was strong. A pace or two behind him stood a short fine-boned girl whom he introduced as his daughter, saying she would drive through the village in the horsebox and settle Golden Malt into his new home. He watched approvingly as she climbed into the high cab beside the driver for the journey, and he invited me into his house, eyeing Ivan's expensive car with reassurance and telling me that Emily had said she was sending her 'special lad' to ensure the safe transit of a special horse.

Jimmy Jennings asked why I was smiling. Was I not Emily's 'special lad'?

'I'm married to her,' I said.

'*Really?*' He looked me up and down. 'Are you that painter feller who ran off and left her?'

'I'm afraid so.'

'Good Lord! Come this way. Come this way.'

He hurried down a hallway, beckoning me to follow, and led me into his office, furnished, like most trainers' such rooms, with ranks of framed photographs on the walls. He stood and pointed in silence, but I didn't need his directing finger: among the clutter hung a painting I'd done and sold four or more years earlier.

As always when I saw my own work freshly after an interval, I felt a mixture of excitement and shock. The picture was of a jockey plodding back to the stands after a fall, disappointment in his shoulders, a tear in his grass-stained breeches. I remembered the intensity of feeling in the brushstrokes, the stoicism and the loneliness of that man's defeat.

'Feller I trained for couldn't pay his bill,' Jimmy Jennings explained. 'He offered me that picture instead. He swore it would be worth a fortune one day, but I took it because I liked it. Whether you realise it or not, that picture just about sums up a jump jockey's life. Endurance. Courage. Persistence. All those things. Do you see?'

I said lamely, 'I'm glad you like it.'

He thrust out his chin, a defiant gesture against an imminent and inevitable fate.

'That picture keeps me going,' he said.

I drove back to London, having briefly checked on Golden Malt in his isolated splendour, Jimmy Jennings' daughter tending him with years of experience showing.

The horsebox driver had already unloaded and gone, as agreed with his firm. The hiding of Ivan's horse should, barring accidents, be complete.

I left Ivan's car in its underground lair and returned to his house to learn that Patsy had spent the afternoon with him, complaining that I had attacked Surtees so murderously as to leave him concussed, that I had committed child abuse against Xenia, and had brazenly stolen Golden Malt for my own illegal ends, such as holding him for ransom.

'I listened to her,' Ivan said judiciously. 'Is my horse safe?'

'Yes.'

'And a ransom?'

I said tiredly, 'Don't be silly.'

He actually laughed. 'I listened to her, and she's my daughter, but when she went on and on about how devious and dishonest you are, I slowly realised that I've truly been trusting you all along, that my inner instinct has held firm, even though to you I may sometimes have shown indecision. I love my daughter, but I think she's wrong. I said once impulsively that I wished you were my son. I didn't think I meant it when I said it. I do mean it now.'

My mother embraced him with uncharacteristic delight and he stroked her arm happily, content to have pleased her. I saw in them both the youthful faces they had left behind, and thought I might paint that perception, one day soon.

There was time after that for the three of us to eat dinner calmly before I left for the night train. We drank wine in friendship, Ivan and I, and had come nearer than ever before to an appreciative and lasting understanding. I did believe, against all previous experience, that Patsy could not henceforth sow overthrowing doubts of me in his decent mind.

He insisted on returning to my care the unopened envelope containing the codicil to his Will.

'Don't argue, Alexander,' he said. 'It will be safest with you.'

'We won't need it for years. By then it will be out of date.'

'Yes. Perhaps. Anyway, I've decided to tell you what's in it.'

'You don't have to.'

'I need to,' he said, and told me.

I smiled and hugged him for the first time ever.

I hugged my mother, and went to Scotland.

CHAPTER 10

To my surprise Jed was waiting at Dalwhinnie in the dawn. Himself had telephoned my mother late the previous evening, he said, and she'd told him I was on the train. Himself wanted me to go directly from train to castle, a command automatically to be obeyed.

On the way Jed told me that I now had a new bed and a new armchair in the bothy (chosen by Jed, paid for by Himself) and I was to write a list of other things I would need. My uncle would foot the bill unconditionally.

'But he doesn't have to,' I protested.

'If you ask me, he feels guilty. Let him atone.'

I glanced at Jed sideways. 'A shrink, are you?' I asked.

'He told me you wouldn't think, let alone suggest, that he ought to make good your losses. I explained that you'd cleared out the bothy and he had me get that pile of muck removed. I hope to God the hilt wasn't hidden in it.'

'Your prayers are answered. Where's the painting, the one in the sheet?'

'In my house, with all the other things you gave me.'

I sighed with relief.

'Flora looked at it,' he said. 'She says it's the portrait of a ghost.'

Flora, his wife, had 'the sight', the ability deep in the Scottish gene-pool of being able sometimes to see the future.

'The word ghost means spirit,' I said. 'If Flora sees a spirit, that's what I painted.'

'You make it sound so prosaic.'

'It isn't finished,' I said.

'No. Flora said not.' He paused. 'She said she saw that ghost weeping.'

'*Weeping?*'

'She said so.' He sounded apologetic. 'You know how she gets, sometimes.'

I nodded.

Weeping and Dr Zoë Lang weren't concepts that sat easily together, and I had no intention of trying to paint regret, but only a statement that while the outer shell aged, the inner spirit might not. The task was hard enough already. Weeping for lost youth would have to be a sequel.

As before I found Himself in his dining-room eating toast. He raised his big head at my entrance and gave me his formal greeting.

'Alexander.'

'My lord.'

'Breakfast?' He waved a hand.

'Thank you.'

There were three places laid that morning, one used. James, I learned, had already gone out on the moors.

'He wants a round of golf,' Himself said. 'How about this afternoon? He's leaving tomorrow. I've asked Jed to fix you up with wheels, and also with a portable telephone of your own, and don't object that you can't recharge the batteries, Jed is getting you extra ones and he'll call on you every day with replacements. It may not be to your liking for solitude, but please humour me in this.'

He looked at my silent face and smiled. 'You would no doubt die for me as your clan chief. You can suffer a portable telephone.'

'Put like that . . .'

'You can go back to your damned paints tomorrow.'

Resignedly, I ate toast. The old feudal obligations might be thought to be extinct, but in fact were not. The freedom of the wild mountains that I so prized was my uncle's gift. I owed him an allegiance both decreed by my ancestry and reinforced by present favours and, besides, I liked him very much.

He wanted to know what I'd been doing in the south, and he kept prodding me for details. I told him fairly fully about the codicil, about Patsy's chatty involvement with Oliver Grantchester, about the discovery of Norman Quorn's body, and about my fracas with Surtees in Emily's yard.

'Two things emerge from all that,' he said eventually. 'Surtees is a dangerous fool, and where is the brewery's money?'

'The brewery's auditor can't find it.'

'No,' he said thoughtfully, 'but can *you*?'

'I?' I no doubt sounded as surprised as I felt. 'If the accountant and the insolvency lady say finding it is impossible, how can I, who knows next to nothing about international transfers, how can I even know where to begin?'

'It will come to you,' he said.

'But I don't have access . . .'

'What to?' he said, when I stopped.

'Well . . . to whatever is left of Norman Quorn's office in the brewery.'

He wrinkled his forehead. 'Would there be anything still there?'

'If the dragons didn't guard the gates, I'd take a look.'

'Dragons?'

'Patsy, and the brewery's manager, Desmond Finch.'

'You would think they would *want* the money found.'

'But not by me.'

'That woman,' he said, meaning Patsy, 'is a menace.'

I told him of the friendly evening I'd spent with Ivan, and he said that my stepfather seemed to have come to his silly senses at last.

'He's a good man,' I observed mildly. 'If your son James told you over and over again for years and years that I was trying to worm my way into your regard and your Will, would you believe him?'

Himself thought long and intensely. 'I might,' he at last acknowledged.

'Patsy is afraid of losing her father's love,' I said. 'Not just her inheritance.'

'She's in danger of bringing about what she fears.'

'People do,' I agreed.

The two of us made a complete circuit outside of the whole castle and its wings, as he liked to do, only to find on our return, outside the entrance door the family now used, a small white car that drew from him frowns and disgust.

'That bloody woman.'

'Who?'

'That Lang woman. She lives on my doorstep! Why did I ever ask her here?'

Himself might rue the day, but I was fascinated to see her again. She and her eighty-year-old wrinkles climbed out of the car and stood stalwartly in our path.

'She has joined the conservationists who look after the castle,' Himself said. 'Joined them? She *rules* them. This past week she's somehow got herself appointed chief custodian of the castle's historic contents . . . and you can guess what she's chiefly after.'

'The hilt,' I said.

'The hilt.' He raised his voice as we approached the white car. 'Good morning, Dr Lang.'

'Lord Kinloch.' She shook his hand, then looked me briefly up and down, unsure of my name.

'My nephew,' Himself said.

'Oh, yes.' She extended her hand again and shook mine perfunctorily. 'Lord Kinloch, I've come to discuss the Treasures of Scotland exhibition being planned for the Edinburgh Festival next year . . .'

Himself with faultless courtesy showed her not into the dining-room this time, nor into his private room, but into the fairly grand drawing-room into which his best pieces of furniture had been moved at the time of the handover. Dr Lang eyed two French commodes with a mixture of admiration for their beauty and workmanship and disapproval of their private ownership. She believed, as she said later, that they should have been included in the transfer, despite their having been personally bought and imported by a nineteenth-century Kinloch earl with cultured taste.

My uncle offered sherry. Dr Lang accepted.

'Al?' he enquired.

'Not right now.'

Himself took a polite tokenful. 'The flying eagle,' he said cheerfully, 'will look magnificent in the Treasures of Scotland.'

The flying eagle stood in the castle's main entrance hall, a splendid treble-life-sized marble sculpture with wing feathers shining with gold leaf, the wings high and wide as if the fabulous bird were about to alight on the onyx ball at its feet. Transporting the flying eagle to the Edinburgh exhibition would mean cranes and crates and a slow low-loader. Himself had been heard to remark (tactlessly) that the castle's conservationists still had charge of the eagle only because its weight made stealing it difficult.

'We must insist,' Dr Lang said crisply, 'on taking charge of the Kinloch hilt.'

'Mm,' my uncle made a non-committal humming noise and offered nothing more.

'You can't hide it away for ever.'

Himself said with regret, 'Thieves grow more ingenious every year.'

'You know my views,' she told him crossly. 'The hilt belongs to Scotland.'

Zoë Lang looked half the size of her adversary, and was neat and precise where he moved clumsily. Belief in their cause stiffened them both. While he controlled the whereabouts of his treasure, she couldn't claim it: if once she'd found it, she would never relinquish it. I could see that for each of them it was all hardening into a relentless battle of wills, a mortal duel fought over dry La Ina sherry in cut lead crystal.

I said to Zoë Lang, 'Do you mind if I draw you?'

'*Draw* me?'

'Just a pencil sketch.'

She looked astonished. 'Whatever for?'

'He's an artist,' Himself explained casually. 'He painted that large picture over there.' He pointed briefly. 'Al, if you want any paper, there's some in my room, in the desk drawers.'

Gratefully I went to fetch some: high grade typing paper, but anything would do. I sorted out a reasonable pencil and returned to the drawing-room to find my uncle and his enemy standing side by side in front of the gloomiest painting I'd ever attempted.

'Glen Coe,' Dr Lang said with certainty. 'The sun never shines.'

It was true that the shape of the terrain caused orographic cloud formation more days than not over the unhappy valley, but the dark grey morning when the perfidious Campbells murdered their hosts the Macdonalds – thirty-seven of them, including women and children – seemed to brood forever over the heather-clad hills. A place of shivers, of horror, of betrayal.

Zoë Lang stepped closer to the picture for a long inspection, then turned my way.

'The shadows,' she told me, 'the dark places round the roots of the heather, they're all painted like tiny patches of *tartan*, the red of the Macdonalds and the yellow of the Campbells, little ragged lines of shading. You can only see them when you're up close . . .'

'He knows,' my uncle said calmly.

'Oh.' She looked from me to the picture and back again. There were glazes of shadow over the hillsides and atmospheric double shadows over many of the tartan pools round the heather roots. I'd felt ill all the time, painting it. The massacre of Glen Coe could still churn in the gut of a world that had seen much worse genocide in plenty since.

She said, 'Where do you want me to sit?'

'Oh.' I was grateful. 'By the window, if you would.'

I got her to sit where the light fell on her face at the same angle as I'd painted her, and I drew the face in pencil as it appeared now to my eyes, an old face with folds and lines in the skin and taut sinews in the neck. It was clear and accurate, and predictably she didn't like it.

'You're cruel,' she said.

I shook my head. 'It's time that's cruel.'

'Tear it up.'

Himself peered at the drawing and shrugged, and said in my defence, 'He usually paints nice-looking golf scenes, all sunshine with people enjoying themselves. Sells them to America faster than he can paint them, don't you, Al?'

'Why *golf*?' Zoë Lang demanded. 'Why America?'

I answered easily, 'Golf courses in America are built to look good, with lots of water hazards. Water looks great in paintings.' I painted water-washed pebbles in metal paints, gold, silver and copper, and they always sold instantly. 'American golfers buy more golf pictures than British golfers do. So I paint what sells. I paint to live.'

She looked as if she thought the commercial attitude all wrong, as if any painter not starving in a garret were somehow reprehensible: I wondered what she would think if I told her I amplified my income nicely via royalties from postcards, thousands of copies of my paintings for golfers to send to each other from places like Augusta (the Masters) and from Pebble Beach and Oakland Hills (the Open) and even, in Britain, from Muirfield, St Andrews and The Belfry.

She sparred a little more with my uncle. He offered unstinting help with the eagle and smiled blandly to all else. She asked if King Alfred's chalice had turned up, as her friend was still waiting to put a value on the 'glass ornaments' (her words) embedded in the gold.

'Not yet,' Himself said unworriedly. 'One of my family will no doubt have it safe.'

She couldn't understand his carefree attitude, and it wasn't until after she had left that I told him the glass ornaments, if they were the original gems, were in fact genuine sapphires, emeralds and rubies.

'The King Alfred Gold Cup,' I said, 'is almost certainly worth far more intrinsically than the hilt. There's far more gold by weight, and the gems are nearly double the carats.'

'You don't mean it! How do you know?'

'I had it traced to the firm that made it. It cost an absolute fortune.'

'My God. My God. And young Andrew was playing with it on the kitchen floor!'

'Upside down,' I agreed, smiling.

'Does Ivan know where it is?'

'Not exactly,' I said, and told him where to look.

'You're a rogue, Alexander.'

I had put him in great good humour. He marched us into his own room for a 'decent drink' – Scotch whisky – and I stunned him speechless by suggesting that next time Zoë Lang vowed the hilt belonged to the nation he tell her then OK, the nation would lose on the deal.

'How do you mean?'

'Generation by generation – ever since the invention of inheritance taxes, the Kinlochs have paid for that hilt. The same object, but taxed after a death and retaxed and taxed again. It never ends. If you give it into public ownership, the country forfeits the tax. It's a case of kill the goose ... Dr Lang never thinks of the golden tax eggs.'

He said thoughtfully, 'James will not have to pay crippling death duties on the castle, as I did. It was my greatest reason for handing it over.'

'One is taxed for giving a big present to one's son,' I smiled, 'but not for losing the same amount at the casino. Nor for winning. Screwy. But that's spite and envy for you. All feeling and no addition.'

'What brought all this on?'

'Thinking about the hilt.'

'Do you seriously think we should surrender it?'

'No,' I said, 'but arithmetic might cool Dr Lang's ardour.'

'I'll try it.' He lavishly poured more gold into my glass. 'By God, Al.'

'If you get me drunk,' I said, 'James will beat me at golf.'

James beat me at golf.

'Whatever did you say to Himself?' he asked. 'Nothing but catching a twenty-pound salmon puts him into such a high mood.'

'He's good to me.'

'The sun shines out of your arse.'

The difference between James and Patsy was that my cousin felt secure enough to make a joke of his father's occasional glance in my direction. James would inherit his title and an entailed estate. He had none of Patsy's devilish doubts sitting bleakly on his sunny shoulders.

As always we went amicably round eighteen holes, laughing, cursing, helplessly incompetent, racking up scores we would never confess to, happy in each other's undemanding company, cousins in the simplest sense, family attitudes and loyalties taken for granted.

We pulled our golf bags along behind us on their little trolleys, and if I were careful replacing my clubs each time, sliding them gently into the bag instead of ramming them home, it was because the handles rested not on the firm base of the bag but in the wide bowl of the grey cloth-wrapped shape within it, the jewelled gold treasure fashioned by Maxim in 1867.

We finished our round lightheartedly, and in the club house I wiped clean my woods and irons and stowed them upright in the bag in the locker, sentinels guarding King Alfred's Gold Cup.

Owing to the rigid divisions at the top of the golf bags, which held the clubs apart to prevent their damaging each other, I had had to buy a bag that could be taken apart at the bottom – for cleaning – and in the castle's drying-room I had undone the necessary screws to take the bag apart, and had lodged the Cup inside. It fitted there snugly: and as a bonus for having to undo the bag to get it out again, it could never be tipped out by accident.

The locker's flat grey doors were uniform and anonymous. Changing my shoes, I put the black-and-white studs on the shelf and closed everything unremarkably away, and with amusement returned with James to the castle.

By mid-morning the next day my life in the bothy had taken shape again, and in greater comfort than before when it came to mattress and armchair. A hired jeep stood outside my front door, the portable phone (with spare batteries) was working, and Zoë Lang's portrait stood unwrapped on the easel.

With a thankful feeling of coming home I set out the paints I needed, feeling their texture on knife and brush, darkening the background again, adding the shadows that had flashed into imagination in my travels, putting a glow on the skin and life-lights in the water-like surfaces of the eyes.

The woman lived on the canvas, as vital as I knew how to make her.

At five o'clock, when the quality of the light subtly changed, I put down the brushes, washed them for the last time that day and made sure that all the brilliant colours were airtight in their pots and tubes, a routine as natural as breathing. Then I lit my lamp and put it by the window, and took my bagpipes out of their case, and walked with them up the rocky hillside until the bothy lay far below.

It was weeks since I'd played the pipes. My fingers were rusty on the chanter. I filled the bag with air and tuned the drones, swinging them along my shoulder and waiting for such skill as I had to reawaken in my ear; and at length began to feel and to remember the fingering of one of the long ancient laments of a time earlier than Prince Charles Edward. The sadness that had enveloped Scotland for centuries before him, the untamable independence that no Act of Union could undo, all the dark Celtic mysteries pulsed in the old elemental endlessly recurring tunes that slowly wove a mood more of endurance than hope.

I had learned to play laments – the pibrochs – as a boy, chiefly for the unromantic reason that their slowness meant I had more time to get the notes right. I'd progressed to marches later, but a lament suited my painting of Zoë Lang better, and I stood on the Monadhliath Mountains while the moon rose, and played for her a mixture of an old tune called 'The King's Taxes' and a new one that I made up as I went along. And it was just as well, I thought, as stray squeaks and wrong notes made me wince, that my old army teacher wasn't there to hear.

Scottish piping laments could go on for hours, but earthly hunger put a stop to them usually in my case, and I returned in the dark to the bothy, filled with a pleasant melancholy but with no feeling of despair, and cooked paella in contentment.

I always woke early in the mountains, even in the dark winters, and the next day I sat in front of the easel watching the slow change of light on that face; the growth, as it almost seemed, of the emerging personality taking place before me; and I wondered if anyone would ever again see that gradual birth. If the picture were successful, if it ever hung in a gallery, passing visitors might give it a glance under a bright light and view it as a conjuring trick: now you see youth, now you don't.

When daylight was fully established I still sat comfortably in my new armchair, trying to tap into that courage I was supposed to have. It was one thing to imagine, another to *do*. And if I didn't do, I would know for ever that I'd failed in courage, even though, as it now stood, the portrait of an unknown woman was complete and workmanlike.

I had ransacked my mother's kitchen for a sharp-pointed knife, and in the end I'd borrowed from her not a knife but a meat thermometer. This unlikely tool had proved to have a spike whose tip was both sharp and abrasive. The spike was for sticking into joints of meat: the round dial from which it

protruded measured the inner heat and the state of cooking –
rare, medium, well done.

'Of course you can borrow it,' my mother said, puzzled, 'but
whatever for?'

'It's scratchy. It's rigid. The dial gives it good grip. It's pretty
well perfect.'

She sweetly humoured her unfathomable son.

So I had the perfect tool. I had the light. I had the vision.

I sat and quaked.

I had the pencil drawing of the real Zoë Lang. I'd drawn
her at the same angle. It should have been easy.

I had to see the old face over the young.

I had to see it clearly, unmistakably, down to the soul.

I had to play the lament for time past. I had to play the
lament as a fact but not necessarily as a tragedy. I had to depict
the persistence of the spirit inside the transient flesh.

I couldn't.

Time passed.

When I finally picked up the meat thermometer and stood
in front of Zoë Lang and made the first scratch down to the
Payne's grey, it was as if I had surrendered to an inner force.

I started with the neck, conscious that if the whole concept
were in fact beyond my ability, I could overpaint a fluffy scarf
or jewel decoration to conceal the failure.

I saw the outer shell of age as larger than the face within,
as if the external presentation were the cage, the prison, of the
spirit. I held the pencil drawing beside the painting and put
dots of reference at pivotal points: at the outer lines of the eye
sockets, at the upper edges of the jaw bones, at the rear exten-
sion of the skull.

With almost an abandonment of rational thought I swept
the sharp scratching point across my careful painting. I let go
with instinct. I drew the old Zoë in grey scratches, as if the
flesh colours weren't anything but background; I scratched
the prison bars with the cruelty she'd sensed in me, with the
inability to soften or compromise the brutal conception.

I left as little to chance as I could. I traced the direction of each line in my mind until I could see the effect, and that could take ten minutes or half an hour. The result might be a sweeping stroke that looked spontaneous and inevitable, but in nerving myself each time to scrape down to the grey I was cravenly aware that a mistake couldn't be put right.

It was a cold day, and I sweated.

By five o'clock the shape of Zoë Lang's old face was clearly established over the inner spirit. I put down the meat thermometer, stretched and flexed my cramped fingers, took the portable phone with me and went for a walk outside.

Sitting on a granite boulder, looking down on the bothy, looking away down the valley to the tiny cars crawling along the distant road, I phoned my mother. Bad reception: crackle and static.

Ivan, she assured me, was at last and slowly shedding his depression. He had dressed. He was talking of not needing Wilfred any longer. Keith Robbiston had paid one of his flying visits and had been pleased with the patient's progress. She herself felt more settled and less anxious.

'Great,' I said.

She wanted to know how the meat-thermometer picture was coming along.

Medium rare, I said.

She laughed and said she was pleased Himself had insisted on a phone.

I told her the number.

She was calm, cool and collected, her normal serene self.

I said I would call her again on Sunday, the day after tomorrow, when I had finished the picture.

'Take care of yourself, Alexander.'

'You too,' I said.

I went down again to the bothy and ate the remaining half of the paella, and sat outside in the dark thinking of what needed to be done to the picture to complete its meaning; and chiefly I thought of not muddling the outlines by too many more strong grey scratches but of not going down so deep, not nearly down to the canvas, but only as far as the ultramarine blue layer, so that the wrinkles and sagging areas of old skin would be gentler, though still unmistakable, and I would end, if I could manage it, with a blue-grey mist-like top portrait, so that the eye could see both portraits separately, the outer or the inner, according to the chosen focus, or could see both together as an interpretation of what all life was like, the outward relentless change of cell-structure decreed by the passing of time.

I slept only in snatches that night and dreamed a lot and in the morning again watched the light grow on Zoë Lang, and spent the day with rigidly governed finger muscles until my arms and neck ached with tension, but by late afternoon I had gone to the limit of what I could understand and show, and whatever the picture might be judged to lack, it was because the lack was in *me*.

Only the eyes of the finished portrait looked blazingly young, whichever other aspect one chose to see. I put suggestions of bags under the lower lids with a few blue lines, and drooped upper lids in faintly, but that unchanging spirit of Zoë Lang looked out, present and past identical.

I couldn't sleep. I lay for a while in the dark wondering what I could have done better, and coming to a realisation that I would probably go on wondering that for weeks and months, if not for my whole life.

I would wrap the picture in its sheet and put its face to the wall, and when I looked at it again, when I'd forgotten the strength and direction and feeling of each individual brush-stroke or scratch, when I could see the whole with time's perspective, then I would know if I'd done something worth keeping, or whether the whole idea had been a mistake and beyond me.

Restlessly I got up at about four in the morning and, locking my door behind me, took my bagpipes up into the mountains, seeing my way by starlight, humbled by the distance of those flaming unvisited worlds, melancholy with the insignificance of one self in the cosmos and thinking such unoriginal thoughts as that it was much easier to do harm than good, even unintentionally.

As always the melancholy drifted away into space and left acceptance. Some people clung to angst as if it were a virtue. I let it go with relief. Optimism was a gift at birth. Bottles were half full, not half empty. When I took up the pipes in the dawn and blew the bag full of air, it was marches and strathspeys I played into the brightening silence, no longer the sad regrets of the piobaireachd.

Zoë Lang, the real Zoë Lang, now lived in an old body. Through all her ages, persisting into her fanaticism, the essence of Zoë Lang had triumphed. The shell was but a crab's carapace, grown, hardened, shed and grown again. I played marches for her this time as a salutation.

She would never find the Kinloch hilt if I could prevent it, but I would pay my foe the most intense respect (short of capitulation) that I could.

I never counted time up there on the granite heights. The grey dawn turned to a brilliant blue sparkling day and I reckoned I would go down to the bothy only when the lack of breakfast gave me a shove. Meanwhile I played the pipes and marched to the beat and filled the whole optimism bottle slowly with uncomplicated joy at being there in that wilderness, alive.

Too good to last, I supposed.

I was aware first of a buzzing noise that increasingly interfered with the drone of the pipes, and then a helicopter rose fast over the ridge of the mountain at my back and flew overhead, drowning out all sound but the deafening roar of its rotor.

I stopped playing. The helicopter swooped and wheeled and clattered and circled, and while I still half-cursed its insistent penetrating din and half wondered what on earth anyone would be looking for in that deserted area at that early time on a Sunday, the helicopter seemed like a falcon spotting a kill, and dropped purposefully towards its prey.

The prey, I realised in dismay, was the bothy. I sat down and folded the pipes across my knees, and watched.

The helicopter made a sort of circuit and approached the bothy from in front, hovering unsteadily over the small plateau there, sliding through the air to one side of my parked replacement jeep and finally settling onto the ground the longitudinal bars of the landing support.

The noise of the engine faded, and the speed of the rotor fell away.

I watched in extreme apprehension. I sat as motionless as the mountain itself, aware that unless I moved or put my head above the skyline I was invisible from below against the jumble of rocks.

If the four robbers had come . . .

If the four robbers had come they wouldn't catch me up in the mountains, but they could again break into my house.

They could destroy my painting.

I felt as if it were a child I'd left there. A sleeping child. Irreplaceable. I wondered how I could bear it, if they destroyed it.

After what seemed time for several deaths the rotor blades came to rest. The side door of the helicopter opened and one man jumped out. A small figure, far below.

One.

Not four.

He looked around him then walked forward out of my sight, and I knew he must be trying the front door of the bothy. He reappeared, looked into the truck, stuck his head into the helicopter door as if talking to someone there, and then in obvious frustration walked to the edge of the plateau and stood looking down the valley towards the road.

Something about the set of his shoulders as he turned back towards the helicopter brought me recognition and floods of relief.

Jed, I thought. It's Jed.

Blowing a scant lungful of air into the bag on my knees I squeezed it and played four or five random notes on the chanter.

In the clear silent air Jed heard them immediately. He whirled and looked up towards the mountains, shading his eyes against the eastern sun. I stood up and waved, and after a few moments he spotted me, and made huge circular movements with an arm, beckoning, beseeching me to come down.

Not good news, I thought. Helicopters were extreme.

I went down to join him, though not with happy haste.

'Where the hell have you been?' he demanded, as soon as I was within earshot. 'We've been trying to phone you for hours.'

'Good morning,' I said.

'Oh, shut up. Why do you think you've got that portable phone?'

'Not for lugging around on the mountains. What's happened?'

'Well . . .' he hesitated.

'You'd better tell me.'

'It's Sir Ivan. He's had another heart attack.'

'No! How bad?'

'He's dead.'

I stood motionless, just staring at him.

I said stupidly, 'He can't be dead. He was better.'

'I'm sorry.'

I hadn't thought I would care so much but I found I cared very much indeed. I'd grown fond of the old guy in the past three weeks without realising the depth of my feeling.

'When?' I said. As if it mattered.

'Some time late yesterday. I don't know exactly. Your mother phoned Himself before six this morning. She said you'd given her your number but she'd phoned you from five onwards and you didn't answer.'

I said blankly, 'I'd better phone her at once.'

'Himself said to tell you that Sir Ivan's daughter is now re-routing all calls, and she wouldn't let him get back to your mother. He says she has taken complete charge and is being unreasonable. So he told me to find you by helicopter and fly you direct to Edinburgh to catch the first flight south. He said you could do without arguing with Patsy Benchmark.'

He was right.

We went into the bothy. Jed seemed struck dumb by the

painting but agreed to take care of it again, wrapped in its sheet. We loaded it into the jeep: also my pipes and other belongings. I collected a few travelling things into the duffle bag. We locked the bothy door.

'Jed,' I said awkwardly, aware of how much I owed him.

'Get going.'

We didn't need, I supposed, to say more. He waved me away into the helicopter and watched until it was circling in the air before setting off homewards in the jeep.

CHAPTER 11

My mother wept.

I held her tight while she shook with near-silent sobs, the grief deep and terrible.

I wondered if she had ever cried in the dark for my father, privately broken up under the public composure. I'd been too young then to be of understanding comfort to her, and also I'd been too immersed in my own feelings.

This time, when I arrived at Park Crescent, she turned to me on every level, and there was no doubt at all that her emotions were intense and overwhelming.

From life-long habit, though, after the first revealing half-hour, she stiffened her whole body, damped all movements, powdered her face and presented, at least to the world if no longer to me, the outward semblance of serenity.

Ivan was not in the house.

When she could talk, she told me that at bedtime the previous evening she'd heard Ivan cry out, and she'd found him lying on the stairs.

'Such pain . . .'

'Don't talk,' I said.

She told me at intervals.

She had been in her nightclothes, and he in his. She didn't know why he had been downstairs. There was no need for him to go down to the kitchen for anything. He had water and a glass beside his bed, and there was the tray of other drinks in his study. He hadn't told her why he was coming upstairs. He seemed to be out of breath, as if he'd been *hurrying*, but why should he have been hurrying, it was after ten o'clock?

He had said her name, 'Viv . . . Vivienne . . .'

I squeezed my mother's hand.

She said, 'I loved him.'

'I know.'

A long pause. She had been very frightened. They had given Wilfred the night off because Ivan had been so much better. They had said they wouldn't need him much longer. He had left the box of heart-attack remedies at hand on Ivan's bedside table and my mother had run to fetch them. She had put one of the tiny nitroglycerine tablets under Ivan's tongue, and although he had tried to cling to her she had run to the telephone and had miraculously reached Keith Robbiston at his home, and he had said he would send an ambulance immediately.

She had put a second pill under Ivan's tongue, and then a third.

They hadn't stopped the pain.

She had sat on the stairs, holding him.

When the front door bell had rung she had had to go down to answer it as there was no one else in the house. The ambulancemen had been very quick. They had carried a stretcher upstairs and had given him an injection and oxygen, and had put him on the stretcher and had fastened straps round him and carried him down.

She was wearing only her nightdress.

The men were kind to her. They said that they were taking him just along the road to the London Clinic, as he had been a patient there and Dr Robbiston had arranged it. They were a private firm. They gave my mother a card.

'A *card*,' she said blankly.

She had gone down the stairs with Ivan, holding his hand.

Keith Robbiston had arrived.

He had waited while she put some clothes on, and he had driven her to the Clinic.

A long, long pause.

'I wasn't with him when he died,' she said.

I squeezed her hand.

'Keith said they did everything possible.'

'I'm sure they did.'

'He died before they could get him to the operating theatre.'

I simply held her.

'*What am I going to do?*'

It was the unanswerable cry, I guessed, of all the bereaved.

It wasn't until the next day, Monday, that Patsy swept in. She wasn't pleased to see me but seemed to realise my presence was inevitable.

She was brisk, decisive, the manager. Her grief for her father, and to be charitable one had to believe her own description of her feelings as 'distraught' (that excellent but over-used word) were chiefly expressed by a white tissue clutched valiantly ready for stemming tears.

'Darling Father,' she announced, 'will be cremated . . .' she applied the tissue gently to her nose, '. . . on Thursday at Cock-fosters crematorium, where they have a slot at ten o'clock owing to someone else's postponement. It's so difficult to arrange this sort of thing, you would be appalled . . . but I agreed to that, so I hope, Vivienne, that you don't mind the early hour? And of course I've asked everyone to come here afterwards, and I've booked a caterer for drinks and a buffet lunch . . .'

She went on talking about the arrangements and the announcements in the papers and the seating in the chapel, and she'd notified the Jockey Club and invited Ivan's colleagues to the wake; and it seemed she had done most of all this that morning, while I had been seeing to breakfast. I had to admit to relief not to be doing it all myself, and my mother, who seemed mesmerised, simply said, 'Thank you, Patsy,' over and over.

'Do you want flowers?' Patsy demanded of her. 'I've put "no flowers" in the announcement to the papers. Just a wreath from you on the coffin, don't you think? And one from me, of course. Do you want me to arrange it? I've asked the caterers to bring flowers here for the buffet table, of course ... And I'll just go down now and talk to Lois about cleaning the silver ...'

My mother looked exhausted when Patsy left.

'She loved him,' she said weakly, as if defending her.

I nodded. 'All the activity is her way of showing it.'

'I don't know how you understand her, when she's always so beastly to you.'

I shrugged. No amount of understanding would make her a friend.

We struggled through the next few days somehow. I cooked for my mother; Edna tossed her head. When my mother asked forlornly if I thought she should wear a black hat to the funeral, because she couldn't face shopping, I went out and bought her one, and pinned a big white silk rose to its sweeping brim so that she looked good enough to paint, though I just refrained from saying so.

We went one afternoon to see Ivan in his coffin at the undertaker. He looked pale and peaceful; my mother kissed his forehead and said on the way home how icy cold he was; nothing like life; and I didn't tell her that it wasn't the chill of death but of efficient refrigeration.

For Thursday morning I engaged a car with a chauffeur to take the two of us to the crematorium and back again. I had personally asked a fair number of Ivan's friends and business people to turn up at Park Crescent even if they couldn't face the crematorium but, in the event, the old boy drew a full house at Cockfosters, an eloquent and moving tribute to a good man.

'All the brewery people are here,' my mother murmured. 'All the workpeople!'

They had come in a chartered bus, we found, and were working extra hours to make up.

The racing people had come. Many bigwigs and owners. Several lads from her yard accompanied Emily.

Himself came, with his countess. Jamie came, ever cheerful, with his pretty wife.

Patsy, with husband and daughter, received everyone graciously.

My mother looked ethereal and shed no tears.

Chris Young showed up at my shoulder, dressed as the secretary, lighthearted about his task of guarding my back against Surtees.

Patsy, at her administrative best, had briefed the presiding cleric thoroughly, so that he spoke knowledgeably and well about Ivan's life; and Himself, delivering a eulogy, quoted, to my surprise, from the translation of Bede's Death Song: 'No one is wiser in thought than he needs to be, in considering, before his departure, what will be adjudged to his soul, of good or evil, after his death-day,' he said, and declared that Ivan Westering had behaved on earth with such uprightness that only good would be adjudged to him now, after his death-day.

All in all, impressive.

The grand drawing-room at Park Crescent was packed afterwards with mourners, and I had to acknowledge that Patsy had been far more accurate in her estimation than I would have been. The caterers nevertheless sent their van away early for reinforcements.

Tobias Tollright came, and also Margaret Morden. I asked them both to linger for a while after the crush had cleared to discuss a brewery plan of action, and I was reminded triumphantly by Desmond Finch that all my powers of attorney had been cancelled by Ivan's death, and nothing I might say or do mattered any more in Ivan's or the brewery's affairs.

Oliver Grantchester made his large presence benevolently felt both at the crematorium and Park Crescent, behaving rather as if Ivan had been his own personal achievement; as if he, Oliver, had been responsible for all Ivan's good decisions and successes. 'Of course Ivan regularly took my advice,' I heard him saying, and he saw me listening and gave me a sideways Patsy-inspired glare of disapproval. I had no need to ask him to stay on for a conference; he showed every sign of wanting to conduct one.

I had invited Lois and Edna to join the gathering, but they stayed obstinately below stairs. Wilfred took a brief glass of farewell champagne, spoke a few words to Patsy and descended to join them. Wilfred thought I hadn't appreciated his services sufficiently: Edna had told me Wilfred thought it was my fault he hadn't been there when Ivan had needed him. The fact that I'd been in Scotland didn't excuse me.

Emily's lads ate and drank with an eye on the scales, made awkward but genuine little speeches to my mother, and left Emily behind when they departed.

Emily eyed Chris with obvious speculation, not doubting his/her gender but wondering if the tall leggy dark-haired presence in black tights, short inappropriate skirt and baggy black sweater, were a serious girlfriend, in view of the glue that kept her ever and only a short pace away from my side.

Chris wore white frilled shirt-cuffs over the thick wrists, and a small discreet white frill round his neck. He carried a small black handbag. Tobias attempted to chat him up. They could both hardly speak for laughing. 'This is a *funeral*, for God's sake,' I told them.

Keith Robbiston dashed in, glancing at his watch. He kissed my mother's cheek and murmured comfort quietly into her ear, so that she smiled at him gratefully. He shook my hand, nodding, and made a sort of sketchy bow to Patsy, who looked forbidding, as if Ivan's death were the doctor's fault. She had said, in fact, during the past few days, that clearly Ivan should have stayed in the Clinic and been shielded from stress, though she hadn't said it when he was alive, and had herself generated a good deal of the stress.

Keith Robbiston shook hands with Oliver Grantchester, their mutual disregard stiff in their spines, then, duty done, the doctor gave my mother another cheek-to-cheek fondness and hurried away.

I wandered round the room, thanking people for coming, carrying a glass of champagne that I didn't feel like drinking.

The champagne was good. So were the canapé snacks. Patsy had ordered the best.

There was a woman standing apart in a far corner of the room, talking to no one and looking a little lost, so I drifted that way to draw her in.

'You have no champagne,' I said.

'It's all right.'

She was undemanding and not at home among Ivan's friends. She wore a tweed skirt, a shiny pale blue blouse, a brown cardigan, flat shoes and pearls. Sixty, or thereabouts.

'Take my champagne,' I said, holding it out to her. 'I haven't drunk any. I'll get some more.'

'Oh no, I couldn't.' She took the glass, though, and sipped, eyeing me over the rim.

'I'm Lady Westering's son,' I said.

'Yes, I know. I've seen you coming and going.' Then, seeing my surprise, added, 'I live next door. I'm the caretaker there, you see. I've just popped in to pay my respects to Sir Ivan. Lady Westering invited me. Always so kind to me, both of them. Really nice people.'

'Yes.'

'I'm ever so sorry Sir Ivan died. Did he find what he was looking for?'

'Er . . .' I said. 'What was he looking for?'

'Ever so distressed he was, poor man.'

'Was he?' I asked, only half interested. 'When was that?'

'Why, the night he died, of course.'

She sensed in me the sudden acute sharpening of attention and began to look nervous.

'It's all right, Mrs . . . er . . .' I assured her, calming us both. 'I'm sorry, I'm afraid I don't know your name.'

'Hall. Connie Hall.'

'Mrs Hall. Please do tell me about the night Sir Ivan died.'

'I was walking my little dog, you see, same as I always do before going to bed.'

'Yes, of course,' I said, nodding.

Reassured, she went on, 'When I got back to the house – next door, that is, of course – there was Sir Ivan down in the

195

road, and in his pyjamas and dressing-gown poor man, and *frantic*, there's no other word for it. *Frantic.*'

'Mrs Hall,' I said intensely, 'what was he frantic *about*?'

She began to lose her nervousness and to enjoy telling me her tale.

'It was ever so unlike him, you see. I mean, I never thought of him in *pyjamas* like everyone else, and I didn't recognise him at first and told him pretty sharply to take himself off and leave the black plastic rubbish bags alone, because he was scrabbling about in them, and it wasn't until he turned and spoke to me that I realised who he was, and he said, "Oh, Mrs Hall, when do they collect the rubbish?" I mean, it was after ten o'clock at night! So I told him they collected the bags every Monday, Wednesday and Friday morning – we have a good service round here, this being a wealthy sort of place and not a once-a-week-if-you're-lucky back street – and he was tearing open some of the bags with his *fingernails* . . . and looking inside them . . . he was ever so . . . *upset* . . . and I asked him if I could help him, and . . . and . . .'

Connie Hall stopped, herself distressed at the memory, and emptied her glass.

I pivoted one-eighty degrees, aware of Chris close behind me, and fielded his full glass of bubbles.

'Hey!' he objected.

'Get some more.'

I turned back to Connie Hall and exchanged Chris's glass for the empty one she held.

'You'll get me tiddly,' she said.

'What was Sir Ivan looking for in the black bags?' I asked. 'Did he tell you?'

'I mean,' she said, 'it didn't make sense, him emptying some of the bags like that.'

I waited, smiling vaguely, while she sipped.

'He said he was looking for an empty box,' she frowned. 'I asked him what empty box and he said Lois must have thrown it away. He was so fearfully upset . . .'

'What sort of box?'

'I think he said a tissue-box. I *think* that's what he said. But why should anyone worry so much about an empty tissue-box?'

Dear God, I thought: *what had been written on it?*

I said, 'Have you told my mother about this?'

'No.' She shook her grey-haired head. 'I didn't want to upset her. Sir Ivan left all the rubbish just lying there and went in through his front door, which was open, of course, and said he would look in the kitchen, and I said goodnight to him and went in myself with my little dog, and it was a terrible shock the next day when I heard Sir Ivan had died.'

'It must have been . . . I suppose Sir Ivan didn't tell you *why* he was looking for the box?'

'No, but he was sort of talking to himself. I think it was something about Lois always moving things.'

'Nothing else?'

'No, poor man. He can't have been himself, can he, poor Sir Ivan, to be scrabbling about in a rubbish bag in his night-clothes?'

'Well . . . Thank you for telling me, Mrs Hall. Would you like some smoked salmon?'

I collected a plate of goodies for her and found her another Park Crescent neighbour to talk to, but later on I saw her talking to Patsy, and from her gestures and her pleasure in the drama I suspected she was telling her the same story, and felt a deep thrust of unease, but wasn't quite sure why.

Surtees stood beside Patsy, listening, and when he saw me looking at him he gave me a stare of such high-voltage malevo-lence that Chris said '*Jeeze*' into my ear.

Maddened and murderous, I thought. It wasn't the restrained and sensible who sought to kill. Surtees might, to my mind, be a fool, but I felt him also to be as unstable and volatile as hydrogen.

Himself also fielded Surtees's raw exhibition of an obses-sional hatred fast ballooning past Patsy's enduring antagonism and, startled, asked, 'Whatever did you do to deserve that?'

'Probably didn't care being shut in the box in Emily's yard.'

'In retrospect, a bad move.'

'Mm.' I shrugged. 'It can't be helped.'

'Introduce me to your friend,' my uncle said, looking at Chris.

'Oh . . . er . . . Lord Kinloch,' I said to Chris, and to my uncle, 'Christina.'

Himself said, 'How do you do?'

Chris shook his head, silently, though shooting a frilled cuff with panache. My uncle looked at me quizzically. I smiled back without explanation. Chris stuck to my back.

The room gradually cleared until only those close to Ivan and his affairs were left. There was to be no formal reading of his Will as its general provisions had been much discussed and were well-known – the brewery to Patsy, everything else to my mother for her lifetime, reverting to Patsy on her death. For all her fears, Ivan had never swerved from his promises to his daughter, though all she displayed to me was triumph, not apology.

Oliver Grantchester who, true to his loud-voiced authoritative manner, had taken it as his natural province to orchestrate the semi-business meeting, cleared his throat noisily and said, 'I say, I say' a few times until everyone was listening. 'I suggest we all sit down,' he said, 'and discuss the immediate future.'

Everyone acted on his suggestion, and I looked round at the haphazard circle of sofas, chairs and footstools, and at my mother, with me on one side of her and Emily on the other, then at Patsy and at Surtees (scowling) and Xenia (fidgeting), and at Margaret Morden and at Tobe, at Himself (alone, having sent his countess off with James and his wife), at Oliver (in charge), at Desmond Finch (smirking) and finally at Chris, beside me.

Chris crossed his long legs in their black tights, showing a stretch of thigh. The legs ended below the ankles in black patent medium-heeled court shoes. ('Don't worry, I can run in them,' he'd said.)

Oliver stared at him with displeasure. 'You may leave now,' he said.

I started to say, 'I want him to stay . . .' and almost choked on the 'him', turning it to 'her' at the last fraction of credibility. 'I asked Christina to stay,' I repeated. 'She is my guest in my mother's house.'

No one protested further. Tobe put his face in his hands. His body shook.

Oliver said with satisfaction, 'We all know that the power of attorney that Ivan gave to Alexander expired with his death. Alexander has no authority from now on to conduct any business for Ivan's estate. Patsy, indeed, forbids it.'

Patsy nodded vigorously. Surtees sneered. Xenia, not old enough to understand the words, simply transmitted second-hand hate.

I said mildly, 'There's the codicil . . .'

Oliver interrupted, 'Ivan may have written a codicil, but it can't be found. We can assume he tore it up, as he suggested he would.'

'He didn't tear it up. He gave it to me for safe-keeping.'

'Yes, we know that,' Oliver said impatiently, 'and he made you give it back again. We were all there. He made you give it back.'

'It isn't in this house,' Patsy said.

'Have you searched?' I asked with interest.

She glared.

'It isn't in my office,' Grantchester said smoothly. 'We can safely assume it no longer exists.'

'No, we can't,' I said. 'Ivan gave it back to me again later, and I have got it here today.'

Both Patsy and Grantchester looked furiously disconcerted. My mother was nodding, 'Ivan gave it back to Alexander,' and no one else seemed to mind one way or another.

'Give it to me, then, and I'll read it out,' Grantchester said.

I hesitated. 'I think,' I said politely, 'that I'll give it to Tobias to read out. If you don't mind, Tobe?'

He had with difficulty stopped laughing. He said he would be of any service he could.

I put a hand out towards Chris, who opened his black leather handbag and took out the codicil in its envelope. Also in the handbag, I knew, were a scent-laden lace handkerchief, a lipstick and a thoroughly illegal set of brass knuckles. It wasn't only Tobe who had trouble with giggles.

I took the envelope and crossed to Tobias, saying, 'Ivan signed and dated this twice across the stick-down flap. You can verify that I haven't tampered with it.'

Soberly Tobias examined the envelope, reported on its secure state, and ripped it open, pulling out the single sheet of paper inside.

He read the introduction, then:

'I bequeath my racehorses to Emily Jane Kinloch, known as Emily Jane Cox.'

Emily gasped, wide-eyed, moved beyond tears.

Tobias continued, 'I bequeath the chalice known as King Alfred's Gold Cup to my friend Robert, Earl of Kinloch.'

Himself looked stricken dumb.

Tobias read, 'I appoint Alexander Kinloch, my stepson, to be my executor, in conjunction with my two executors already appointed in my Will, namely Oliver Grantchester and Robert, Earl of Kinloch.'

Patsy stood up, stiffly angry, and demanded, 'What does that mean, appointing Alexander as executor?'

'It means,' Himself told her neutrally, 'that Alexander has a duty to help bring your father's estate to probate.'

'Are you telling me he still has any say in the brewery's affairs?'

'Yes. Until your father's estate is wound up, he does.'

'It's impossible.' She turned to the lawyer. 'Oliver! Say he's wrong.'

Grantchester said regretfully, 'If the codicil was properly drawn and witnessed, then Lord Kinloch is correct.'

Tobias stood and walked round the room, showing the paper to everyone in turn. 'It is written in Sir Ivan's own handwriting,' he said.

'But the witnesses?' Patsy demanded, before he reached her. 'Who were *they*?'

'The witnesses,' my mother said, 'were Wilfred, his nurse, and Lois, our cleaner. I watched them witness Ivan's signature. It was all done properly. Ivan was very careful.'

Patsy stared long at the paper. 'He had no *right* . . .'

'He had every right,' Himself said. 'Alexander will work with Mr Grantchester and me to do the best we can for a good resolution to your father's affairs. Why do you not acknowledge that the continued existence of the brewery today is altogether thanks to Alexander's efforts, in conjunction with Mr Tollright and Mrs Morden . . .' he gave them one of his little bows, '. . . and why do you not realise that your father knew what he was doing when he put his trust in Alexander's integrity . . . ?'

'Don't,' I said, trying to stop him.

'You never stand up for yourself, Al.'

'Let it be.'

He shook his head at me.

I reflected that Ivan's trust had wandered in and out a bit, and also that he'd trusted Norman Quorn, but anything that might dampen Patsy's animosity, I supposed, couldn't be bad.

Oliver Grantchester moved smoothly back to his intended overview, this time accepting the codicil's provisions as fact, whatever he privately thought of them.

'The horse Golden Malt –' he began.

'Will run in the King Alfred Gold Cup a week on Saturday,' Emily said firmly.

Grantchester raised his eyebrows and said, 'No one seems to know where the horse is.'

Surtees stood up convulsively and pointed at me in accusation. '*He* knows where it is.' He was unnecessarily shouting. 'Make him tell you.'

Himself said, 'After probate the horse will belong to Emily. Until then it can run in races by order of the executors.'

Surtees obstinately shouted, 'It belongs to the brewery. Alexander stole it. I'll see he goes to jail.'

Even the lawyer began to lose patience with him. He said, 'Whether Mrs Cox or the brewery is ultimately judged to be the owner, the executors can still authorise the horse to race, as it may lose value as an asset if it doesn't, for which the executors might be held accountable. If Mrs Cox can assure us that she can produce the horse at Cheltenham while complying with all racing regulations, then as executors, Lord Kinloch, Alexander and I will, at the appropriate time, declare him a runner.'

Well, bravo, I thought.

Surtees seethed.

Emily said sweetly that she was sure she could abide by all the regulations.

Surtees sat down like a cocked volcano, steaming, ever ready to erupt.

'Now,' Oliver Grantchester said, moving along the agenda majestically, 'The prize, the King Alfred chalice. Where is it?'

No one answered.

My mother said eventually, almost weakly, 'Ivan never sends . . . oh dear, *sent* . . . the real chalice to the races. It's far too valuable to risk. But he had several smaller replicas made only a few years ago. There must be one or two left. A replica is given to the winning owner each year.'

Desmond Finch made throat-clearing noises and flashed the silver frames of his glasses as he reported that two replicas remained in the locked glass-fronted cabinet in Sir Ivan's office.

'That's the trophy settled, then,' Himself said cheerfully, but Patsy told him with spite, 'Your precious Alexander stole the real one. Make him give it back. And whatever my father said, the chalice belongs to the brewery. It belongs to *me*.'

'I'm sure,' Himself said with courteous worldliness, 'that we can come to a civilised solution to our differences out of court. It would be so unwise, don't you agree, to hang out the brewery's private troubles on the public washing line? That's why your father thought it best to swallow in silence the frightful financial losses. He wouldn't, I feel sure, want you to discard out of pique the fortune he worked so hard to give you.'

I didn't look at Patsy. Her hatred of me always drastically interfered with her common sense. I'd taken so many insults from her over the years that it was only for Ivan's memory that I now cared what happened to the brewery. I wanted to go back to the mountains. It was like a physical ache.

Oliver Grantchester droned on, a committee man to his fingertips. The executors would be doing this and the executors would be doing that, and as my uncle made no protest or suggestion, nor did I.

Tobias finally broke up the session by parking a chewed toothpick and apologising to my mother that he had a plane to catch: he was off to Paris for the weekend.

'I'll be back on Monday,' he said to me. 'In the office on Tuesday, if you have any brilliant ideas.'

Patsy, overhearing, demanded to know what I could possibly have brilliant ideas about.

'Finding the brewery's lost millions,' he said and, correctly interpreting and anticipating her automatic denigration, added, 'and you should pray, Mrs Benchmark, that he does have a brilliant idea, because those lost millions are yours now, don't you understand? See you,' he finished, lightly punching my arm. 'Don't play on the railway lines.'

When Tobias had gone, Chris asked me what I wanted him to do.

'Follow Surtees,' I said promptly. 'I want to know where he is.'

Chris looked down at his clothes. 'He knows what I look like.'

'Go up two floors,' I said. 'Turn right up there. You'll find my room. Take what you need. There's money on the chest of drawers. Take it.'

He nodded and quietly left the room, and only Emily, appearing at my elbow, seemed to notice.

'Are you bedding Christina?' she asked blandly. 'She knows you well.'

I nearly laughed but made it a smile. 'She's not my bed mate and never will be.'

'She never takes her eyes off you.'

'How's Golden Malt?'

'Fine. You're exasperating.'

'Has Surtees bothered you?'

Emily glanced at him where he stood across the room talking to Grantchester and stabbing the air with a vigorous forefinger. 'He hasn't found the horse. He won't, either. I've driven over to Jimmy Jennings' place twice. It's all quiet there. And actually I think the change of scene is doing the horse good. He was really on his toes two days ago.'

'He's yours now.'

She blinked hard. 'Did you know Ivan was going to do that?'

I nodded. 'He told me.'

'I liked him.'

It seemed natural to me to put my arms round her. She hugged me back.

'Jimmy showed me your painting of the jockey,' she said. 'He told me you gave him courage.'

I silently kissed her hair. We had said everything we needed to. She stepped back, composed, and went to comfort my mother.

People gradually left. Himself (positively grinning) patted me on the shoulder, told me he would be in residence in his London home for the following ten days, asserted his intention of going to Cheltenham races and kissed my mother's cheek affectionately, calling her 'my dear, dear Vivienne'.

Emily waved goodbye. Fussy Desmond Finch twittered away. Margaret Morden paid her respects. Oliver Grantchester ponderously closed his briefcase.

Chris Young ran lightly down the stairs, crossed past the open door of the drawing-room and left quickly by the front door.

'Who was that?' asked my mother unsuspiciously, watching through the window as the fleeting backview of cropped light brown hair, loose jacket, rolled up jeans and too-big trainers made a fast sloppy shuffle out of sight.

'One of the caterers?' I casually guessed.

She lost interest. 'Did you talk to Connie Hall from next door?'

'Yes, I did.'

She looked distressed. 'Patsy told me what Connie Hall said about Ivan searching the rubbish bags.'

Patsy *would*. I said, 'Mrs Hall didn't want to upset you.'

My mother said unhappily, 'I think Patsy has gone down to the kitchen to talk to Lois about it.'

I glanced round the room. Surtees, Xenia, Grantchester still, but no Patsy.

'Let's go down, then,' I suggested, and moved her with me below stairs, where Lois was tossing her head and bridling with umbrage at any insinuation that her work wasn't perfect. Edna stood beside her, nodding rhythmically in support.

The caterers, spread all around the extensive room, were packing away their equipment. I threaded a path through them, my mother following, and fetched up by Patsy's side in time to hear Lois saying indignantly, '. . . of course I threw the box away. There were only a couple of tissues left in it, which I used. I gave Sir Ivan a fresh box, what's wrong with *that*?'

'Didn't you check whether anything was written on the bottom of the box you threw away?'

'Of course not,' Lois said scornfully. 'Whoever looks on the bottom of empty tissue-boxes?'

'But you must have known my father wrote on the bottom of a tissue-box all the time.'

'Why should I know that?'

'You kept moving his notepad onto the desk, out of his reach.'

Patsy was right, of course, but predictably (like most legislation) she achieved the opposite result to that intended.

Lois inflated her lungs and stuck out her considerable frontage, her hoity-toity level at boiling-over point. 'Sir Ivan never complained,' she announced with self-righteousness, 'and if you're implying some stupid tissue-box gave him a heart attack and that it's my fault I'll . . . I'll . . . I'll consult my lawyer!'

She tossed her head grandly. Everyone knew she didn't *have* a lawyer. Even Patsy wasn't fool enough to point it out.

My mother, looking exhausted, said soothingly, 'Of course,

it wasn't your fault, Lois.' Turning to go, she stopped and said to me, 'I think I'll go up to my sitting-room. Alexander, would you bring me some tea?'

'Of course.'

'Patsy . . .' My mother hesitated, '. . . thank you, dear, for arranging everything so well. I couldn't have done it. Ivan would have been so pleased.'

She went slowly and desolately out of the kitchen and Patsy spoiled the moment by giving me the grim glare of habit.

'Go on, say it,' she said. 'You could have done it better.'

'No, I couldn't. It was a brilliantly managed funeral, and she's right, Ivan would have been proud.' I meant it sincerely, which she didn't believe.

She said bitterly over her shoulder, stalking away, 'I can do without your sarcasm,' and Edna, touching my arm, said kindly, 'You go on up, I'll make Lady Westering's tea.'

Lois, in unspent pique, slammed a few pots together to make a noise. She had been Patsy's appointee and, I guessed, Patsy's informant as to my comings and goings in that house, but she was discovering, as everyone did in the end, that Patsy's beauty and charm were questionable pointers to her core nature.

I followed her up the stairs to where my mother was bidding goodbye on the doorstep to Oliver Grantchester and, after him, to Patsy, Surtees and Xenia.

A taxi cruised past slowly on the road outside. Chris Young didn't look our way out of the window, but I saw his profile clearly. I wouldn't have known how to begin to follow Surtees, but when Chris was trying he seldom lost him. Since the dust-up in Emily's yard, Surtees hadn't often left home without a tail.

I went up to my mother's sitting-room where she soon joined me, followed by Edna with the tea. When Edna had gone I poured the hot liquid and squeezed lemon slices and handed the tea as she liked it to a woman who looked frail and spent and unable to answer questions.

She told me what I wanted to know, however, without my asking.

'You're bursting to know if I saw what Ivan wrote on that

terrible box of tissues. Do you really think he was frantic to find it? I can't bear it, Alexander. *I* would have looked for the box, if he'd told me. But we'd kissed goodnight . . . he didn't say anything then about the box. I'm certain it wasn't in his mind. He'd been so much better . . . calmer . . . saying he relied on your strength . . . we were truly *happy* that evening . . .'

'Yes.'

'Connie Hall didn't say anything about Ivan being in the street, not until today.'

'She would have caused you pain if she had.'

She drank the tea and said slowly, reluctantly, 'Whatever was written on the box of tissues . . . I wrote it.'

'My dearest Ma . . .'

'But I don't remember what it was. I haven't given it a thought. I wish I'd known . . .'

The cup rattled in its saucer. I took them from her and kneeled beside her.

'I wish he was *here*,' she said.

I waited through the inconsolable bout of grief. I knew, after four days, that it would sweep through her like a physical disturbance, making her tremble, and then would subside back into a general state of misery.

'Someone telephoned – it was a woman,' she said, 'and she wanted to speak to Ivan, and he was in the bathroom or something, and I said he would phone her back, and you know how there was never a notepad beside the phone, so I wrote what she said on the back of the box, like Ivan does, and I told him . . . but . . .' She stopped, trying to remember, and shook her head. 'I didn't think it was important.'

'It probably wasn't,' I said.

'But if he went down to the street to find it . . .'

'Well . . . when did the woman phone? What time of day?'

She thought. 'She phoned in the morning, when Ivan was dressing. He did phone her back, but she was out, I think. There was no reply.'

'And Lois was cleaning?'

'Yes. She always comes on Saturday mornings, just to tidy

up.' She drank her tea, thinking. 'All I wrote on the box was the woman's phone number.'

'And you don't know who she was?'

She frowned. 'I remember that she wouldn't say.' A few moments passed, then she exclaimed, 'She said it was something to do with Leicestershire.'

'Leicestershire?'

'I think so.'

Leicestershire to me at that time meant Norman Quorn, and anything to do with Norman Quorn would have caught Ivan's attention.

I said slowly, 'Do you think it could possibly have been Norman Quorn's sister, that we met in Leicestershire, at that mortuary?'

'That poor woman! She wouldn't stop crying.'

She had just seen something pretty frightful, I thought. Enough to make me feel sick. 'Could it have been her?'

'I don't know.'

'Do you by any chance remember her name?'

My mother looked blank. 'No, I don't.'

I couldn't remember having heard it at all, though I suppose I must have been told. Perhaps, I speculated, that it had been only when he was going to bed that Ivan remembered that he hadn't phoned back again to Norman Quorn's sister, and had then discovered that he had lost her phone number, and had gone to look for the box . . . and had thought of something to upset him badly.

How could I find Norman Quorn's sister if I didn't know her name . . . ?

I phoned the brewery.

Total blank. No one even seemed to know he had had a sister at all.

Who else?

Via directory enquiries (because yet another tissue-box was long gone) I asked for Chief Detective Inspector Reynolds. Off duty. Impossible to be given his home number. Try in the morning.

I sought out and telephoned the mortuary. All they could or would tell me was the name of the undertaker to whom they had released the body of Norman Quorn. I phoned the undertaker, asking who had arranged cremation and paid the bills. Sir Ivan Westering, I was told, had written them a single cheque to cover all expenses.

How like him, I thought.

CHAPTER 12

I reached Chief Inspector Reynolds in the morning. He hummed and hahhed and told me to phone him back in ten minutes, and when I did he told me the answers.

Norman Quorn's sister was a Mrs Audrey Newton, widow, living at 4, Minton Terrace, in the village of Bloxham, Oxford-shire. Telephone number supplied.

I thanked him wholeheartedly. Let him know, he said, if I found anything he should add to his files.

'Like, where did Norman Quorn die?' I asked.

'Exactly like that.'

I promised.

Using the portable phone, as I had for all the calls I'd made from the Park Crescent house, I tried Mrs Audrey Newton's number and found her at home. She agreed that yes, nearly a week ago she had tried to talk to Sir Ivan Westering, but he hadn't called back, and she would have quite understood if he didn't want to talk to her, but he'd been ever so kind in paying for the cremation, and she'd thought things over, and since her brother couldn't get into any more trouble, poor man, she had decided to give Sir Ivan something Norman had left with her.

'What thing?' I asked.

'A paper. A list really. Very short. But Norman thought it important.'

I cleared my throat, trying to disregard sudden breathlessness, and asked if she would give the list to me instead.

After a pause she said, 'I'll give it to Lady Westering. Ever so kind, she was, that day I had to identify Norman.'

Her voice shook at the memory.

I said I would bring Lady Westering to her house, and please could she tell me how to find it.

My mother disliked the project.

'*Please*,' I said. 'And the drive will do you good.'

I drove her north-west out of London in Ivan's car and came to a large village, almost a small town, not far from the big bustling spread of modern Banbury, where no fair lady would be allowed anywhere near the Cross on a white horse, bells on her toes notwithstanding.

Minton Terrace proved to be a row of very small cottages with thatched roofs, and at No. 4 the front door was opened by the rounded woman we'd met at the mortuary.

She invited us in. She was nervous. She had set out sherry glasses and a plate of small cakes on round white crocheted mats which smelled of cedar, for deterring moths.

Audrey Newton, plain and honest, was ashamed of the brother she had spent years admiring. It took a great deal of sherry-drinking and cake-eating to bring her, not just to give the list to my mother, but to explain how and why Norman had given it to *her*.

'I was over in Wantage, staying with him for a few days. I did that sometimes, there was only the two of us, you see. He never married, of course. Anyway, he was going away on holi-day, he always liked to go alone, and he was going that day, and I was going to catch a bus to start on my way home.'

She paused to see if we understood. We nodded.

'He was going to go in a taxi to Didcot railway station, but someone, I think from the brewery, came to collect him first. We happened to be both standing by the window on the upstairs landing when the car drew up at the gate.' She frowned. 'Norman wasn't pleased. It's extraordinary, but look-ing back I might almost say he was *frightened*, though at the time it didn't occur to me. I mean, the brewery was his *life*.'

And his death, I thought.

'Norman said he'd better go,' she went on, 'but all of a sudden he took an envelope out of the inner pocket of his jacket – and I saw his passport there because he was going to Spain for his holiday, as he usually did – and he pushed the envelope into my hands and told me to keep it for him until he sent for it . . . and of course he never sent for it. And it wasn't until I was clearing out his house after the cremation that I remembered the envelope and wondered what was in it, so I opened it when I got home here and found this little list, and I wondered if it had anything to do with the brewery . . . if I should give it to Sir Ivan, as he had been so good to me, paying for everything he didn't need to, considering Norman stole all that money, which I can hardly believe, even now.'

I sorted my way through the flood of words.

I said, 'You brought the envelope home with you—'

'That's right,' she interrupted. 'Norman told me to take his taxi, which he'd ordered, when it came, and he gave me the money for it to take me all the way home – such a *treat*, he was so generous – and I would never get him into trouble if he was alive.'

'We do know that, Mrs Newton,' I said. 'So you only opened the envelope one day last week . . . ?'

'Yes, that's right.'

'And you phoned Sir Ivan . . .'

'But I didn't get him.'

'And you still have the list.'

'Yes.' She crossed to a sideboard and took an envelope out of a drawer. 'I do hope I'm doing right,' she said, handing the envelope to my mother. 'The brewery man telephoned only about an hour ago asking if Norman had left anything with me, and I said only a small list, nothing important, but he said he would send someone over for it early this afternoon.'

I looked at my watch. It was then twelve o'clock, noon.

I asked my mother, 'Did you tell anyone we were coming here?'

'Only Lois.' She was puzzled by the question. 'I said we were going to see a lady in Bloxham and wouldn't be needing lunch.'

I looked at her and at Audrey Newton. Neither woman had the slightest understanding of the possible consequences of what they had just said.

I turned to Mrs Newton. 'The brewery told me they didn't know your name. They said they didn't know Norman Quorn *had* a sister.'

She said, surprised, 'But of course I'm known there. Norman sometimes used to take me to the Directors' parties. Ever so proud, he was, of being made Director of Finance.'

'Who was it at the brewery who phoned you today?'

'Desmond Finch.' She made a face. 'I've never liked him much. But he definitely knows me, even if no one else does.'

I took the envelope from my mother and removed the paper from inside which was, as Audrey Newton had said, a short list. There were two sections, one of six lines, each line a series of numbers, and another section, also of six lines, each line either a personal or corporate name. I put the list back into the envelope and held it loosely.

A silence passed, which seemed long to me, in which I did some very rapid thinking.

I said to Audrey Newton, 'I think it would be a marvellous idea if you would go away for a lovely long weekend at the seaside.' And I said to my mother, 'And it would be a marvellous idea if you would go with Mrs Newton, and get away just for a few days from the sadness of Park Crescent.'

My mother looked astonished. 'I don't want to go,' she said.

'I so seldom ask anything,' I said. 'I wouldn't ask this if it were not important.' To Audrey Newton I said, 'I'll pay for you to go to a super hotel if you would go upstairs now and pack what you would need for a few days.'

'But it's so sudden,' she objected.

'Yes, but spur-of-the-moment treats are often the best, don't you think?'

She responded almost girlishly and, with an air of growing excitement, went upstairs out of earshot.

My mother said, 'What on earth is all this about?'

'Keeping you safe,' I said flatly. 'Just do it, Ma.'

'I haven't any clothes!'

'Buy some.'

'You're truly eccentric, Alexander.'

'Just as well,' I said.

I picked up my mobile phone and pressed the numbers of the pager Chris carried always and spoke the message, 'This is Al, phone me at once.'

We waited barely thirty seconds before my mobile buzzed, 'It's Chris.'

'Where are you?'

'Outside Surtees's house.'

'Is he home?'

'I saw him five minutes ago, wandering around, looking at his horses.'

'Good. Can Young and Uttley do a chauffeur-and-nice-car job?'

'No problem.'

'Chauffeur's hat. Comfortable car for three ladies.'

'When and where?'

'Like five minutes ago. Leave Surtees's, get the chauffeur to Emily Cox's yard in Lambourn. I'll meet you there.'

'Urgent?'

'Ultra urgent.'

'I'm on my way.'

My mother fluttered her hands. 'What is ultra urgent?'

'Have you by any chance got a safety pin?'

She looked at me wildly.

'Have you? You always used to have, in a baby sewing kit.'

She dug into her handbag and produced the credit-card-sized travelling sewing kit that she carried for emergencies from life-long habit, and speechlessly she opened it and gave me the small safety pin it contained.

I was as usual wearing a shirt under a sweater. I put the Quorn envelope in my shirt pocket, pinned it to the shirt to prevent its falling out, and pulled my sweater down over it.

'And paper,' I said. 'Have you anything I could draw on?'

She had a letter from a friend in her handbag. I took the envelope, opened it out flat, and on its clean inside, with my mother's ball point pen, had time to make nine small outline drawings of familiar people – Desmond Finch, Patsy, Surtees, Tobias included – before Audrey Newton came happily downstairs in holiday mood carrying a suitcase.

I showed her the page of small heads. 'The person who came to pick up your brother on the first day of his holiday . . . was it one of these?'

She looked carefully and, as if the request were nothing out of the ordinary, pointed firmly. 'That one,' she said.

'You're sure?'

'Positive.'

'Let's get going,' I said.

Audrey Newton having locked her house, we drove away and headed for Lambourn.

'Why Lambourn?' my mother asked.

'I want to talk to Emily.'

'What's wrong with a telephone?'

'Insects,' I said. 'Bugs.'

Friday lunchtime. If Emily had gone to the races it would have complicated things a little, but she was at home, in her office, busy at paperwork with her secretary.

Nothing I did surprised her any more, she said. She agreed easily to my making lunch and pouring wine for her unexpected guests but adamantly refused to join them in any flight from Egypt. She was not, she pointed out, Moses.

I persuaded her to go as far as her drawing-room and there explained the explosive dangers of the present situation.

'You're exaggerating,' she objected.

'Well, I hope so.'

'And anyway, I'm not afraid.'

'But I am,' I said.

She stared.

'Em,' I said, 'if someone were standing behind you now with a knife, threatening to cut your throat if I didn't shoot myself, and I believed it, then . . .' I hesitated.

'Then what?'

'Then,' I said matter-of-factly, 'I would shoot myself.'

After a long pause, she said, 'It won't come to that.'

'Please, Em.'

'What about my horses?'

'Your head lad must have a home number. You can phone him.'

'Where from?'

'I don't know yet,' I said. 'But wherever you are, use your portable phone.'

'It's all mad.'

'I wish I were in Scotland,' I said. 'I wish I were painting. But I'm here. I'm walking over an abyss that no one else seems to see. I want you safe.'

'Al . . .' She breathed out on a long, capitulating sigh. 'Why you?'

Why me?

The cry of ages.

Unanswerable.

Why did I care about right and wrong?

What made a policeman a policeman?

Emily went quickly out of the room and left me looking at the painting I had given her, that was not about an amateur game of golf in bad weather, but about the persistence of the human spirit.

After a while I unpinned the Quorn envelope from my shirt pocket. I lifted the golf picture off its hook and turned it over, and I slotted the envelope between the canvas and the frame, in the lower left-hand corner, so that it was held there securely, out of sight.

I hung the picture back on its hook and went out to see how lunch and life was passing in the kitchen.

Although not natural friends my mother and Audrey were being punctiliously civil to each other and were talking about how to pot cuttings from geraniums. I listened with the disjointed unreality-perception of an alien. At any minute the brewery might be breaking into the house in Bloxham. One should dip the slant-cut stem into fertiliser, Audrey said, and stick it into a peat container full of potting compost.

A large car rolled up the drive and stopped outside the kitchen window. The driver, a chauffeur in a dark navy blue suit, flat cap with shiny peak, and black leather gloves, climbed out and looked enquiringly at the building, and I went out to talk to him.

'Where am I going?' he said.

'Somewhere like Torbay. Find a good hotel with a sea view. Make them happy.'

'They?'

'My mother, my wife and the sister of the man who stole the brewery's money. Hide them.'

'Safe from Surtees?'

'And other thugs.'

'Your mother and your wife might recognise me.'

'Not without the wig, the rouge, the mascara, the high heels and the white frills.'

Chris Young grinned. 'I'll phone you when I've parked them,' he said.

'What's your name today?'

'Uttley.'

When I went back into the kitchen Emily, having made herself a sandwich, was talking to the head lad on the telephone.

'I'll be away this weekend . . . no, I'll phone you . . .' She gave her instructions about the horses. 'Severence runs at Fontwell tomorrow. I'll talk to the owners, don't forget to send the colours . . .'

She finished the details and hung up; not happy, not reassured.

'My dears,' I said lightly, looking at all three women, 'just have a good time.'

My mother asked, 'But why are we going? I don't really understand.'

'Um . . . Emily knows. It's to do with hostages. A hostage is a lever. If you hold a hostage you hold a lever. I'm afraid,

217

if any of you were taken hostage, that I might have to do what I don't want to do, so I want you safely out of sight, and if that sounds a bit improbable and melodramatic, then it's better than being sorry. So go and enjoy yourselves ... and please don't tell *anyone* where you are, and only use Emily's mobile phone if you *have* to phone someone, like Emily to her head lad, because it wouldn't be much fun to be taken hostage.'

'You might get your throat cut,' Emily said nonchalantly, munching her sandwich, and although my mother and Audrey Newton looked suitably horrified, it seemed Emily's words did the trick.

'How long are we going for?' my mother asked.

'Monday or Tuesday,' I said. Or Wednesday or Thursday. I had no idea.

I hugged my mother goodbye and kissed Emily and warmly clasped Audrey Newton's soft hand.

'The chauffeur's name is Mr Uttley,' I told them.

'Call me C.Y.,' he said, and winked at me, and drove them cheerfully away.

I sat in Ivan's car in a shopping centre's car park and tried to reach Margaret Morden by phone.

She was at a meeting, her office reported, and no, they couldn't break in with an urgent message, the meeting was out of town, and she would not be available until Monday, and even then she had meetings all day.

So kind.

Tobias had said he was going to Paris: back in the office on Tuesday.

I hated weekends. Other people's weekends. In my usual life, weekends flowed indistinguishably, work continuing regardless of the day. I sat indecisively, working out what to do next, and jumped when the mobile phone rang in my hand.

It was, surprisingly, Himself.

'Where are you?' he said.

'In the car somewhere. God knows where.'

'And your mother?'

'Gone away for a long weekend with friends.'

'So, if you're alone, come for a drink.'

'Do you mean in London?'

'Of course in London.'

'I'll be an hour or so.'

I drove to Chesham Place, home of the Earl in the capital, and parked on a meter.

Himself had a single malt ready, a sign of good humour.

'A good send-off, yesterday,' he observed, pouring generously. 'Ivan would have approved.'

'Yes.'

After a long silence he said, 'What's on your mind, Al?' I didn't answer at once and he said, 'I know your silences, so what gives?'

'Well . . .' I said, searching for an image, something pictorial, 'it's as if there's a high wall with a path along each side of it, stretching into the distance,' I said, 'and I am on one side of the wall and Patsy and some other people are on the other side, and we are all trying to go in the same direction to find the same pot of gold at the end, and I can't see what they are doing and they can't see what I am doing. The way forward on both sides of the wall is difficult and full of pot-holes and one keeps making mistakes.'

He listened, frowning.

I went on, 'Yesterday at the wake, Mrs Connie Hall, who lives next door to Ivan, told me that, on the night he died, Ivan was very upset because he couldn't find a tissue-box that had a phone number written on the bottom of it. He couldn't find it because it had been thrown away. Mrs Hall, the neighbour, told Patsy the same thing, so there we are, Patsy and I, one on each side of the wall, starting off together.' I paused. 'My mother told me that it was she who had written the telephone number on the bottom of the box, and it was something to do with someone we met in Leicestershire. She had forgotten all about it until yesterday, because of Ivan dying. The woman we had met in Leicestershire was Norman Quorn's sister, but

I didn't know her name, so I phoned the brewery and asked them for it, which was a very stupid mistake.'

'But, Al,' Himself said, 'how could it have been a mistake?'

'Because,' I said, 'it set an alarm bell somewhere jangling.'

'What alarm bell?'

'It gave rise to the question – *Why* did I suddenly want to know Norman Quorn's sister's name and phone number? And I think that, on Patsy's side of the wall, messages and specu-lations began fizzing about.'

Himself sat still, listening.

I said, 'This morning I found out Norman Quorn's sister's name and address from the police in Leicestershire, where Norman Quorn's body was found, and I took my mother to see her, because she said she had a list that her brother had given her, that she had been going to give to Ivan. She said she would give it to my mother, and she did.' I drank some whisky. 'On the other side of the wall, which I can only guess at, someone decided to ask Norman Quorn's sister if her brother had given her anything to look after before he went on his holidays, and she told them that yes he had, but it was nothing very important, only some little list.' I stopped.

Himself said, 'What little list?'

'I think it is the signpost to the pot of gold. In fact, I don't think the gold can be found without it.'

Himself stared.

'So here I am on one side of the wall and, on the other side of the wall, they will know by now I have the list. So if you want to know what's troubling me, it is how to find the treasure safely.'

'But Al . . .'

'They know I've had a lot of practice in hiding things, start-ing with the Kinloch hilt.'

'I'm sorry about that. Sorry, I mean, that I talked to Ivan about it when Patsy could hear.'

'It can't be helped.'

'And you've hidden the list?'

'Sort of.'

'And – am I understanding you right – you think that list alone will lead to the brewery's lost money?'

'It's possible.'

'But surely . . . Patsy will want that money, won't she, to put the brewery back on its feet?'

'The problem is,' I sighed, 'that the brewery will survive *without* that money, partly as a result of my own efforts. The coffers will slowly fill up again, the pensioners will eventually get back to their old levels, the poor little widows will be able to stop recycling their teabags, the brewery may re-employ the workers they are having to sack and the firm will be as prosperous as it was before. There's no guarantee, really, that Patsy, or anyone else who finds the money, will use it to pay off the brewery's debts.'

Himself looked horrified.

'Theoretically,' I said, 'after a year or two of prosperity, the brewery could be plundered again.'

'Al . . . !'

'That would be the end of the brewery, because the creditors would not stand for it twice.'

'But you surely don't think Patsy is as dishonest as that?'

'Perhaps not Patsy, but Surtees . . . ? People do often kill the golden goose.'

'Is Surtees bright enough?'

'He's dumb enough to think a double whammy a good idea.'

'But *Patsy*. I simply can't believe it.'

My uncle's goodness interfered with his perception of sin.

I said, 'Patsy has henchmen. She has people she talks to, who are entranced by her and lead her on. There are people like Desmond Finch and Oliver Grantchester and others, who scramble to please her. There's Lois who cleans at Park Crescent. Patsy gave her that job, and Lois has been faithful to her, even though yesterday I think Lois began to see the stiletto behind the smile. But she has the *habit* of reporting to Patsy, and I would expect that to go on, at least for a while, so I don't think I'll go back to Ivan's house just now.'

Himself said, as if baffled, 'But Patsy must know you have the good of the brewery at heart!'

I shook my head. 'She's resented me for twelve years and feared I would cut her out with Ivan, and although she now knows I didn't, I'm sure she's wide open to the suggestion that I'm trying to find the brewery's millions in order to hide them away for myself.'

'Oh no, Al.'

'Why not? She tells everyone I stole the King Alfred Gold Cup. I don't know if she really believes that. But I'm certain she can be persuaded I'm after the money.'

'But who would persuade her?'

'Anyone who's looking for it, who wants her attention and ill will fixed on *me*. A bit of distraction, as in conjuring tricks – watch my right hand while I vanish your wallet with my left.'

Himself said, frowning, 'Why don't you try telling her all that?'

I smiled. 'I paid her a compliment yesterday on how well she'd organised the funeral. She automatically thought I was being sarcastic. In her eyes, I'm a villain, so anything I do is suspect.' I shrugged. 'Don't worry, I'm used to it. But just now it's one big complication.'

'She's an idiot.'

'Not in her own estimation.'

He poured more whisky.

'You'll get me drunk,' I said.

'James says it's the only way he can beat you at golf.'

It wasn't golf that I was presently engaged in. I had better stay sober, I thought.

I declined my uncle's offer of a bed for the night and stayed instead in one of the hundreds of small hotels catering for London tourists. I ate a hamburger for dinner and wandered around under the bright lights among the back-packing youth of Europe. No demons. I felt old.

I took with me the portable phone and spoke to Chris while I sat beside the fountains and bronze lions in Trafalgar Square.

'I'm back home,' he said. 'My passengers have nice sea-view rooms in a hotel in Paignton, in Devon.'

'Which hotel?'

'The Redcliffe. Your mother wouldn't stay at the Imperial in Torquay because she'd been there with Sir Ivan. The Redcliffe is about three miles from there, round Torbay. They all seemed quite happy. They talked about *shopping*.'

'My mother had no suitcase.'

'So I gathered. So, anyway, what do you want done next? More Surtees-watching? That's the most unproductive job on earth, bar looking for your four thugs.'

He had had no luck with the boxing gyms. Had I any idea how many of them there were in south-east England? Sorry, I'd said.

'You can charge me double-time,' I promised, 'if you watch Surtees all weekend.'

'Right,' he said, 'you're on.'

He had assured me, laughing, that if Surtees spent all his time looking out of his front gate, which he didn't, he would seldom see the same person there. There were cyclists with baseball caps on backwards, there were council employees measuring the road, there were housewives waiting for a bus, there were aged gentlemen walking dogs; there were beer drinkers sitting on the wall outside the pub up the road, and there were people tinkering with the innards of a variety of rented cars. Surtees never saw the skinhead or the secretary-bird.

Patsy's and Surtees's stud farm lay on the outskirts of a village south of Hungerford. I had never been there myself, but I felt I knew it well from Chris's reports.

I tried to phone Margaret Morden at her home, but there was no reply. I tried again in the morning, and reached her.

'It's Saturday,' she objected.

'It's always Saturday.'

'It had better be worth it.'

'How about some numbers and names that Norman Quorn gave to his sister?'

After a silent moment she said, 'Are you talking about routes and destinations?'

'I think so.'

'We can't do anything until Monday.'

Bugger weekends, I thought.

'I can't change my Monday meetings. It'll have to be Tuesday.'

'Tobias said he was going to Paris and wouldn't be back in his office until Tuesday.'

'On Monday morning,' Margaret said, 'I will liaise with Tobias's office for an appointment and I will rope in the big bank cheese. Say ten o'clock, Tuesday, at the bank? Will you bring the numbers?'

I agreed resignedly to what seemed to me an endless and endlessly dangerous delay. The weekend stretched ahead like a boring monochrome desert, so it was quite a relief when, early in the afternoon, Himself decided to give me a buzz.

'Where are you?' he said.

'Little Venice, looking at the narrow boats, and thinking about paddling.' Thinking about the mountains, thinking about paint. Ah well.

'I have been talking to Patsy,' my uncle said.

'Who phoned who?' I asked.

'She phoned me. What does it matter? She wanted to know if I knew where you were.'

'What did you say?'

'I said you could be anywhere. She sounded quite different, Al. She sounded as if she had suddenly woken up. I told her that you had been working for her all along, at the brewery, and that she had misjudged you, and you had never tried to cause trouble between her and her father, very much the opposite, and that she had been grossly unfair to you all these years.'

'What did she say?'

'She said she wanted to talk to you. Al, do talk to her, at least it's a beginning.'

'Do you mean,' I said, 'talk to her on the phone?'

'It would be a start. She said she would be at home all afternoon. Do you have her number?' He read it out to me.

'I can't believe this,' I said.

'Give her a chance,' my uncle pleaded. 'It can't do any harm just to talk to her.'

I said, 'Any olive branch is worth the grasping.' And, ten minutes later, I was talking to her.

She sounded, as Himself had said, quite different. She *apologised*. She said that my uncle had given her a proper ticking-off for never seeing that I was no threat to her, and she was willing, if I were, to try and sort things out between us. She asked if I would let bygones be bygones, and perhaps we could come to an understanding for the future.

'What sort of understanding?' I asked.

'Well,' she said, 'just that we don't fight all the time.'

I agreed to a truce.

Would I, she suggested diffidently, would I come for a drink?

'Where?' I asked.

'Well . . . here?'

'Where is here?'

'At home,' she said. She mentioned the name of the village.

'Do you really mean it?' I asked.

'Oh, Alexander, your uncle has made me see how prejudiced I have been about you. I just want to start to put things right.'

I told her I would turn up for a drink at about six thirty and then, disconnecting, I phoned Chris's pager. He called back.

'I said, 'Are you outside Surtees' house?'

'You betya.'

'Is anything happening?'

'Bugger all.'

'I have been invited for a drink.'

'Belladonna? Aconite? Gin and toadstools?'

I sighed. 'But if she is genuine . . .'

'She is never genuine, you said.'

I was truly undecided. 'I think I'll go for the drink,' I said.

'Bad choice.'

'I'll take you with me. Have you got the "secretary" handy?'

'In the car, zipped bag number five.'

I laughed. 'What are in numbers one, two, three and four?'

'The skinhead. Various Mr Youngs, various Mr Uttleys.'

'And at present?'

'I'm in a jogging suit, in a rented car, reading a map.'

'I'll pick up the "secretary" in the road at half past six.'

'Fair enough.'

I spent a couple of hours wondering if it were possible that Patsy had undergone a sea-change. I had either to believe it or not believe it. I had either to try for peace or fear a trap.

I would go, I thought, and take Chris with me. Peace treaties had to start somewhere, after all. So, in the late afternoon, I followed the map and arrived in Patsy's village at dusk and came across a long black-legged figure thumbing a lift.

I stopped beside him and he oozed into the car, wafting billows of expensive scent and doubling up with chuckles.

'Is anything happening?' I asked.

'Half an hour ago Surtees and his missus came out of the house, got into the car, and drove down the road, and I followed them in my car and I was just about to phone you when they turned into the gates of a house about half a mile away from here. They have got fairy lights all around the garden in the trees there, and several cars outside, and it looks as if it's some sort of party. So what do you want to do, try the house where Surtees lives, or join the party?'

'The house,' I said.

I walked from the road to the front door with Chris a step behind me and rang the bell. A young woman opened it. Beside her stood Xenia, unforgiving as always, with, behind, two younger children.

'Mrs Benchmark is expecting you,' the young woman said when I introduced myself. 'She says that she is very sorry but, when she was talking to you earlier, she forgot that she and Mr Benchmark were going to a drinks party. It's through the village, past the pub, along on the right-hand side, and you can't miss it. It is all decorated with lights. Mrs Benchmark asked me just to phone when you got here, so that she can meet you when you arrive at the party.'

I thanked her, and Chris and I walked back to the car.

'What do you think?' I asked.

'A toss-up.'

I tossed up mentally, heads you win, tails you lose, and lost.

CHAPTER 13

Chris and I drove along past the pub and came to the house with the lights. When we reached the driveway, which was full of cars, we parked in the roadway. As we climbed out, Chris stumbled and broke the heel off one of his high-heeled patents. He swore, stopped, and said he would break off the other one to level himself up. I laughed, and set off towards the house a few steps ahead of him.

It was as if the bushes themselves erupted.

One moment I was walking unsuspectingly along, and the next I was being enmeshed in nets and ropes and being overwhelmed and pushed and dragged, not into the looming shadowy house but through some sort of rustic gate from the drive into a garden.

The garden, I was hazily aware, was lit by more festoons of fairy lights and by big multicoloured bulbs installed against many trees which, shining upwards, made canopies of illuminated branches and leaves; it was all strikingly theatrical, dramatically magnificent, a brilliant setting for a party.

No party that I'd been to before had started with one of the guests being tied to the trunk of a maple tree next to a bunch of red light bulbs that shone upwards into autumn-red leaves, creating a scarlet canopy above his head. My back was against the tree. There was rope round my ankles, and round my wrists, drawing them backwards, and – worst – round my neck.

At no party that I'd attended before had there been four

familiar thugs as guests, one of them busy putting on boxing gloves.

Red leather boxing gloves.

The only other guests were Patsy and Surtees and Oliver Grantchester.

Surtees looked triumphant, Grantchester serious and Patsy astounded.

I looked round the garden for possible exits and could see precious few. There was a lawn ringed with bushes, lit on the garden side, shadowy beyond. There was a flower bed with straggling chrysanthemums. There was an ornamental goldfish pond with an artificial stream running down into it over a pile of rocks.

There was a big house to the left, mostly dark, but with a brightly lit conservatory facing the garden.

There was Oliver Grantchester.

Oliver Grantchester.

The one crucial piece of information I hadn't learned was that he had a place in the country half a mile along the road from Patsy's house. The only address and telephone number for Oliver Grantchester in Ivan's address book had been in London.

Audrey Newton had firmly pointed to Oliver Grantchester's sketched head as the person who had collected her brother on the day he left Wantage to go on holiday.

I'd known *who* would be looking for me, but not *where*.

There weren't swear words bad enough to describe my stupidity.

Patsy would never change. Why had I ever thought that she would?

I'd *wanted* to believe that she had. I'd wanted an end to the long pointless feud.

Serve me right.

Grantchester stood six feet away from me and said, 'Where is the Kinloch hilt?'

I looked at him in bewilderment. I could think of no reason why he would want to know. He made some sort of signal to the wearer of the boxing gloves, who hit me low down, in the abdomen, which hurt.

My neck jerked forwards against the rope. Dire.

Grantchester said, 'Where is the King Alfred Gold Cup?'

Golf bag. Locker. Clubhouse. Scotland. Out of his grasp.

A bash in the ribs. Reverberations. Altogether too much, and quite likely only the beginning. *Shit.*

'Ivan sent you the Cup. Where is it?'

Ask Himself.

Another fast, hard, pin-pointed bash. Shudder country.

Where the hell, I wondered, was my bodyguard?

Surtees strode to Grantchester's side.

'Where's the horse?' he yelled. 'Make him tell you where he's put the horse.'

The thug with the gloves was the one who had been demanding 'Where is it?' at the bothy.

'Where's the horse?' Grantchester said.

I didn't tell him. Painful decision.

Surtees positively jumped up and down.

'Make him tell you. Hit him harder.'

I thought detachedly that I would quite likely prefer to die than give in to Surtees.

Oliver Grantchester hadn't the same priorities as Patsy's husband.

He said to me, 'Where's your mother?'

In Devon, I thought: thank God.

Bash.

He had to be mad, if he thought I would tell him.

'Where's Emily Cox?'

Safe. Same thing.

Bash.

'Where is Norman Quorn's sister?'

I was by then fairly breathless. It would have been difficult to tell him even if I'd wanted to.

He stepped forward to within three feet of me, and with quiet intensity said, 'Where's the list?'

The list.

The point of all the battering, I supposed, was to make it

more likely that I would answer the one question that really mattered.

'Where's the list?'

He had never liked me, he had seen me always as a threat to his domination of Ivan. He had encouraged Patsy's obsessive suspicions of me. I remembered his dismay and fury when Ivan had given his powers of attorney to me, not to Patsy or himself. He hadn't wanted me looking into the brewery's affairs. He had been right to fear it.

His big body, his heavy personality faced me now with thunderous malevolence. He didn't care how much he hurt me. He was enjoying it. He might not be hitting me himself, but he was swaying in a sort of ecstasy as each blow landed. He wanted my surrender, but wanted it difficult; intended that I should crumble, but not too soon.

I saw the pleasure in his eyes. The full lips smiled. I hated him. Shook with hate.

'Tell me,' he said.

I saw it was my defeat he wanted almost as much as the list itself: and I saw also that he was wholly confident of achieving both. If I could deny him . . . then I would.

'Where's the list?'

The boxing gloves thudded here and there. Face, ribs, belly. Head. I lost count.

'Where's the list?'

Such a pretty garden, I groggily thought.

The punch-bag practice stopped. Grantchester went away. The four thugs stood around me watchfully, as if I could slide out of their ropes and knots, which I couldn't, but not for lack of trying.

Patsy's face swam into my close vision.

'What list?' she said.

It made no sense. Surely she knew what list.

I would have said she looked worried. Horrified even. But she'd lured me there. My own fault.

'Why,' she said, 'why did Oliver ask where your mother and Emily are?'

I dredged up an answer, 'How does he know they are not at home?' My face felt stiff. The rest just felt.

'Alexander,' Patsy said in distress, not working it out, 'whatever Oliver wants, for God's sake give it to him. This . . . this . . .' she gestured to my trussed state, and to the thugs, '. . . this is *awful*.'

I agreed with her. I also couldn't believe she didn't know what her friendly neighbourhood lawyer wanted. I'd done believing Patsy. Finished for life. Finished for what was left of life.

Oliver Grantchester was playing for millions, and boxing gloves were getting him nowhere. He returned from the direction of his house, pulling behind him a barbecue cooker on wheels.

Oh God, I thought. Oh no.

I can't do this. I'll tell him. I know I will. They're not my millions.

Grantchester took the grill grid off the barbecue and propped it against one of the wheeled legs. Then he went back into his bright conservatory and returned carrying a bag of charcoal briquettes and a bottle of lighter fuel. He poured briquettes from the bag into the fire-box of the barbecue and then poured the whole bottleful of lighter fuel over the briquettes.

He struck a match and tossed it onto the fuel.

Flame rushed upward in a roaring plume, scarlet and gold and eternally untamed. The flame was reflected in Grantchester's eyes, so that for a moment it looked as if the fire were inside his head, looking out.

Then, satisfied, he picked up the grill with a pair of long tongs and settled it in place, to get hot.

I could see the thugs' faces. They showed no surprise. One showed sickened revulsion, but still no surprise.

I thought: *they've seen this before.*

They'd seen Norman Quorn.

Norman Quorn . . . burned in a garden, with grass cuttings in his clothes . . .

Patsy looked merely puzzled. So did Surtees.

The briquettes flamed, heating up quickly.

I would tell him, I thought. Enough was enough. My entire body already hurt abominably. There was a point beyond which it wasn't sensible to go. There were out-of-date abstractions like the persistence of the human spirit, and they might be all right for paintings but didn't apply in pretty country gardens in the evening of the second Saturday in October.

Norman Quorn had burned down to his ribs, and died, and he hadn't told.

I wasn't Norman Quorn. I hadn't millions to lose. They were Patsy's millions. God damn her soul.

Grantchester waited with lip-licking anticipation for frightful ages while the heat built up, and when the briquettes glowed a bright searing red, he lifted the barred grill off the fire with his pair of long tongs and dropped it flat on the lawn, where it sizzled and singed the grass.

'You'll lie on that if you don't tell me,' he said. He was enjoying himself. 'Where's the list?'

Cussed, rebellious, stubborn ... I might be all those by nature: but I knew I would tell him.

Defeat lay there at my feet, blackening the grass. Money was of no importance. The decision was a matter of will. Of pride, even. And such pride came too expensive.

Tell him ... you have to.

'Where is it?' he said.

I meant to tell him. I tried to tell him. But when it came to the point, I couldn't.

So I burned.

Some of the marks will be there always, but I can't see them unless I look in a mirror.

I could hear someone screaming and I remembered Surtees promising 'next time you'll scream', but it wasn't I, after all, who was screaming; it was Patsy.

Her high urgent voice, screaming.

'No. No. *You can't. For God's sake, stop it. Oliver. Surtees. You can't do this. Stop it. For God's sake. Stop it . . .*'

The noise I made wasn't a scream. From deep inside, like an age-old recognition of a primeval torment, starting low in my gut and ending like a growl in the throat, the sound I heard in myself, that was at one with myself, that was all there was of existence, that unified every feeling, every nerve's message into one consuming elemental protest, that noise was a deep sort of groan.

I could hear him repeating, 'Where is it? Where is it?'

Irrelevant.

It all lasted, I dare say, not much more than a minute. Two minutes, perhaps.

Half a lifetime, condensed.

I'd gone beyond speech when the scene blew apart.

With crashes and bangs and shrieking metal the driving cab and entire front half of a large travelling coach smashed down the fence and gate between the drive and the garden. Out of the bus and onto the lawn poured a half-drunk mob of football supporters, all dressed in orange (it seemed) with orange scarves and heavy boots and raucous shouting voices.

'Where's the beer, then? Where's the beer?'

Scrambling through the demolished fence came more and more orange scarves. Hooligan faces. 'Where's the beer?'

The four thugs who'd been pinning down my arms and legs decided to quit and took their weight off me so that I was blessedly able to roll off the grill and lie face down on the cool grass: and a pair of long legs in black tights appeared in my limited field of vision, with a familiar voice above me saying, 'Jesus Christ, Al,' and I tried to say, 'What took you so long?' but it didn't come out.

The brightly lit garden went on filling with noise and orange scarves and demands for beer. Surrealism, I thought.

Chris went away and came back and poured a container of cold water over me, and squatted down beside me and said, 'Your sweater was *smouldering*, for God's sake,' and I agreed

234

with him silently that water was better than fire any day.

'Al,' he said worriedly, 'are you OK?'

'Yuh.'

A goldfish flapped on the grass. Poor little bugger. A goldfish out of the pond. Pond water, that Chris had used.

Goldfish pond. Cold water.

Great idea.

I made an attempt to crawl and stagger there, and Chris, seeing the point, unwound the ropes from my arms and legs and neck and hooked an arm under my armpit and gave me a haul, so that somehow or other I crossed the short distance of grass and lay down full-length in the cold pond, my head using the surrounding stones like a pillow, leaves of waterlilies on my chest, the overall relief enormous.

'Did bloody Surtees do this?' Chris demanded with fury.

'Bloody Grantchester.'

He went away.

There were more people in the garden. Policemen. Uniforms. The monstrous front half of the coach rose over the scene like a giant incarnation of Chaos, yellow, white and silver with windows like eyes. I lay in the pond and watched the football fans scurry about looking for free beer and turning violent when they couldn't find any, and I watched the police slapping handcuffs on everyone moving, including the four thugs, who had over-estimated the window of escape, and I watched Patsy's bewilderment and Surtees's swings from glee to non-comprehension and back.

I heard one of the football crowd telling policemen that it was a *girl* who had stolen the coach from outside the pub where they had pulled up for some refreshment; a girl who had yelled that there was free beer at the party along the road, a girl – 'a bit of all right', 'a knock-out' – who'd said she was up for grabs for the quickest pair of boots after her into the garden.

When they'd drifted away, Chris came back.

'I caught bloody Grantchester trying to sneak out through the garage,' he said with satisfaction. 'He'll be going nowhere for a while.'

'Chris,' I said. 'Get lost.'

'Do you mean it?'

'The police are looking for the young woman who drove the bus.'

A shiny object splashed down onto my chest.

A set of brass knuckles, gleaming wetly. I swept them off my chest into deeper, concealing water.

Chris's hand briefly squeezed my shoulder and I had only one more glimpse of his dark shape as he passed from the lit side of the bushes into the shadows.

The farce continued. A large uniformed policeman told me to get out of the pond, and when I failed to obey he clicked a pair of handcuffs on my wrists and walked off, deaf to protests.

It gradually appeared that a couple of people in the garden were neither uniformed police nor uniformed fanatics but the law in plain clothes or, in other words, tweed jackets with leather patches on the elbows.

The artificial waterfall splashed cold water over my throbbing head. I lifted my handcuffed hands and steered the water delicately over my face.

A new voice said, 'Get out of the pond.'

I opened my closed eyes. The voice held police authority. Just behind him stood Patsy.

He was a middle-aged man, not unkind, but my occupancy of the pond, the length of my wet hair and the presence of the handcuffs could hardly have been encouraging.

'Get out,' he said. 'Stand up.'

'I don't know if he can,' Patsy said worriedly. 'They were hitting him . . .'

'Who were?'

She looked over to where bunches of handcuffed figures sat gloomily on the grass. No beer. No fun at all.

'And they burnt him,' Patsy said. 'I couldn't stop them.'

The policeman looked at the barbecue with its glowing coals.

'No,' Patsy said, pointing, 'on that grill thing, over there.'

One of the uniformed policemen bent down to pick the grill up and snatched his hand away, cursing and sucking his fingers.

I laughed.

Patsy said as if shattered, 'Alexander, it's not *funny.*'

The policeman said, 'Mrs Benchmark, do you know this man?'

'Of course I know him.' She stared down at me. I looked expressionlessly back, resigned to the usual abuse. 'He's . . . *he's my brother,*' she said.

It came nearer to breaking me up than all Grantchester's attentions.

She saw that it did, and it made her cry.

Patsy, my implacable enemy, wept.

She brushed the tears away brusquely and told the policeman she would point out my attackers among the football crowd, and when they moved off their place was taken by Surtees, who was very far from a change of heart and had clearly enjoyed the earlier entertainment.

'Where's the horse?' he said. He sneered. His feet quivered, I thought he might kick my head.

I said with threat, 'Surtees, any more shit from you and I'll tell Patsy where you go on Wednesday afternoons. I'll tell her the address of the little house on the outskirts of Guildford and I'll tell her the name of the prostitute who lives there, and I'll tell her what sort of sex you go there for.'

Surtees's mouth opened in absolute horror. When he could control his throat, he stuttered.

'How . . . how . . . how . . . ? I'll deny it.'

I said, smiling, 'I paid a skinhead to follow you.'

His eyes seemed to bulge.

'So you keep your hands to yourself as far as I'm concerned, and your mouth *shut*, Surtees,' I said, 'and if you're still what Patsy wants, I won't disillusion her.'

He looked sick. He physically backed away from me, as if I'd touched him with the plague. I gazed up peacefully at the bright coloured lights in the trees. Life had its sweet moments, after all.

*

No one had actually seen Oliver Grantchester being attacked and tied up securely in his own garage. He had been swiftly knocked out and had seen no one. He was found, when he recovered consciousness, to be suffering not only from a blow to the back of the skull but also from a broken nose, a broken jaw, and extensive damage to his lower abdomen and genitals, as if he'd been well kicked while knowing nothing about it.

Whoever would do such a thing! Tut tut.

The police put him in a prison hospital and provided him with a doctor.

Patsy organised things, which she was good at.

Patsy organised me into a private hospital that specialised in burns with an elderly woman doctor able to deal with anything on a Saturday evening.

'Dear me,' she said. 'Nasty. Very painful. But you're a healthy young man. You'll heal.'

She wrapped me in bio-synthetic burn-healing artificial skin and large bandages and in her grandmotherly way enquired, 'And a couple of cracked ribs, too, wouldn't you say?'

'I would.'

She smiled. 'I'll see that you sleep.'

She efficiently drugged me out until six in the morning, when I phoned Chris's bleeper and got his return call five minutes later.

'Where the hell are you?' he demanded aggrievedly.

I told him.

'That hospital's strictly for millionaires,' he objected.

'Then get me out. Bring some clothes.'

He brought my own clothes, the ones he'd borrowed for his departure from the wake at Park Crescent three days earlier, and he arrived to find me standing by the window watching the grey dawn return to the perilous earth.

'Hospital gowns,' he said, as I turned to greet him, 'shouldn't be visited even on the damned.'

'They cut my clothes off last night.'

'Sue them.'

'Mm.'

'To be frank,' he said, almost awkwardly, 'I didn't expect you to be on your feet.'

'More comfortable,' I said succinctly. 'That bus, if I may say so, was brilliant.'

He grinned. 'Yes, it was, wasn't it?'

'Go on then, tell me all.'

He dumped the carrier bag with the clothes in and came over to join me by the window, the familiar face alight with enjoyment. High cheekbones, light brown hair, bright brown eyes, natural air of impishness. Solemnity sat unnaturally upon him, and he couldn't tell me what had happened without making lighthearted jokes about it.

'Those thugs that jumped out of the bushes at you, they were the real McCoy. Brutal bastards. There was no mistaking they were the ones I'd been looking for. And to be honest, Al, I couldn't handle four of them at once on my own, any more than you could.'

I nodded, understanding.

'So,' Chris said, 'I thought the best thing to do would be to find out how big a posse would be needed to round up the outlaws, so to speak, so I shunted round in the shelter of a sort of high wooden fence that's all round that garden, until I could see through the bushes. All those lights . . . and there they were, your four thugs, tying you up to that tree and bashing you about, and there were three other people there too, which made seven, and I couldn't manage seven . . .'

'No,' I said.

'There was that big fat slob, the lawyer from your step-father's funeral.'

'Yes,' I said.

'And bloody Surtees . . .'

'Yes,' I said again.

'And his wife.'

I nodded.

'So,' Chris said again, 'I had to go for reinforcements, and I ran down the road to the pub and used their telephone and told the police there was a riot going on, and those bastards told me there were a dozen riots going on every Saturday evening, and they wanted to know *where* exactly, so I asked the barman in the pub if he knew whose house it was with all those lights in the garden, and he said it belongs to Mr Oliver Grantchester, a very well-known lawyer, so I told the police, but they didn't show up, or anything, and to tell you the truth, mate, I was jumping up and down a bit by that time.'

So would I have been, I thought.

'So then,' Chris said, 'this bloody big coachload of fervent psychos in orange scarves invaded the bar, and I thought then, "manna dropped from heaven", so I went outside where half of them were still in the bus, and I yelled at them that there was free beer down the road at a party, and I just got into the driver's seat and drove that damned jumbo straight through Grantchester's fence into the garden.'

'It did the trick,' I said, smiling.

'Yes, but . . . my God . . . !'

'Best forgotten,' I said.

'I'll never forget it,' he said, 'and nor will you.'

'You came, though.'

'So did the bloody police, in the end. Too many of them.'

'What exactly,' I asked him contentedly, 'did you do to Oliver Grantchester?'

'Kicked him a good many times in the goolies.' Chris had been wearing, I remembered, pointed black patent shoes, sharp enough even without heels. 'And I smashed him round the face a bit with the hard knuckles. I mean, there's villains, and there's villains. Boxing gloves is one thing, but burning people . . . that's diabolical. I could have killed him. Lucky I didn't.'

'The police asked me,' I said, 'if I knew who had tied him up. I said how could I possibly know anything. I was lying in the pond.'

Chris laughed. 'I'll work for you any time,' he said. 'Attending to Grantchester will be extra.'

Patsy arrived silently while I was sitting on the edge of the bed, dressed in trousers and shirt, head hanging, feeling rotten. Of all the people I would have preferred not to see me like that, she would have been tops.

'Go away,' I said, and she went, and the next person through the door was a nurse with a syringeful of relief.

Around mid-morning I had a visit from a Detective Inspector Vernon, whom I'd met, it transpired, in the garden.

'Mrs Benchmark said you were dressed,' he remarked, not shaking hands.

'Do you know her well?'

'She's a patron of local police charities.'

'Oh.'

He joined me by the window. There were scudding clouds in the sky. A good day for mountains.

'Mrs Benchmark says that Mr Grantchester, who is another of our patrons, was instructing four other men to ill-treat you.'

'You could put it like that,' I agreed.

He was a bulky short man, going grey: never, at that rank, at that age, going to climb high in police hierarchy, but maybe a more down-to-earth and dogged investigator because of it.

'Can you tell me why?' he said.

'You'll have to ask Mr Grantchester.'

'His lower jaw's badly broken. This morning he can't speak. He's badly bruised in the abdomen, too. Doubled over. Black and blue.'

Vernon asked me again if I knew who had attacked him. I'd been in the pond, I repeated. As he knew.

I said helpfully, however, that the same four thugs had battered me earlier in Scotland, and told him where I'd given a statement to the police there. I suggested that he might also talk to Chief Inspector Reynolds of the Leicestershire police about people being burned on barbecue grills on mown grass. Vernon wrote everything down methodically. If I had recovered enough, he said, he would appreciate it if I would attend his police station the following morning. They could send an unmarked car for me, he offered.

'See you down the nick,' Chris would have said, but all I raised was 'OK'.

The day passed somehow, and the night.

Bruises blackened. The cracked ribs were all on my right side: a south-paw puncher's doing.

The burns got inspected again. No sign of infection. Very lucky, I was told, considering the unsterile nature of goldfish ponds.

On Monday morning I discharged myself from the hospital against their advice. I had too much to do, I said.

A plain-clothes police car came to transport me to Vernon's official stamping ground, where I was instantly invited to look through a window into a brightly lit room, and to say if I'd seen any of eight men at any earlier time in my life.

No problem. Numbers one, three, seven and eight.

'They deny they touched you.'

I gave Vernon a glowering come-off-it glare. 'You saw them yourself in that garden. You arrested them there.'

'I didn't see them in the act of committing grievous bodily harm.'

I closed my eyes briefly, took a grip on my pain-driven temper, and said, on a deep breath, 'Number three wore boxing gloves and caused the damage you can see in my face. He is left-handed. The others watched. All four assisted in compelling me to lie on that hot grill. All four also attacked me outside my home in Scotland. I don't know their names, but I do know their faces.'

It had seemed to me on other occasions that the great British police force not only never apologised, but also never saw the need for it: however, Inspector Vernon ushered me politely into a bare interview room and offered me coffee, which in his terms came into the category of tender loving care.

'Mrs Benchmark couldn't identify them for certain,' he observed.

I asked if he had talked to Sergeant Berrick in Scotland, and to Chief Inspector Reynolds in Leicestershire. They had been off duty, he said.

Bugger weekends.

Could I use a telephone, I asked.

Who did I want to talk to? Long-distance calls were not free.

'A doctor in London,' I said.

I reached, miraculously, Keith Robbiston; alert, in a hurry.

'Could I have a handful of your wipe-out pills?' I asked.

'What's happened?' he said.

'I got bashed again.'

'More thugs?'

'The same ones.'

'Oh . . . as bad as before?'

'Well, actually . . . worse.'

'How much worse?'

'Cracked ribs and some burns.'

'*Burns?*'

'Nothing to do with "Auld Lang Syne".'

He laughed, and talked to Inspector Vernon, and said my mother would kill him if he failed me, and pills would be motor-biked door to door within two hours.

If nothing else, Keith Robbiston's speed impressed the Inspector. He went off to telephone outside. When the coffee came, it was in a pot, on a tray.

I sat and waited for unmeasurable time, thinking. When Vernon returned I told him that number seven in the line-up had been wearing what looked like my father's gold watch, stolen from me in Scotland.

'Also,' I said, 'number seven didn't relish the burning.'

'That won't excuse him.'

'No . . . but if you could make it worth his while, he might tell you what happened to a Norman Quorn.'

The Inspector didn't say, 'Who?' He went quietly away. A uniformed constable brought me a sandwich lunch.

My pills arrived. Things got better.

After another couple of hours Inspector Vernon came into the room, sat down opposite me across the table and told me that the following conversation was not taking place. Positively *not*. It was his private thanks. Understood?

'OK,' I said.

'First of all, can you identify your father's gold watch?'

'It has an engraving on the back, "Alistair from Vivienne".'

Vernon faintly smiled. In all the time I spent with him it was the nearest he came to showing pleasure.

'Number seven in the line-up may be known as Bernie,' he said. 'Bernie, as you saw, is a worried man.' He paused. 'Can I totally trust you not to repeat this? Can I rely on you?'

I said dryly, 'To the hilt,' which he didn't understand beyond the simple words, but he took them as I meant them: utterly. 'But,' I added, 'why all this cloak-and-dagger stuff?'

He spent a moment thinking, then said, 'In Britain one isn't, as you may or may not know, allowed to make bargains with people accused of crimes. One can't *promise* a light sentence in return for information. That's a myth. You can persuade someone unofficially to plead guilty to a lesser charge, like in this case, *actual* bodily harm, rather than *grievous* bodily harm, GBH, which is a far more serious crime, and can carry a long jail sentence. But some authorities can be perverse, and if they suspect a deal has been struck, they're perfectly capable of upsetting it. Follow?'

'I follow.'

'Also the business of what is and what isn't admissible evidence is a minefield.'

'So I've heard.'

'If you hadn't told me to ask Bernie questions about Norman Quorn I wouldn't have thought of doing it. But Bernie split wide open, and now my superiors here are patting me on the back and thinking of going to the Crown Prosecution Service – who, of course, decide whether or not a trial should take place – not with a GBH involving *you*, but with a charge against Oliver Grantchester for manslaughter. The manslaughter of Norman Quorn.'

'Hell's teeth.'

'At this point in such proceedings everyone gets very touchy indeed about who knows what, in order not to jeopardise any useful testimony. It wouldn't do for you to have heard Bernie's confession. It could have compromised the case. So I'll tell you what he said . . . but I shouldn't.'

'You're safe.'

He nevertheless looked around cautiously, as if listeners had entered unseen.

'Bernie said,' he finally managed, 'that they – the four you call the thugs – all go to a gym in London, east of the City, which Oliver Grantchester has been visiting for fitness sessions for the past few years. Grantchester goes on the treadmill, lifts a few weights and so on, but isn't a boxer.'

'No.'

'So when he wanted a rough job done, he recruited your four thugs. Bernie was willing. The up-front money was good. So was the pay-off afterwards, though the job went wrong.'

'Quorn died.'

Vernon nodded.

'Grantchester,' he said, 'told them to turn up at his house in the country. He told them the name of the village and said they would know his house because it had Christmas lights all over the driveway, and he would turn them on, even though it would be daylight and not Christmas. Grantchester arrived at his house with an older man, who was Norman Quorn, and he took him through the gate in the fence into the garden. The four thugs tied the man – whose name they didn't yet know –

to the same tree as they tied you, but they didn't belt him, like you. Grantchester lit the barbecue and told Quorn he would burn him if he didn't come across with some information.'

Vernon paused, then went on. 'Bernie didn't know what the information was, and still doesn't. Quorn was shitting himself, Bernie says, and Grantchester waited until the fire was very hot, and then he threw the grill onto the grass, and told Quorn he would lie on it until he told him – Grantchester – what he wanted to know. Quorn told him he would tell him at once, but Grantchester got the four thugs to throw Quorn onto the grill anyway, and hold him there, and although he was scream-ing and hollering that he would tell, Grantchester wouldn't let him up, and seemed to be enjoying it, and when he did let him up, Quorn dropped down dead.'

Vernon stopped. I listened in fascinated horror.

'Bernie,' Vernon said, 'was near to puking, describing it.'

'I'm not surprised.'

'Grantchester was furious. There was this dead body on the ground and he hadn't found out what he wanted to know. He got Bernie and the others to put Quorn into the boot of his car in the garage, and in the house he made them put their hands round empty glasses, so that he had all their fingerprints, and he threatened that if they ever spoke of what they'd seen they would be in mortal trouble. Then he paid them and told them to go away, which they did. Bernie doesn't know what Grantchester did with Quorn's body.'

After a while I said, 'Did you ask Bernie about Scotland?'

Vernon nodded. 'Grantchester paid them again to go to your house and beat you up a bit until you gave them something to give to him. He didn't tell them what it was. He just told them to say, "Where is it?" to you, and you would know what it was. Bernie said you didn't give them anything, and Grant-chester was furious, and told them they should have made sure you were dead before they threw you down the mountain.'

'Well, well,' I said.

'Bernie says he complained that beating up people was one thing, but murder was another, and Grantchester threatened that Bernie would do as he was told, because of his finger-prints.'

'Bernie is simple,' I said.

Vernon nodded. 'Just as well, from our point of view. Any-way, the pay was good, so when Grantchester told them to turn up again at his house the day before yesterday, they did.'

'Yes.'

'Grantchester told them that you would be coming, and that they were to tie you to the same tree, like Quorn before, only this time there was no talk of burning.' He paused. 'The one with the boxing gloves is known as Jazzo. He thought you got knocked out too soon in Scotland. He told Grantchester you wouldn't like another dose. He said he wouldn't knock you out and he would guarantee you would answer any question you were asked.'

I listened without comment.

'Of course, it didn't turn out that way,' Vernon said. 'So Grantchester brought out his barbecue again, because it had worked the first time, and that's when Bernie's bottle deserted him, he says.'

'It didn't stop him sitting on my legs,' I remarked with satire.

'He didn't mention sitting on your legs.'

'You don't say.'

'He said Mrs Benchmark was there, and she was screaming and screaming to Grantchester to stop, and he wouldn't. I asked Bernie if you were screaming too.'

'That's an unfair bloody question.'

Vernon gave me a sideways glance. 'He said the only noise you made was a sort of moan.'

Charming, I thought.

'And that's when the bus crashed into the garden.' Vernon paused and looked at me straight. 'Is Bernie's account of things accurate?'

'As far as I'm concerned, yes.'

Vernon stood up and walked around the room twice, as if disturbed.

'Mrs Benchmark,' he said, 'called you her brother, but you're not, are you?'

'Her father was married to my mother. He died a week ago.'

Vernon nodded. 'Mrs Benchmark is devastated by what happened in the garden. She doesn't understand it. The poor lady is very upset.'

I again made no comment.

'She said your girlfriend was there. We released all the football supporters yesterday, but half of them agreed that the bus was driven from the pub to the garden by a young woman. Was she your girlfriend?'

I said, 'She is a friend. She was walking a few steps behind me when the thugs hustled me into the garden. They didn't notice her. She told me yesterday that when she saw what was happening she ran down to the pub and called the police. Then, it seems, the busload of happy revellers arrived, so she drove the bus to the rescue, for which I'll always be grateful.'

'In other words,' Vernon said, 'you are not going to get her into trouble.'

'Quite right.'

He gave me a long slow look. 'And you're not going to give us her name and address.'

'She lives with a man,' I said, 'who wouldn't like to see her in court. You don't really need her, do you?'

'Probably not.'

'If there was any damage to the bus,' I said, 'I'll pay for it.'

Vernon went over to the door, opened it, and shouted to someone outside to bring tea. When he came back he said, 'We obtained a warrant yesterday to search Grantchester's house.'

He waited for me to ask if he'd found anything useful, so I did.

He didn't answer straightforwardly. He said, 'The policeman in Scotland sent us faxes today of the drawings you did of the thugs the day they attacked you at your home. Bernie almost collapsed when we showed them to him. Your policeman also sent the list of things that were stolen from you. In Grantchester's house we found four paintings of golf courses.'

'You didn't!'

Vernon nodded. 'Your policeman, Sergeant Berrick, said that the pictures had stickers on the backs, and if other stickers had been stuck over them, your name would still be visible under X-ray. So this afternoon we X-rayed the stickers.' He almost smiled. 'Your Scottish policeman said that you promised to paint a portrait of his wife if he helped to find your pictures.'

'I did,' I said. 'And I will.'

Vernon suggested, 'Mine, too?'

'A pleasure,' I said.

CHAPTER 14

On Tuesday morning I went to the bank meeting in Reading and was shown into a small private conference room where the area bank manager, Margaret Morden and Tobias were already sitting round a table with coffee cups in front of them.

When I went in, they stood up.

'Don't,' I said awkwardly. 'Am I late?'

'No,' Tobe said.

They all sat. I took the one empty chair.

'Did you bring the list?' the bank man said.

I was wearing an open-necked white shirt with no tie, and carrying a jacket. I dug into a jacket pocket and handed Norman Quorn's envelope to Tobias.

They were staring at me, rather.

'Sorry about the bruises,' I said, making a gesture towards my face. 'I got a bit clobbered again. Very careless.'

Tobias said, 'I've talked to Chris. He told me about . . . Grantchester's barbecue.'

'Oh.'

Tobias had also, clearly, relayed to the bank man and to Margaret what Chris had said. All of them were embarrassed. I too. Very British.

'Well,' I said, 'can we find the money?'

They had no doubt of it. With a relieved air of eagerness and satisfaction they passed to each other the piece of paper, the riddle that Quorn had left; it soon became apparent that, although the numbers and names belonged to bank accounts, the brewery's Finance Director had been coy about setting down on paper which account referred to which bank. The list had been an aide memoire to himself. He had never meant anyone else to have to decipher it.

Thoughtfully they each copied out for themselves the whole list, numbers and names. (He wouldn't trust it to the office copier, the bank man said; the information was so hot it would not be allowed to leave that room.)

Each of them had brought a personal computer that was not connected to anything else and could not be hacked into from outside. Each of them fed into their separate computer a disc recording what each of them, separately, knew. The bank had supplied a fax machine dedicated to this one job.

The room grew silent except for the tapping of keys and the drumming of thoughtful fingers when the solutions didn't quickly appear.

I waited without fret. They knew their business, and I didn't.

Tobias and the bank man wore the suits of their trade, dark confidence-builders with gravitas. Margaret had come in flowery printed wool, soft and rose-red and disarming, hiding the steel-hard brain. How ridiculous, I thought, that the male mind could often accept a female as equal only if she pretended to be in need of help. Margaret amused me. She caught me looking at her, read my thought, and winked. Men were right to be afraid of women, I concluded: the witch lived near the surface in all of them.

They burned witches . . . God help them.

I moved stiffly on my chair, leaning forward, resting my elbows on the table, taking shallow breaths. Body management, learned fast.

At the police station the previous afternoon Inspector Vernon had told me that Ivan's car (the wheels I'd driven to the party) had been identified by Mrs Benchmark and towed by the police and was, in fact, at that moment right outside in the station's car park.

'Can I take it?' I asked, surprised.

'If you think you're fit to drive.'

I had the car keys, among other things, in my restored trousers pocket.

Fit or not, I drove the car to Lambourn, found Emily's spare house key on its old familiar nail in the tack room, made inroads into her whisky and spent a disturbed night lying on my side in my clothes on the sofa in her drawing-room, lacking energy for anything else, feeling shivery and sick.

In the morning I'd made it upstairs to the bathroom, found a throw-away razor, combed my hair and rinsed my mouth. Well, I told myself, my physical state was my own stubborn fault: just put up with it. Swallow the tablets and be grateful for mercies.

I phoned Chris who said he'd been trying without success to reach my mobile number.

'The phone's in the car,' I said. 'I expect the battery's flat.'

'For hell's sake, charge it.'

'Yes.'

'Are you all right, Al? And where are you?'

'Lambourn. Could you drive to Paignton and then come here?'

'Today? Bring all three ladies?'

'If you can. I'll phone the hotel.'

'Chauffeur's togs coming up. Zipped bag nine.'

We disconnected on a smile. I phoned the Redcliffe and left messages for Emily and my mother. Then I retrieved the Quorn list from the back of the golf picture and drove to Reading.

By lunchtime the experts had got nowhere nearer the end of the rainbow.

They sent out for sandwiches, and we drank more coffee.

'The trouble is,' the bank man explained to me, 'that we have here three lots of variables. We have to match the account numbers on the list with a name on the list and with a bank identification number that we already have, and then we have to send that combination to the bank in question and hope to get a response from them to acknowledge that that account exists. We haven't so far been able to do that. The nearest we have come is matching one of the account numbers to one of the banks, but we supplied the wrong name for the account, and the bank told us by return fax, just now, that as our enquiry is incomplete, they cannot answer it. No one is being helpful. On top of that, the account numbers are the wrong way round.'

I said, 'How do you mean, the wrong way round?'

'All the numbers on the list end with two zeros. As a rule account numbers *begin* with two zeros. We have tried reversing the numbers, so far without success. I am still sure that all of the numbers have been reversed, but if Quorn jumbled them up further, or multiplied by two, for instance, we are in real trouble.'

Tobias and Margaret nodded in depression.

Tobias said, 'Quorn may have sent the money on a circular route involving all of these numbers – like the beach towels on the poolside chairs – or he may have sent it direct from Panama to any one place, but so far we haven't found a single trace of it. I have been working on the belief that one of these numbers or names must mean something to the Global Bank in Panama, but they will not admit it.'

'All banks are secretive,' the big bank man said. 'And so are we.'

'Don't despair,' Margaret said, 'we'll find the money. It's just taking longer than we hoped.'

By the end of the afternoon, however, they themselves were looking cast down; they said they would think of a new strategy for the next day. The time change alone was making things difficult. It was already mid-afternoon in Reading when the bank in Panama opened for business.

They carefully shredded every scrap of used fax and working paper and locked Norman Quorn's list into the manager's private safe. I drove a shade dispiritedly back to Lambourn and found that Emily, my mother and Audrey Newton had arrived a bare five minutes before me.

C.Y. Uttley was busy unloading suitcases from the boot.

I gave my mother a minimum hug, kissed Emily and planted an air kiss beside Audrey Newton's buxom cheek.

'We've had a lovely weekend,' she said, beaming. 'Thank you ever so much. You've bruised your face, dear, did you know?'

'Walked into a door.'

Emily took Audrey and my mother into the house and Chris gave me an assessing inspection.

'You look lousy,' he said. 'Worse than Sunday.'

'Thanks.'

'Your bus-stealing Grantchester-immobilising friend no longer exists,' he assured me. 'I dumped her today, bit by bit, in a succession of wheelybins on my way to Devon.'

'So wise.'

'How do blonde bubble curls and D-cup knockers grab you?'

'I wouldn't be seen dead with her.'

'At least the lawyer didn't cauterise your sense of humour.'

'A close-run thing.'

'Do you want anything else done?'

'Just take Audrey Newton home to Bloxham.'

'After that?'

We stared at each other.

'A friend for life,' I suggested.

'I'll send my bill.'

Emily proposed that my mother and I stay the night in Lambourn and met with little resistance.

The telephone rang in the kitchen while we were sitting round the big table watching Emily search for supper in the freezer. Emily picked up the receiver and in a moment said with surprise, 'Yes, he's here. So is Vivienne.' She held out the receiver in my direction. 'It's Himself. He's been looking for you.'

I took the instrument and said, 'My lord.'

'Al, where have you been? I've had Patsy on the line all day. She sounds practically hysterical. She wants to talk to you. She says you signed yourself out of some hospital she put you in. She won't tell me why she put you in hospital. What the hell's happened?'

'Er . . . I ran out of wall.'

'Al, talk sense.'

My mother and Emily could both hear what I said. I thought through five seconds of silence and said, 'Can I come for a drink with you at about six tomorrow evening?'

'Of course.'

'Well . . . please don't tell Patsy where I am. Ask her if she'll meet me at two o'clock tomorrow afternoon in the car park of the brewery's bank's head office in Reading. And tell her . . .' I paused. 'Tell her thanks for the help.'

Emily said, astounded, as I put the phone down, 'Patsy *helped* you?'

'Mm.'

They would have to know, so I told them as unemotionally as possible that Oliver Grantchester had been trying to lay his hands on the brewery's missing millions. 'He had either conspired with Norman Quorn to steal the money in the first place, or tried to wrest it from him afterwards,' I said. 'I'm not yet sure which.'

'Not *Oliver*!' my mother protested in total disbelief. 'We've known him for years. He's always been Ivan's solicitor, and the brewery's too . . .' her voice faded. 'Ivan trusted him.'

I said, 'Ivan trusted Norman Quorn. Quorn and Grant-chester . . . they were two normal men, good at their jobs, but fatally attracted by what looked like an easy path to a bucket of gold – and I'm not talking about the literal bucket of gold, the King Alfred Gold Cup, which Grantchester thought he could lay his hands on as a consolation when the serious prize slipped through his fingers. Grantchester may have been a good lawyer but he's an inefficient crook. He hasn't got the Gold Cup and he hasn't got the brewery's money, and Patsy has woken up to the fact that her dear darling avuncular Oliver had been trying his damnedest to rob *her*, as she now owns the brewery complete with its losses.'

My mother had her own concern, 'You didn't really walk into a door, did you, Alexander?'

I smiled. 'I walked into Grantchester's fist man. You'd think I'd know better.'

'And no one took hostages,' Emily said thoughtfully, with much understanding.

We went to bed. Emily expected and invited me between her sheets, but I simply had no stamina left for the oldest of games.

She asked what was under the bandages that was making me sweat.

'The wages of pride,' I said. 'Go to sleep.'

I drove my mother to Reading in the morning and saw her onto the London train, promising to spend the evening and night in Park Crescent after my six o'clock date with Himself.

Frail from grief, my calm and exquisite parent showed me in a single trembling hug on the railway platform how close we both were to being stretched too far. I understood suddenly that it was from her I had learned the way to hide fear and pain and humiliation, and that if I'd extended that ability into material things like hilts and chalices and dynamite lists, it had been because of her ultra-controlled outer face that I had all my life taken to be an absence – or at least a deficiency — of emotion.

'Ma,' I said on Reading station, 'I adore you.'

The train came, quiet and rapid, slowing to whisk her away.

'Alexander,' she said, 'don't be ridiculous.'

In the bank Tobias, Margaret and the big financial cheese were gloomily studying the electronic messages on the one machine they had left alive to receive them overnight.

Useful information from around the globe: zero.

The experts had drawn up ways of approaching the problem from so far untried angles, but nothing worked. By lunchtime

they were saying they couldn't dedicate more than that afternoon to the search, as they had other unbreakable commit-
ments ahead.

When I asked if I could bring Patsy to the afternoon session
they said I could do anything I liked but Tobias, chewing hard
on a toothpick, asked if I remembered what had happened to
me four days ago, on the one time I'd believed in her good
faith.

I was leaning forward, elbows on table, the morning's pills
wearing off. I remembered, I said, and I would rely on Tobe
to defend me from the maiden.

I could joke, he said, but I should also remember the sirens
whose seductive songs lured foolish sailors to shipwreck and
death.

Not in this bank, I said.

I met her in the car park, as arranged.

'Hello,' I said.

'Alexander . . .'

She was unsure of herself. Awkward. I'd never seen her like
that.

She wore a shirt, a cardigan, long skirt, flat shoes: wholesome, well-groomed.

I explained that she should come into the bank with me and
listen to the difficulties that had arisen in finding the brewery's
millions.

For someone whose main fears for twelve years or so had
been that I would somehow manage to rob her, she seemed
less than anxious about the success of the search.

'I promise you,' I said, 'they are trying everything they know
to find your money.'

'My father's money,' she said. 'Everything you have done
was for him, wasn't it?'

'I suppose so.'

'You would never have done it for *me*.'

I said, 'His whole life was the brewery. He built it up. It
was his pride. The heartless betrayal of Norman Quorn devastated him, and yes, I believe it killed him. And for his sake,

257

and for my mother's sake I would have done anything to put things right. I've tried. I haven't managed it. I want the bank people to tell you that I am not trying to steal from you. I am trying to restore what Ivan built.'

'Alexander . . .'

'I did believe on Saturday,' I said, 'that you were sincerely offering a truce. I hope you didn't know exactly what you were beckoning me into. I know you tried to stop that little lark with the barbecue . . . I could hear you. I know you got me help. Anyway,' I finished, running out of impetus, 'will you come into the bank?'

She nodded speechlessly and went with me into the conference room, where of course her looks and natural charm immediately enslaved the bank man who hadn't encountered her before. He fussed over a chair for her and offered her coffee, and she smiled at him sweetly, as she could.

We all sat down round the table. The bank man obligingly outlined all the measures so far taken to keep the brewery alive, and he explained that they were trying to find the missing millions by using the list.

'That list!' she murmured. 'What's on that list?'

'Don't let her see it,' Tobe said abruptly.

The bank man asked, 'Why ever not?'

'Because of what it cost to bring it here. Al may sit at this table with us hour after hour pretending there's nothing the matter, but he's halfway to fainting most of the time . . .'

'No,' I objected.

'Yeah, yeah.' He waved his toothpick in my direction. 'It was Oliver Grantchester, I'll bet you, who got Patsy to offer you a truce and to inveigle you into that garden. He may be in the lock-up at this moment, but he'll get out sometime, and he may know a way of using this list that we haven't fathomed, and he may have told her what to look for, so don't let her see it.'

There was an intense silence.

Patsy slowly stood up.

'Oliver used me,' she said. 'You are right. It's not easy to admit it.' She swallowed. 'I didn't know anything about any list before Oliver tried to make Alexander give it to him. Don't show it to me. I don't want to see it.' She looked directly at me, and said, 'I'm sorry.'

I stood up also. She gave me a long look, and a nod, and went away.

At the end of the afternoon that produced nothing but baffling frustration I drove back to London and Chesham Place and told my uncle, over a tumblerful of single malt, that three clever financial brains had spent two whole working days trying to make sense of Norman Quorn's list of bank accounts, and failing.

'They'll succeed tomorrow,' he said encouragingly.

I shook my head. 'They've given up. They've got other things they have to do.'

'You've done your best, Al.'

I was sitting forward, forearms on knees, holding my glass with both hands, trying not to sound as spent as I felt. I told him about Patsy's visit to the bank and about her understanding of Oliver Grantchester's intention of robbing the brewery. 'But between them,' I said, 'he and Norman Quorn have fumbled the ball. The millions are lost. I'm glad Ivan didn't know.'

After a while Himself asked, 'What were you doing in hospital? Patsy wouldn't tell me.'

'Sleeping, mostly.'

'Al!'

'Well ... it was Grantchester who sent the thugs to the bothy, thinking you'd given me the King Alfred Gold Cup to look after. He didn't tell them exactly what they were looking for, I suppose because he was afraid they would steal it for themselves if they knew how valuable it was. Anyway, when he found out I had that damned list, that has proved useless, he got the same thugs to persuade me to hand it over, but I still didn't like them – or him – so I didn't.'

He looked aghast.

'Some of my ribs are cracked. Grantchester's in a police hospital ward. Patsy and I may come to that truce in the end. You're making me drunk.'

My mother and I ate an Edna-cooked dinner and afterwards played Scrabble.

My mother won.

I took a pill at bedtime and stayed asleep for hours, and was astounded to meet Keith Robbiston on the stairs when I dawdled on my way down to breakfast.

'Come in here,' he said, pointing me into Ivan's lifeless study. 'Your uncle and your mother are both worried about you.'

I said, 'Why?'

'Your mother said she beat you at Scrabble and your uncle says you're not telling him the whole truth.' He studied my face, from which the swelling and bruises had largely faded, but which did, as I had to acknowledge, show grey fatigue and strain. 'You didn't tell either of them about any burns.'

'They worry too much.'

'So where are these burns?'

I took off my shirt, and he unwound the bandages. His silence, I thought, was ominous.

'They told me,' I said, 'that there wasn't any sign of infection, and that I would heal OK.'

'Well, yes.'

He got from me the name of the hospital and on Ivan's phone traced the grandmotherly doctor. He listened to her for quite a long time, staring at me throughout, his gaze slowly intensifying and darkening. 'Thank you,' he said eventually. 'Thank you very much.'

'Don't tell my mother,' I begged him. 'It's too soon after Ivan.'

'All right.'

He said he would not disturb the synthetic skin dressings, and re-wrapped the damage from armpits to waist.

'They gave you several injections of morphine in the

hospital,' he said. 'And those pills I've given you, they too contain morphine.'

'I thought they were pretty strong.'

'You'll get addicted, Al. And I'm not being funny.'

'I'll deal with that later.'

He gave me enough pills for another four days. I thanked him, and meant it.

'Don't take more than you can help. And driving a car,' he observed, 'is only making things worse.'

I phoned Tobe's office and didn't get him. He had gone away for the weekend.

'But it's only Thursday,' I protested.

He would probably be back on Monday.

God damn him, I thought.

Margaret was 'unavailable'.

The big bank cheese had left me a message. 'All the King Alfred Gold Cup race expenses will be honoured by the bank, working closely with Mrs Benchmark who is now organising everything for the day at Cheltenham.'

Bully for Patsy. Big cheeses were putty in her hands.

I drifted through a quiet morning and companionable lunch with my mother and in the afternoon drove to Lambourn, arriving in the hour of maximum bustle; evening stables.

Emily, in her natural element, walked confidently around her yard in her usual fawn cavalry twill trousers, neat and businesslike, instructing the lads, feeling horses' legs, patting necks and rumps, offering treats of carrots, delivering messages of positive love to the powerful shining creatures that rubbed their noses against her in response.

I watched her for some time before she realised I was there, and I vividly understood again how comprehensively she belonged in that life, and how essential it was to her mind's well-being.

While I was still sitting in Ivan's car, a horsebox drove into the yard and unloaded Golden Malt.

He came out forwards, muscles quivering, hooves placed delicately on the ramp as he sought for secure footing, the whole process jerky and precarious: once out, he moved with liquid perfection, his feet on springs, his chestnut coat like fire in the evening sun, the arrogance of great thoroughbreds in every toss of his head.

Impossible not to be moved. He had twice let me lead him into misty unknown distances, taking me on faith. Looking at his splendid homecoming, I didn't know how I'd dared.

I stood up out of the car. Emily, seeing me, came to stand beside me, and together we watched the horse being led a few times round the yard to loosen his leg muscles after the confines of his journey.

'He looks great,' I said.

Emily nodded. 'The short change of scene suited him.'

'And Saturday?'

'He won't disgrace himself.' Her words were judicious, but trembled with the hard-to-control excitement of any trainer who felt there was a chance of winning a big race.

We went into the house where it proved impossible for her to do anything as ordinary as cooking dinner. I hadn't the energy, either.

We ate bread and cheese.

At ten o'clock she went out into her stable-yard, as she was accustomed, to check that all her charges were happily settled for the night. I followed her and stood irresolutely in the yard looking up at the stars and the rising moon.

'Em,' I said, as she came towards me, 'will you lend me a horse?'

'What horse?' she asked, puzzled.

'Any.'

'But . . . what for?'

'I want . . .' How could I explain it? 'I want to go up onto the Downs . . . to be alone.'

'*Now?*'

I nodded.

'Even for you,' she said, 'you've been very silent this evening.'

'Things need thinking out,' I said.

'And it's a matter of the hundred and twenty-first psalm?'

'What?'

'I will lift up mine eyes unto the hills,' she said, 'from whence cometh my help.'

'*Em.*'

'And the Downs will have to do, instead of your mountains.'

Her understanding took my voice away entirely.

Without questions, without arguing, she went across to the tack room and reappeared with a saddle and a bridle. Then she crossed to one of the boxes in the yard and switched on its internal light.

I joined her there.

'This is one of Ivan's other horses. He's not much good, but he's a friendly old fellow. I suppose he's mine now . . . and as you're Ivan's executor, you've every right to ride him . . . but don't let him get loose if you can help it.'

'No.'

She saddled the horse expertly, pulling the girth tight.

'Wait,' she said, and made a fast detour back to the house, returning with the blue crash helmet and a padded jacket. Looking at my cotton shirt, she said, 'It'll be cold up there.'

She held the jacket for me to put on. Even though she was careful, it hurt.

'Oliver Grantchester can burn in hell,' she said.

'Em . . . how do you know?'

'Margaret Morden phoned me today to ask how you were feeling. She told me. She thought I knew.'

She bridled up the horse and unemotionally gave me a leg-up onto his back. She offered me the helmet, but made no fuss when I shook my head. She knew I preferred free air, and I was not going out to gallop.

'Thanks, Em,' I said.

She understood that it was a comprehensive sort of gratitude.

'Get going,' she said.

*

263

King Alfred, I thought, had perhaps sat on a horse on the exact place where I'd reined to a halt after a slow walk uphill from Lambourn.

I was on one of the highest points of the Downs, looking east to the valleys where the uplands slid away towards the Thames, that hadn't been a grand waterway in Alfred's lifetime, more a long winding drainage system from the Cotswolds to the North Sea.

King Alfred had been a scholar, a negotiator, a poet, a warrior, a strategist, a historian, an educator, a law-giver. I wished a fraction of him could be inhaled to give me wisdom, but he had ridden this land eleven hundred and more years ago, when villainy wore its selfsame face but nothing much else was familiar.

It was odd to reflect that it was, of all things, *ale* that was least changed. The brewery named for the king still flowed with the drink that had sustained and comforted his people.

Ivan's horse walked onwards, plodding slowly, going nowhere under my aimless direction.

The clear sky and weak moonlight were millions of years old. Chill threads of the earth's wind moved in my hair. The perspective of time could cool any fever if one gave it a chance.

One could learn, perhaps, that failure was bearable: make peace with the certainty that all wasn't enough.

I came to the long fallen tree trunk that many trainers on the Downs made use of to give young horses an introduction to jumping. I slid off Ivan's horse to let him rest and sat on the log, holding the reins loosely while the horse bent his head unexcitedly to graze. His presence was in its own way a balm, an undemanding kinship with the natural ancient world.

I had caused in myself more pain than I really knew how to deal with, and the fact that it had been for nothing had to be faced.

It was five days now since I'd been dragged into Grantchester's garden. Five days since the thug called Jazzo, with his boxing gloves and his well-trained technique, had cracked my ribs and hit me with such force that I flinched from the memory as sorely as I still ached in places. I hadn't been able to dodge or in any way defend myself, and the helplessness had only added to the burden.

I could call him a bastard.

Bastard.

It didn't make anything better. Cracked ribs were like daggers stabbing at every movement. Much better not to cough.

As for the grill . . .

I looked out over the quiet age of the Downs.

Even with the pills, I was spending too long on the absolute edge of normal behaviour. I didn't want to retreat to a drugged inertia while my skin grew back, but it was an option with terrible temptations. I wanted not oblivion but fortitude. More fortitude than I found easy.

The horse scrunched and munched, the bit clinking.

What I had done had been irrational.

I should have told Grantchester where to find the list.

There was no saying, of course, that even if I'd told him the minute I'd set foot in his garden, he would have let me walk out of there untouched. I had seen the sickening enjoyment in his face . . . I'd heard from Bernie's confession to the police that Grantchester had burned Norman Quorn even though the frantic Finance Director would have told him anything to escape the fire. Grantchester's pleasure in prolonging Quorn's agony had directly led to Quorn's sudden death . . . from heart failure, from stroke or from shock; one or another. Grantchester's pleasure had in itself denied him the knowledge he sought. The only bright outcome of the whole mess.

Poor Norman Quorn, non-violent embezzler, had been sixty-five and frightened.

I'd been twenty-nine . . . and frightened . . . and irrational . . . and I'd been let off in time not to die.

I'd been let off with multiple bars of first, second and third degree burns, that would heal.

I'd been let off in time to know that burning had been a gesture for nothing, because whatever information Norman Quorn had entrusted to his sister in that benighted envelope, it hadn't turned out to be an indication of what he'd done with the brewery's money.

I could admit to myself that I'd burned from pride.

Harder to accept that it had been pointless.

Essential to accept that it had been pointless, and to go on from there.

I stood up stiffly and walked for a while, leading the horse.

If I'd been in Scotland I would have gone up into the mountains and let the wild pipes skirl out the raw sorrow, as they always had in turbulent history. Yet . . . would a lament be enough? A pibroch would cry for the wounded man but I needed more – I needed something tougher. Something to tell me, well OK, too bad, don't whine, you did it to yourself. Get out the paints.

When I went back to the mountains, I would play a march.

I rode for a while and walked by turns through the consoling night, and when the first grey seeped into the dark sky I turned the horse westwards and let him amble that way until we came to landmarks we both recognised as the right way home.

CHAPTER 15

Friday morning, Lambourn, Emily's house.

I telephoned Margaret Morden.

No, she said, no one had thought of any new way of finding the money. The list, if it held the secret, had humbled them so far, but . . .

'It was a false hope,' I said. 'Useless. Forget it. Give it up.'

'Don't talk like that!'

'It's all right. Truly. Will you come to the races?'

'If you want me . . .'

'Of course we want you. Without you, there would be no race.'

'Without *you*.'

'We're brilliant,' I said, laughing, 'but no one will give us our due.'

'You do sound better.'

'I promise you, I'm fine.'

I was floating on a recent pill. Well, one had to, sometimes.

Inspector Vernon telephoned. 'Oliver Grantchester,' he said.

'What about him?'

'Someone viciously assaulted him last Saturday, in his garage . . . as you know.'

'The poor fellow.'

'Was it your girlfriend who kicked hell out of him?'

'Inspector,' I said reasonably, 'I was lying in that pond. How could I know?'

'She might have told you who did it.'

'No, she didn't – and, anyway, I don't repeat what I'm told.'

After a moment he said, 'Fair enough.'

I smiled. He could hear it in my voice. 'I do hope,' I said, 'that poor Mr Grantchester is still in a bad way.'

'I can tell you, off the record,' he said austerely, 'that the testicular damage inflicted on Mr Grantchester was of a severity that involved irreparable rupture and ... er ... surgical removal.'

'What a shame,' I said happily.

'Mr Kinloch!'

'My friend has gone abroad, and she won't be back,' I said. 'Don't bother looking. She wouldn't have attacked anyone, I'm sure.'

Vernon didn't sound convinced, but apart from no witnesses, it seemed he had no factual clues. The unknown assailant seemed to be getting away with it.

'How awful,' I said.

I supposed that, when Chris found out, the gelding of Oliver Grantchester would cost me extra. Money well spent.

I said to Vernon, 'Give Grantchester my best regards for a falsetto future.'

'That's heartless.'

'You don't say.'

I slept on the pill for three or four hours. Out in the yard life bustled along in the same old way, and by lunchtime I found myself falling into the same old role of general dogsbody, 'popping' down to the village for such-and-such, ferrying blood samples to the vet's office, collecting tack from repair.

Emily and I ate dinner together and went to bed together, and even though this time I easily raised the necessary enthusiasm, she lay in my arms afterwards and told me it broke her heart.

'What does?' I asked.

'Seeing you try to be a husband.'

'But I am . . .'

'No.' She kissed my shoulder above the bandages. 'You know you don't belong here. Just come back sometimes. That'll do.'

Patsy had organised the race day. Patsy had consulted with the tent-erectors and caterers who were out to please. At Patsy's command, the hundred or so commercial guests – creditors, suppliers, landlords of tied houses – were given a big welcome, unlimited drinks, free racecards, tickets to every enclosure, press-release photographs, lunch, tea.

Cheltenham's racecourse, always forward-looking, had extended to King Alfred's brewery, in Ivan's memory, every red-carpet courtesy they could give to the chief sponsor of one of their top crowd-pulling early-season afternoons. Patsy had the whole racecourse executive committee tumbling over themselves to please her. Patsy's social gifts were priceless.

To Patsy had been allocated the Sponsors' Box in the grandstand, next best thing to the plushed-up suite designed for crowned heads and other princes.

Patsy had organised, in the Sponsors' Box, a private family lunch for my mother, her stepmother, so that Ivan's widow could be both present and apart.

Having met my mother at the Club entrance, I walked with her to the Sponsors' Box. Patsy faultlessly welcomed her with kisses. Patsy was dressed in dark grey, in mourning for her father but with a bright Hermès silk scarf round her neck. She looked grave, businesslike, and in full control of the day.

Behind her stood Surtees, who would not meet my eyes. Surtees shifted from foot to foot, gave my mother a desultory peck on the cheek, and altogether behaved as if he wished he weren't there.

'Hello, Surtees,' I said, to be annoying.

He gave me a silent, frustrated look, and took two paces backwards. What a grand change, I thought, from days gone by.

Patsy gave us both a puzzled look, and at one point later in the afternoon said, 'What have you said to Surtees? He won't talk about you at all. If I mention you he finds some reason for leaving the room, I don't understand it.'

'Surtees and I,' I said, 'have come to an understanding. He keeps his mouth shut, and so do I.'

'What about?'

'On my side about his behaviour in Oliver Grantchester's garden.'

'He didn't really mean what he said.'

I clearly remembered Surtees urging Jazzo to hit me harder, when Jazzo was already hitting me as hard as he could. Surtees had meant it, all right: his revenge for my making him look foolish in Emily's yard.

I said, 'For quite a while I believed it was Surtees who sent those thugs to my house in Scotland, to find the King Alfred Gold Cup.'

It shook her. 'But why?'

'Because he said, "Next time you'll scream".'

Her eyes darkened. She said slowly, 'He was wrong about that.'

I shrugged. 'You were telling everyone that I'd stolen the Cup. Surtees, of course, believed it.'

'You wouldn't steal.'

I listened to the certainty in her voice, and asked, trying to suppress bitterness, 'How long have you known that?'

Obliquely she told me the truth, opening to my understanding her own long years of unhappy fear. She said, 'He would have given you anything you asked for.'

'Ivan?'

She nodded.

I said, 'I would never have taken anything that was yours.'

'I thought you would.' She paused. 'I did hate you.'

She made no more admissions, nor any excuses, but in the garden she had called me her brother, and in the bank she had said, 'I'm sorry.' Perhaps, just perhaps, things had really changed.

'I suppose,' she began, 'that it's too late . . .' She left the sentence unfinished, but it was a statement of acceptance, not a plea.

'Call it quits,' I said, 'if you like.'

When Himself and his countess arrived to keep my mother company, I went down to find out how things were going in the hospitality tent, and found that the mood, in spite of the brewery's troubles, was up-beat, alcoholic and forgiving.

Margaret Morden greeted me with the sort of embrace that would have been over the top in any office but seemed appropriate to the abandon of a race day. Dressed in soft blue, with a reliable-looking husband by her side, she said she knew nothing about horses but would back Golden Malt.

She followed my gaze across the tent to where Patsy, flanked not by Surtees but by the perfect lieutenant, Desmond Finch, was encouraging everyone's future.

'You know,' I said to Margaret, 'Patsy will make a great success of running the brewery. She's a born manager. Better than her father. He was conscientious and a good man. She can bend and manipulate people to achieve her own ends . . . and I'd guess she'll lug the brewery out of the threat of bankruptcy faster than you can imagine.'

'How can you *possibly* forgive her?'

'I didn't say I forgave her. I said she would be a good manager.'

'It was in your voice.'

I smiled into the clever eyes. 'Find out for me,' I said, 'whether Oliver Grantchester suggested the embezzlement, or just stumbled across it and muscled in. Not that it really matters, I just wonder, that's all.'

'I can tell you now. It was Grantchester's idea all along. Then Norman Quorn did some fancy footwork to keep the loot himself, and misjudged the strength and cruelty of his partner.'

'How do you know?' I asked entranced.

'That weasel Desmond Finch told me. I leaned on him the

tiniest bit. I said that as deputy managing director he should have spotted irregularities in the finance department, and he fell over himself to tell me that Norman Quorn had practically cried on his shoulder. I think – and to be honest I don't see how we can prove it unless Grantchester confesses, which I can't see him doing . . .'

'He's not the man he used to be,' I murmured.

'I think,' Margaret said, not hearing, or at least not understanding, 'that Norman Quorn must have said in all good faith to Ivan's trusted friend and lawyer Oliver, how easy it would be in these days of electronic transfers to make oneself seriously rich. I think they worked it out together, maybe even as an academic exercise to begin with, and then, when the trial run succeeded, they did it in earnest, and then Quorn tried at the last minute to back out.'

'He did steal the money,' I said flatly. 'He tried to cut his partner out.'

She agreed bleakly. 'They both did.'

We drank champagne. Sweetish. Patsy was no spendthrift fool.

I sighed. 'I wish Tobe could have been here today,' I said.

Margaret hesitated. 'He couldn't bear that we hadn't been able to find the money with that list, when you suffered so much to bring it to us.'

'Tell him not to be so soft.'

She bent forward and unexpectedly kissed my cheek. 'Soft,' she said, 'is the last word I would apply to Alexander Kinloch.'

Himself and I, as two of the executors in whose name the horse was running, stood by the saddling boxes and watched Emily fasten the racing-size saddle onto Golden Malt.

Himself said to me conversationally, 'Word gets around, you know.'

'What word?'

'What Oliver Grantchester put you through in his garden.'

'Forget it.'

'If you say so. But it is rippling outward, and you can't stop it.'

(He was right to the extent that a short while later I got a postcard from young Andrew at his prep school. 'Is it true you were lying fully clothed in a goldfish pond one cold night in October?' – and I sent him back a single-word answer, 'Yes.')

Mad, weird Alexander. Who cared? Some have weirdness thrust upon them.

'Al,' Himself said, 'would you have burned for the Kinloch hilt?'

'It wasn't for the list,' I said.

He smiled. He knew. He was the one person who wholly understood.

We stood in the parade ring with Emily, watching Golden Malt stride round, led by his lad.

Emily's jockey joined us, dressed in Ivan's racing colours of gold, green checks, gold cap.

Emily was all business, no excitement obvious, a shortness of breath the only sign. She told the jockey to be handy in fourth place all the way, if he could, and make his move only after he'd rounded the last bend and straightened up for the uphill run to the winning post.

'Don't forget,' she said, 'that he won't accelerate on a curve. Wait, even though it hurts. He'll deliver if you do. He's a great fighter uphill.'

When the horses had gone out onto the track, Himself, Emily and I joined my mother up in the Sponsors' Box.

My mother, in the black clothes she had worn to Ivan's funeral, and the black sweeping hat with the white rose, gazed out over the autumnal racecourse and yearned for her lost consort, for the steadfast man of no great fire who had been all she needed as a companion.

It was Ivan's race. Ivan's day. Nothing would comfort her.

Patsy arrived, with Surtees. Patsy's manner to her husband was impatient: she was looking at him with the fresh cold eyes of disillusion. I would give that marriage another year at most, I thought. The Surtees looks wouldn't for ever make up for the void inside.

Golden Malt looked splendid on the turf, but he faced no easy task: the generous money prize alongside the prestige of taking home the King Alfred Gold Cup, even in replica, had drawn out the best. Of the nine provenly fast steeplechasers lining up, Golden Malt was generally counted only fourth or fifth in the hierarchy.

White knuckle time. Emily watched the start through race-glasses without trembling. Probably no one else in the box could have managed it. Emily stood rock still for nearly all of the two miles.

It was one of those races at Cheltenham when neither the fences nor the undulating curves sorted the runners out into a straggling line: all nine runners went round in a bunch, no one fell, the crowd on the grandstands yelled and drowned out the commentator, and Golden Malt came round the last bend in close fourth place and headed for glory up the hill.

Emily put down her race-glasses and breathlessly watched.

Himself was shouting with powerful lungs. My mother clasped her hands over her heart.

Patsy murmured, 'Oh, come *on* . . .'

Three horses crossed the line together.

One couldn't tell by eye which head had nodded forward. We all went down to the unsaddling area for first, second and third, and none of the little group could disguise the agony of the wait for the photograph.

When the result came it was in the impersonal voice of the course announcer.

'First, number five.'

Number five: Golden Malt.

There was a lot of kissing. Patsy gave me an uncomplicated smile, with no acid. Emily's eyes outshone the stars.

Patsy had ordained that the trophy should be presented to the winning owner by my mother, as Ivan's wife; so it happened that at the ceremony my mother presented the replica of the

King Alfred Gold Cup to Emily, to universal cheers and a blaze of flashing cameras.

Ivan would have loved it.

When my mother and I were placidly breakfasting and reading congratulatory newspapers, my uncle Robert telephoned with a full-head of steam.

'Whatever you're doing, stop doing it. I've had Jed on the line. He is more or less foaming at the mouth. The conservationists have invaded the bothy with spades and pickaxes and metal detectors, and are tearing everything apart. He has told them they are trespassing, but it makes no difference, they won't go away, and Zoë Lang is there, with the light of battle in her eyes as if she were on a crusade.'

'Does Jed mean they are there now?'

'Indeed he does,' he said. 'They intend to stay all day and they are digging up all the ground round the bothy. He begs me to fly up there at once.'

'Do you want me to come with you?'

'Of course I do,' he bellowed. 'Meet me at Heathrow, terminal one, as soon as you can.'

I explained to my mother that I would have to go. Resignedly, she told me to finish my toast.

I laughed and hugged her, and found a taxi which would go to Heathrow on a Sunday morning.

Himself was striding up and down, an awesome sight. We caught a flight to Edinburgh where we were met by the helicopter pilot who had risked the bothy's plateau once before.

Our arrival alarmed the crowd at the bothy who scattered outwards like ants under an insect-killing spray. When the rotor stopped, the ants came back, led by Jed but with Zoë Lang close on his heels.

'How dare you?' Himself thundered to the fanatical lady.

She straightened, as if she would add inches to her stature. 'This bothy,' she insisted, 'was given to the nation with the castle.'

'It certainly was not,' my uncle said furiously. 'It comes under the heading of my private apartment.'

Behind both of their backs, Jed raised his eyebrows to heaven.

No doubt the courts would decide, I thought, but meanwhile the conservationists were making almost as much mess of my home as the four thugs had done in the first place. There were holes in the ground everywhere. Beside each hole lay a little heap of empty Coke cans and other metal debris.

In the ruined section of bothy that housed the rubbish bins, the corner that held the old bread oven had been excavated to a depth of three feet and the oven left belly up. At the carport end, the earth had more or less been ploughed, revealing old spanners and ancient pieces of iron machinery.

Staggered by the extent of the ruthless search, I left Himself arguing with Zoë Lang and went into my home to see what damage had been done inside.

To my surprise and relief, very little. Jed had brought back my pipes. The place looked tidy. The picture, wrapped in its sheet, stood on the easel. It seemed the searchers had left the core of the search until last.

I went out to protest to Zoë Lang about the work of her fanatical friends, about ten of whom were still digging holes in every direction, but as I approached her my mobile phone, which I by now carried around out of habit, buzzed weakly in my hand, demanding attention.

Because of the bad reception in the mountains, and the whining noise of the metal detectors and yelling all around of the conservationists, I could hear nothing in the receiver but a crackle, with the faintest of voices in the background.

To obliterate at least some of the noise, I carried the mobile phone into the bothy and closed the door.

I said loudly into the receiver, 'Whoever you are, shout.'

I heard an earful of crackle, and one word, 'Tobias.'

I shouted, unbelieving, 'Tobias?'

Crackle.

His faint voice said, 'I've found it.'

Another load of static.

His voice said again, 'Al, I've found the money.'

I couldn't believe it. His voice said, 'Are you there?'

I bellowed, 'Yes. Where are you?'

Crackle. Crackle. 'In Bogota. In Columbia.'

I still couldn't believe it. There was a sudden clearing of the static and I could hear his voice plainly. 'The money is all here. I found it by accident. The account here had three names on it, not just one or two. A person's name and two corporate names. I put them all on an application form by mistake, and it was like pressing a button, a door opened, and they are asking for my onward directions. The money will be back in Reading next week.'

'I can't believe it. I thought you went away for the week-end.'

He laughed. 'I went to Panama. We were getting nowhere electronically. I went to bang a fist . . . and the trail led to Bogota.'

'Tobe . . .'

'See you soon,' he said.

The crackle came back. I switched off the telephone and felt my knees weakening as in the phrase 'weak at the knees' which I had never believed in before.

After a while I took the wrapping sheet off the picture, and even to me the force of it filled the small room.

I had thought I would need time's perspective to know what I'd done, but the power of the concept seemed to have taken over and made me its instrument. The picture might not comfort, but one wouldn't forget it.

During the past few weeks I had painted that picture, the brewery's money had been found, and I'd discovered how far – how deep – I could go into myself.

I had met Tobe and Margaret and Chris.

I'd slept again with Emily and would stay married for as long as she wanted.

I had come to a compact with Patsy.

There wasn't a great deal I would undo.

Shakily, I went out of the bothy and walked on the weak knees to where Himself and Zoë Lang were gesticulating in each other's air-space with none too gentlemanly fury.

Himself stopped abruptly, alerted by whatever he saw in my face.

'What is it?' he said.

'The money is found.'

'What money?' Zoë Lang demanded.

Himself didn't answer her. He stared at me alone with the realisation that what had been paid for had been miraculously delivered.

Zoë Lang, thinking that I had found some treasure or other within the bothy, strode off in that direction and disappeared inside.

'Tobias found the money in Bogota,' I said.

'Using the list?'

'Yes.'

Himself's rejoicing was like my own; unexpressed except in the eyes, a matter of central warmth rather than triumphal whoops.

'Prince Charles Edward's hilt,' he said, 'is irrelevant.'

We looked around at the determined searchers. None of them was now metal-detecting in the right place, but they might succeed if they went on long enough. The prize had been within their reach: they had dug quite near it.

I thought ruefully that this lot wouldn't burn me to make me tell them where to look. Zoë Lang wouldn't strike a match. I wouldn't have wanted her to be Grantchester.

'Will they find it, Al?' my uncle asked.

'Would you mind it very much?'

'Of course I would. That woman would crow.'

I said, 'If she perseveres long enough . . . she will.'

'No, Al,' he protested.

'When I hid it,' I said, 'it was from burglars, not from a zealot with a mission. When her cohorts give up, that's when she'll start thinking. Up until now, I'd guess she believes she's dealing with simple minds, yours and mine. She suffers from the arrogance of the very brainy. She doesn't expect anyone to keep up with her on level terms.'

'Your mind is far from simple.'

'She doesn't know that. And my mind is simpler than hers. She will find the hilt. We could go away and not watch her gloat.'

'Leave the battlefield?' He was outraged. 'Defeat may be unavoidable, but we will meet it with pride.'

Spoken like a true Kinloch, I thought, and remembered briquettes flaming.

Zoë Lang came out of the bothy and walked towards us still carrying a metal detector, basically a long black stick with a white control box near the top and a flat white plate at the bottom.

When she reached us she ignored Himself and spoke directly and with penetration to me alone. 'You will tell me the truth,' she said in her old voice. 'I am sure you are a very good liar, but this time you will tell me the truth.'

I made no reply. She took it as assent, which it was.

She said, 'I saw that picture. Did you paint it?'

'Yes.'

'Is it you who has hidden the Kinloch hilt?'

'Yes.'

'Is it here . . . in your bothy? And would I find it?'

I said, after a pause, 'Yes . . . and yes.'

My uncle's mouth opened in protest. Zoë Lang flicked him a glance and thrust the metal detector into his arms.

'You can keep the hilt,' she said. 'I'll look for it no longer.'

Himself watched in bewilderment while she told one of her helpers to round up the searchers, that they were leaving.

'But, Dr Lang . . .' her helper objected.

'The hilt isn't here,' she said. 'We are going home.'

We watched while they picked up their spades and pickaxes and metal detectors and drifted across to their mini-van transport, and when they'd gone Zoë Lang said to Himself, 'Don't you understand?'

'No, I frankly don't.'

'He hasn't seen the picture,' I said.

'Oh.' She blinked. 'What is it called? Does it have a name?'

'Portrait of Zoë Lang.'

A tear appeared in each of her eyes and ran down her wrinkled old cheeks, as Jed's wife Flora had foreseen.

'I will not fight you,' she said to me. 'You have made me immortal.'

Himself looked long at the picture when Zoë Lang had driven away in her small white car.

'Immortal,' he said thoughtfully. 'Is it?'

'Time will tell.'

'Mad Alexander, who messes about with paints . . .'

I smiled. 'One has to be slightly mad to do almost anything such as hiding a treasure.'

'Yes,' he said. 'Where is it?'

'Well,' I said, 'when you gave me the hilt to hide all those years ago, the first thing I thought about was metal detectors because those things find gold almost more easily than any other metal. So I had to think of a hiding place safe from metal detectors, which is actually almost impossible unless you dig down six feet or more . . . and under water is no good because water is no barrier.'

He interrupted. 'How does a metal detector *work*?'

'Well,' I said, 'inside that flat white plate thing there is a coil of very thin wire. The batteries in that white box, when you switch them on, produce a high-frequency alternating current in the coil, which in turn produces an oscillating magnetic field which will induce a responding current in any metal near it, which will, in turn, excite the coil even more, whose increased activity can be interpreted as a whine – and that's putting it simply.'

'You've lost me,' Himself said.

'I had to look it up,' I agreed. 'It's a bit hard to understand.'

He looked around at all the little dug up heaps of unprecious metal.

'Well, yes,' I grinned. 'I buried a lot of things to keep searchers busy.'

'Really, Al.'

'The childish mind,' I said. 'I couldn't help it. I did it five years ago. I might not do it now.'

'So where is the hilt?'

'It's where I hid it when you gave it to me.'

'But *where?*'

'Everyone talks about buried treasure . . .' I said, 'so I didn't bury it.'

He stared.

I said, 'The metal that most confuses a detector is a sheet of aluminium foil. So to start with I wrapped the hilt in several loose layers of foil, until it was a shapeless bundle about the size of a pillow. Then I took a length of cotton duck – that's the stuff I paint the pictures on – and I primed it with several coats of gesso to stiffen it and make it waterproof, and then I painted it all over with burnt-umber acrylic paint, which is a dark brown colour and also waterproof.'

'Go *on,*' he said when I paused. 'What then?'

'Then I wrapped the foil bundle in the cotton duck, and super-glued it so that it wouldn't fall undone. Then all over the surface I super-glued pieces of granite.' I waved a hand at the grey stony ground of the plateau. 'And then . . . well, the more metal you offer to a detector the more it gets confused, so I put the hilt bundle where it was more or less surrounded by metal . . .'

'But,' he objected, 'they dug up that whole old oven and the hilt wasn't in it . . .'

'I told you,' I said, 'I didn't bury it. I glued it onto the mountain.'

'You did . . . *what?*'

'I glued it granite to granite, and covered it with more granite pieces until you can't distinguish it by eye from the rock around it. I check it fairly often. It never moves.'

He looked at the metal detector in his hands.

'Turn it upside down,' I said.

He did as I said, waving the flat round plate in the air.

'Now I'll switch it on,' I said, and did so. 'And,' I said formally, laughing, 'My lord, follow me.'

I walked not up onto the hill, as he obviously expected, but into my corrugated iron-topped carport.

The waving upside-down metal detector whined non-stop.

'If you go to the rear wall,' I said, 'and stand just there,' I pointed, 'you will hear the indistinguishable noise of the Honour of the Kinlochs, which is up on the carport roof where it joins the mountain. If you stand just there, the hilt of Prince Charles Edward Stuart's ceremonial sword will be straight above your head.'